ON WINGS OF HATE

Bruce Summa

Dedication

For Josh and Jessica, Jay and Barb, Shawn, Faith, Bridget, and my loving wife Julie. You guys have gamed with me for decades and let me practice my storytelling on you and your characters. Without the confidence you gave me, I could never have done it.

Acknowledgement

With many thanks to my wife Julie for listening to me walk through ideas and to Authors Arsenal for holding my hand through self-publishing.

About The Author

Law enforcement by day, storyteller by night, Bruce Summa grew up telling bedtime stories to his siblings and then graduated to storytelling through tabletop roleplaying games. Always dreaming of different people in different worlds, writing it all down became a hobby that gives voices to the people in his head.

Table of Contents

Chapter One:
Hate Takes Flight

Karen Ashter waved her arm in the general direction of the sound in the sub-basement of the old church, and the shadows seemed to dim as light magnified its effect. It wasn't like Karen had turned on a flashlight or even used some kind of light spell from some old Dungeons and Dragons game; instead, the light in the room just suddenly got more assertive. "Wolves," Karen screamed in a blind rage! "Rick, they want to hurt Britney, kill them!"

Rick Bradshaw was dead, not in the future tense like he was about to fight an unwinnable battle, but in the current tense like he had died a year ago and she had reanimated him. Karen was a witch, complete with magic powers, and this basement was strong in the magic surrounding everyone. Magic was everywhere but spread so thinly that only very few people still had the power to collect it and then form it into something useful. To be a witch or a warlock, your soul had to be heavier than usual. It was like a reincarnation, but a little different. One soul in different bodies in different places and at different points in history, but from their point of view, all live simultaneously. The net effect was one soul reincarnated into different people but effectively being used at the same time, thus magnifying the soul's impact on the magic around it. Now imagine what would happen to the human mind if you could sometimes hear the voices of your other lives, voices from one life could be heard by other heads. The more people in history who shared the same soul, the stronger the witch or warlock, the more voices. Modern mental health professionals had a word for it, auditory hallucination, and the people who were most famous for having it were known as schizophrenics.

This was her chance to make her daughter beautiful again. Karen's daughter, Britney, and Rick had been in a terrible accident. Rick had died, and Britney had been paralyzed. Poor Karen's already damaged mind couldn't take it, and her already shaky grasp on sanity had finally snapped. Now Karen was in the sub-basement of a hundred-year-old church with Rick and Britney and her 'spell component', one of Britney's rivals named Angela. Karen's plan was so close to being done. She had worked so hard, so much research and testing, so much money to hire people to steal Rick's dead body back. Her plan had even cost her the support of her own witches' coven when they found out about her plan. She had done the almost impossible when she brought Rick's soul back from the other side to make him pay for his crime of damaging her daughter. Now she was going to break new ground in magical theory by stripping the memories and soul out of that bitch Angela and then swapping them for her beautiful daughter's. She was going to pull her daughter out of her broken body and put her in a new one. It was only fair; Angela had everything handed to her on a silver platter. She didn't have to work as hard as Britney had, didn't have to fight for every win constantly, didn't have to suffer like Karen had suffered. So Angela was going to give up her body and swap places with Britney's broken body. It didn't matter that Angela didn't agree to the swap; that was just part of the price Angela would have to pay to balance the scales of fate.

Then the wolves got involved. Werewolves, those self-righteous self-appointed guardians of humanity. Werewolves kept the paranaturals, what humans would call supernaturals, from taking their rightful place. Humans had been created to be ruled, the fodder for the mighty, to be ground down and stepped on until the rightful rulers were where they belonged…where she belonged. It had been a bastard human, her now deceased husband, who had gotten her pregnant and forced a daughter on her. It had been another bastard human who had been driving the sports car the night of Britney's accident. Rick had broken her daughter, and now Rick suffered for it as an undead servant. It was all going perfectly; she had all the pieces in place, but the wolves had shown up.

Karen stood between the two tables, one holding the girl that was now little more than a spell component, and the other holding her broken daughter. Karen wore almost nothing, just her underwear; it wasn't seemly, but it was necessary. She needed to feel the Aether, what humans called magic, flowing through this nexus point, a place where the Aether naturally collected. If she couldn't feel its ebb and flow, she couldn't hold the spell together to switch their bodies. She looked one last time at the twin circles she had carved into the floor. Each circle would act like a spinning top, collecting the soul's energy and the memories of each girl as Karen pulled them free. Then, when she was ready, she would open the gate between them and exchange one circle for the other. The hard part was just like working a spinning top, as long as she put just enough energy into it to keep it spinning. The process would work, but if one side of the circle began to slow compared to the other, then the tops might rub together and would wobble, causing the whole thing to come apart.

Out of the corner of her eye, she watched Rick's fight as she started the daunting process of gathering in enough raw power to do her part. Rick was doing surprisingly well; his first attack had taken one of the wolves out in mid shift from human to wolf, and now he was fighting two others. Karen hadn't paid much attention, but the wolf looked like it had been a young girl about Britney's age. Now that girl lay unmoving across the room from a single punch from her servant's hand. Karen hoped that Rick had already killed the wolf. She hated werewolves; she would have burned them all down if she weren't busy. One of the intruders, an older woman, was checking on the downed wolf while Rick fought the other two.

"They are coming," the woman's voice in Karen's head warned. "I told you this plan would fail. You're not strong enough."

"You don't deserve to have her," another voice agreed, this one an older male by the sound.

"They will come and take her away from you and then you'll be a failure again, like you always are," a third voice agreed, this one a younger woman's voice.

"Shut up," Karen thought in answer. She hated the voices and her other selves but needed them tonight. "You're going to help me, or the wolves will tear me apart, and then where will we all be? Think of how it's going to feel, me getting torn apart. We all share this soul, what's going to happen to yours after they are done with me? So you're going to help me or risk all of this coming to an end."

The voices were silent as they thought about the horror of her statement. Karen was strong, but even her skills would need help. "We have no choice," they answered together as the older female wolf began to shift and charge at her.

"NO," Karen screamed. Once again, she waved her hand towards the approaching danger and flipped her hand over in mid-swing. The approaching wolf dodged to its left and put a masonry support pillar between her and Karen's hand as the air in front of Karen superheated. Karen's manipulation of the laws of nature excited the air molecules until the air almost exploded in ripples of heat, immediately igniting the loose debris and old scraps of wood scattered around the basement. The wolf would have been part of that fire if it hadn't dodged at the last moment.

"We will hold the wall but you have to do your part," the voices said in unison. "It is all we can do to hold this part."

Karen moved purposefully and picked up the leather headband she had created as part of the link between her spell and the girl she was using as a spell component. Britney was yelling at her, something unimportant, so Karen ignored her. A simple leather band by itself wasn't magical, but Karen's belief in it made it so. Function, or more accurately, the belief of function, was more important than the nature of the item itself. People believed that calculators could do math, so they did. In the hands of a witch or wizard, they would still do math, even if the calculator was broken and the batteries were gone. Karen made this headband, carved the images onto its surface, and believed each carving would serve its purpose. That's why when the leather band touched the girl and Karen put her power into it, the girl screamed.

Now the female wolf was in her human form again and was yelling something, even having the gall to throw something at her. Karen ignored the distraction; she couldn't risk a second of distraction, or the whole spell would come apart.

Immediately, Karen could feel the strain and the raw power of the Aether in this place as it flowed through her so intensely that it felt hot to the touch. She had only felt the power of this place once before, when she brought Rick back from the dead, but this time, it was a more substantial magnitude of power—compared to the spell she was working now, bringing Rick back had been as easy as screwing in a light bulb. Somewhere, in the back of her mind, she heard her daughter's voice screaming something about Rick but she dared not pay attention to it. Her spell wound through the girl's brain, memory by memory, unwinding the things that made Angela an individual. With each passing second, Angela began to empty like water poured out of a glass and collected in the incantation ring surrounding the table. She dared to look away from the vessel under her hand when she had the first half balanced and spinning.

"Just a little longer, dear, now you have to be brave," Karen's bat crap crazy voice sounded in a perfectly calm manner, like she was asking someone to pass the salt. Karen reached down, picked up the matching headband from Britney's table, and placed it on her daughter's head. Both girls screamed in unison as the leather band touched her daughter's skin. Karen wanted to dance joyfully; the screams were a good sign, and both girls were already beginning to link. She added more power to her daughter's headband and started the unwinding process when she felt the snap of her binding spell. It was the snapping of the spell that held Rick to his body and kept him under her control. That little bit of her power snapped back at her and stung her like a bee sting, but that was all it took. The tops began to wobble.

Rick stepped through her wall of superheated air, and the stench of burning flesh stung her nose. Rick screamed, "Britney!" as he lunged for Karen. She was still trying to stabilize the wobbling spell when his burning body wrapped around her as it was collapsing. The pain was like a sudden shock of cold water, and she screamed, first in physical pain and then in mental pain as her powerful spell spun out of control. Across time, other voices screamed out as their shared soul also felt the backlash. All that power and Aether energy she had been channeling and focusing spun apart. Torn from its home and now released, Angela's memories flooded back into her body, but they pulled so hard that part of Britney went with them. Forever, the two girls would now be linked, but that would be the start of an adventure for another day.

Karen's mind burned with the backlash from the energy she had been controlling just as her physical body began to burn. The process she had used to create Rick, to preserve his physical body, had also made him combustible. She tried to scream again, but already her body was beyond that point. All that was left for her was the screaming torture of her burning flesh and a hate so hot that it burned her soul. It had been those wolves; they had caused this. She had been so close to regaining all that had been taken from her, and then they stole even her hope away. Her body burned, and the old church burned around her as the fires from her forgotten wall of heat continued to grow. Even as she died, her body twisting and sizzling like overcooked meat, her soul burned and tattered but refused to leave. Karen refused to be beaten, to have all her dreams torn from her again. She refused to let go of her hate. Somewhere in all that hate and pain, the thing that used to be Karen saw the wolves escape with her daughter and Angela.

The old building with its hundred-year-old timbers went up like an inferno, heating the red brick like a blacksmith's forge. When the firefighters arrived, they took the safest approach, surround and drown. The old structure, now off balance, superheated, and lacking the majority of its support beams, collapsed in on itself and crushed what was left of her burned body. The hot brick turned the sub-basement into an oven, and what was left of her and Rick's bodies continued to bake. When the firefighter's water reached the sub-basement, the heat turned the water into steam. Even if someone had been standing right beside her, no one could have noticed the wisp of oily black vapor as it oozed out of her charred and broken remains. The vapor flowed into the night sky and disappeared on wings of hate. What it left behind was nothing more than bits of bone and ash, the mortal remains of Karen Ashter.

All that existed now was this vapor; it felt nothing but the burning hate for everything. It was confused, not knowing what it was or where, just that it wished to kill and destroy all it found. The vapor's hate had no bounds, but without form, it could take no actions, so it raged against the universe and screamed out in fury without a voice. It floated on the Aether through the back ways, through the forgotten places in the city, like a moving shadow in the night, and learned. For days, it would travel before it learned enough, got strong enough, before it could act.

Chapter Two:
New Body, Old Mistakes

Eight days later…

Chief of Police Stephen Butler reached over and turned off the alarm on his phone before staring at the ceiling. It was early, too damn early for his taste, but he had made an appointment to go for a run with his good right arm, Lieutenant Deon Chase. Deon was the patrol division commander, a werewolf, and one of Stephen's best friends. He had to go to work, but one of the advantages of being the boss was that you were never late for work. Stephen led the Moser City Police Department. The men and women in blue who put their lives on the line every day to protect and serve a growing community. Moser City had reached that magic population point, and now businesses and people were actively trying to move to town instead of being begged to come. If he thought his life as Chief of Police of a growing, vibrant community had been demanding before, somewhere in some dark cave, one of the three Fates reached out to her sisters and said, "Here, hold my beer".

It had been a hell of a month and a half, maybe a little more? His best friend, Dr Malcolm Roberts, had been alive and drinking coffee with him at the Bit and Byte, a coffee shop slash Internet cafe. Five weeks ago, he found out that Malcolm, a Mensa level genius and research geneticist, had infected him with a serum that turned him into a werewolf. Two weeks ago, he met four other werewolves when they showed up to oversee his first change, his first Shift from man to wolf. Eight days ago, he fought a real spell-throwing witch and her undead creation with his new roommates, the three women who had shown up at the beginning of the week. Seven days ago, Stephen went to a nudist resort and fought a guy almost to the death to become the Alpha male werewolf, essentially the king of the pack. Six days ago, his three roommates, Kara, Veronica, and Kaitlin, agreed to move in with him permanently.

Stephen stared at the ceiling and tried to make sense of it all. So much had been going on that he didn't have time to understand it all totally. When his fight for Alpha ended, he did something that he thought would be impossible for him, until he had done it. He had taken his first act as Alpha by ordering the execution of another living being. Marcus Dobson was a drug dealer, a rapist, and was guilty of five counts of conspiracy to commit murder, not counting all the other murders that he was probably involved in with his drug trade. He had conspired with another pack to have Stephen and Deon murdered, paying with the lives of three of his own pack's women. Marcus had been a danger to the pack and human society and had to be killed. There was no such thing as going to prison for werewolves. One of the side effects of being a werewolf was that they aged at least half of what was normal for a human. Kaitlin, the youngest of his roommates, was twenty-three years old but had a body that made her look like she was sixteen or seventeen. She would stay looking that age until she hit her thirties. The girl had it tough; she was a sexually motivated young woman trapped in a body that made people think of jail sentences just for looking at her too long. Even when he saw her naked for the first time, he had thought he was going on a list, until she explained that she was twenty-three. If he had been able to reason at that moment, he would have asked for ID. Even then, he couldn't look at her without feeling creeped out by finding her body attractive.

To make matters worse, Kaitlin had even played up the part of looking like a kid. He had learned that she didn't want to act like a little kid, but her pack was dying, and it made them all feel better to think of her like a child. It gave the pack hope that there was still young life in a pack of slowly dying off werewolves.

Her pack…his pack was dying. Werewolves had been around since the first humans banged two rocks together and started the first fire. After all these hundreds of thousands of years, the genetic lottery called evolution was finally catching up to them. Werewolves led a life of blood and pain in the best of times. They never had high birth rates, which was probably why they evolved such long-life spans, but now even their typically low birth rates were dropping off. Then comes Dr Malcolm Roberts, riding his white horse of genetic modification named, CRISPR, to play a little genetic card game. Malcolm had spent his life trying to reshuffle the deck and find a cure. He may have seen one, but he hadn't been certain. Malcolm was the former Alpha male of the pack and had experimented on his people to try to improve their fertility rates. He wasn't sure if he had succeeded, so he started a second phase of the master rescue plan. He created a werewolf from scratch. He found that his best friend, Stephen, was genetically compatible, so he infected Stephen with a virus that either rewrote his genetic code or unlocked what had already been there. Malcolm didn't just turn him into a werewolf; he became the genetically perfect werewolf. Now all Stephen had to do was go out and screw every female werewolf he could find, hopefully get her knocked up, and spread his superior genes, if the cure worked at all.

Well, there was a step three to the plan, one that Malcolm had left for Stephen before Malcolm ate a shotgun to bring an end to a lifetime of pressure and depression. Stephen had to convince the other remaining werewolf packs to try out Dr Malcolm Roberts' all-natural super cure, guaranteed to improve birth rates and even regrow hair. Not hard at all, just find a way to convince a bunch of terrified, panicky killing machines to trust each other long enough to take a medical procedure designed to mess with their DNA that was as far from FDA approval as anything could get. Nope, nothing big at all, give Stephen a week and he'd have it done…

"Stephen, you need to get out of bed, you're going to be late," Veronica Hughes called through his closed bedroom door. That was another thing about living with werewolves: there was very little privacy.

When you had senses that bordered on the lines of superpowers, privacy was one of the things he was still learning to do without. That and werewolves could sense each other's emotions, sort of like understanding body language and pheromones, somewhere on a subconscious level. They didn't fully understand how they did it, but they couldn't lie to each other. Regardless of how it was done, they just knew when another werewolf was in a crappy mood.

"I'm awake, just laying here thinking," Stephen answered.

Veronica cracked the door open slightly and walked in when he didn't complain. She closed the door behind her before walking to his bed and sitting on its edge. Veronica's hair needed brushing, she rarely bothered with makeup, and she wore just a pair of old sweatpants and a comfy shirt. Even in her 'morning' face, she was still beautiful; her shoulder length reddish brown hair was still damp from her shower, but it was her eyes that Stephen always noticed first. She had bright greenish blue eyes that told you that she had seen some bad shit in her life, but she had come through it all and kept her gentle soul. She was intelligent and compassionate, but a force to be reckoned with on the battlefield, and if he believed what she had told him before, she was in the bedroom too. "So…wanna talk?" she asked.

"I'm alright," he said dismissively, "just thinking about everything. I guess it's all finally settling in. It's all been just a blur of trying to stay alive and find a kidnapped girl. I really didn't have a lot of time to fully process everything and now I've got to learn how to pick up the pieces that are left over and make sense of it all."

"Kind of like Angela and Britney," Veronica answered. "They're alive today because of what you and the rest of us did. They get the chance to put their lives back together because you were there for them."

Stephen smiled half-heartedly. "Ya that is a good part, I guess Angela was right, when her parents found out that Britney had risked her own life to keep their daughter alive, they took her in immediately. I'm told they are even filing adoption papers. Then of course there's the three of you girls moving in, that's a good part too."

"Wait till you see the water bill or have to clean hair out of the bathroom drains."

He smiled again, and this time it reached all the way up to his eyes. "I never thought of that part before, the honey do's start up again."

"Well maybe, but we're pretty self-sufficient," Veronica said with a mock pout. "Just remember, there's more to living with us than just honey do's. You're Alpha now, we'd be more than willing to…help you out too. In case you ever got tired of sleeping alone."

That was part of what had been on his mind, too. There is a saying that "it's good to be King". As the Alpha male, the pack king, it was Stephen's duty to do everything he could to improve the pack's health. That meant sex and a lot of it was expected. If he was the cure for the pack's failing gene code, he would have to spread that cure as far as possible. Even women in relationships were expected to be his sexual partners. If he got a married woman pregnant, that child would be raised by the mother and her husband. Their status would be raised within the pack, and he'd saunter off to the next bed. Werewolves were sexual creatures at the best of times, enjoying sex with almost none of the taboos of his human upbringing. Now that they were dying off and birthrates were so low, people should change the phrase "fucking like bunnies" to "fucking like werewolves".

"I...", he started before Veronica cut him off.

"I know, you're not comfortable with that idea yet. Don't worry about it; we all understand, and I think Kara is glad you're taking it slowly, too. Kaitlin is another story, but now that you gave the rest of the males permission, she's enjoying having an active sex life. She'd still prefer you, of course." That had been one cure he'd already been able to spread. Malcolm had treated Kaitlin publicly like a little girl, even though she was long past that age, so no man dared treat her differently. Kaitlin took the treatment as a snub, like she wasn't good enough to be a sexual partner and ended up feeling like a wallflower at the high school dance. When Stephen had put on display that he was treating her as an adult, her dance card filled up immediately.

"That's part of what is confusing me," Stephen explained. "Part of me really likes the idea, I mean come on, all three of you are beautiful and any man would be lucky to be invited to your bed. It just seems…I don't know, like I'm taking advantage or something, like it's just because I'm Alpha now."

"We've told you that in our society sex isn't always about romance, it's about reproduction and its good for pack bonds, but…I think I understand what you're trying to say."

"Ya, I mean, I know it's expected and is my duty now, but I don't want people to think that just because I'm Alpha that I'm expecting women to just give it up," Stephen answered almost excitedly. "Especially with you three, I…worry you know."

Veronica smiled and leaned forward to kiss him on his forehead. "Stephen, you worry too much. We were raised in this lifestyle. The Alpha must spread his genes for the wellbeing of the entire pack. We've explained that no one will care if you are sleeping with the three of us, it's what the pack needs right now; especially if Malcolm's treatments really do work and we're more fertile than we had been. The pack has very high expectations of you and so did Malcolm. That's why being an Alpha is a game of life and death, you're always being tested to make sure you're the right one. You can't get too comfortable being the Alpha or there will be someone else in the wings ready to take the job from you. They need you to be sexually active. The only person worried about you becoming a 'man whore' as Malcolm called it, is you."

"OK so maybe I can see it with the other women in the pack, like it's a one-night stand that everyone is fine with for the good of the many; but with you three it just feels different."

"Different how?"

"I don't know, it's just…like I want you three to know that you can say no. That I don't expect you three to want to have sex with me or to have a relationship with me, unless you wanted to. I understand that the Alpha male thing but with you three it just doesn't feel right. Like I'm taking advantage of you and your society."

"Our society," Veronica corrected. "You're one of us; you're the Alpha one of us now. This is your society too. Stephen why do you think we moved in here?"

"Well at the time I thought it was because you all enjoyed your time here, that you wanted to move in but now I don't know. Did you move in because you wanted to or because your Alpha asked you? I mean think about it, Kara hated me until just a few days ago, and you and Kaitlin just moved in with a guy you've really just met. None of that makes sense. I've kissed all three of you already, well Kara was an accident, and none of you complained; but is that because you wanted me to kiss you or because your…our society says I can get away with it. For that matter, why are you three even interested in me at all, is it because I'm Alpha and it's expected or is it because you're interested in me?"

"So, you're asking, do we like you or do we like the Alpha? I've offered you sex and you didn't know if I wanted to fuck you or fuck the Alpha," Veronica answered, her voice turning hard. "So, you can't tell if I'm just trying to sleep up the social ladder or if I'm interested in you as Stephen? Do you actually think that any of the three of us give a damn about you being Alpha? Kara is an Alpha female; she has nothing to gain at all from moving in here or sleeping with you. She can sleep with any man she wants, actually, we all can. We all risked our lives trying to protect you, and you can't tell now why we wanted to move in?"

"Well…I think I know, but maybe I'm just overthinking this," Stephen said, his voice beginning to get a touch of sadness. "I mean, seriously, have you looked in the mirror lately? You just got out of the shower and are so beautiful that you could stop traffic. It's not just you either, Kara is probably the closest thing to a Greek goddess I've ever seen. Kaitlin, if springtime were a person, so full of beauty and energy, springtime would look like Kaitlin. Then there's me, forty-eight, starting to go grey, and utterly clueless about being a werewolf. The only interesting thing I have going is a compatible genetic structure; otherwise, I'm as dull as any other human. I've been out of this whole dating game for many years and was never very good at it back then. When Becky was in my life, it all seemed to make more sense. Now, after losing her, I don't know…maybe I'm afraid of losing you guys too."

Veronica took a deep breath and slowly let it out, her anger at his confusion trying to go out with it. She was angry that he had thought so little of them, so little of her, not to know why they were all there or why they were willing to be with him. Sure, he was Alpha, but she started liking him when they talked in the hospital. Part of her felt betrayed and angry at him, but the other parts reminded her to be patient; he was like a new baby in the pack. "Stephen," she said slowly, trying to control every syllable, "we are all here because we chose to be. Not because the Alpha asked us. Not because living or sleeping with you would gain us political advantage, and if you don't understand that by now, then you're just being stupid. I think you are right, I think you're afraid of losing something again that you honestly care about. I think you found not one but three women to have feelings for, and it's freaking you out, so you look for any reason you can find to put up barriers; and I think you're being an ass right now." Veronica snapped to her feet, losing her attempt to be patient with him, and walked out of the room, closing the door behind her like a woman closing a chapter in her life. Stephen watched her go and could sense her frustration and anger. His feelings matched hers, frustration and anger at himself; anger at doing something that hurt her. All he wanted to do was pull the covers back over his head and hide from his entire day, but the day wouldn't be denied.

Stephen threw back the covers and got dressed without throwing or breaking anything. He called that part a win at least. He was pissed off, he didn't know why, but he was still mad as hell. All the emotions he had been avoiding or bottling up all the feelings of helpless frustration, and they started to come out as his teeth began to clench tighter. Getting up early wasn't helping anything either; he hated mornings, hated running, and was just generally in a crappy mood. Stephen flopped back down on the bed and tied on his tennis shoes just as he heard Deon's car rolling up the driveway. One of the advantages of being a werewolf now was that he could hear cars coming when they turned off the pavement and hit the gravel of his driveway, through the trees, from almost three acres away, from inside his house.

He stepped out the front door just as Deon was about to knock. "Well good morning," Deon said in surprise.

"Morning."

"Well, you're all pissed off about something." Stephen was about to deny it when he remembered Deon would know better; he could sense Stephen's mood. Besides, even humans would see how his body language transmitted his mood.

"Ya, I hate mornings, and I hate running. I'm not really sure why I let you talk me into this," Stephen said as he started to stretch his legs. He wasn't a runner, but he knew enough that if he didn't stretch, he'd cramp up or pull something.

"Well, I noticed something when you were fighting, and I thought we'd go for a run to discuss it," Deon answered as he began to stretch. After a few more seconds, both men started at a light jog down the driveway. It was still before sunrise, and the woods around his thirty-acre property were coming alive. Stephen could smell the animals in the woods and track them by sound if he actively tried. However, he still hadn't mastered his new hyper-senses yet and would just as likely end up with a splitting headache and sick to his stomach. They started their jog slowly, but Deon was a big man, and his longer legs meant that Stephen's pace had to be just a little bit faster to keep up.

"So, you want to talk about it," Deon asked. "I know it's not about running, so it has to be the girls."

After a few seconds' pause, Stephen agreed it wasn't worth resisting. "I pissed off Veronica this morning, and I'm not really sure how or even why. I've had more time to think now that everything has slowed down, and I can't wrap my mind around it. Why would the girls be interested in living with me or even being sexually interested? I mean, they're all freaking sex on legs hot, and well I'm not. Plus they've only known me about a couple of weeks now, but sex was on the table much earlier, and they all decided to move in when I asked. So, I figured it had to be because I'm the Alpha now or was going to be Alpha then, so it's the only reason that makes sense."

"And you asked her if she was interested in you because you're the Alpha now," Deon deduced.

"What else was I supposed to do, I mean it's really the only reason that make sense."

Deon sighed at the situation before he answered. "For such a good cop, you sure do have trouble reading those girls don't you."

"Well…it just doesn't make sense, unless you can explain it to me or is this a Stephen, you're being human again thing."

"No, this isn't about you being human, it's about you being a stupid human," Deon answered with a slight laugh. "You're trying to use logic to an emotional situation. The girls met you a couple of weeks ago and then spent that week living in your house, eating your food, fighting your battles with you, and even risking their lives for you; and that was before you became Alpha. They did that for you… Stephen you…not Alpha werewolf you. What makes you think that they don't like the Stephen you? Believe me, those three could give two shits about you being Alpha."

"So, you think they like me then, enough to live here, and even agree to sex because of me and not the position or because they have to? Are they interested in a relationship then, or is this just a casual sex thing?"

"That I don't know, you'll have to ask them; but the only one worried about if your good enough for them is you."

"I don't get it. They can have so much better, it just doesn't make sense that they would be interested in me when they could have, I don't know, like better; you know," Stephen said at a loss for words.

"OK if you don't get it then turn it around, what did you ask Veronica from her point of view."

"I just asked if she was interested in me for me or for me being Alpha. I was just trying to figure out the why behind her interest."

"And from her point of view," Deon asked? Stephen jogged in silence for a few more steps before it started to dawn on him.

"Oh hell…I basically asked her if she was wanting to sleep with me for me or if she was being a whore and using her body for position and pack duty. I told her that it didn't make sense for her to like me so I was basically calling her a whore and dismissing any real feelings that she may actually have for me. Oh I fucked up…," Stephen exclaimed as the weight of being a stupid human hit home.

"No shit Sherlock," Deon answered. "And she was the worst possible choice to fuck up with."

"I don't get it?"

"Well, that part isn't your fault; you couldn't know, but you'll still pay the price. Kara is the Alpha female and was born to that position. She's always been strong and confident in just about every situation. You couldn't stop Kaitlin if you hit her with a truck. She's always been full of life and so outgoing that she's in your face. Veronica though she's Kaitlin's opposite, until you come along, she's always been quiet and most comfortable in the background. She started taking martial arts as a kid, so she'd start building some confidence. It surprised everyone when she started coming out of her shell around you. When you were in the hospital, she gave us daily reports about you and how you were doing. The more time she spent with you, the more excited she became. The girl who usually sits in the back and reads a book at pack meetings was standing out in front with you. You must break yourself out of this human idea that just because you look older, means she can't be interested in you. When you can live to well over two hundred years old, being fifty isn't even a quarter of the way through. When people say age is just a number, for us, it's true. In this case, fifty is the new twenty-five. Veronica was getting interested in you before you even left the hospital, and it had nothing to do with your age or being Alpha material."

"And I just told her that I couldn't accept the idea of her feelings, or any of the girls having feelings, without there being some kind of ulterior motive."

"Sure did."

Stephen and Deon turned from the driveway to the side of the road. Stephen lived well out of town on one of the many county secondary roads, which meant there usually wasn't much traffic, especially at this god forsaken morning time. Deon wasn't even breathing hard, but Stephen was beginning to huff and puff from all the work of running and still trying to talk.

"So…what do I do now? How do I fix this?" Stephen asked.

"Same way you fix it with any woman. Apologize, explain that you've figured out how you screwed up, and then do something nice for her."

"I'll have to think about it," Stephen answered, breathing hard.

"Which brings me to why we are running," Deon answered. "I noticed this when you were fighting Marcus, your mind is also still thinking like you're human."

"Huh?"

"Right now, you're breathing hard and you're struggling to keep up, why? I'm not breathing hard at all."

"Better shape," Stephen answered.

"Maybe, or maybe my mind knows that I'm a werewolf and this isn't even a fast walk yet. Let's try something, take a deep breath and hold it."

"Can't, not while running," Stephen answered between puffs.

"Just do it," Deon commanded. After a pause, Stephen gave it a shot and breathed in a deep lungful of air. He held his breath and kept running. The first few steps didn't feel any different, but then he felt uncomfortable and needed to breathe. "Don't breathe," Deon said. "You really don't need to, not at this pace. We have to convince your mind of it, too." The feeling got worse, but Stephen fought to hold his breath, and to his surprise, the burning lung feeling started to fade slowly. The longer he fought to hold his breath, the easier it became. After running this far, he should have been blowing like a bellows, but he was running while holding his breath. After about thirty more steps, he let out the breath, and when he started to breathe again, it was at a casual rate, like he was sitting on the couch in the living room.

"This is weird," Stephen said casually.

"I never thought about it," Deon answered. "Your body is changing, and with your first complete Shift done now, it'll change just a little more, but your brain still thinks it's human. It's like driving a car with the computer settings wrong; it's still working, but you're not getting all the performance you should get. During the fight, you were still moving like you're human, at human speeds. Marcus was cocky at first and didn't capitalize on the speed difference, and then when your dire wolf surprise came out, he was too scared to notice. If he had been operating at full potential and not taking you for granted, he could have kicked your ass."

"So, what do we do? How to we upgrade my brain for the new werewolf 1.0 operating system?"

"First, we make you notice the difference. That's why we're going on a run. You don't realize it yet just how much faster you are, how much more powerful your legs are. So, just try to keep up." Deon doubled his speed. It was like a long-distance runner going from cruise to sprint, but he just kept pounding the pavement without looking like it was much effort. Stephen leaned forward just a little, and to his surprise, his legs kept up with him. Every time he tried to push them a little faster, they complied. Stephen caught up with Deon in just a few steps. "Excellent! Now let's really go." Deon took off at an even faster sprint, and it looked like something Stephen had seen while watching Olympic sprinters, except Deon was keeping up the pace for a lot longer. Stephen demanded more from his legs, and they kept on moving faster. Only now, running long distances at sprinter speeds, Stephen started to feel the need to breathe a little harder. Still, the closer he got to catching Deon, the faster Deon would run and to Stephen's amazement, so did he. Deon turned on a dime and took off towards the ditch beside the road. Without missing a step, he jumped the ditch and the fence on the other side, only to land in the field on the other side in perfect stride, a distance of about twenty feet. It wasn't a world record running long jump, but it was stupid far as much as Stephan was concerned. Stephen turned to match Deon but thought better of it at the last second and instead came sliding to a halt just before the fence. Deon stopped and waited for him on the other side.

Breathing a little harder than usual, Stephen looked wide-eyed at Deon. "How fast was that?"

"About, twenty-three or twenty-four miles per hour roughly, not super-fast."

"The fuck it isn't," Stephen countered.

"Scientists have crunched the numbers and think that the top speed for the human body is about forty and is only limited by the maximum contraction speed of the muscles. Our muscles work the same as humans but our muscle fibers are denser and our lungs are more efficient. That means we have more fast twitch muscle in comparison. Even at my size, I top out around thirty at a sprint but I can cruise long distances at about twenty four pretty comfortably."

"That's just crazy," Stephen answered, trying to catch his breath again.

"You think that's fast, watch Kaitlin sometime, now that girl can run. I don't think she gets tired even at sprint speeds and you should see her run as a wolf, she's easily pushing forty five or maybe fifty in a sprint there. My point here Stephen is your body and your mind have to get on the same page about a lot of things. Next time you're in a fight, and there will be a next time, you have to be used to your new speed and strength because you won't get a second chance. Word has gotten out about you already, the other packs know we have a new Alpha and maybe what you are. Right now they are probably trying to figure out just how much is rumor and how much is fact so we don't have to expect them any time soon. The exception to that being the pack that sent those assassins after us. Depending on how much Marcus told them, they know exactly what's going on and assuming that they've tried to reach him, they probably know he's dead."

"They really that hard to get along with? Malcolm said I had to convince them to try his treatment but if they are going to try and kill me on sight then how's that going to work?"

"They aren't going to try and kill you on sight, there are some social rules we all follow, but if they sense weakness in you, it'll only invite them to attack. Like you said, the only currency they all respect right now is breeding, and if they can kidnap our women, they'll try. Until we know how the assassin's pack will react, you can probably expect them all to be a threat. Now…before you are late for work, lets head back to the house. I'll race you."

Chapter Three:
Maxwell Pack

Commander Kaden Maxwell stepped off the international flight and was greeted by his Beta, Ted Branson. Kaden walked with the smooth confidence of a leader—a man on a mission, someone who got things done. People around him subconsciously took notice, lesser men got out of his way, and he caught the eye of every woman he passed. He was a good-looking young man, apparently in his mid-twenties; Kaden was actually pushing almost forty. He chose to keep his auburn hair close-cropped, in a military style, and made a point of keeping his body fit for combat at all times. With his high cheekbones and geometrically pleasing face, Kaden often imagined himself being depicted in marble as a twin to one of Alexander the Great's busts. He could have passed for any other overly handsome soldier; except he wasn't wearing a uniform and would never be able to serve. He was Alpha of the Maxwell pack, but he preferred the term "Commander". Truthfully, though, Kaden wasn't a strategist; he was a warrior, preferring to charge headlong into battle rather than plot and scheme. Military advantage had its place in his view, but the best attack was head-on. That was part of why he had resisted taking this trip; it seemed too underhanded. The other reason was that Kaden hated to fly; humans and their rules deprived him of the weapons that he always wore, but flying out of the country had been necessary, or so Ted had repeatedly said. Now back from his "retreat" in the Canadian wilderness, Kaden was ready for the report of their victory.

"Ted."

"My Commander, it is good to see you. I assumed your spiritual retreat went well?"

"Yes, I will admit that, as opposed as I was to your insistence on plausible denial-ability, Saber and I enjoyed running through the back woods. We hunted and were hunted in return. A local wolf pack caught our scent and chased us, thinking us a lobo, but a kill left on the trail persuaded them to leave us in peace," Kaden answered, referring to Saber his wolf's name. "Now let's get my bags and head home. I feel naked without my weapons."

"This way Sir."

Kaden put up with the drudgery of human society long enough to reach their car before he asked about the mission. "You seem hesitant to discuss the mission," Kaden started, "I assume you have something to discuss."

"Yes, Sir, the mission did not go was well as planned."

"I assume Marcus did something terribly foolish like tried to renege on our agreement. What countermeasures have you taken to ensure his delivery?"

"Actually, Marcus didn't renege, we were unable to complete our side of the agreement; and we now believe that Marcus is dead as well."

"What?" Kaden all but screamed as he turned and stared at Ted wide-eyed! "What went wrong? I assume you debriefed our troops?"

Ted paused again. This was going to be the hard part. "Commander, they didn't make it back. The entire strike team is presumed lost. We've tried to reach out to Marcus through normal and our back-channel methods for the past week, but neither has worked, so we assume he is also dead. From what we can tell at this point, Malcolm may have succeeded in creating a new werewolf, and this Stephen Butler may be the new pack Alpha."

Cold fury rolled off Kaden for just the briefest of seconds before he got his emotions under control again. There was a risk to any military maneuver, but the loss of four of his troops had been a surprise. They had been given detailed intelligence, knew the target's movements and locations, knew the opposition forces' numbers and capabilities; they even had the element of surprise, but no action could be perfectly planned. "No battle plan survives first contact with the enemy." It was an old saying, but apparently true.

"What has their response been?"

"Nothing yet, with a new Alpha taking over we believe that he is still securing his hold over the pack. Since he has not acted yet, I have. We've sent word to their Alpha female requesting a meeting. I thought that this would be the best way for you to judge this new Alpha and prevent them from making a counter play without loss of face with the other packs. We could delay the meeting by tying up the negotiations until you returned and we've had the chance to gain more information on Stephen Butler."

Kaden didn't always agree with Ted, but the man had a keen sense of strategy, and he trusted his Beta's advice. "Good. I'm not fond of politics, but in this case, it's probably better to gather more intelligence before considering a follow-up strike. You're right, assuming this Butler person cares for pack politics, this will delay him long enough for us to be ready for any strike he may want to make. You have done well to protect the pack."

"Thank you, Commander. What are your orders?"

Kaden paused and thought it out for a few minutes. Malcolm had been mentally weak, but when forced to fight, rumor was that he was formidable. Marcus, though, had been ruthless and dangerous, making him someone Kaden would have liked to face in battle.

Stephen Butler, though, was an unknown, and that worried him. He recalled what Malcolm had promised at their last meeting: a scientific cure to halt the low birth rates and to renew the strength of the packs. He even promised that he could reintroduce the werewolf genes back into the pack, making his short-term fix permanent. Kaden had thought him a fool and had quit listening a third of the way through what Malcolm had been trying to explain. He didn't need any cure or new werewolf genes; he just needed to cull the herd, removing the weak and diseased werewolves to make the rest stronger. People like Malcolm had to be removed so that stronger wolves would lead. Now, with this unknown threat, Kaden was forced to reconsider what Malcolm had said. If he had been able to "make" a werewolf and Stephen had been that product, how would that change things? There were too many questions, and a good leader hated unknown factors. "Send in our human spies. Learn everything we can about Stephen Butler, especially whether he was a lobo or actually was made into a werewolf by Malcolm. Most importantly, we put our troops on alert. Anyone not on patrols needs to be training. Keep moving forward with our meeting. I want to meet Mr. Stephen Butler for myself."

"Of course, my Commander, so I move forward with assault planning as well?"

"Yes, depending on what I find, we may have one more weakness to cull."

Chapter Four:
A Quiet Night with a Queen

The one thing they never show you in cop dramas on television is all the hours of paperwork. Stephen and Deon pulled in at the police department just a few minutes after seven on Monday morning, and Stephen had a mountain of work on his desk. He had been out of the office for weeks after Malcolm's suicide, a memory that he was still trying hard not to remember, and then there was a kidnapping when he got back. The result was about fourteen inches of paperwork piled on his desk and hundreds of emails to go through. Even after working on it for a week, he still had more work to do. Lieutenant Michelle Wong, commander of the investigations division, probably had it worse. In addition to still trying to wrap up the paperwork on the kidnapping of Angela Witherspoon, she still had to approve and close out all the other routine investigations that never seemed to stop coming.

Stephen got to work the moment he closed his office door and had gotten mostly through his emails before his mind started to wander. His screw up with Veronica was still bothering him, and he was having trouble leaving the home life at home. He was going to have to come up with something special to fix it with her; the only question was what he could do. He had just shaken it off to get back to work when his phone intercom rang and the blur of his workday began for real. The real reason that Chiefs never seem to get enough work done is all the meetings they have to attend. It's like the city officials and the public think that Chiefs can be in two places at once. Come to all these meetings, speak at these engagements, oh and have all your office work done at the same time. That was the worst part of being a salaried employee; there were always more hours you could work. Today, though, Stephen didn't have the option of working too late, so he just worked through lunch and an extra hour at the end. By four pm, he was walking out the door with stiff shoulders and a touch of eye strain.

"So, you figured out what to do about Veronica," Deon asked as he pushed off from the wall he was leaning against by the front door. For a guy the size of Deon, pushing off the wall looked more like pushing the wall down. Some people had no right to grow that big.

"I've got an idea, but it'll take a little work to get ready. She's on second shift today at the hospital so she's not going to be home until later."

"Stephen you're forgetting about the other two. You're living with three women remember. Pardon the pun but if you're in the doghouse with one then you're going to be in the doghouse with the other two."

"Oh shit, really? Kara opened the coffee shop this morning, so she probably didn't get home in time before Veronica left."

"But if Veronica saw Kaitlin and they talked, then Kaitlin will tell Kara, and…"

"And I'm a dead man the moment I walk in the door." The realities of living with three women suddenly became clearer for Stephen. When he was married to Becky, he had one woman to keep happy, which, at first, was hard enough. Now there were going to be three in the house. He had always felt like a minority in his own home when Becky had been alive, like being his wife and woman of the house gave her an extra vote. If Becky had gotten two votes, then three women would get... "Maybe this wasn't my best decision ever. Sure, you don't want to stay for dinner?"

"Oh, hell no," Deon said with a laugh as they both got into his car, "I'm gay for a reason, pissed off women scare the crap out of me." They drove to Stephen's in silence as Stephen stewed over the problem. All too quickly, Deon stopped the car in front of Stephen's house and started to pull away the moment Stephen stepped out. "Dead man walking," Deon called out with only a hint of a smile in his voice as he pulled away.

"Fuck you, Deon," Stephen answered, but couldn't dispute the description. Taking a deep breath, he opened the front door to find Kara waiting for him at the dining room table.

"Afternoon, Kara," Stephen began, trying to start as neutrally as possible. Kara looked up at him and smiled, which threw him off even more.

"Kaitlin got called in early, I guess the casino is short-handed this afternoon, and she wanted to make up some time that she lost from last week," Kara answered. "Guess it's just you and me for dinner tonight."

Stephen sighed with resignation. He didn't want to bring it up, but he needed Kara's help, and it was like pulling off a Band-Aid. Sometimes, it was better to jerk it off and get it over with. "Kara, I screwed up with Veronica this morning. I didn't mean it the way it sounded but I said something wrong, and I think she's pretty pissed at me. She was trying to help me work some stuff out this morning, and I said some things that I didn't think through. I hurt her feelings and was a jerk, but I didn't mean it. I'm going to try and fix it with her, but I didn't want to call her at work." Stephen explained in a rush before he relayed the situation. By the time he had finished retelling his stupidity, Kara's expression wasn't nearly as friendly as it had been when he walked in.

"So," she said carefully to keep her emotions under control, "I can see why she might be mad. I am too, but...if I try to think it through from your point of view, I can understand your thinking."

"Deon helped to point that out too this morning. I'm sorry for what I said, to her and to you and Kaitlin too; I know you guys don't understand where I'm coming from right now, but I am trying to change my thinking. It's just really hard, I've had an entire life of social programming that says that age and appearance matters. Men my age are starting on the downhill side of being attractive to most women. Sure, there's women with daddy issues that still might find me attractive, but this is the age where most women, especially younger women, just see me as being old. Deon reminded me that in werewolf years, my age now isn't all that old anymore and even younger woman could be attracted to me. I've spent my whole life knowing that it was one guy and one girl, or guy guy or girl girl; you didn't get to add in others along the way. That whole monogamy thing, and now I'm living with three women, and I'm expected to have sex with all of them, plus a pack full of other women." Stephen's mouth finally stopped moving as his thoughts rambled out of it in a broken flow of thought.

"Stephen this has nothing to do with your age, and is only partly about your upbringing," Kara corrected sternly but with a touch of compassion seeping in, "it's all about your confidence. Before all of this, you were self-assured, you were the Chief, a man at his emotional prime, and you knew exactly how your life was going to turn out. Now everything has changed and you're scared, like being a teenager again, trying to figure life out. The funniest part is you can't see yourself how we see you...how I see you. Remember, I know the Stephen before he became Alpha, Malcolm told me every little detail and every little secret. Even back then you were confident and motivated, brave and loyal, hardworking and determined; everything that we need in an Alpha werewolf. The girls don't see you as an Alpha, or really even as a fellow werewolf yet; you're just Stephen, but they do see all those traits I just said and that's what they are attracted to. Malcolm saw those in you from day one, but now you've had your world shaken up so you're doubting yourself… which is making you a little stupid and doubting us now too."

Stephen thought for a bit before he slowly nodded. "Like I told her, I think I'm overthinking this too much. It's like I have this new pressure on me to perform…in all kinds of ways…and I'm not sure I can do it. If I can't live up to expectations, then what? I don't want to let you girls or the pack down. Hell, I don't even know all their names yet, but I keep thinking about what I can do that's best for the pack. Then there's the part after sex, the becoming a father part. I've never had children and never thought that I ever would. Becky was too high-risk to have kids, so we never really put much thought into it. Still, that's a problem for another day. First, though, I need to fix it with Veronica."

"Yes, you do, and I have confidence that you'll be able to do that too. She really likes you…a lot… and you're smart, you'll figure it out. But speaking of the pack, I do have some official business we need to talk about," Kara said, changing the mood to a different serious topic. "I got a call this afternoon, from Kaden Maxwell's people, he's Alpha of the Maxwell pack to our west. He's asking for a meeting concerning, as he put it, recent misunderstandings of his orders by some of his pack. He's wanting to meet at the border between our two territories to meet you. From what he was saying,

I'm pretty certain that Marcus made the deal with his pack to hire the assassins that came after us."

"So, you think he's trying to smooth things out or finish the job?"

"With Kaden, it's hard to tell. Kaden's pack is a little bigger than ours and his people are all tough. About ten years ago, before Malcolm started to get really bad, we got into a war with the Hampton pack to our north. The war lasted a couple of months but there was some pretty bad fighting, and we got a reputation as good fighters so we got a little of Kaden's respect, but not much. He runs his pack like a military operation and he's all about combat strength. They train and drill all the time but that also means that they don't have the resources that we do. He doesn't spend as much time keeping his real-world businesses going or keeping up relations with the other paranaturals. If he joined with Marcus to hit us here, then he might be trying to see if we're going to hit back."

"Apparently he wasn't worried enough to turn Marcus down, and what's up with the weird pack names?"

"Weird? … Oh! Packs are named after the last name of the current Alpha male. It's just simpler to keep track of them that way. Before we used locations but when the pack numbers fell and packs started covering larger parts of the country, it just got to be easier to go by name."

"So, what, we're now the Butler pack?"

"Yep, as soon as everyone finds out your name and that you're the new Alpha, we'll be the Butler pack."

"That's just weird, but by now I should be getting used to weird. Anyway, so what do we do about the meeting?"

"Kaden Maxwell is young, he's only been Alpha for about four years and with his obsession with being all military, it's hard to guess what he really wants. You don't turn your pack into a bunch of soldiers for nothing. Taking Marcus' offer and sending in people to assassinate you and Deon, that's ballsy. Kaden isn't stupid though, war with us would be messy and costly, but I think he's a bit of a hawk and might be looking for a war. Malcolm went to the other packs and told them he could make them strong again, but no one believed him. Now you're showing up out of nowhere to become Alpha might make some of them rethink it. If Kaden does think we have a cure, he might want to hit us before we become too strong or he might want to take the cure for his pack. At the very least, if he goes to war now, he has a chance to bring more women into his pack."

"I'm not interested in going to war with anyone, right now we need to be making allies not enemies. Marcus was the one that made them the offer, and we sent their people to the cleaners. I don't want to fight a war that doesn't need to be fought. That's just a waste of life."

"That is my thought as well, let's just hope that Kaden agrees that a war wouldn't be cost-effective. This is a dangerous time for us. You're new all the way around, so some packs will fear you and some that will see this as an opportunity. How we deal with Kaden and the Maxwells is going to set a tone for the others."

"So how do we proceed? Is there a protocol or something," Stephen asked.

"There's a negotiation process on the terms and location of the meeting. How many people each side can bring, assurances that neither side will be armed, or a declaration that all parties will be armed, that sorta thing. Meetings between two Alphas are rare and difficult at the best of times. Security is always an issue both from the other pack and from the packs not invited to the meeting. Two Alpha males at the same place is a tempting target for the others."

"Fuck how does anyone get anything done with all this suspicion and backstabbing?"

"Sometimes, we don't get anything done. We take care of the creatures of the night in our territory and hope that the other packs can do the same. Malcolm was always careful with his people, so we've kept our numbers higher than some of the other packs. By now…smaller packs must be getting pushed really hard just to keep their own territories under control, let alone something as stupid as fighting another pack."

"OK, so if he wants to meet, do I need to call him or something?"

"Deon and I will take care of the details. We'll send envoys with our demands and they'll send theirs. Then we negotiate a fair middle ground somewhere, something that both sides feel is safe enough and still saves face."

"This is so dumb," Stephen complained as he got up from the table and started to pace in frustration. "We're supposed to be protecting humanity and finding a way to keep from going extinct but we're spending all this time and energy with politics. We need to be making allies, finding friends to help while we try to grow the packs again, but instead we're trying to find ways not to go to war."

"No one ever said that werewolves made sense or that being Alpha was easy," Kara answered as she got up and put her arms around him. Kara's hug was like cool water, calming his spirit and refreshing him at the same time. She was queen, his queen, the pack's queen, and they couldn't have been any better choice than her. Just her touch seemed to melt his stress away, like she could erase his worries with her own strength. Kara held onto him a little longer than he was expecting and maybe the momentary confusion bled through his emotions. "I know, I should let go now," she explained still holding on, "but all the sudden I don't want to let go." Stephen held on a little tighter and tried to read her emotions. To his surprise, it felt like she wanted to cry, emotionally she was trembling inside. "You're not the only one that feels the pressure of leadership. I never had a choice, from the very beginning people were telling me that Malcolm and I would be pack leaders someday. I heard it so much that I never thought anything different. I understand how it feels, always having someone watching, always having to be perfect; I couldn't even tell you how scared I was during your fight with Marcus. I couldn't flinch when he tore up your arm because someone in the pack would notice. I was so scared that we'd lose you too and now we have Kaden's shit to deal with."

Stephen buried his face in her hair trying to curl himself closer to her as they stood in his little dining room nook and held each other. "Can you make me a promise," Stephen started as a whisper through her hair. "Never hide from me. If you want to cry, then cry. If you want to scream, then scream. You're right, I'm off my game because I'm scared and in new territory; but that doesn't mean that I'm not here for you. I understand having a game face, I do it all the time at work too, but now I have to learn how to do that with my emotions just like you. You don't have to do that around me. I understand the pressure you're feeling, always having to look like you have your shit together when you're just trying to keep from screaming. Cops want to look up to their boss like he's super cop, especially during the times when we aren't. Promise me that at least here, while we're together in this house, you are just going to be you."

Kara pulled away a little just so she could look into Stephen's eyes. "I promise that I'll try. When Malcolm and I were together I couldn't show him either, I couldn't let go, I didn't want my stress to trigger him so I held it all in with him too. I've been so practiced at holding everything in for so long that I don't know if I can just be myself, but I promise that I'll try."

"May I ask a question," Stephen said gently.

Kara chuckled lightly in response, like his question had been funny. "Of course, but I can't promise you'll like the answer."

"May I kiss you? Not by accident like when you made me breakfast, Becky used to do that and it was part of our morning routine, but because I really want to kiss you. Not Alphas, not werewolves, just me Stephen, a guy in the arms of a beautiful woman who he really cares for; kissing you, Kara."

"Ah, hell," Kara answered with mock frustration and then leaned into him, letting him kiss her for the first time that wasn't accidental, or during the Shift. Kara's lips were warm and so very gentle for a woman of such strength. They kissed easily, like they were made to kiss each other, and the gentle kiss slowly turned into something a little more. Kara finally broke the kiss before it could turn into something…hotter.

"Ah, hell," Stephen asked with a stupid high school grin on his face, he looked like the prom queen had just agreed to go out with him? Kara couldn't help but smile and even laugh a little.

"Being asked for permission for a kiss," she answered, finally beginning to pull away from their hug too. "It's no wonder that the other two are falling in love with you so fast. Maybe I am too…but just a little," she added with a mischievous look. "Now…before I make myself even more embarrassed than I am already, and start talking way too much, or too loud, or something very juvenile like that; I think it's time we start looking for dinner. Ya, dinner, what sounds good?"

Now it was Stephen's turn to laugh just a little. He had never imagined the mighty Kara, werewolf queen, being embarrassed or being suddenly just that damn cute. "Just about anything sounds good right now, but something with a lot of protein. Deon and I went for a run this morning and I guess the body is craving protein, I've been dying for a good burger all day."

Together they stepped around the L shaped bar that divided the kitchen from the rest of the room and set to work. Stephen's house was large, much bigger than he or Becky had needed when his wife had been alive. She had been the social engagement diva, though, hosting monthly house parties, so the large house had been well used. Becky had been a gifted investment broker so hosting parties for her clients, friends, and future business partners had just been part of the deal. There were bedrooms and enough bathrooms for ten or more people with space left over. The front room had been designed specifically for entertaining people. It was an open floor plan design that combined a dining room, kitchen, and family room all into one open space. Walk into the kitchen by stepping around the bar. To get from the dining room to the living room, just take a few steps down into a sunken nook area and have a seat in front of the huge fireplace. Off the living room two large doors led into the sunroom, extra space for those times when just the living room wouldn't be enough. Off the sunroom, the large wrap around deck for the outside entertainment space. Next to the doors going out to the sunroom was the library, which doubled as Stephen's man cave and office. Becky had thought about everything when they built the house. Stephen thought about Becky a lot, especially with all the new changes in his life. He often wondered what she would think of him now being an Alpha werewolf and living with three women. Would she be happy for him? Would she even understand? They had both been faithful to each other for their entire marriage, and even before that, would she understand that he was beginning to have serious feelings for more than one woman?

"You got quiet, what are you thinking about," Kara asked as she checked the cooking of the burgers.

"Becky," he answered, a little uncomfortable talking about his deceased wife with a woman now living in her house. "I was just wondering what she would think about the whole werewolf thing and our current domestic arrangements."

"Most humans can't or won't believe in real werewolves. Werewolves in movies and books are fine but having one standing beside you is different. Now, about having the three of us living with you; that's a harder question. I'd hope that she would be happy for you. I know that if I had been her, I wouldn't want you to give up on things like love and physical intimacy. Even in human years, you still have a lot of life to live, I hope she would understand that and want you to live it the most fulfilling way possible. As long as you're happy with the three of us, then I'd hope she'd be happy for you too."

"How do you do that," Stephan asked, "how do you turn it on and off? You were in love with Malcolm, but you knew that he was having sex and was in love with other women too. Veronica told me that they had been in love with each other but said it was just a different love from what you and he had, how do you turn it off and not get jealous?"

Now it was Kara's turn to pause in thought before she answered. "You don't turn anything on or off, you accept that love is love even if it involves people other than you. When Malcolm and I were together, we were there because we both chose to be; our love for each other wasn't a form of ownership. Maybe it's different for humans; we were brought up thinking like this, but for me and him, our love didn't mean that we owned each other. He and I were still different people; we had different interests, and neither of us expected or asked the other to give anything up because we were together. Just the opposite, I wanted him to be happy and fulfilled both sexually and emotionally. No one person can fulfill the other completely and denying your partner the chance to find fulfilment is just greed. Veronica is different from me; she could meet needs I couldn't and add things to his life I couldn't add. That didn't mean that I was any less or any more than her, we were just different. In a way, I'd argue that it's a more powerful love than what other people feel with monogamy. With monogamy, you're socially bound, you're commanded to stay together and love each other or else, and the only escape or way to find fulfilment if it's missing is to either cheat or walk away. I loved Malcolm enough to let him walk away, to find what else he was needing, knowing and trusting that he loved me enough to come back."

"And was he able to do that for you too? I mean with your duties as Alpha female, the pack needs you to be sexually active too."

"Again, we were raised like that, our social rules were set from day one; but yes, he knew I had other lovers. I had other people in my life, but I didn't love any of them like I loved him, I just loved them differently. The secret that makes this work is being totally honest with yourself and the person that you're with. Honesty is a byproduct of being a werewolf, our biology kind of forces you to tell the truth or get really really good at hiding your emotions. Now don't get me wrong, there are couples in the pack that are almost monogamous, being exclusive to each other and the Alphas; but marriage like what you and Becky had isn't as common. There are some humans that are living like this now too, I think they call it polyamory. Another way to look at it, Kaitlin and Veronica are both my daughters. In a monogamy world, I could only love one but not the other. Parents don't do that though; they love both and value each child for being individuals. You love them both but just differently."

Stephen thought about it, and Kara could feel his tension brewing. She waited patiently for him to be ready. "So…this is hard for me, like you said I wasn't brought up this way, but I'm trying to be honest here so I have to ask. So…it's OK then if I think I'm having feelings for or building relationships with Kaitlin and Veronica, that wouldn't bother you? And, maybe, if you and I could maybe consider having a relationship, I'd really like that too," Stephen said, almost like a kid asking for permission to eat dessert before dinner. "I mean only if you're interested in something like that, you know maybe, kind of seeing what it would be like…oh hell I sound like an idiot."

"Yes, you do," Kara said, smiling, but not in a way that made fun of him. She could feel his sincerity, even his fear of rejection. Stephen had taken a big step into trying to accept and adapt to the werewolf world and to move past a problem that had been bothering him since he was first introduced to his new life. "Would it bother me if you started a relationship or fell in love with one or both of them? Of course not, I'd be happy for all of you, I want them and you to be happy. If that's the way this all goes then great! Now, you and me —we've discussed my feelings about who I thought you were. I hated you, and some emotions take a little time to let go of, but that was me being greedy. You were human so I guess I didn't think about it the same way that I would have if he had been spending time with another werewolf. I wasn't being fair to him or to you but since I've met the real you, I can see how wrong I was now." This time, it was Kara who needed to pause for a second to get herself prepared. "I'm also not over Malcolm being gone yet. I loved him so much I think sometimes I'm going to die knowing that he's gone but being here, with you and the girls, helps. So, to answer your very eloquent question about if you and I could maybe start building something more than just friendship…I'm not against that either, just don't expect the big L word right away and give me some time to get over Malcolm's loss."

"Oh, absolutely," Stephan answered sincerely and with a kid-like excitement, "slow and easy sounds like a great idea! Becky has been gone for several years, and I'm just now getting to a point where I can even consider emotional commitment to another woman. Most important, though, if this does start getting weird for you, I want you to tell me, you're too important to me to screw any of…this…up," he said as he waved his hand vaguely around the room.

"We're all werewolves, getting messed up emotionally isn't something we hide very well, but I promise. Now…food is done and I'm starving too so let's eat."

Stephen helped her to plate the food, and then they ate together on the couch in front of the cold fireplace. They spent the rest of the evening together, laughing, telling stories, talking about people they knew, and about places that they had always wanted to see. No one looked at their phone or checked their social media page. They had started the evening with each of them at one end of the coach, but by the end, Kara was leaning against him, and Stephen had his arm wrapped around her shoulders.

"It's getting late and you work tomorrow morning," Kara said with a twinge of disappointment in her voice, "but I really am enjoying just sitting here with you."

"I'm having a good time too," Stephen answered as he leaned his head over on top of hers, pulling their cuddle a little closer, "but you're right I have work and don't you open tomorrow?"

"No, one of the guys needed off early tomorrow so I swapped shifts, I don't go in till nine."

"Wow, sleeping in and everything, it's good to be the owner I guess."

"Too bad I don't get overtime for all the extra hours the owner has to work to make the Bit and Byte work. You need to go to bed," Kara said reluctantly as she pulled away and got to her feet. She paused for a moment as she stood above him while he was still sitting on the couch. Smiling, she bent down and kissed his forehead. "Thank you."

"For?"

"For being Stephen." Kara walked away with a sense of ease and contentment that she hadn't felt in years. She still missed and loved Malcolm; some nights, she still cried herself to sleep with her face buried in a pillow but tonight had helped. With a smile and a twinkle in her eyes, Kara walked towards the back of the house and headed for bed.

Chapter Five:
A Badly Timed Phone Call

Stephen went to bed not long after Kara with a smile on his face. The evening had been simple but amazing, reminding him of just how much he had missed the simple evenings he had with Becky before the cancer came. Standing in the bathroom, staring at the mirror with a toothbrush hanging out of his mouth, he tried to laugh at himself and almost gagged. Sure, things were going… different than he had expected, but that just meant his life wasn't going to be boring. Spit, rinse, toilet, and then bed was next on his agenda. Last week's cold snap over, Stephen threw on some old cotton running shorts and climbed into bed.

He promptly…stayed wide awake. He tried to settle his mind, count sheep, fluff the pillow, roll over to the right spot, but nothing helped. Stephen checked his phone and social media, then tried to go to sleep again. Still, nothing was helping. Concentrating carefully, he reached out with his new hearing abilities and tried to hear what Kara was doing in the room just down the hall from him. Sounds came rushing in, louder than they should be, all mixed together, like trying to pick out the individual tomatoes in a bottle of ketchup. He needed more practice, but after a few moments he started to pick apart the sounds, and his mind began to filter them out. It was painful and took way longer than the girls took to do the same trick, but he was making progress. When all he could hear was Kara, he was almost disappointed to listen to her even and deep breathing.

Minutes ticked by but still sleep wouldn't come. He had been having this problem off and on since he became Alpha and had his first complete Shift. Last night hadn't been much better so he finally gave up and grabbed a blanket off his bed. Resigned to another restless night, Stephen decided that he'd at least be productive. Grabbing his cell phone charger and phone, Stephen snuck out of his room as quietly as he could and grabbed his laptop, a pad of paper, and his favorite pen. You knew when a man had reached that particular age, when he had a favorite pen. If he couldn't sleep, then he could at least get something else done. It was already getting late for people who had to work in the morning, but Veronica and Kaitlin would both be home around midnight, assuming they didn't have to stay late. Kaitlin worked at the casino so their clients would sometimes keep them busy into the early hours, and Veronica, well, she worked at a hospital, enough said.

Stephen plugged in the various chargers, wrapped the blanket around himself, and settled into one of the fluffy chairs on the back deck. The weather was still a touch cool at night, being spring, but it wouldn't be long before the warm nights of summer came, and a blanket would be overkill. Mostly, he wrapped himself in the blanket just because he liked it. It was a beautiful night, though, with clear skies lit by the sun's reflected light off the moon. Wolf senses were terrific; even by the light of the moon, the whole night seemed to light up for him. Looking up into the sky, it looked so different to his senses that it was like looking at the stars while standing on an alien world. The stars seemed like they were closer, being easier to focus on, and new stars he'd never seen were now visible. Shaking himself out of his amazement, Stephen took a pad and pen and started making notes and working on ideas. Productivity began to eat away the minutes and then the hours, only releasing him when the crunch of driveway gravel could be heard. A glance at his phone showed that enough time had slipped away that it was twelve thirty.

Veronica slipped inside the house and thought, not for the first time, how much nicer it was than her apartment. She still needed to pack up her stuff and close out the apartment, but having a "just in case" fallback wasn't always a bad thing either. She really liked living with her mom and sister…and Stephen when he wasn't being stupid. Still, he was still human in his head, and this new life might all come crashing down, and she didn't want to find herself without a place suddenly. She was surprised when the light from the back deck caught her eye, his silhouette visible from the light from his laptop screen. Veronica knew he had to work in the morning, so she hadn't prepared herself to have to see him again this early, not after what he said this morning. With a sigh of resignation, Veronica laid her small bag on the table and made for the back door.

"Waiting up," she asked as she slid the back door closed behind her.

"Partly," he answered carefully, looking up from his work. "I tried to sleep but it wasn't happening so I thought I would get some ideas down on paper. I was doing some research."

Veronica glanced over at the screen before she settled down in the deck chair across from him. Stephen had chosen a lounge chair, his legs out in front of him so he had a place to rest his laptop; she had chosen a regular padded deck chair. She wasn't sure how this conversation was going to go, so formality had won out over comfort.

"Polyamory huh," she said without judgment.

He could feel her emotions, what she was letting slip through at least, and she was still pissed off at him. She was being cautious, waiting to see how he proceeded, but he knew that under the surface, she was still hurt. "Just trying to learn. Obviously, we need to talk," he started, "but before that you've had a long day, and I didn't make it any better. Do you feel like talking now, or do you want to wait till tomorrow?"

"Now," she answered, leaving no room for argument. "I probably wouldn't be able to sleep either."

"Alright," he answered, shoring up his mental walls. Whatever came next, he deserved it. "I…," they both started at the same time, stumbling over the conversation like a dancer with two left feet.

Stephen smiled lightly before he asked if he could go first. With her nod, he started. "What I said this morning was terrible, it was hurtful, it wasn't fair, and it was completely wrong. I know that now and deep down I knew that then too. Deon and Kara both helped me work some things out today and I wanted to say that I'm sorry. I really didn't mean to hurt you or say that you…any of you…were with me for petty reasons like that. Kara pointed out that this thing I've got going on in my head is really about me losing my confidence, about me being afraid. Before all of this, before you guys, I had my life all together. I was in control. Now…now I can see stars that weren't there before, I can tell if my roommate is asleep by listening to her breathing from down the hall, and I can feel the anger and pain coming off of you. That's not me in control anymore and as Kara pointed out, I'm scared. I'm scared of getting hurt because I can't keep up with all this stuff going on. I'm scared of hurting you girls. I'm scared that I'm not good enough for you or for the pack. I'm worried that I am some kind of genetic cure all pill and at the same time I'm worried that I'm not. I knew things were progressing between you and me, that night on the couch was…just wow, but I think things are changing between me and Kara too. Don't even get me started on Kaitlin, I have no idea what's going on there yet. All these emotions are mixing up inside and I didn't know the rules anymore, not until I really got time to talk with Kara this evening. So…ya, I fucked up this morning, and I'm really sorry."

"I'm glad she helped you," Veronica answered carefully when Stephen paused, "and yes, you fucked up this morning. If it makes you feel any better, I guess I'm scared too. My life is changing too. I never really put myself out there like this before. Sure, there's been other men before, Malcolm and the others, but they all came to me. You're the first man I've really…tried to go after before and like I said before I'm not really the 'out there' kind of woman. So…ya…I'm a little scared too, but I don't want to hurt you or the others either. I'm not mad at you anymore, but I still have my apartment, and I'll pack things up in the morning if you want. Maybe it would be easier for you if we weren't all living in the same house, give you some time to adjust to your new life and get your control back. Then when you are ready and in a better place, I'll still be there."

Fear and panic rolled off Stephen so hard that Veronica could almost feel the impact against her skin. His fear woke up his wolf. "No," he said in the same voice he had used at the pack meeting, waves of command and Alpha authority pouring off of him. Deep inside of him, in that metaphysical realm, his wolf paced back and forth on its side of the dividing line. Stephen didn't want her to leave, and neither did the wolf.

Veronica's breath caught in her throat as she shuddered with the feelings. Inside her, in her metaphysical space, her wolf reacted too. "Stephen," she answered with effort, "calm down, please. Your wolf is…calling, and my wolf is trying to answer. Plus, you're going to wake Kara."

Her reaction and the touch of excited fear in her voice were all he needed to get back in control. "No," Stephen answered, but this time only with his voice. "I'm sorry, this is your decision, not an Alpha thing. I didn't mean for this to feel like a command, but I really don't want you to leave."

"I can tell," Veronica answered, finally catching her breath, trying to put her wolf back to bed. "He can be pretty…demanding when he tries." Inside her head, she was dancing. Sure, he had been an epic level jerk this morning and deserved a good beating for it, but what she just saw made her happier than she had expected. He wanted her —wanted her to stay with him —so much so that he was scared she would leave.

"So, are we good then? You'll stay…because you want to?"

"What do you think?" Veronica answered as she got up and started to climb up the length of the recliner on her hands and knees, giving Stephan just enough time to get his laptop out of the way. When she reached his chest, Veronica slid her hand under the blanket and across his bare chest, the genetic lottery having left him hairless. "Ohhhhh," she said, drawing out the word like the touch of his skin under her hand was intoxicating. With a flourish, she threw open the blanket and stared down at him with an almost hungry look in her eyes. Even before becoming a werewolf, Stephen had taken care of himself in the gym, but now the changes were even more noticeable. Muscles that hadn't been there a couple of weeks ago were clearly defined, and his chest had grown broad enough that some of his shirts were getting snug. Veronica straddled his waist as she leaned forward and ran her tongue up the middle of his chest, tasting and smelling him at the same time. When her mouth reached his neck, she gave him a little touch of a bite and then went to his mouth. She kissed him hard, wantonly, and any worries that he had about age or performance disappeared. Stephen kissed her back, matching her desires, his fingers digging into her back as he tried to pull her down closer to him. Wanting even more, Veronica broke the kiss and reared up as she ground her hips against his. Still in her work clothes, she grabbed at her scrubs top and all but tore it off over her head, revealing the simple black sports bra underneath. Somewhere in the tiniest of portions of her mind, that little bitty part that was still thinking like a rational person, two thoughts danced through, "I probably smell like the hospital," and "I'm not even wearing one of my pretty bras". Stephen's hands grabbed her by her hips, fingers digging in slightly before sliding his hands up her sides. When his fingers reached the sports bra, they slid under the elastic, and the bra slipped off as his hands kept rising. Freed from their elastic prison, Veronica's breasts bounced slightly as they fell. They were beautiful, round and full, with nipples that were already sharp enough to cut glass as they pointed upwards at him. She threw the bra to the side before he pulled her back down on top of him, her bare skin now pressing against his.

Stephen's cell phone sprang to life, buzzing and playing its offending ringtone. "Dammit," answered three voices in unison. Veronica sat back up, and Stephen reached for his phone, but both stared at the doorway to the sunroom, where Kaitlin stood, one hand under her shirt and the other down the front of her pants. Unapologetically, she just shrugged as she answered their unspoken question, "It's not my fault, that was a hell of a show, and Big Black can be…persuasive."

"Who," Stephen asked just as he grabbed the phone.

"Your wolf, that's what the women in the pack have already named it, Big Black," Veronica answered, the disappointment rolling off her. It didn't take a rocket scientist to know what it meant when the Chief's phone rang at one in the morning. Grabbing up her clothes, she followed Kaitlin back into the house. "You know where he keeps the batteries," she asked when the door closed behind them as they walked through the sunroom back into the living room.

"I was going to ask you that," Kaitlin answered with a teasing smirk in her voice.

Matching their teasing tone, Kara's voice answered from the hallway leading back to the bedrooms, apparently woken by Big Black after all. "In the kitchen, second drawer on the right from the fridge. Add it to the shopping list, he's running low."

"He'll be out at this rate," Veronica answered, still smiling but with a twinge of frustration peeking through.

"I told you; you needed to buy the rechargeable one I showed you," Kaitlin answered playfully.

"This is Stephen," he answered between the third and fourth ring. Caller ID said that it was Lieutenant Michelle Wong on the other end, the investigations division commander, and one of the key people in his department.

"Sorry if I woke you up, Stephen," she began with her Texas twang thick in her voice. Michelle was Chinese, grew up in Texas, was above average in height for a Chinese woman, loved driving too fast, and hated Chinese cooking. She was such a mix of contrasting features that few people knew how to handle her, and when she did make the rare joke, most people were too uncomfortable to laugh.

What she really was was a damn good detective who knew her job and her people. "There's been a break-in at the University."

"Oh hell, please don't tell me we have some missing science project,"

Stephen answered, thoughts of following Veronica to her room quickly fading.

"I'm just leaving my house now," Michelle answered, ignoring his poor attempt at humor, "patrol said it's the sword."

Bradford University of Research Arts was the local high-end, elite private college that specialized in degrees for people who were hard-science or research-oriented. It wasn't a huge school by university standards, but it was famous in certain circles. The university was founded by an old railroad tycoon back in the 1800s on the idea that, regardless of background, only the elite minds would be admitted. The entrance exams were brutal, but once accepted, the students never paid for a thing until the day they graduated. For some budding scientists or researchers, they'd do their best work at the university. Bradford University's crowning glory, though, was the library. Holding over a million books, many of which are unique or exceptionally rare, the library was a researcher's dream. Stephen had been there just a week ago and met one of their employees, who had been a little less of a dream than expected.

Six months ago, well before any of this werewolf stuff started, the university dean called him one bright Monday morning and told him the good news. The Japanese government had finally agreed to bring a travelling cultural history exhibit to the US, and Bradford University was on the list of venues. This was the kind of exhibit that people and scholars alike interested in Japanese history would travel hundreds of miles to see. The crowning glory of the show was the Onimaru Kunitsuna, a 13th-century Tachi-style samurai sword considered one of Japan's legendary "Five Swords Under Heaven". The sword was of such cultural significance that it was even held by the Imperial Household Agency, the government agency responsible for preserving only the most important treasures. Obviously, when the dean had expressed his excitement, he couldn't have been more overjoyed to host such an exhibit. Stephen only heard drama and dealing with the Feds. There was no way an exhibit like that could come to the US without the State Department's hands all over it. Now…Michelle had just told him that the sword had been stolen.

"Let me get changed and I'll meet you there," he replied and then hung up. His department had just got out of the news, recovering a missing girl, alive and healthy, and now they were going to be in the spotlight again. "Whatever happened to the days of trying to bust drug dealers?" Stephen thought to himself as he grabbed his stuff and moved with purpose back inside.

"So," Kara asked, the other two girls reading his emotional change and stopping too.

"The university had a break in; a famous sword has been stolen from a traveling exhibit from Japan. State Department is going to be all up my ass on this one and I'll be stepping on Feds all over the office."

"The Onimaru's been stolen," Veronica said with obvious shock. "Jason worked for three years trying to get the Japanese government to approve the exhibit to come here."

"Who?"

"Sorry, you haven't met yet, Master Jason Sato, I told you about him, he's my martial arts teacher and one of the pack. Jason's father was a Japanese American at the start of World War Two. He got picked up during the internment camp thing and met Jason's mom. When he got released, they moved back to Washington DC and got married. Jason's Dad worked for the government after the war, I think the State Department, but for whatever reason the family traveled a lot. Jason ended up being born in the US but lived in Japan most of his life. He had his first Shift in Japan and stayed with a very small pack there until his parents died and he decided to move back to the US. He took a job working at the university and was accepted into our pack just before I was born. Jason's going to be devastated, this was one of his greatest achievements and brought great honor to him and the school. The loss of the sword will be terrible for him."

"Well, it's going to suck for us too, the PD is going to take a pounding if we can't recover the sword," Stephen answered as he moved towards his bedroom in a rush to get dressed. Finally breaking his mind away from the problem, he remembered his other problem and stopped to look back at Veronica. "Sorry about…you know…this."

"It's you're duty, just one of the things I like about you, and it goes along with being in your life. You're not the only one who has to adapt," she answered. Over her shoulder, Kara smiled broadly, glad they had made up and mouthed the words, "told you so" back to him.

"Well, it sucks for me too," Kaitlin complained teasingly, lightening the mood. "I really liked that show too. You think I'll get to watch it again later?"

"Go to bed, perv," Veronica teased back. Memories flooded back to his mind as Stephen watched the girls teasing and showing their love for each other. One of the hardest parts about being a cop was having to leave a loving family behind when you had to go to work, a feeling he had forgotten since Becky's death. Now he had a new family, and the sense of missing out on life came rushing back. Here he was, off saving the world and fixing everyone's problems, when all he wanted to do was stay home with these three. His plans weren't quite ready yet; he still wanted to do some more research, but he knew he couldn't leave them, leave her, like this yet.

Pausing at the door to his bedroom, Stephen looked back at the group. "I'm not quite done planning yet, and I really wanted to surprise you all, but now seems like a good time as any. You three have been very good to me —much better than I probably deserved — and I really feel like I owe you all. Plus, I wanted a way to get to know you all better, something fun, so what would you guys think if I took each of you out on a date?"

It was Veronica who answered first. "A date, in public, just the two of us, but all three of us get a turn? I think that sounds amazing!"

"I agree, I think that would be very nice, I'll look forward to it," Kara agreed, putting on just a touch of formality in her voice. It was Kaitlin who surprised them.

"Pass," she answered calmly, but her pain wasn't easy to hide. "Thanks for the offer, but unless Dad wants to take his little girl to the movies or something, I don't think it's going to work for me. Thanks for the thought," she answered as she walked towards her room just a little faster than necessary. It was a boon for most werewolves, the ability to age at less than half the normal rate, but Kaitlin wasn't enjoying it as much. She had her first Shift just a few years ago when she was sixteen. Now at twenty-three, her body still looked like it was the same sixteen or seventeen-year-old young adult. As she passed him, Stephen grabbed her suddenly and pulled her up close. He kissed her like he meant it before he said anything.

"You're not a little girl and I don't see you like that. I'm sorry I didn't think that through, but I won't leave you out. Give me a chance to come up with an idea before you just say no."

Tears in the edges of her eyes, she looked up at him, almost like she was pleading for her body to grow up faster. "You don't have to, I know it's going to be hard enough for the Chief of Police to be seen on dates with two different women. We could go out, but you couldn't show any affection, and we'd be too worried about what people thought. Face it, I'm sixteen to most people, but thank you for the thought." Kaitlin reached up and kissed him back on the cheek, then headed to bed. He wanted to call after her, wanted to make it right, to find something to make her feel like she was an equal, but in the end, she was right.

"We'll help you think of something," Kara replied, knowing what he was thinking. "You need to go; they need you. We'll be here when you get home."

Chapter Six:
Onimaru Kunitsuna

Stephen arrived on scene a little before two thirty in the morning, but there was still plenty of activity. Police lights flashing around the library reflected off the glass-fronted building, turning the night into a red-and-blue disco, and, like any good dance club, it was drawing the teenage crowd. Students, almost all with IQs higher than his, milled around outside the police tape watching what was going on. When he got out of his car, Stephen grabbed the first uniformed cop he saw.

"Brad."

"Ya, Chief."

"Do me a favor, start getting pictures of the crowd, good face shots, but make it subtle, I don't want them knowing. When you're done give them to Lieutenant Wong."

With a nod, the officer headed towards his patrol car and the digital camera stored inside. There was no way to know the motivation for the burglary yet. Whoever stole the sword could be after ransom, a collector seeking the sword itself, or someone with a political agenda trying to make a statement. Depending on the motivation, it wasn't uncommon for the criminals to return to the scene to see what the police found. Stephen walked past several more officers until he got inside the library.

"Morning Stephen," Chief Alex Caldwell greeted morosely. "Sorry about this, we doubled the building checks and patrols around the library and whoever did this still got through." Alex was the Chief of Police for the campus security forces. They were fully commissioned and certified officers, but had jurisdiction only on campus property, which gave most of the officers minimal experience with major crimes. Stephen and Alex had been friendly for years, and their two departments had trained together often because one group routinely backed up the other.

"Don't worry about it Alex, we both know that a locked door only keeps out an honest man. Motivated criminals always find a way; we just need to work together on this one and get the sword back before the Feds and State can fuck it all up. Can your guys start with the student population? Who had a political motive against Japan, who was a sword freak, someone who was unusually interested in the sword; that sorta thing. Your guys know the student population a lot better than mine, so you'll be able to weed out suspect faster, saves my detectives time doing useless interviews."

"Sure thing, I'll get everyone started on that. I assume you want our info forwarded to Lieutenant Wong?"

"That would be perfect, thanks, that's going to be a big help."

Stephen continued walking through the library following the sounds of voices. For once, no one was talking in hushed tones in the library. The exhibit had been held in a special wing of the library, usually reserved for only local history museum pieces. That didn't mean the library's security was lax; it held several rare and costly books, so security was taken seriously. Turning the last corner, Stephen couldn't help but smile when he heard Michelle's Texas twang.

"Look, I don't care and changing languages isn't going to make me listen right now," Michelle barked at someone Stephen couldn't see yet, "you're in an active crime scene and until we're ready to talk to you, you need to leave."

As Stephen approached, the target of Michelle's wrath came into view. He was an average-looking man, probably middle-aged, of mixed Japanese descent, who was obviously very concerned that his information wasn't being taken seriously. Stephen had seen this throughout his career; crime victims often tried to do the job of the police, sometimes out of distrust or a lack of confidence in the investigation, but often they felt the need to be involved to regain part of their sense of security. Being a crime victim, especially in cases like residential burglaries, left the owners feeling violated, as if even their own homes were no longer safe.

"Dr. Sato," Stephen said confidentially, immediately drawing the slightly shorter man's attention. "I'm Chief Stephen Butler, is there someplace private that you and I could talk while Lieutenant Wong and her team does their work?"

Dr Sato's eyes widened slightly, and Stephen could sense a twinge of fear mixed in with his apprehension and worry. For a passing second, Stephen had time to wonder why he could feel the emotions coming off of werewolves and not humans, too, but that would be a thought for another day. "Yes, of course, my apologies Lieutenant Wong for interfering. Chief Butler we can talk over here in one of the private study rooms." Stephen followed Dr. Sato into a small study area and closed the door behind himself. The moment the door closed, Dr Sato dropped to one knee and bowed his head. "My apologies my Alpha for not being able to attend your ascension trial, my duties here would not permit me to attend. The exhibit just opened this weekend, and I was needed here. I meant no disrespect, I am very glad that you won, Marcus would not have made a good leader."

"Stand up, Jason," Stephen answered quickly, still not used to being treated like royalty. "You didn't offend anyone by not attending. Veronica speaks very highly of you, so I'm sure you did only what was right."

Jason smiled with evident pride when he spoke next. "Veronica is my best student and the pride of my teachings. When I came back to America, I was lost and a lobo. Getting a job with the university and then starting my martial arts teaching helped me learn to fit in with American culture. I was born American but raised Japanese, so there was a lot to learn. Even as a young child, Veronica went out of her way to make me feel welcomed and tried to explain the culture to me. She has grown into quite a woman."

"I agree," Stephen replied as he returned the smile. "Kara, Veronica, and Kaitlin are living with me now. Without them, I would have never even made it to the trial, they've been teaching me since day one and I still feel lost most of the time. Now, let's talk about the sword."

Dr Sato's mood soured again as the reality of the burglary returned. "I cannot believe that it's been stolen. The fallout is going to be terrible. Politically, the sword is irreplaceable, and its loss will damage our relationship with Japan for years to come."

"Maybe I don't understand, I agree it's embarrassing to the campus and the PD, but the loss of this sword will really damage the political relations between the United States and Japan?"

"Absolutely," Jason replied with a sense of desperation in his voice. "The sword is named Onimaru or the Demon Sword. It was forged sometime in the thirteenth century and is considered one of the finest examples of Tachi sword smithing in history. It's so well acclaimed that it is considered to be Tenka-Goken, or one of five greatest swords under heaven. Even the history of the sword itself is important. The sword was said to have come to Shogun Hojo Tokiyori in a dream. Tokiyori was being plagued by terrible nightmares about being tormented by a demon. The sword came to him in the image of an old man and promised that if Tokiyori would clean the sword, that the sword would destroy the demon. The legend says that Tokiyori cleaned the sword of every speck of rust and then put it in a place of honor. The sword then moved on its own and fell from the scabbard, striking the foot of a fire blazer. The foot had been carved to look like the face of an oni, a demon, and the blade struck the demon on the neck, cutting it from the blazer. Tokiyori was never troubled by the demon again and gave the sword the name Onimaru. The sword became a prized treasure of the Hojo family, and several Shoguns wore the sword over the generations. It eventually was passed to the Ashikaga family and has been passed down through history. For Americans, it would be like us lending out the original Constitution and then having it stolen in a foreign country."

Stephen nodded as Jason explained and started to feel ill with every word. If Dr Sato was right which, of course, he would be then the State Department would be on a rampage. The Feds would come in, take over the case, run over anyone and anything in their path, and blame Stephen's department when they couldn't find the sword either. This was the kind of case that ended careers or made them famous.

"I think I understand now," Stephen replied seriously. "I'll do my best to make sure we recover the sword as quickly as possible and I'm sure the State Department is already on their way too. Do you know of anyone who would have an interest in the sword, maybe a collector, or someone who strongly opposed the sword coming to America?"

"I don't normally deal in Asian antiquities beyond my own personal interests so I'm not familiar with any of the possible collectors. The sword has worldwide renown so if it is a collector, they could have come from anywhere. There was some opposition to the sword leaving Japan, but I doubt that a Japanese official would be involved in stealing the sword back. I'll do some digging and talk to some of my other academic contacts, see if I can't help putting a list together. It won't be easy though, stolen antiquities have a huge market worldwide so the sword could have a buyer anywhere."

"How much could a sword like this cost," Stephen asked.

"To the right buyer, a sword of this magnitude could go for eighty maybe ninety million dollars, but that's just a guess. If Excalibur really existed, how much would it go for?"

"Thank you, Doctor, I'll make sure to pass this information along to Lieutenant Wong. Sometime when we aren't all so busy, I'd like to talk to you about your martial arts form that you developed. Veronica says it's called the Way of the Wolf Warrior."

Jason Sato chuckled lightly but nodded, "It kind of loses a little in translation. Growing up I was exposed to several different martial arts forms and even mastered a couple. My parents didn't have a lot of time for me growing up so sending me off to a dojo made for an easy babysitter. I've taken little bits of different forms and tweaked them to take advantage of our unique physical abilities and limitations. Veronica is by far my best student and is more than capable of teaching you if you wished to learn."

"I'll talk to her about that, she's shown me a little, but I'd like to learn more. Apparently, my life has gotten a lot more combat oriented lately and I'll take any advantage that I can get."

"Of course, my Alpha, it would be an honor to instruct you," Dr. Sato said with a little bow from his shoulders. When Stephen opened the door again, Jason hurried out.

Stephen wandered back to Michelle who was still working on the crime scene with her people. The scene looked like one would expect, rows of glass cases showing little bits of Japanese history, each with a little card explaining the importance and rarity of each peace. The first thing that struck Stephen was all the glitzes. Several of the cases held items made of gold and encrusted with gems of various sorts. Jade, opal, and other semi-precious stones were scattered on several different items across the whole exhibit. Whoever had broken in hadn't touched a single case other than the sword's case. He had time to only take one quick look around before Michelle approached him.

Without preamble, Michelle started with her report. "Point of entry looks like it was one of the back service doors, it's the only door that was found unlocked and all the windows are secure. The door had an electronic lock with a manual key override, so it was either left unlocked, they bypassed the electronics or had the key. The outside keypad looks like it's intact so I'm leaning towards they had a code or the key. Interior alarm didn't go off either and looks like it's also intact, so another point for someone having the codes. Interior cameras were all operational, but the DVR is missing out of the security office. We may have gotten lucky there, they took the DVR but the university had been backing up the video to the cloud so we may have video. We're still checking on that; we're trying to get a hold of their IT security guy. The university keeps its own security staff for the library but they brought on six more when the exhibit announced. Chief Caldwell is pulling their background investigation files now but they were vetted by him and the outside security company that the university contracted with so who knows how much we'll find. We're still trying to interview the night security staff, there were only two guards last night, one watched cameras while the other walked the floors. One guard, Brenda Cross, said she was walking the floor. Her job was to stay on the exhibit wing but she's already admitted that she wondered the library sometimes as well. She was the one who found the open display case and made the call. The other guard, Ted Crossland, was on camera duty but said that he had fallen asleep. He said that he didn't wake up until Brenda called it in on her radio and that's when he saw the cameras were all down. He's still groggy and a little out of it so I've called for the medics to check him out."

"Drugged maybe?"

"I don't know, kind of cloak and dagger if he was, but it's possible. We'll take him to the hospital and see if he'll consent to a blood draw. Brenda says that she wasn't off the exhibit floor for more than ten minutes before she found the burglary. She's claiming that she made a loop but then had to go to the bathroom, so she left the floor for about ten minutes. She's saying that she was feeling nauseous and had the shits," Michelle twanged in her Texan accent, ever the lady. "Just in case, I want to take her too and see if she's just got a stomach bug or maybe something else got her stuck on the toilet."

"Dr. Sato said this could be an eighty-million-dollar job to the right collector and there would be buyers all over the world," Stephen added. "Don't rule out professionals on this so cloak and dagger might be a thing. I assume the various government powers have been called already."

"Ya, the university called State, and we called the FBI. I'm sure they'll have all kinds of people showing up to stomp around the place in another hour or two."

"OK so make sure you're ready when they start showing up. Where do you want to start in the meantime?"

Michelle stuck her pen in her mouth and started chewing as she thought, the cop version of a stereotypical hillbilly chewing on a blade of grass. "I'm thinking inside guy, someone who knew enough of the codes to get in and shut off the exterior door alarms. Someone knew the layout, including where the security office was and that Brenda liked to go walk about. If the guards were drugged, someone had access to their food, or access to the guards enough to slip them something. Only part that makes me wonder about that is the cloud backup. Why take the DVR when it was being backed up and if they knew enough to get it, why didn't they know about the backups?"

"So, we locate and interview all the guards and IT staff. We start at the top and go down. Speaking of which, why isn't the security director here already," Stephen asked?

"I've got a squad car going to her house now. We're told that the director, Mrs. Cindy Hendrix, had been taking a lot of time off lately due to domestic issues but was a good boss and was still getting her job done. She's been employed with the university for years and passed all the background screenings before the exhibit came in. Ted said that she'd been pulling a lot of hours in the last few days on the final checks before opening weekend, so he just assumed she had taken today off."

"So, she didn't come in today," Stephen asked?

"Nope," Michelle answered with the same sinking feeling. "I'll check the keypad logs, see who was the last one to use the back door keypad."

"And get Chief Caldwell to open her office, see if anything is off there too. Who did you send to her house?"

"I don't know," Michelle answered as she started to walk away in a hurry. "I just called dispatch and gave them the address I got from Caldwell."

Stephen grabbed his phone.

"Moser City Police Dispatch, what is the nature of your emergency?"

"It's Chief Butler, who did you send to Cindy Hendrix's house for Lieutenant Wong?"

"634, he just went on scene about five minutes ago."

"Status check him."

"Dispatch 634…," pause. "Dispatch 634…," pause. "Dispatch 634 status check," the dispatcher said, stress bleeding through, but silence only answered her.

"Put out an officer needs assistance and text me the address," Stephen ordered, reaching down he turned up the handheld radio he wore on his belt and started for the front door. Seconds later every officer who could hear a radio froze as the alert tones sounded, it was a sound designed to get everyone's attention, a sound that every officer dreaded.

"BEEEEEEEEEEE!   Dispatch to any available officer, officer needs assistance, 312 Hillcrest Road, 312 Hillcrest road, officer needs assistance. 634 is on scene and non-responsive." Anyone who had ever worn a badge before would know exactly what was happening next. It didn't matter who 634 was, if he was well liked or a jerk. It didn't matter what color of uniform you wore or who you worked for, if you heard that call and wore a gun, you went. Light bars would flash to life, sirens would be screaming their warnings, tires would be squealing, and cops would be cussing every slow driver who didn't get out of the way fast enough.

"I'm going," Stephen called out to anyone who cared to hear. Already he could hear sirens and tires coming to life in the parking lot as officers not immediately needed were jumping in cars.

"Call me," Michelle yelled back as the front doors banged open just barely in time to let Stephen through.

Stephen sprinted across the parking lot, only barely remembering to run at a human pace, only to come to a screeching halt at his car door. Sitting in the passenger seat was a woman he hadn't expected to see tonight.

"Get out Leann, I don't have time," he commanded the woman in his car. Leann Kingsly was a unique individual in many ways. She was transitioning from male to female, she was a diagnosed Schizophrenic, she worked and probably lived in the library's basement, and she was a witch. Stephen had only met her a little over a week ago and barely understood the metaphysics behind being a witch. Still, somehow witches and warlock were sharing their souls with multiple people throughout history at the same time. From their point of view, each life was happening at the same instant. The result was often diagnosed as Schizophrenia since the voices from one life frequently bled through to the others. The other side effect was that Leann's soul was now heavy enough to make a wake through the Aether, the realm of magic, what scientists were currently calling dark energy. When he had first met, Leann had been wearing a full-length evening gown with elbow-length opera gloves. Now she was wearing leopard striped yoga pants, a short pink lace skirt complete with ruffles, and a yellow loose-fitting top with a blue denim jacket. She looked like something that 1980s fashion had thrown up.

"We needed to talk to the Chief Idiot and there was no other way," Leann answered calmly. That was another part of her unique charm; Leann referred to herself in the plural and didn't think much of the intelligence of other people. "Now you can waste our time arguing with us, which you will still end up losing, or you can get in, and we'll talk as you drive."

Stephen got in and lit up his emergency equipment. Leann winced in discomfort; she didn't like loud noises. When they first met, she complained because Deon and he had taken the elevator instead of the stairs. "OK, I'm driving," Stephen answered curtly.

"Excising your dominant male gruffness won't get you very far here so don't even bother, believe us we're not overly happy about being here either. We needed to talk but we're certain that you might wreck the car if we force you to think too hard, so let us explain and you just try not to kill us in this screaming death trap." Stephen didn't answer. Emergency driving in an urban setting was hard enough without someone like Leann in the front seat. "There is more to your stolen sword than just politics. We didn't want the damn thing in the building, but no one would listen to us. The sword is a Tsukuyomi."

"A what?"

"Four winds preserve us, read a book already," Leann barked in frustration. "We'll be there before we can even explain this all to you. OK, small words…Tsukuyomi is a Japanese philosophy that says that if a tool exists long enough and is used regularly enough that it can gain a kami, a soul, of its own. Many ancient sword makers believed that the best swords could gain a soul while being forged. The Onimaru has been around for almost eight hundred years and has been passed down from generation to generation, used over and over to kill the bearers' enemies, and it has its own soul. Now think about our computer downstairs and how we explained how the Aether works, remember what we said about form and function."

"Belief in the function is more important than the current form. Believing a calculator can do math is more important to a witch than the fact that the calculator is currently broken."

"Exactly, you do have a few grey cells that work," Leann answered. "Now what did we say about how souls work for witches?"

"Your soul is heavier than normal humans because you have multiple people using it at the same time. The more people, the heavier the soul, the stronger the witch or warlock."

"So, what do you think would happen to a sword whose soul could be eight hundred years old, and for that entire time has had an entire country of people believing in its story. A country's worth of people believing day after day that the sword's function was to kill demons, to be the Onimaru, the Demon Sword. Now…and this is the hard part so we'll go slow…what do you think would happen if a witch or wizard got a hold of a sword like that?"

Stephen tried to think through it while driving and still trying to listen to his car's police radio for updates. "You'd get a sword that actually could kill demons, that had a soul heavy enough to have access to the Aether."

"Not just access," Leann corrected, "but could be used as a magical fetish, a tool to make access to the Aether easier and more efficient. Why do you think witches use brooms or magic wands? The older these tools are, the stronger they get and the more readily they grant access to magic. Say a warlock tries to cast a spell on his own, it might take days to gather enough power depending on what he's trying to do; but with a good wand the warlock might be able to cast the same spell in minutes or even immediately."

"So Onimaru can be used as a potent weapon, capable of killing demons, and could be a powerful spell casting tool."

"Ah teaching the children is such a fulfilling feeling," Leann answered in mock pleasure. "Now the Japanese had a very broad definition for the word Oni, or demon, so the sword will probably be pretty damn affective on all kinds of creatures, including witches and werewolves."

"Hold on," Stephan warned as he took a hard right turn before he continued. "Leann, I have a question, werewolves have packs ruled by Alphas, how are witches and warlocks set up?"

"Many of us are solo, us for example, we do our own thing," Leann answered hesitantly. "Some gather together in small groups of three or four, rarely as large as six, which are called covens. The covens and even the solos are overseen by the Cabal, sort of a high council. Oversight is very loose; we magic users aren't much for following the rules of 'the man'; but it's the Cabal that keeps everyone in sort of a straight line. The Cabal and fear of werewolves actually," Leann corrected. "What do you want with the Cabal?"

"From what you said, every warlock and witch alive now have a motive to steal the sword and after Karen Ashter raising the dead to kidnap an innocent teenager, I think I need to talk to this Cabal. Is there a Cabal locally or how do I reach them."

Stephen didn't need superpowers to read Leann's sudden change in mood. She wasn't happy talking about this and now boarded on scared. "Stephen," she answered, shocking him that her insulting attitude had been replaced by using his first name. "You're new to this world so we'll explain. Werewolves aren't that popular with many paranaturals, a lot of them are scared to death of you guys. We're one of them too. We've known Deon for years and still have trouble trusting him; you, you're completely unknown. It's been the werewolves that have kept us all in the shadows for all these centuries, even the races that didn't want to hide do now because of your people. We know you're not personally to blame but werewolves have always kept the peace by killing anyone who broke it. A werewolf showing up at the front door meant that someone had been sentenced and the executioner was knocking. We're not sure we should tell you how to find the Cabal."

"Dispatch all units responding to 312 Hillcrest Road, we've made contact with 634 by phone, all units can stand down from code response. 634 requesting medical and supervisors to continue to respond. 600, call dispatch for more information."

"600, copy," Stephen answered into his radio before he turned off the lights and siren. Slowing back down to a reasonable speed, he turned his thoughts back to Leann. "I'm sure you know that werewolves have a mandate that they believe in, to protect humanity from the enemies in the night. That's meant keeping the paranatural away from the human world and in the past that was enforced upon pain of death. I wasn't part of that and until just a little while ago, I didn't even know that any of this really existed," Stephan began. "I'm also sure that you and the rest of the paranatural world know that werewolves are dying out, that soon we won't have the numbers to police ourselves, let alone anyone else. That means the nastier things out there that I don't even want to know about yet, are going to have free rein real soon to do whatever they want to whomever they want. I'm also pretty sure that they won't care if their target is human, or another paranatural, as long as they think they can get away with it. That leaves everyone else just two choices, either hope that they are hidden well enough not to be found, or that they are strong enough to fight back when they are found; either way humanity is going to find out. What happens then, when humanity finds out that they aren't the dominant predator anymore, what will they do? I know what they'll do, I was human until a month ago, they're going to lash out with everything they have. Paranaturals will go from predator to prey overnight. Sure, we'll take a lot of them with us, we've been really good at hiding for a really long time, and one on one humans don't stand a chance: but there's a crap ton of them. In the end, maybe even in my lifetime, all paranaturals will either be hunted to extinction or we'll become lab specimens. I know you probably have every right to be afraid of me, of us, because of how the rules were enforced, but I really just want to make this all better for everyone, humans and paranaturals." It was only when Stephen paused that he realized what had just happened. For the first time, he had thought of himself as a paranatural by default. He had an us vs. them moment, and he was now counting himself on the paranatural side. Somewhere deep inside, a little bit of his humanity cried at the loss.

Leann got quiet and even squeezed herself tightly. "I agree," she answered, talking about herself only this time. Usually, her plural form referred to her and her other lives. When she spoke in the singular, she was only speaking for her current life. "I've hated werewolves and their self-appointed righteousness, but they've kept us safe from humanity just as much as they've saved humanity from us. That doesn't mean that this still doesn't scare me straight, but I guess trust must start somewhere. Deon has never treated us badly. So, what's your plan?"

"I need to talk to the Cabal. I need their help to find the sword, and I need their help to build a future that keeps everyone alive. I need you to tell me how to find them."

Leann didn't answer at first, but finally she just reached into a pocket of her jacket and slid a small rectangular piece of plastic towards him but didn't let go for a few more seconds. "We are trusting you, only because we think you're not quite human and not quite werewolf. We know how that feels, being lost in both worlds' and not comfortable even in your own skin. We are hoping that you can be something different, maybe be a bridge between human and paranatural, maybe we just like to dream of a place where we can all live and be accepted for who we are."

Stephen glanced down at the piece of plastic and read it with a laugh. "Magical Wizard Con! All Access Pass". Stephen was going to a comic book convention.

Chapter Seven:
312 Hillcrest

Leann's presence had been inconvenient but also full of disturbing information. With Michelle tied up at the library still, Deon had been called out to respond to this new crime scene that had one of his junior patrol officers so rattled. Stephen didn't have any choice; he called Deon and diverted him to come pick up Leann to take her back to the library. The last thing he needed was for the Chief of Police to show up at a crime scene with a woman in transition dressed like it was still 1980. Deon hadn't been far away, already responding to the officer needs assistance call and was very surprised when he saw Leann with Stephen. Deon had known her for ten years and had never once known her to leave the library. He wasn't happy about being diverted; one of his guys had needed him after all, but he knew the importance of returning Leann before anyone noticed. As soon as Deon left with Leann, Stephen called dispatch and was told that 634 had called in to report a homicide, apparently a pretty bad one.

With Deon's sacrifice, Chief Stephen Butler was able to arrive on scene just before four in the morning. Officer needs assistance calls didn't come out all that often, so even after being called off, several patrol vehicles had responded anyway, mostly to see what all the fuss was about. Several of the officers looked like they regretted showing up now. When Stephen arrived and made his presence known, several of the zone cars suddenly found better things to do.

312 Hillcrest Drive was a modest home in a middle-class neighborhood. Painted light blue with white trim, the small ranch home was probably only a two- or three-bedroom house, what some would call a starter home. It had a single-car garage attached, but one vehicle was still in the driveway. He hadn't even reached the front porch before he caught the smell of vomit and something fouler in the air using just his normal human sense of smell. This was one of those times he didn't even want to consider trying his werewolf senses. The local paramedics were already inside, leaving Officer 634 outside on the porch.

"Chief I'm really sorry, I heard dispatch, but I was…, I was getting sick sir and couldn't call back." Stephen knew all his people and officer 634 went by the name of Chase Andrews.

"It's alright Chase, I'm just glad you weren't in any real trouble. So, tell me what you've got."

"I responded to the house to contact Cindy Hendrix and to have her respond to the library but something just kind of felt wrong when I got to the front door. It was past three when I got here but the lights were still on, and the car was still in the drive. If someone was home, then why didn't they answer the phone? I got a little nervous, so I peeked in the front window and that's when…she's dead, sir, in a chair in the front room. Since I had a medical emergency, I forced the front door and tried to go in but…well the smell and there was so much blood and the kids," Chase reported as he started to turn green and his shoulders convulsed in a gag reflex. Stephen turned the young man away and guided him towards some bushes away from the front door. Thankfully, there wasn't much left in the rookie's stomach.

"Don't worry about it Chase, we've all done it," Stephen lied. He'd come close to blowing chunks on a couple of calls but had never actually done it. "I've got a bottle of water in my car, go drink it and get some air, I'll take it from here."

"Yes sir," Chase answered too uncomfortable to be embarrassed about puking in front of the Chief.

Stephen walked up the front porch and made it to the door just in time to get shoved to the side by a paramedic making for the door and the fresh air outside. He didn't need werewolf senses to smell what was coming from the front room. Cindy Hendrix, or what was left of her, was tied to a chair in the front room and the bodies of two small children were dead at her feet. Stephen risked a quick look at the two children. Each child had a single gunshot wound to the head, but the weapon had been of a large caliber and from close range, which turned their small heads into V shapes. From the position of their small bodies, Cindy had been made to watch as the children were shot. Cindy for her part had been tortured. Her body was covered in small cuts, nothing overly deep individually but enough to be painful and to bleed. Stephen guessed that the work had gone on for most of the day based on the amount of dried blood on her and pooled beneath her. He didn't have to be a detective to guess what had happened, she had gotten taken sometime early yesterday morning, so she didn't make it to work on time. The kids looked like they were of school age, so had probably already been on the bus when their mother had been taken. Whoever took her had worked her over for most of the day, slowly, like they were playing with the process. Stephen guessed that she probably had resisted giving up the key codes and other information at first, she had been a loyal employee for years; but when they started to hurt her…well everyone breaks eventually. By the end, she probably told them everything they wanted to know just hoping that they would leave before her kids got home, but they didn't. Maybe she had held out or maybe they were just sick fucks, but they grabbed the kids the second they got home and the rest, the rest was laying on the floor. Whoever had done this wasn't afraid of hurting people and was comfortable using a knife to do it. Cindy had probably been the last to die, a deep cut across her stomach had released her intestines out onto her lap and finally let her bleed out. It was a terrible way to die; disembowelment was maddeningly painful and a slow way to go. Stephen could imagine Cindy's feelings, the terrible pain, the mindless terror, looking down and seeing her own internal organs laying in her lap and begging for death to come. This wasn't murder, this was torture, the kind designed to deliver pain without purpose. Sick fuck, didn't even come close to describing the suspect.

None of the paramedics said a word as they packed up and got out of the way. As they walked out, the lead paramedic simply handed the EKG strips to Stephen showing that none of the bodies had any heart rhythm left. Stephen made a mental note to call the fire chief; those guys would need an after-incident debriefing and so would his patrol guys. Gone were the days of looking at stuff like this and then just going back to work, now we knew enough about the long-term effects of seeing shit like this to know that people needed to talk. Officer Andrews would probably need some time off and some time to talk to a professional. In a perfect world, Stephen would too, maybe he'd call that counselor from the hospital again, Jeff something.

Stephen walked back out into the front yard and used what few people were still around to start setting up a crime scene perimeter. As patrol was stringing tape, Stephen grabbed his phone.

"Deon," Stephen started immediately when the big man answered on the first ring. "It's a bad one, three DOA, two were kids. Get someone to come in and relieve Andrews, he walked in on it and needs to decompress. As soon as you're freed up from dropping off Leann, I need you back here, I don't want to break Michelle away from the library yet until she's done. As soon as I'm off the phone with you, I'll call the Coroner. I'll also call Michelle, let her know that her burglary just probably became a triple homicide and see if she has any crime scene techs that she can break free, if not I'll call the investigation squad, but their guys will take a while to get here." There was never enough manpower in law enforcement. Officers had to be experts in so many different skill sets that no one agency was ever prepared for everything. Thus regional manpower sharing agreements was the only way to cover all the bases, in this case a regional investigators squad.

"OK," Deon answered neutrally, already knowing how bad it was going to be just by Stephen's reaction over the phone. Stephen was in cop mode, see a task complete the task, but don't process anything else. The last time that Stephen had been like this was when he had watched Malcolm kill himself. Deon made his apologies to Leann and all but threw her from the car the moment they had pulled up to the library. His Alpha was alone and there was a murderer out there, the place of the Beta was at the Alpha's side. What scared Deon even more was Stephen's own mental health. PTSD just didn't go away overnight or even in a few months. He had watched his best friend kill himself and had been unable to stop it, leaving Stephen with baggage that he probably hadn't even noticed yet. Hell, after being forced to sit there unable to move and watch your best friend blow the top of his head off, baggage wasn't even close to the right word.

Chapter Eight:
Puppy Pile

Cop mode had lasted until almost nine in the morning. Deon had arrived and started taking over the investigation. Michelle freed up some of her lab techs and then bailed from the library as soon as she could to come to the new scene. Stephen had stayed on scene the whole time. There was a process for homicide investigations, and they all knew it, so he hadn't needed to give much in the way of advice. Truth be told, Stephen trusted his people and didn't even need to be there; they knew their jobs and could do them just as well without him. He needed himself to be there; the victims needed him to be there. It wasn't much, but he could at least stand vigil, acknowledge that the pieces of meat left behind had been people. He needed to watch, because somehow his continued presence meant that he was still working and didn't have to feel anything yet. He was the Chief of Police, the Alpha werewolf; he didn't let things like this bother him. He had a job to do, the citizens of his community needed him, his officers needed him, his pack needed him, the whole damn paranatural world needed him; those kids needed him. He needed sleep.

Stephen left the scene a little after nine. Crime scene had packed up, the building was taped off, Michelle had made her notes, and three people who called that place home had been loaded into bags and put in a cargo van to be taken to the morgue. Michelle had already made the critical notifications. Prosecutors had been woken up, and search warrant applications had been started to search the house and vehicle. Cindy's ex-husband got a knock on the door, and her mother's out-of-town address had been found. In another town miles away, a cop would be knocking on her door, too. Stephen would continue to live; his day had to go on, but those two kids wouldn't be going to school today; their day was done. He made a mental note to have someone call the school and let them know the Hendrix kids wouldn't be coming back. Somehow, he had driven back to the PD. Apparently, his patrol car knew the way because he didn't recall anything. Looking at the front of the building from his private parking place, Stephen took a deep breath and let it out slowly. He did what all good cops did: he clung to the memories, memorized the names, and buried the pain. He looked up into the rear-view mirror and saw his wolf's eyes looking back at him, brought out by his emotions. Stephen made a promise to himself, to his wolf, and to Cindy and her kids; when they found the people responsible, they'd see justice, and if the suspects weren't human people, they'd see his justice.

Chief Stephen Butler, game face securely back on, took a quick look around the parking lot before he walked to the front doors. Government-issued vehicles and airport rental cars littered the lot. Moser City wasn't the biggest city around; it didn't have an airport, it didn't have Federal zone offices or regional headquarters, so the Feds had to drive in if they were close enough or jump on a red-eye flight and then drive the rest. There weren't as many vehicles as he had expected; the others were probably still on their way. All the high dollar command posts, the special response vans, and probably even assistant directors of various three-letter organizations were still coming. It was his job to be ready for them, to brief them, and, if possible, to make nice with them enough that everyone got the job done. The conference room wouldn't be big enough; they'd have to use the investigations squad room again, like they had when Stephen had pulled in the whole department during the kidnapping. Stephen grabbed the front door and pulled it open. It was time to go to work.

The support staff of any police department are unsung heroes in Stephen's book. Cops got to go out and get the glory, make the arrests, chase the bad guys, but the support staff made it all possible. IT people kept the tech running, admin assistants kept the paperwork flowing and made the bosses look good, records division and evidence techs kept the important stuff found and got rid of the unimportant stuff, and somehow, they made it all just work right. Once word had gotten out what had happened, support staff had jumped into action; some probably even got called in early, and when Stephen walked in, they were all working in overdrive.

Stephen had just made it to the investigations squad room when Mathew, his personal assistant, walked up beside him. Any administrator knows that a great personal assistant is like Superman's cape; the Man of Steel might still be able to fly, but he'd look silly doing it without one. "Morning, Boss."

"Where we at Mathew?"

"Lucky, I guess," the young man started, "we still had the squad room partly set up for the FBI guys that helped with the kidnapping, so IT is already in place. I assumed you'd want to use the investigations squad room again, so we've been getting ready for the briefing there. We've got some Feds already here and they're already chomping at the bit, but I think they're waiting on more brass to show up. Your phone has been blowing up from the Assistant Director of Diplomatic Partnerships Unit of the State Department. I guess they helped arrange the exhibit as part of a cultural exchange program and this guy's blowing a blood vessel about the sword."

"I assume I'm supposed to drop absolutely everything and call this person back."

"I've tried to explain that the burglary has now turned into a triple homicide but apparently this Mr. Thomas Gordan is worried that his boss is going to have to call the Japanese ambassador personally to apologize for the gross disrespect we've personally shown to the country of Japan by allowing one of their most important cultural treasures to be stolen."

Stephen sighed and tried to blow out the evil and suck in the good. "Remind me after the briefing, what's the rest of the alphabet soup looking like?"

"FBI has three here already and their regional major crimes squad is still incoming. ICE is here with four, I didn't know it but I guess they have a Cultural Property, Art, and Antiquities Investigation division, I think they have more coming too. I think State called ICE and asked them to show up but FBI doesn't seem too thrilled. I'm told that State is even sending their own cops, Diplomatic Security Services I guess has a Special Investigations group that is supposed to coordinate law enforcement actions when dealing with State's projects."

"Please tell me they aren't whipping out their jurisdictions to see who's got the biggest one."

"Well, the FBI guys don't look like they're going to be the easiest to get along with, I overheard one already talking about trying to get us off the case so 'the locals don't get in the way'."

"Damn, I thought they got over that crap. We're all supposed to be on the same team now, aren't they doing the 'get along with people' training now? Hey! If State is sending these DSS people, then why am I calling the DC guy?"

"Actually I told him you'd call as soon as you got in the door, I guess he isn't big on waiting for up to date information."

"So…find the sword immediately so Japan's ambassador doesn't get offended, keep a room full of federal egos from stepping all over each other, make sure all the logistics are in place to support all these folks until their toys arrive, keep the press updated, oh and when I get around to it I should probably let the Mayor and City Administrator know too. That about it?"

"You forgot the university dean, he's called twice concerned about his donors who paid big dollars to make this exhibit a thing."

"Oh ya, I knew that was too easy. Mathew, I think I might be getting too old for this crap."

"I wasn't going to say it boss, but when was the last time you got any sleep? You're not looking quite your best."

"Let's see, what day is this?"

"Tuesday."

"Sunday, I think, depends on how you define sleep. Right now, I've got other things to do besides try and sleep, I assume they've all been demanding to go see the crime scenes."

"Not so much, they're mostly waiting on their bosses and tech support to arrive, that and arguing 'politely' about who's in charge. They look like the young up and comers, all of them looking to tie their name to the case with hopes that the sword gets recovered and their name gets on the news or read by director somebody."

"And probably not a one of them happens to care about the three people who died over some stupid eight-hundred-year-old hunk of scrap metal," Stephen growled, almost literally. "So, what's your schedule?"

"I've coordinated with them, most of their brass will be here by noon. State's DSS admins won't be in till tomorrow. I've scheduled the briefing for 12:30, assuming Michelle has enough time to get her notes in order."

"You're amazing Mathew, I don't know how we could do it without you."

"Ya, well, remember that when it's time for the annual reviews and pay raises," Mathew joked. He was a single dad with two little girls, and even the admin assistant to the Chief of Police didn't get the biggest of checks.

Stephen gave Mathew a weak smile and then walked out without saying another word. He made a beeline for his office, hoping that some bit of normalcy could be hidden in the files on his desk. He had thought about trying to sneak in a nap for an hour or two before the briefing, but try as he might, his mind wouldn't stop. Frustration began to turn to anger; this was his town, his people, his territory, and someone or something had the gall to challenge him here. At some point, he did drift off, but not into a sleep that would matter; it was restless, filled with flashes of memories. He remembered the dead family, the look on Marcus' face when Stephen had shifted for the first time, the feeling of power and horror when he sentenced Marcus to be hunted down, and the look of relief on Malcolm's face just before the shotgun blast tore it off. He woke up before the alarm he'd set went off, left his office, and then had a few moments to splash some water on his face in the bathroom before he headed to the meeting.

He could hear them still arguing in the investigations squad room before he had even opened the door. It was junior agents mostly, each trying to make the case that their senior agent or special agent in charge would agree that their agency should take the lead. ICE argued that they had a division that did nothing but investigate and intercept stolen antiquities, so they had better experience and resources. The FBI claimed that all they did was investigate, and that they had the most powerful law enforcement resources in the world to call upon. No one even mentioned his team or that the locals were the only ones that had actually done anything so far. People were still filing into the back of the room when Stephen had finally had enough. Without a word, he walked over to the computer Michelle was planning to use for the briefing and started scrolling through photos. There were well over a hundred for each crime scene, but he was looking for a certain few. When he found them, he grabbed the remote, turned on the projector, and then slapped the closest light switch. When the room suddenly went dark, the voices paused and the various agents began looking around. The image on the wall kept their attention.

Stephen started speaking, but his anger dripped from every word. He didn't yell, he didn't even raise his voice, but he made his opinion known. "Sometime yesterday, a mom got up and got her kids ready for school. She fed them breakfast, probably had to find a missing shoe or got them ready, and then sent them off. Her name was Cindy Hendrix, and she became a target because she worked in campus security. It was her job to help secure an eight-hundred-year-old hunk of steel that isn't worth a damn compared to her or her kids, but it was her job to protect it. She got targeted, and some evil people came into her house and tortured her. See these cuts here," Stephen said slowly as he pointed at the picture, "this is where they took a knife and cut through her skin over and over just to watch her bleed. I wonder how many times they had to cut her before she gave up the back door codes. The specialists will get a better count, but when I was standing over her body, I counted over forty. I'll admit, it was hard to stand there and count them, her body stank of piss where her bladder had let go at some point, and her bowels were sitting in her lap, so you imagine the rest." Stephen clicked through the following pictures, one at a time, slowly, until he found the ones he wanted to talk about. "I think Cindy lasted all day, but the Coroner will have to be the one to tell. I think she made it until it was time for her kids to get off the bus. She probably knew exactly what time it was and could feel the desperation that only a mother knows when her kids are about to walk into danger. Then, when these two children got home, these evil bastards grabbed them and made them stand there in front of their mom. I wonder if she lied to them, told them it was all going to be OK, that they shouldn't be afraid, that she was just fine… I wonder if she smiled at them before some asshole put a large caliber gun to the back of their heads and blew their faces off. If you look here and here in this photo, that's brain and skull matter from her own children still stuck to Cindy's body. Then, probably long after they got all the information they needed, the person who liked the knife, cut her belly open, all the way through the abdominal wall and spilled her guts out in her lap." Finally, with slow, deliberate motion, Stephen turned to the room of cops and federal agents. Rage rolled off Stephen as he started to talk again. "I've listened to you all talk about the Onimaru, and some of you even mentioned that there were people killed, but all you saw was fame and glory for your careers. Who gets to be in charge, whose name gets to be on the reports, who gets to be in the press conferences or makes the arrests. If the only reason you're here is because of a fucking piece of steel, then get the fuck out of my building. If you want to help me find the sick fucks that tore that family apart, then shut the fuck up and let's get to work." When Stephen stopped speaking, several of the junior FBI agents were pale, and a couple of the ICE agents looked like they were about to be sick. A few of the colder-hearted agents looked like they were about to do something foolish, like talking back.

"I agree," a strong female voice came from the back of the room from a woman wearing the standard blue FBI jacket with gold lettering. She wasn't overly attractive; her hair had once been almost black but was now more gray than black, but she had the look of an old battle ax that may be old but would still cut you to pieces. "I'm Senior Special Agent Monica Chandler…"

"Chief Stephen Butler," Stephen answered to her apparent question.

"If the Chief had to give you all a reminder like that, then I'm damned embarrassed of all my agents in this room. Chief, I am very sorry. Anyone here who isn't completely committed to the single most important goal, solving a triple murder, I'll personally send them home."

"Thank you," Stephen replied, still trying to fight down his anger. "If everyone is here, I'll let Lieutenant Michelle Wong conduct the briefing." He didn't say anything more, just made for the closest door. The moment the door closed behind him, a cautious voice met him.

"Stephen," Deon said as he stepped into the hallway behind his Alpha. "Try to stay calm, take a slow deep breath and try to relax your shoulders."

"Deon, I?"

"It's a side effect of being a werewolf. I didn't even think about this being a problem, but you didn't grow up with it. Your wolf is right under the surface right now, and you need to send him back before you change right here. The wolf responds to strong emotions; mostly anger and fear, and if you can't control those feelings, it'll be happy to slaughter anything in the room for you, and I mean anything. Your wolf will go on a killing spree and kill everyone in the building before you notice."

Stephen closed his eyes, and almost immediately, he stepped into the metaphysical realm that belonged to his wolf. Every other time he came here, he always arrived a distance away from the wolf's lair, having to walk through the scattered trees and rolling hills before finding the wolf on the other side of a small creek down in a valley. This time, Stephen arrived just a few steps away from the creek. His wolf, "Big Black", as the girls had named him, was already in the creek and pacing back and forth, just inches from Stephen's side. He knew what would happen if the wolf stepped onto the bank on his side; they would swap places, and the wolf would take over. Big Black's amber eyes were all but glowing with rage, and his lips curled up to threaten death to anyone who would challenge him. Big Black and Stephen hadn't gotten along very well when they first met; they'd actually tried to kill each other, but recently they had come to an agreement, or so Stephen had thought. The wolf's intentions were clear; he was going to cross and kill anything that dared to stand in front of him.

From far away, Deon's voice could be heard. "We have amazing abilities, but there are drawbacks too. Humanity gives us the ability to reason and to use logic; but our wolves give us passion and raw, unchecked emotion. They feel pure emotions, not tempered by social restrictions or limitations. You have to keep him in check, you have to be the stronger; you have the reasoning mind, use it to keep control."

Stephen stared down at his wolf, which was actually a little taller than waist high, and tried to make his intentions known. He had been told that the wolves didn't understand language, but they did understand intent, so he made it clear that he intended to be the one in charge. Immediately, Big Black reacted, dropping into a crouch like he was going to leap, teeth bared, ready to tear Stephen apart. Stephen didn't flinch or even move; he just stared into Big Black's eyes and matched the wolf's rage with his own will. "We're both pissed off right now," Stephen finally said, hoping that his feelings would sink in, "but you can't go out there and tear everyone apart. The people in the station didn't kill that family; they were being stupid and I dealt with it. You and I aren't monsters; we aren't going to become the beasts' others fear unless they are the ones doing the evil. We protect, we keep the peace, we fight the monsters, not become one."

Ever so slowly, the wolf's body started to relax. It was like letting the tension off a car's coil spring: do it right, and everything is fine; rush it or make a mistake, and the thing will jump through the ceiling. Carefully, Stephen kept eye contact and kept his will focused on the wolf going back to bed. It took what felt like minutes before Big Black finally stepped out of the creek.

Opening his eyes again, Stephen was in the hallway with Deon. "Stephen, you need to go home, this case has gotten too personal for you and you haven't slept. Now before you argue, just think what would have happened if I hadn't talked you through this and you hadn't gotten your wolf under control. You know I'm right."

Sighing in frustration, Stephen knew he had to agree. "You and Michelle make sure you keep them on task and I'll want updates; but maybe I do need some sleep."

"And I'm going to call Kara too; you need her right now."

"No, I'm fine, just tired; besides I don't want the girls getting too involved in my work life. You know how hard this job is, I don't want them to worry about me like Becky did."

"Stephen," Deon said with a pause, making sure that he had Stephen's attention. "Becky was a fantastic woman, and I know she wouldn't have changed anything. Just because you didn't tell her about what you were going through doesn't mean that she won't feel it, anyway, now think of what the girls will feel. You're thinking like a human again. We're werewolves and they're your pack, pack protects and supports each other. Plus, if I don't call her, you'll do something stupid like go off and try to investigate on your own instead of going to bed where you belong."

Growling in frustration, Stephen was finally forced to comply. "You know, for Beta, you're pretty damn good at ordering me around," he said, finally letting a little smile sneak in.

"That's the job of a good Beta, be there to give the Alpha a kick in the ass when he needs it. Just be glad it wasn't Kara, when she kicks, she's not aiming for your ass. Go get some sleep and I'll come over this evening for a briefing."

Stephen turned and started walking towards the front door, but paused a few steps away. "Hey Deon…thanks. I couldn't do either of these jobs without you. Oh, and make sure to call that assistant director guy, Mathew has the number."

"I am pretty awesome," Deon answered with a smile, "and I guess I'll call him too."

When Stephen opened the front door to his house…their house, not just Kara was waiting for him. Kara, Veronica, and Kaitlin waited at the kitchen table. Stephen could feel their emotions, worry, anxiety, and a touch of annoyance. He had been a fool to think that he could keep his feelings from them. This being a werewolf thing sure was complicated. Veronica and Kaitlin must have had the day off, but Kara was supposed to be covering at work. She owned the place, but he prayed that she hadn't done something crazy like close for the day just to come home and coddle him.

"Deon said you were being human again," Kara started calmly, like her sentence summed up the whole problem, "and that Big Black almost made an appearance."

Stephen sat in the empty chair opposite Kara, who sat at the end of the table, and began his story. He told them everything, every ugly detail. He told them how he hadn't been sleeping well since the Shift and about how this case was the kind that could destroy his department's reputation. They sat quietly and listened, only stopping him to ask a question if he hadn't been clear enough. When he had finished, it was Kaitlin who spoke first in her typically exuberant manner.

"Oh, I know exactly what he needs," she said, jumping to her feet and tearing the She-Ra fan girl t-shirt off that she had been wearing. Kaitlin may have looked like she was seventeen, but she had a body that sent male teachers to jail.

"I don't think that…," Stephen started before being interrupted.

"His room," Veronica asked as she too jumped to her feet and stripped off her shirt.

"Agreed," and to Stephen's extreme surprise, Kara also stood up and stripped off her shirt. All three women, each wearing just a bra from the waist up, turned to Stephen in unison and smiled. He'd never been hunted as prey before but suddenly found himself wondering if this was the same feeling. "Stephen, go take a hot shower. We can smell you from here, and crime scene isn't a good fragrance on you. When you're done, we'll be ready too."

"Uh girls, I don't think that I'm really in the mood," he tried to explain again before getting cut off a second time.

"Oh, this is going to be fun, I love doing these," Kaitlin said with a smile bright enough to light up the room! Then, without preamble, she slid her feet out of her shoes and dropped her pants.

"Stephen, you're being human again and overthinking," Kara said, reminding him of who he was now. "Just go take a shower, please, and leave the rest to us."

Stephen went to his room and closed the bathroom door behind him. He was tired but also desperately trying not to think about what the girls were doing. First the toilet, then a quick toothbrush, and then into the shower. Nope, he wasn't going to think about why all three women that he lived with were getting undressed and telling him to take a shower. He wasn't going to think about all the smooth, beautiful, female flesh that he wanted to touch. He wasn't going to dwell upon his heightened senses and what that would do to change the pleasures of sex. Then a flash of doubt came screaming through; he definitely wasn't going to think about trying to keep up with not one but three women who would usually be way out of his league— nope, just going to stand there in the shower and have an empty mind. That was the problem with men and harem fantasies; in reality, they'd never keep up.

Hoping that he had gotten the Ode'd Crime Scene fragrance off, Stephen stepped out of the shower and grabbed a towel. He could feel them in the next room, excited, mischievous, and a touch hungry. Taking a deep breath, he opened the door, and his breath caught in his chest. Kara was nude and lying slightly on her left side, her strawberry blond hair draped across her shoulder and down, hiding one of her tits as she lay spread across a pile of pillows in the middle of the floor. Veronica wore just her smile, her reddish-brown hair, and bright greenish-blue eyes sparkling in the candlelight that now lit the room. She was stretched along Kara's back, like two goddesses come to earth, each fantastic, but when viewed together, enough to make men lose their minds. Kaitlin wore only an impish smile as she twisted her red and gold hair playfully around her finger. She lay there facing Kara, but with an apparent gap between them. He stood there, unable to think, barely able to breathe, as his mind tried to process the beauty before him but came crashing to a halt at the power of the view.

"Well," Kara asked.

"Uh…," was all that Stephen could get out.

"I think he likes it," Kaitlin answered with more than just a touch of heat in her voice.

"Well part of him definitely does," Veronica teased.

"I, uh…" he tried again.

"Oh…, I'm so sorry," Kara said in mock apology, "I think you might have misunderstood, based on your…reaction. Did you think this was sex?"

"Oh, you perv," Kaitlin teased, "not with our mom in the room!"

Finally, it was Veronica who took pity on him. "Puppy pile, Stephen. This isn't about sex; it's about touch and being reassured that you are safe and that the people that care about you are here. Just like the shower last time. Come lay down and just let everything go. You need sleep but we couldn't keep from teasing you a little bit."

"Looks like we teased him a lot more than 'a little bit'," Kaitlin added. "Besides, you should have known we were teasing, like Kara being here would stop us if this had been about sex." Kara reached out to him, and Stephen just took her hand. He should have thought about it; this should have bothered him somewhere in his mind, but the moment he lay down between Kara and Kaitlin, nothing else mattered. He could feel their skin against his, their touch, their warmth, and their love for him. They wrapped themselves around each other, and for the first time since Malcolm's death, Stephen felt whole. It was like opening up a floodgate that he didn't know had been there. The gates opened, and a dam's worth of stress and emotion flowed out. Tears fell from his eyes, tears that he hadn't even known that he had been holding in. He wasn't usually a crier, but here, in this place, it was allowed. He fell asleep almost immediately after the last tear, and this time he slept well.

Chapter Nine:
Chained to Life

Sirens screamed through the night as all focus was on responding to an officer needs assistance call. No one considered the possibility of other dangers moving through the darkness around them. Humanity was only concerned about its own problems and failed to see that the world was bigger than they thought. Rage floated through the darkness, moved through the alleys, and hunted for vengeance. The oily black vapor was invisible in the darkness, but some could still see it. Cats froze and stared at the shadows until it passed, dogs whimpered and cried for no apparent reason, and small animals fled in unseen terror. Rage fueled the vapor, her rage, rage that no longer even knew why it raged. It had taken days for the vapor to learn, to focus its anger into force, to learn to move by its own will and not that of the breeze. Now it had power, now it could move…it could kill.

The vapor of death floated through the back streets and hunted for prey. The twisted and charred shreds of Karen Ashter's soul knew only that it had been betrayed, that it had to seek vengeance, and that nothing would ever satisfy it. Its first kill had been a small mouse, distracted by the cache of food that it had found, it never saw the vapor sinking on it from above. The vapor was the touch of death itself. In the language of field mice, the tiny creature screamed out in pain and fear, screamed out for salvation, and finally just begged for it to be over. What the vapor left behind was a twisted, broken thing, each tiny bone broken carefully, slowly, so that death would not come too quickly. When the mouse's death did finally come, the smallest of sparks of life fled the body only to be devoured by the oily vapor of death, and death fed. The meal was like a speck of sand in a vast desert, tiny and insignificant, but it was still there. The vapor wanted more, wanted bigger death, wanted so much more death.

The cop driving the screaming police car never had a chance to slow down when he saw the big dog run out of the shadows. The dog, nothing but an unloved and unwanted stray, had been hunting and was so focused on chasing its prey that it, too, never saw the oncoming squad car. Life on the streets was dangerous for humans and animals alike, and dogs learned quickly how to cross the road correctly or would never cross it again. This stray would be one of the unlucky ones. The patrol car barely slowed down when it hit and rolled over the dog, leaving the broken body lying next to the road. The police officer cursed, prayed there wouldn't be too much damage when he had time to check his vehicle, and hoped that his Sergeant would understand.

Broken and dying, the dog, too cursed, cursed the universe that made it a stray and not a pet, cursed its long-lost ancestors who chose to come in by the fire and let man feed it, but mostly just cursed the life it had led. Black inky vapor floated silently towards it from a back alley. The dog knew that it was death but no longer cared; it just wanted the pain to stop. When the shreds of her soul touched the big dog, the dog gave in immediately. It didn't fight to hold onto its life like the other creatures had, no, the dog just wanted an end. It had been chained to a life and a world that it didn't wish to, that was neither fair nor worth having, so the dog gave up to the inky vapor of death. For the briefest of moments, the vapor felt another emotion, not blinding rage, but understanding. As the beast's soul fled and was devoured, the vapor sank into the body.

This was a form that it could use, a body twisted by the same frustration and hate that it felt, and so it sank into the body to replace the dog's soul. The dog's broken body broke even further as the new soul twisted its form. The body grew larger to hold so much rage, and the teeth grew to vent that rage on the world. Black leathery wings ripped out of the dog's shoulders so that rage could take flight as before.

A new creature stood from where the dog's body had fallen, a Kludde, a creature of hate that had once been thought to have been a demon from Hell itself. The Kludde stood up, not as a dog would, but as a Karen Ashter would have, on its back legs. No longer vapor, this new creature saw the world of the living again, like it had when it had been alive. It breathed in the stench of man with every breath, it tasted prey on the wind, and it heard the clink of a chain. The beast looked down in surprise as it moved its left hind leg to find a length of chain had been formed from the Aether. The chain that bound the dog to an unwanted life now bound the Kludde. The hound smiled, as Karen had smiled, and rows of yellowed teeth were revealed. "Yes, this is a good form," the creature now thought to itself. "This is how I will bring death." With a thought, the monster's wings opened and grabbed at the air, pulling the beast from the ground. It took flight to seek out larger prey, to eat larger souls, and to hear larger screams.

Sergeant Major Brent Shakes watched through the tiny slit in his cardboard home as the body of the dying dog started to twist. Shakes had seen war, too much of it, so much that he couldn't be "normal" anymore. He couldn't fit in, couldn't hold a job, and couldn't look his family in the eye; so, he lived in this cardboard home in this forgotten alley. Shakes knew that there were things that moved in the dark, vampires and other monsters that hunted people experiencing homelessness who weren't wary or protected. He had seen other monsters during the war, like terrible fire demons that danced on burning corpses, but this black dog terrified him to his core. Urine ran freely down his legs, but he didn't notice, didn't dare look away from the beast in case it saw him. Shakes had been taught never to look away, because some things only come for you when you're not looking. Whatever this dog was, no, this walking nightmare, it was surrounded by death and hate. The nightmare stood like a man in dog form, looking down at its leg, where a length of chain was forming from smoke. Standing, it was almost six feet tall now, with large bat wings, and bulging red eyes that he hoped he'd never see again. With a nearly silent beat of its wings, the monster took flight and disappeared into the night. He knew what it wanted; he could smell it like the dog had rolled it in, bloodlust smelled the same on a man as it did the beast. It was only after Sergeant Major Shakes was certain that the beast had gone that rational thought started to come back to him. "I have to go," Shakes said to no one, "I have to tell the Marquee." Shakes ran off into the darkness to report what he had seen and prayed that he would never see it again.

Chapter Ten:
Head of the Table

"Stephen," Kaitlin said softly as she gently stroked his arm. "Stephen it's time to wake up."

"Mmmm," he moaned in protest as he pulled the naked woman closer to him and nuzzled his face into her hair.

Kaitlin had stayed with him once he finally got to sleep, not so much by choice, but because he had curled up behind her and thrown an arm over her. If the truth were known, she didn't mind staying with him; the feeling of him wrapped around her made her happy. They hadn't known each other for very long by human terms, but it was long enough for her. Stephen had become so very important to her, to all of them, really, and not because he was the Alpha male or the promised savior of their race, but because he was Stephen.

"Stephen, are you awake?"

"Mmmm...I'm up," he answered from her hair. He hadn't slept with a woman like this since Becky had died, and part...most...of him didn't want to let go yet.

"I can feel that you're up, the Little General, or maybe I should call him Major General, has been poking me in the ass for ten minutes already. I would really love to put him to use, but Kara said I'm supposed to wake you up before Deon gets here."

"Oh shit, sorry," Stephen stammered, now suddenly fully awake as he tried to jump back.

"Hey, morning wood happens, maybe it was the company," Kaitlin answered with a smile as she rolled over and faced him, willingly giving him the full view. Stephen had been exhausted physically and even more mentally when the girls had called him to their puppy pile, so he didn't even think about resisting. Nudity was nothing for werewolves, and up till now, he thought he had finally gotten used to it, but with his "General" at full salute, he suddenly felt very self-conscious. A lifetime of human upbringing took over, and he started staring at a spot on her forehead. Kaitlin could feel his sudden embarrassment and certainly noticed his change in focus. "Stephen, do you remember our conversation we had in the changing room at the resort? That part about if you ignored me when I'm naked around you, that I'd kick you in the nuts?" Stephen's eyes angled down to meet hers, and the smile that lit up her face had enough energy to power a light bulb. Still facing him, she moved closer, and Stephen automatically rearranged to let her get comfortable. This ended with his right arm under her neck and his left wrapped around her while she was cuddled against his chest.

"I've noticed something," he began, "you're not using your kid voice as much."

"Ya, I guess that part of me is over now that I'm… available. It just doesn't seem like it's needed anymore."

"I liked that you, but I like this Kaitlin better I think," Stephen answered. "You seem, I don't know, happier? Maybe more… comfortable?"

"Oh, I'm very comfortable," she answered as she snuggled up against his chest closer and breathed him in deeply. "I like how you smell."

"It's a good body wash, I'll let you borrow it," Stephen joked, knowing full well that she wasn't talking about his brand of body wash. "I do have a question though, when I kind of lost my cool at the office and Deon talked me down, he said that our wolves are pure unchecked emotion and that I was having trouble because I hadn't grown up with it, was he saying that the wolf can influence me?"

Kaitlin lay quietly in his arms for a moment as she thought and tried to arrange her words. She wasn't as good at this as Kara or Veronica, so she wanted to be careful how she explained it to him. "Yes, and at the same time no. When we say two souls in the same body, that's exactly what we mean: two living beings in the same skin. Your wolf doesn't reason like you do but it feels more intensely, so your emotions will be more intense as well. I don't think any of us even thought about that part, we've just sort of grown up with it but for you getting these emotions all the sudden, it probably did mess with you. The emotions you feel are yours, but the wolf makes them more…I don't know, vivid, I guess. The wolf can't make you do things, but it can make you feel things more, sort of like it takes the filters off. Believe me, I'm an expert, hitting puberty and then having your first Shift hit you makes it a really rough time for everyone."

Now it was Stephen's turn to be quiet while he thought, and Kaitlin waited for him to process it all. "So what I feel, everything, about work, about being a werewolf, about…you girls, it's all my emotions just more intense?"

"It's hard for me to describe," Kaitlin answered, "I guess for you that's what it would be like. Your feelings are harder for you to ignore. There's a saying in our society, 'you think with your head but feel with your wolf'."

Stephen was quiet again, thinking for a little bit before he spoke. "It's like wearing sunglasses your whole life and then suddenly taking them off. When Becky died, I closed in on myself. If it hadn't been for work, I probably wouldn't have left the house. I shut it all off and buried it, but I don't remember ever crying. Now I have a bad day at work and I'm sobbing in your arms like a little kid. So much for the macho man code," he joked.

"Without your sunglasses, it forces you to be more honest with yourself," Kaitlin answered tenderly. "When the man code doesn't get in the way, you can let yourself deal with what really hurts instead of just ignoring it all. Ever since I had my first Shift and thought that I was part of the group but wasn't, I've been hurting; you helped me fix that now. I'm happier now, thanks to you."

"If you don't mind me asking, how is that going?"

Kaitlin smiled happily as she answered. "You were right, they did notice me all that time. Ever since the ass grab to end all ass grabs," she teased with a faked purring moan, "I've had inquiries every few days now. After that first night, I've turned most down, but some I've started seeing once in a while." Kaitlin paused for a second before she threw caution to the wind and asked anyway, partly afraid of the answer. "You know we girls talk when you're not around. I know Veronica is really getting attached to you and Kara…she may not want to fully admit it yet, but I think she is too. You've sort of… responded to both already, I think… Uh…," she stammered.

He could feel her anxiety mixed with just a touch of fear. "It's alright, if you have something you need to say, just say it."

"Does it bother you that I've got a sex life now? The other two aren't right now, well Veronica maybe but not much, and Kara hasn't really gotten out there since Malcolm started getting bad, so if it's bothering you I'll stop! I know for most humans sex outside of a relationship isn't acceptable and I know you've been doing your best to adapt to werewolf life but if me having sex with other people bothers you or makes you think that I don't care for you then I'll stop, you just have to say the word and monogamy here I come," she answered like a rushing fire hose of thought. The moment she took a breath to recharge the fire hose, Stephen put a finger against her lips.

"The only thing I want from you and for you, is your happiness," Stephen answered as he stared down into her eyes, adding sincerity to each word. "This life is new to me but knowing how to be happy for someone and knowing what it feels like to really care isn't new. I'd never ask you to give up something so important to you. Now that you've explained about the wolf's emotions, things that I've been feeling and confused about make more sense to me now too. I got really attached to you three very fast and I didn't understand why so it bothered me sometimes. Now it makes more sense. You go out there and enjoy yourself with whoever makes you happy. If you're happy, then I'll be happy with you."

"But…how do you feel…about me," she asked, emotions almost leaking out of her eyes. "I…I can't sense it. I don't know, maybe my own feelings are getting in the way, but I can feel it when you're around the other two. I can sense how you care for them, but I'm not sure about how you feel about me."

Physically, she was smaller than him, and she looked like she should still be in high school. There was a twenty-plus-year age gap between them. Everything, every rule, every moral he had been brought up with, said his feelings were not acceptable, but those were human rules. He was a werewolf now, and they had different rules. Kaitlin had grown up differently, faster than most humans; the things that made a person an adult in the human world happened faster for werewolves. When you grew up in a world of violence and death, when life's experiences hit you harder and faster, age became more of just a number. Stephen moved towards her slowly, gently, and she leaned up to meet him. He kissed her softly, not like the hormone or sex crazed kisses of before, but like a man who loved a woman and wanted it to be known.

"Any questions?" he answered when he broke the kiss.

Kaitlin smiled back at him with a look of returned affection, right up to when her mischievous side poked through. Now smiling like the cat about to eat the canary, she slid her hand down across his bare chest and down towards his hips. "Just one," she answered as her hand kept sliding south. "Is the General still ready for war because I'm really looking forward to an invasion."

The knock at Stephen's bedroom door was not the answer Kaitlin had been wanting. "Hey, you were supposed to be getting him up and around. Deon just pulled in, and he's going to want to talk to Stephen. He can charge up your San Juan Hill later," Veronica's voice said through the door in her own mischievous tone.

"Ugh," Kaitlin answered in protest. "Cock Blocker," she accused as Veronica turned to go back to the living room!

"Join the club," Veronica answered, still with a smile in her voice. "At least I'm not a ringing cell phone."

Five minutes later, Stephen and an obviously pouting Kaitlin were dressed and came out of his bedroom. Imaginary daggers shot from her eyes as she stared down Veronica, who was smiling back gleefully.

"Bitch," Kaitlin said teasingly under her breath, just loud enough for everyone else to hear.

"Slut," Veronica play whispered back.

"No, but I was trying," came Kaitlin's response, and with that banter, all was forgiven.

Stephen walked into the dining room and found them all sitting around the table. Deon and Kara both sat across from each other, an empty chair at the head of the table obviously left open for him. As he reached the table, Veronica and Kaitlin both took their places opposite each other, but further down from Deon and Kara. Thus, his council table had been set, and it waited for its King; it waited for him. Once he sat down, Deon started his report.

"After you left the office, Michelle brought everyone up to speed. Senior Special Agent Monica Chandler and your slide show appear to have gotten everyone back on track. She's really a pretty good person, for a Fed; she's been able to get all the various groups to work together instead of against each other. Oh, she's officially taken over the case now, too, claiming that the multiple homicide in conjunction with the theft of a foreign national treasure should be prosecuted as a federal crime.

"I was expecting that," Stephen answered. "We totally out of the game or is she letting Michelle play too?"

"Oh no, Agent Chandler has done this before apparently, she's made it quite clear that she needs and wants our help. She and Michelle have been all but attached at the hip since the end of the briefing like they were old friends."

"Good, I'm glad they are getting along and we're not out in the cold on this one. Where are we at so far?"

"Chief Caldwell's guys have been running down all the local campus suspects, anyone that would have a political motivation or maybe had a grudge against the campus. So far not a lot of leads there, a campus of super nerds doesn't make for a great suspect list. FBI is going back over both crime scenes fiber by fiber and is still working on getting the security camera backups. I guess Mrs. Hendrix had taken lead on that as well so they are trying to track down passwords to gain access. They've got the first search warrant written for the video but that could take days for a response. The campus is doing everything it can to help as well so they should probably have the videos at any time if they go the password route. ICE has put out a national alert to all the customs stations to be on the lookout for the sword and they're sharing their known smuggler lists. They're also working the overseas angle, trying to hear if someone was in the market or looking for the sword. State Department is taking point with the media and the Japanese embassy. I guess the embassy is mad as Hell and is threating all kinds of stuff but that's above our pay grade so everyone is trying to stay as far from that as possible."

"How are the security guards, Michelle said that she was going to send them both to the hospital to get checked. What were their names again?"

"Brenda Cross and Ted Crossland, they're fine. Michelle was right, Brenda did have something in her system, I don't recall the name right now, but it was why she was on the toilet instead of walking the floor. The FBI is going through her house and food right now trying to find the source. If I had to guess, I'd say it was probably in whatever she took to work to eat or maybe if she got something on the way in; but I suppose that would be hard to set up beforehand unless she's got some kind of routine. Ted came back clean so we don't know if he fell asleep because he was a crap security guard or for some other reason. Could also be we just didn't find it, something in the air would be a lot harder to find."

Stephen sighed and felt the frustration of the case trying to seep in again. "Anything more from Leann? She was pretty damn worried when I talked to her."

"Ya, that's bothering me too," Deon agreed. "I've known her for ten years and she's never shown up like that to give me information, normally I have to goto her and beg. I wonder if she's afraid you'll blame the witches for it since the sword could be some magical device?"

"I guess generations of werewolf punishment has left its mark," Stephen admitted. "She made it really clear that she was taking a risk by trusting us with just coming to us. She did agree to help though and gave me an invitation to meet with the Cabal."

"Really," Deon answered in shock. "The Cabal is really hard to get to. When the Accords were signed, they were the last hold outs."

"OK, explain," Stephen interrupted. "You've said the werewolves have rules that we enforce but what's the Accords?"

This time, it was Kara who answered. "Well, the Accords are a formal agreement that most of the major paranormal powers have signed. It's sort of a mutual protection pact that was put together in the early 1500s as a response to human expansionist activities. Up till then, werewolves had made their rules known by force, which kept everyone in line, but it wasn't working anymore, as humanity expanded, they came into contact with paranormals more and more. Plus, the paranormal powers had always hated and feared the werewolves, so they were also looking for a change. What really tipped the balance was that humanity's technology had finally improved to the point that they were now a threat to the other races. Surprisingly, it was the vampires that called for a meeting first. Really, it was a brilliant move on their part, the Accords set up rules to protect the races from humans and forced the werewolves to agree to certain restrictions. The werewolves would still enforce the rules, but now they were rules that everyone else agreed on, not just what the werewolves decided. As long as the races lived in the shadows and kept their interactions with humans quiet, then everyone was safer. Anyone who stepped out of line was fair game for us wolves. The problem is, times have changed, and only the oldest races remember that the Accords were designed as a mutual defense pact. Most of the races still blame us for forcing the Accords on them. There are also other races, smaller ones, that didn't sign onto the Accords that still want to do their own thing. It's a problem that we still haven't gotten a good solution for yet."

Stephen took it all in and filed it away for later thought. He'd have to see a copy of the Accords pretty soon. If there were rules to the game, he needed to know them before he started playing. "So where are we at with the Maxwell pack?" he asked. Again, it was Kara who answered.

"They're dragging out the negotiations, claiming that Kaden just returned from a retreat to the Canadian wilds. They're still very publicly requesting the meeting but they seem to have a problem with everything we suggest."

"Delaying tactic, maybe," Stephen asked.

"We think so," Deon answered. "It's unusual for them to be so public with their requests for a meeting. Normally that's risky, putting two Alphas in the same place and then letting all the other packs know about it. This time, it's like they want everyone to know."

"So, if we refuse or back out of the talks, they'll all know it was us," Stephen answered.

"Probably. Forces us to the table to talk but doesn't let us move beyond it. It also keeps us from moving against him, we'd lose public face as being untrustworthy if we attacked while he was so publicly trying to talk," Deon said.

"Buys him time to either get his people ready for war, or to try and figure you out," Kara agreed. "With so many question marks about you, he may be trying to just sort you out."

"So it'd keep him from attacking us too, he can't move either or risk losing face."

"Assuming that he cares," Deon countered. "Kaden is very militaristic minded. He's always struck me as the kind that settles things with his fists before his words. I'd guess it's his Beta that's running this play."

"So, it's the Beta that's wanting the answers. How do they get answers, spies, a background check, social media stalkers?" Stephen asked.

"Probably all three," Veronica said with a chuckle. "Unlike most Alphas, you're very public, just look at how many times you were on the news last week. Some discrete questions around town about what kind of a man you are or what skeletons you have in the closest would answer a lot. I mean they already know where you live and that we're staying with you."

"Which opens us up for an attack whenever they want," Kaitlin added. "He sent a strike team last time because Marcus was paying him, and he expected Marcus to take over. Now that Marcus is gone, and we're all living here in one place, he could send in a more serious force and take out both our Alphas at the same time. The pack would be totally in shambles, and he could walk in to either mop up or take over."

The room went quiet at that thought. Malcolm's words came back to Stephen: "She'll be Alpha someday." It made him smile in his head at the thought of Kaitlin becoming the next Kara. Tactically, though, living with the girls was a mistake. Until he was a stronger fighter, better able to protect everyone, it was a risk to have them live with him. Still, he railed at the idea of sending them away. It was like living with a bully; let the bully change how you live, and they win even more. There was also the possibility that sending the girls back to their apartments wouldn't help either. Instead of having a group on defense, it'd be a solo defense.

"This can't be a new problem," Stephen began. "How did Malcolm deal with this?"

"Mutually assured destruction," Deon answered firmly. "The Malcolm you knew wasn't the same person as the Malcolm in combat. He was a thing of bloody beauty to watch."

"Between him and Deon, the body count would just be too high," Kara continued, "and then there was Marcus. For all his faults, he was also a damn good fighter. Any pack that hit us would have to be certain that they got all three of them or there would be unacceptable losses on both sides."

"So now that Marcus is dead and I have a lot to learn in combat…," Stephen trailed off.

"The cost to benefit ratio is better," Veronica finished. "If they find out that you're still a beginner in combat and that Marcus died because Big Black was a surprise…."

"Then we can almost be assured that Kaden will come regardless if it costs him some social standing with the other packs," Stephen finished for her. Stephen leaned back in his chair and stared up at the ceiling. It had been about ten days now since he became Alpha, and already they were facing a total party-kill scenario because he was weak. Malcolm had said he'd be the strongest of them, the genetically perfect werewolf; he felt more like the perfect puppy at the moment. Still, a pity party fixed nothing, and everyone in the room was waiting for his brilliant answer. "So we let them come," he began. "We make this house our home and our castle. Deon, you said the Beta was the Alpha's spy and assassin. Do we have… what…, assets that we could send in and spy for us?"

"Yes, I've got friends in their territory already, what do you have in mind?"

"Just watch, very carefully, nothing that puts our people at risk. Assuming that Kaden will eventually decide to move, we need to know when. Till then we do everything we can to turn the house and land around it into a fortress. Hell, if we had the time I'd say we dig a moat and put a wall around the place, anything we can think of to give us an advantage when they do come. We'll need some firepower around here too, more than just Becky's shotgun and my duty pistol. Last time they came with a damn sniper rifle and I had a pistol, not again."

Deon and Kara both stared at Stephen like they had been struck dumb. "You would be alright with a security detail then," Deon asked.

"Well, I'm not thinking a whole motorcade or anything but we've already been attacked here and they stabbed you, so ya I'm thinking we need more than just the five of us if Kaden or some other pack tries something stupid. Hell at this point I know just enough about the paranatural world to know that there aren't many people out there that do like us. Why, does this surprise you?"

Kara was the first to answer. "We tried for years to get Malcolm to understand that he was at risk. He just said that he didn't want you or his neighbors to think something was weird so he wouldn't let us try and protect him. I begged him to let me move in with him, just to watch his back but he said that he didn't want to have to explain it to you."

"Another thing I'm guilty of without ever knowing," Stephen answered thoughtfully. "Just knowing me put him and the rest of you at risk."

"It was his choice, not yours," Veronica chimed in, "and as it turned out he was right, no one ever came after him."

"The pack does have people that could help," Kara added. "We tried to kill two birds with one stone. We sent some of Marcus' followers off to close protection school just in case we could ever get Malcolm on board with having protection. We thought that if we could get him to agree and they could spend time with him away from Marcus, we could convince them that Malcolm was Alpha for a reason. It was even one of those high dollar schools that trained personal security for high value private targets. We do have other pack members working in construction and one even works for a security company. Elliot works there doesn't he?" Kara asked as she turned to Kaitlin.

"Titan Security and Defense," Kaitlin answered. "I'm supposed to meet up with him tomorrow evening after work, I can call him and get him started. I'm sure he'll be excited to work out a security plan, he really gets excited about his work."

Stephen saw that tiny little look she flashed him when she mentioned this Elliot person. She was being cautious with her emotions at the moment, but Cop Stephen had caught the tell; Elliot was one of her dance partners. He shot her a smile in return and then moved on. "I'll work on ordering some more firepower after work tomorrow. Deon, if you can, get your friends started and then I need you to meet with what's left of Marcus' followers. This will be their chance to show the pack that they're still team players and to prove to us that they have a right to still be here. I know I said that all was forgiven at the meeting but that doesn't mean that they can just lay around either. If they want to be pack, I want to see them supporting the pack. He had what, seven or eight people?"

"Seven dedicated and another four or five wannabes. We got the seven main followers trained, trying to strip Marcus of his support, so they should be good to go. If we needed the extras, they could train them," Deon answered. "I'll meet with them either tonight or maybe tomorrow during lunch. As much as they owe you for not kicking them out with Marcus, or worse, they should be jumping at the chance to show you, their loyalty.

"I don't care what they did in the past, but if they are working for me, they have to stay clean and on the right side of the law. If they're dirty, they're fired, no second chances. I want them legal too, make sure they have all the licenses and federal permits they may need. If they carry a gun, I want it perfect. Then we give them an olive branch to confirm there's no hard feelings. We'll have to make sure they're paid well and maybe some kind of prestige in the pack;

some reason that they'll want to do the job and keep it. The Romans had their Praetorian Guard, let's give these guys a title, have them report directly to you, and you start feeling them out on where they're loyalty lies."

"You know the Praetorian Guard ended up killing the Emperor a couple of times right," Kara said, concern in her voice.

"Good thing I'm not an Emperor then," Stephen joked, but Kara didn't laugh or even smile. "Now, unless there's something more of end-of-the-world importance…I'm starving."

"And you have sword and martial arts practice," Veronica added with what Stephen thought was an evil look in her eye. Maybe being trained by a woman who got sexual pleasure from giving out pain wasn't a great idea.

Chapter Eleven:
I Gotta Date

Wednesday morning, hump day, as some people call it, started like any typical workday for Stephen. After the meeting and dinner last night, Kara and Veronica took turns beating him senseless until almost midnight. Even after sleeping all day, he hit the bed like a bag of rocks. Kaitlin had offered to "assist" in putting him to sleep, something about using nature's most enjoyable sleep aid, but by the time the beatings disguised as training were over, he was in no shape.

Now that the Feds had officially taken over the case, Stephen was freed up to focus more on his own department. There was training to arrange, a budget to manage, personnel to hire, some to discipline, and a near-avalanche level of paperwork on his desk to sort and approve. He had two meetings scheduled for the day, and that was about it. Overall, after all the craziness that had been happening and the looming threat of the Maxwell pack, he had needed just a typical day at the office. His day was so typical that he actually made time to ask a woman out. He had to wait until she got off work, which was by far the hardest part, before he called.

"Yes, Stephen," Kara answered, a touch of stress in her voice. Ever since she gave him her number, he hadn't used it hardly at all.

"Hello, Ms. Hughes, uh…this is Stephen Butler, we met the other day at your coffee shop," Stephen answered in mock, if not slightly funny fake nervous voice. "I…uh…I just haven't been able to stop thinking about you, and I'd really like to know if you would be able to go out with me tonight?"

"I'm sorry, Stephen Butler who," Kara mocked with a smile in her voice. "You're not that older guy with the bad teeth and the limp?"

"No, I was the really good-looking guy about half your age who almost choked on his tongue when he first met you."

"Oh! That guy…the guy who goes to a coffee shop to order tea."

"Yep, that's me," Stephen answered. "So would you be available about four thirty, maybe?"

The phone line went quiet for a few moments, just long enough to make Stephen start to wonder if the cell tower had dropped his call. Just before he checked his phone, Kara answered. "We'll I guess I could be available, I checked my schedule and I can pencil you in between the rock star and the pro football player. What should I wear?"

"Something semi-formal, but you can move in," he answered, enjoying their little game. "I look forward to seeing you then."

The last hour or so dragged on. He could have left early, but he wanted to give Kara enough time to do whatever it was that women did before going on a date. Another advantage of being the Chief of Police was having a private bathroom. He'd gone in to look in the mirror three times already and even brushed his teeth again. Stephen changed out of his uniform and put on some dress clothes, which wasn't unusual for him around the office. When he couldn't wait any longer, Stephen headed for the door, but not before checking in with Michelle, who was also in a pretty good mood. "So what's the good word," Stephen asked. Michelle looked tired, and her Texas twang was heavier than usual, but she looked ready to call it a day, too. Sometimes having the Feds on point meant that the locals got easier jobs and didn't have to pull all the late hours.

"They got the video about noon," Michelle answered as she grabbed her shoulder bag. "They're going through it but it ends about an hour before the burglary. I guess the system was set to upload in three-hour blocks so we're missing the actual burglary footage. They're checking the rest of the footage to see if they can spot anyone casing the place leading up to the break in. Whoever did the job had a lot of inside knowledge so they're working on that for now. ICE says they haven't heard anything overseas or from their normal smuggler suspects, but they've put the alert out to the private shipping companies too. State had another press conference earlier out by the FBI mobile command; they're offering a million-dollar reward for the sword's safe return."

"Too bad cops can't cash in on that when you end up finding it for them," Stephen said with a dry chuckle.

"Na, they got us working on local leads, trying to run down anyone in town that might be a suspect. We're even going to rental companies and hotels to get lists of clients to see if one of the feds recognizes a name or alias. I doubt we'll come across a Japanese katana in the lost and found box."

"So, what's your plans tonight, headed home to watch Nascar?"

"Na, actually I got a date," Michelle answered with just a touch of pride.

"Let me guess, good looking FBI Agent Williams just happened to be in town?"

Michelle Wong, the great and powerful, blushed. "He never left yet. We sorta hit it off after we got Angela back and he called in a favor, took some vacation time."

Stephen stopped as they both walked out of the PD, forcing Michelle to look back at him. "Michelle, that's awesome. I'm really happy for you!"

She smiled and even had just a little bit of the giddy schoolgirl look when she started to tell him how great Mathew was and how much she really liked him. By the time they had made it to the parking lot, she was almost bouncing, which, for Michelle Wong, meant she really, really liked him.

"What do you have going on tonight Chief," Michelle asked, almost as an afterthought, just as Stephen was about to get in his car.

"I've got a date too." When he drove out of the parking lot and looked back into the rear-view mirror, Michelle was still standing by her car staring at him.

Chapter Twelve:
Little Red Dress with a Purple Mackey

Stephen pulled up to his own house promptly at 4:30 pm and parked in the driveway. Checking one last time in the mirror, he got out of the car and walked slowly to the front door. Of course this was his house, Kara was a werewolf with hearing bordering on superpowers, and he'd called to let her know what time he'd be there; but he rang the doorbell anyway.

Kara Hughes, a mature and dignified woman, queen of her pack; had hung up the phone like a giggly schoolgirl. The call had taken her totally by surprise. She knew he wanted to take them all out on dates but the way he had called her, like he was asking her out for the first time, had made her stomach do little flip flops. Malcolm had been her one true love since the day they met all those years ago. Sure, there had been other men, some she even cared for, but she hadn't been asked out on a date since she and Malcolm had been teenagers. The moment she got home from work, she all but ran to her bedroom and stopped in front of her closet. She'd agreed to move in when he asked but most of her stuff was still in boxes or back at her apartment. Stephen had said semi-formal, not one of her clothing strong suits, but she knew the dress she wanted, if it just still fits. It took her a little bit to find it, buried in one of her boxes, but when she freed it from the zipper bag and held it up in front of her so she could look in the mirror; that's when she saw her hair. "Holy crap I need a shower!" After that, the race was on, and just like her youth, she had enjoyed every second of getting ready for him.

Kara opened the front door for the gentleman caller. When Stephen first met her at Bit and Byte, he thought her beautiful and had stammered over his words like a schoolboy. When he had seen her nude for the first time on the night of his first Shift, she looked to be a goddess. Now…he didn't know the words. The English language lacked words that would do justice to what he saw. Kara wore a floor-length off-the-shoulder red dress that hugged her from shoulder to thigh. Below her thighs, the dress changed to red lace and flared out wider, teasing glimpses of her long legs while giving her room to move comfortably. The dress had a peak-a-boo slit over her cleavage that teased and made you want to ask for more. She had chosen to wear her flaming strawberry red hair loose so that it flowed down just past her shoulders and had put on just enough makeup to accent her green eyes. The only jewelry she chose to wear was a thin choker with an emerald-green stone set-in front. The choker actually belonged to Kaitlin, but Kara was sure she wouldn't mind.

"Kara…I," Stephen tried to say, tried to sound like the cool confident man that he usually was. He failed. The waves of shock and awe that she felt rolling off of him were all the answers she really needed.

"I take it you like this old thing," she teased in her best fake southern belle accent. "Why, I just found it in some old dusty box and threw it on."

Stephen had gone with simple light gray slacks, a black long-sleeve shirt, and a thin gray tie. If you had asked him just a minute ago, he'd said that he looked good; now he'd say that he looked like an old gym shoe that the dog liked to chew on, standing next to her.

"I'm afraid that I pale in comparison to your radiance," Stephen said, regaining a bit of the charm that he had practiced on the way over, "but would you care to accompany me on this evening's festivities?" As he spoke, he stepped in beside her and offered her his arm. Sure, it was over-the-top and maybe cheesy, but lord, he hoped it worked. Kara took his arm, and he escorted her to his car. Once she was settled, he almost ran to his side so he could start their date.

They rode together like lifetime friends, laughing and telling old stories. He told her of how he broke his arm when he was a kid trying to jump his bike over a ditch to impress the neighbor girl. She told him of how she'd fallen out of a tree when she tried to get the neighbor's cat off the branch near the top. He told her about his first date and how he had accidentally taken the girl to an R-rated movie that opened with a sex scene. She told him of how she had gotten sick and puked when Malcolm had tried to take her to an amusement park.

Stephen finally stopped the car in an older part of Moser City, not far from the university. In this part of town, the old red brick buildings had been redone, and businesses had moved in to take advantage of the old town charm. Now it caters to a wide variety of people, from college students looking for a break from their research to hipsters getting a double-shot latte with soy milk and two squirts of sugar-free caramel syrup. As soon as he opened the car door for her, he offered her his arm, and they walked together through the light crowd, enjoying the window shopping. Music filled the air as street performers played, and Stephen dropped a few dollars in every open instrument case he found. They walked through the side streets, now designated for foot traffic only, as he guided her to a small, open-air cafe set in a pocket park between the buildings.

"We're still a little early, but are you hungry yet," Stephen asked as they stepped into the park.

"Honestly, famished, I didn't eat lunch and I was so worried about this dress fitting that I didn't eat after you called either," Kara admitted with a smile. "I actually did find it in the bottom of one of my boxes, I haven't worn this in probably ten years. I hope it's still in fashion enough that I'm not making a scene. That's one of the down sides of living so long, you're always having to clean out the closet or your way out of style."

"It looks amazing," he answered as they found an empty table, and he pulled out a metal chair for her. Kara smiled, amazed at how happy she was tonight. She had been like this with Malcolm once, back before his depression and anxiety had gotten so bad. Part of her wondered if she should feel guilty, he hadn't been dead for two months yet, and here she was on a date with his best friend. For just a moment, her smile fell away, and her mood changed.

"What are you thinking about?" Stephen asked.

"That I'm having a really great time," Kara answered with a fading smile, "and wondering if I should be feeling guilty for it. I wasn't expecting to feel like…this. He hasn't been gone two months yet and I'm already on a date with his best friend. Stephen, I loved him so much it hurts sometimes. I knew he cared, he always had, but he never treated me like this, like I was a princess. Once he got obsessed with his work, and you, I just kind of got forgotten."

"Kara, I understand. I felt the same way when Becky died, like I wasn't going to be happy again; and for years, I was probably right.

Then you came along with your strength and grace, Veronica with her compassion and inner fire, even Kaitlin with her…well just Kaitlin. Now I can't imagine life without you. So, if this is too soon, I understand. We can go home if you want, there will be other nights."

"No…," she answered firmly with a hint of resentment leaking through. "No, I deserve this…we deserve this. Since I met you, you've done nothing but care for me and be there when I needed you. You've fought for me and pushed yourself so hard to adapt to a world that you never wanted to see. I loved him and so did you and he'd be the last person to ever tell us not to be happy together. So…no, I don't want to go home. I want to have an amazing night with the man that I'm falling in love with and eat some amazing food because I think my stomach is growling." Stephen stared at her for just a moment, looking at her with half a grin on his face as he let her own words sink in. "Oh…damn," Kara said with a blank look on her face when it hit her. "I said I wasn't going to use the L word."

"You didn't," Stephen answered with his silly grin still in place. "Falling means you're still headed that direction, you haven't gotten there yet; but when you do get there…would you let me know?"

"I will, keep up doing things like this, and it'll be a short trip," Kara answered with her own silly smile. By the time dinner was served, the sun was starting to dip behind the buildings, so they ate by the light of the candle on their table and the strings of tiny twinkling fairy lights that the cafe had hung in the trees. They ate happily, comfortably, like two friends who could be honest with each other. They chatted between bites, and Stephen even told a bad joke that Kara laughed at anyway. He tried to get her to order dessert; the cheesecake was always amazing at this little cafe, but she declined, so he decided to move on to the next adventure.

"Now that we've eaten, do you feel like working it off?" Stephen asked.

"Absolutely," Kara answered as they stood from the table. Stephen paid the check, and then they walked through more of the side streets. Music still filled the evening air as more people were coming out, mostly couples walking hand in hand on cobblestone paths lit by flickering gas lights. After walking past the third couple holding hands, Stephen reached out for Kara, and she took his hand with a smile. He walked with her through the crowds and couldn't help but notice all the looks they were getting. Men stared openly at Kara, and several of the women did too, for their own reasons. What surprised Stephen was the amount of pride he felt, the 'I'm with her' feeling, which made him appreciate her even more. So wrapped up in her was he that Stephen almost startled when she spoke. "Where are we going now?" she asked, leaning in so their shoulders would touch as they walked, obviously reading his emotions.

"Right here," he answered, and was almost disappointed that they couldn't walk farther as he stopped at a set of small stairs going down towards an outside entrance to what had to be an old basement. A heavy wooden door, painted a dark forest green and bearing a simple wooden sign, waited for them at the bottom of the stairs. The sign read, "The Bootleg Club". Stephen guided her down and opened the door for her as they walked into the basement. Immediately, they were surrounded by upbeat jazz music, playing just loud enough to make you want to dance. The room was alive with people talking, and several were on the dance floor, moving to the rhythm that the small four-piece jazz band was laying down.

"Oh…Stephen…I don't dance," Kara said and started to pull back.

"Yes, you do, just imagine you have the Widow's Tears in your hands," he countered, referring to the twin swords she was training him to use, as he dragged her out towards the open dance floor. "If you can't do that, then just close your eyes and hold onto me." She did as he asked, wrapping her arms around him as the music started to work its magic. In his arms, she forgot where she was, that there were people there that could be watching her, and she danced.

Kara half fell up the stairs as she and Stephen walked out of the club, now well past midnight, and into the night. She had danced and laughed and talked and fed off the power in the room until she wanted to scream to the heavens. "Oh, Stephen," Kara said as she twirled in the street, "I love that place! I feel so…alive! Like there's magic in the air and I'm drunk on it!" Kara grabbed Stephen's hand and spun him around with her like two kids who were playing pretend so well that the world had disappeared from around them. She spun in circles with him, then fell into his arms and into a kiss. She kissed him hard, wantonly, like she'd take him right there on the cobblestone side street if he'd say the word. He kissed her back with the same intensity and the same desire, but no magic lasts forever, and he pulled back as the reality of where they were set in.

"We probably should go home," Stephen said as he stared into her eyes. In this light, he could have sworn her green eyes were glowing with their own energy.

"Ya…we probably should," Kara answered breathlessly. "Either that or we might get arrested." Stephen smiled as he took her hand and led her back to his car. It was all she could do to contain herself as she, for the first time in a very long time, allowed herself to let go. Kara turned back and forth as she danced on their way back, her dress flaring out around her, but never letting go of his hand. "How did you ever find that place, in a basement of all things, and what was that amazing purple drink again?"

"They call it a Purple Mackey, one of their signature house drinks their bartender came up with. I worked on a case with the owner a couple of years ago, he had some employees skimming the cash register, so I helped him with prosecution. I've been meaning to go back for years but…didn't really feel like it until now."

"I wish you had tried the drink, but you're driving."

"That would be quite the headline, Chief of Police Drinks and Drives," said a voice from nowhere. Gone was Kara, the free spirit; here was Kara, the warrior queen. She was a blur of motion as she put herself between Stephen and a set of bushes near the parking lot. Her wolf was immediately just below the surface, waiting for a threat to destroy. Stephen stared at the sound, but the bushes must have been a better hiding spot than he thought because there was nothing there, just bushes and the shadow from gaslights and a nearby tree. Even trying to focus on his vision, trying the same werewolf trick that the girls had made look so easy, didn't do anything; he just got eye strain from the sudden surge in brightness. Slowly, right before his eyes, the shadows began to move, and a misshapen form began to appear. If the thing had been human, it would have been the size of a fifth or sixth grader, but it was impossible to tell what it was, as it was covered from head to toe in layers of cast-off clothes and bits of cloth.

"Name yourself goblin and your purpose," Kara growled…literally growled. Interrupting date night had made her cranky.

"I mean no harm, Queen of Wolves," the creature answered in a voice that sounded like gravel grinding. "I am Authorabanak, herald of the Twilight Marquee, and as per the scripture of the Accords, I bear notice to the King of Wolves that my Lord would parlay with him."

"I," Stephen started, but a hand from Kara waved him off.

Kara stood formally and recalled her wolf but didn't relax from combat-ready status. "Authorabanak, my King, acknowledges the Twilight Marquee's summons and respectfully asks for the Marquee's terms of meeting," Kara answered formally and with obvious care.

"I am told that it is a matter of great importance and as such my Lord demands that the terms be expedited with all due haste. I am commanded to convey that my Lord would consider it...a favor...if the King of Wolves would agree to meet at the basketball courts in Baker's Memorial Park at the hour of the Witch. The King of Wolves, his beautiful Queen, and the Alpha's Fang are asked to attend."

Kara looked back at Stephen and gave him a very slight nod, with a question in her eyes. He answered with his own slight nod but didn't say a word. "Honorable Authorabanak, you have served the Twilight Marquee well this night. The King of Wolves accepts the terms of meeting, and we look forward to hearing your Lord's words."

"And so the deal is struck," Authorabanak answered and then simply faded from view. Kara didn't waste a second but grabbed Stephen's hand and ran for his car.

"Kara?"

"In the car, we're on the clock," she answered and cursed that she didn't bring a bag...or a weapon; a mistake that she wouldn't make again if there were another date night. Stephen didn't bother to open the door for her this time, and Kara was barely belted in before he made for the parking lot exit. "We need to wake up, Deon. Can you call him? I didn't bring my phone. No pockets." A few keystrokes later, and he put the ringing phone on speaker.

"What…" Deon answered in frustration, making it more of a demand than a question.

"Deon," Kara answered, "the Twilight Marquee wants a meeting, 3 AM the basketball courts at the Baker's Memorial Park. He even called it, 'a favor'".

"Fuck," Deon answered, no longer in his sleep-deprived voice. "I'm up. I assume Stephen's with you since you're on his phone. Can you brief him?"

"As soon as we hang up," she answered. "We're on our way home to change and weapon up. Deon, he referred to you as the Alpha's Fang."

"Damn. What the fuck is going on, any clue?"

"He sent Authorabanak so he was sticking with the formalities. I couldn't ask without risking offense. Stephen didn't say anything."

"Good, I'm getting dressed and ready. I can be there by… 1:30ish, if I hurry, to scope the place first. Brief Stephen and I'll meet you there."

The moment the phone beeped to show the end of the call, Stephen started in. "OK, now can you please explain this!"

Kara took a deep breath and tried to slow her heart rate. "What do you know about goblins?"

"Well, I assume they probably aren't like the ones in my DnD game when I was a kid. Deon told me that they're real but he was focusing more on other things when we were talking."

"I've never played DnD so I have no idea, but yes goblins are very real. They're a group of related creatures, kind of like dogs, there's all kinds of breeds and they are different but they're still dogs. Some of the human movies and television stories are right; goblins are fairly small, usually about four feet or less and they have nasty tempers. They're greedy, arrogant, and deceitful; but if you can get one to give his word, he'll never break it. Don't ever make a contract or a deal with a goblin unless there is no other choice, they'll keep to the very strictest letter of the agreement but if you break it even in the slightest, their vengeance will be terrible."

"So, lawyers basically, minus the keeping their word part," Stephen said, only half joking.

Kara only half-smiled at his joke before she continued. "The old mythology about babies disappearing in the night, that was goblins because someone broke a deal. Don't underestimate them in combat either; they're faster than they look and much stronger than they should be. Most of them even have some minor magic, that disappearing trick that Authorabanak did was one of their invisibility illusions. Another thing about goblins, they're all thieves but don't call them that, they'll take offense to just about anything and will hold a grudge for decades."

"So I'm assuming that the Twilight Marquee is kind of like there Alpha then?"

"More like he's their crime boss and chief bully all in one. They like stealing things, anything that isn't theirs already is fair game, and if they didn't steal it then they probably know who did. Deon knows more about that than I do but from what I know, they only usually get into murder and kidnapping if someone breaks a contract."

"I wonder if they were involved in the sword burglary?"

"They could do it, goblins given enough time can steal anything. They have some kind of natural power or ability with locks; most locks will open with a touch. The really hard locks they take as a challenge and gain prestige in their troop if they can open a lock no one else can."

"So how do we prepare, they have to have some kind of weakness or something?"

"The paranormal world has its own myths, just like humans, some stories may be true and some probably aren't," Kara started to explain. "Right now, all goblins are male, but according to the old stories the Keeper told me growing up, they used to have females, too. The story, she said, was that, around the fall of the Roman Empire, a horde of goblins invaded Rome and began stealing all the treasures collected from across the Empire. The Goblin King, at the time, broke into the Temple of Venus, the Roman goddess of love, beauty, and fertility. The story says that, in addition to being the greatest and most wealthy King of the Goblin Hordes, he also wanted to be so virile that his line would go on forever. He broke in looking for…well, the story gets a little vague here, but basically he tried to steal the sex toys belonging to Venus herself, only to find out that one of his wives had already beaten him to it. Since she had already stolen from a goddess, the King of Goblins lost the prestige of the theft. All he could do now was steal from his own wife, and that wouldn't get him anything. In a fit of rage, he attacked his wife and threw her to the ground, screaming that he wished a curse on her and all the scheming and deceitful women like her. Some think that Venus granted his wish as punishment for invading her temple and for stealing her…toys. Others believe that it was some natural selection or maybe a disease that targeted the females. Again, this is just a story, but after that, all the goblins everywhere stopped having female babies. No matter what they tried, only males were born until it was just the males that were left.”

“So the curse took her and since all the goblins are deceitful and scheming, the curse took all the female goblins like her too,” Stephen reasoned. “If there aren't any females left, then how do they reproduce and… how can we use this?”

“I don't know if the story is true but we do know that the goblin females did die out and that's about the same time that stories of goblins stealing babies started. If a goblin can get a human baby less than ten days old, they start feeding the child a mixture of goblin blood and milk for the next ten days. On the morning of the eleventh day, the baby has changed to a male goblin.”

“Wait…,” Stephen interrupted, indignant anger beginning to rise. “They steal other people's children…”

“They used to,” Kara corrected, “nowadays they buy most of them, mostly from homeless women or drug addicts. In exchange, the goblins take the mothers in and care for them for the rest of their lives. Goblins have mostly claimed all of the homeless community, actually. The homeless act like eyes and ears while the goblins provide just enough to get by on…no such thing as a free meal when dealing with goblins.”

With a sigh, he swallowed his earlier emotional outburst and continued with his questions. “Back to the other question, then, how do we use any of this to our advantage. If they are paranormal rules lawyers and obviously the Twilight Marquee wants something from us, how do we keep from getting on the wrong side of one of their contracts?"

This time, it was Kara's turn to sigh and swallow emotions. "With… me. Since goblins don't have their own women anymore, they've become obsessed with other women, mostly humans. They can't successfully mate with them to have children, but that's not for a lack of trying. Imagine being some sex starved teenager your whole life, and everyone has a girlfriend but you. They're fascinated by women but also hate them because they aren't goblins. What women they do have in the clans are little more than sex slaves or production stock. At the best of times, they saw women as second-class, and now it's a point of pride for a goblin to have a woman to push around."

"Still not getting it, how do you become an advantage. Don't even consider something stupid like me trading you or anything."

"No…oh Gods no… Ick," Kara answered, half gagging at the thought. "You'll need to show your power at the meeting, something that they'll respect and crave but can't have. We play to their greed and avaricious nature by putting me on display. The more I can make them want me by climbing all over you, and the more you disregard me, the more the Twilight Marquee will be off his game. Other than that, you listen to every word he says and look for secondary meanings, and unless there is no other way, don't agree to anything remotely like a contract."

Stephen went quiet as he thought through things the rest of the drive home. By the time he turned down the driveway, he felt he had the beginning of a plan. "Kara, do we have an actual written copy of these Accords? I know you said it's from the 1500s, but if I'm going up against the lawyers, I'd better know the law."

Chapter Thirteen:
On the Move

Veronica and Kaitlin sat on the living room couch, knees pulled to their chins, and shoveled ice cream into their mouths. Neither had had a good day at work. Kaitlin's "meeting" with Elliot had been a bust; the guy never showed and only texted her that he wasn't going to be able to make it after he was already late. For Veronica, it was annual review time, and the crap-taco boss she had to answer to hadn't been kind with his review. Sure, it wasn't her fault that she'd been taking so much time off lately, but she really couldn't explain that her werewolf duties had demanded her attention. Then, when they each got home, there was a note on the table that read, "I've got a date. Love, Kara." Of course, they were both excited for her, and neither was jealous, but they had both been looking forward to having everyone home. Werewolves were like that; when one was stressed, their natural comfort place was the family and pack. A single werewolf a lobo was a sad and lonely thing. So, when they heard the crunch of tires on gravel coming down the driveway, both looked up expectantly until they noticed that the tires weren't slowing down.

Kara opened the door like a woman on a mission, her red dress flaring out with the motion. "Kara, you look amazing," Veronica started as the girls stood waiting for them to get home. They had worked out a little teasing routine before, hoping to make fun of the returning dating couple, but Kara's obvious mood had killed the fun time.

Kara stopped, the compliment and her girls waiting at the door, resetting her attention. "What? Oh, thank you, I'm glad the dress still fit," she answered like any woman would. "We had an amazing time; I'll tell you both later, but now we've got a surprise meeting with the Twilight Marque to prepare for and very little time."

"Yes, my Alpha," both girls answered, obviously reading Kara's change in attitude that it was time to go to work.

"We are to meet at 3 AM at Baker's Memorial Park. Deon is probably just now leaving to check the park. Veronica, Stephen needs a copy of the Accords. Kaitlin, I need you to help me get changed. Stephen will need an advantage with the goblins."

Neither questioned Kara; they simply obeyed. Kaitlin fell in step behind her mother as they headed to Kara's bedroom. Veronica grabbed her phone and started going through her files. "I don't have an actual hard copy," Veronica explained, "but I have a scan of the original. I'll email it to you."

"That'll be perfect," Stephen agreed as he watched Kara and Kaitlin disappear down the hallway. He really didn't like the idea of putting Kara on display just to distract the Twilight Marque. Kara was a queen she was a strong and independent woman and she was… special to him; he didn't like the idea of the misogynistic crap that the goblins apparently thought was normal.

"She'll be fine," Veronica answered to Stephen's obvious concerns. "She's had to do this before for Malcolm. The Marque has a thing for her well, for her legs specifically. Just the idea that you've seen Kara naked and slept in the same puppy pile with her would drive him nuts. He's wanted her for her body and for the challenge for years."

"Challenge?"

"To break her will and probably her body too," Veronica said. "Goblins like their women beautiful and compliant. No matter how many women they try to collect, it's never enough for them, and Kara is a very sought-after commodity."

"I still don't like it," Stephen complained. "She's better than this. The idea of her putting herself on display just kind of twists my stomach."

"I have to go help them, and you need to read the Accords. If you're going up against a goblin, you better have them memorized."

Veronica's words hit home, and Stephen wasted no time curling up on the couch and starting to go through Veronica's email on his tablet. The Accords were almost impossible for him to read. First, they were in French the official court language of the day and old French at that. Veronica had other copies, though, thankfully in English, that must have been modern translations. The Accords read like a modern contract, each race agreeing to abide by certain conditions and taking on specific responsibilities. It set up a method of mutual defense, set terms on when the werewolves could enforce violations, and most importantly, apparently set the terms for when the various races could call on the werewolves for intervention. There was an entire section on how the races would arbitrate disagreements to prevent them from going to war. Anytime he found a section that was important, he'd go back to the original French and then to the internet for a translation. He wanted to make sure that the English copy he had matched the original French and, more importantly, that the French wording didn't have other possible meanings. He wanted to work on the project longer, but it had only taken Kara and the girls about thirty minutes to change again.

Kara walked down the hall first, and Stephen stood to meet her. She still wore her red dress, but the lace from thigh down had been removed. Now the off-the-shoulder dress with its peek-a-boo slit over her cleavage ended about mid-thigh. She had added black lace stockings that accented her legs' natural appeal and teased bare skin through the lace. Her previous choker necklace had been replaced with a simple red satin choker with a small ring in the center. For some sections of human society, the choker ring marked her as a taken sub with her own dom. It advertised that Kara was submissive, something that couldn't have been further from the truth. Kara was in full Queen mode; her walk screamed power and grace, which made her look even more amazing. The girls had changed her hair too. Gone was the free-flowing mane of fiery red and yellow she had before; now her hair was twisted up into a tight bun on the back of her head, held in place with two hair sticks. The Kara from earlier in the evening was elegant and suave; this Kara was a woman on the hunt. Stephen wanted to make a comment to tell her how beautiful she was or how amazing she looked but this look wasn't her choice and wasn't for him. This was the look of duty, of dedication to one's pack. She had sacrificed her favorite red dress and had decided to put herself on display for a sex-crazed goblin because it was expected of her. If anyone ever questioned whether Kara was Queen or whether she loved her people, here was their answer. It just made Stephen admire her even more.

Behind Kara came her two daughters, and both were ready for war. Kaitlin and Veronica were both in their body suits, and Kaitlin wore her Widow's Tears short swords on her hips in what looked like scabbards attached to the suit itself. Veronica was also in her body suit, which made Stephen pause for a moment to admire the view. Kara was built tall with long lines ending in curves. She was harder, almost Amazonian in appearance. Kaitlin was smaller-framed, the shortest in the room, with a more hourglass figure accented by her self-proclaimed amazing breasts and curving hips. Like Kara, Kaitlin's musculature was just under the skin, but hers was more subtly defined. Veronica, on the other hand, was softer, more rounded, with curves and more obvious padding in places the other two didn't have. On her hip was a weapon Stephen hadn't seen before.

"What?" Veronica asked. "You're staring."

"Sorry," Stephen answered, slightly embarrassed at getting caught. All three girls smiled when they felt his emotions still so very human. "I, uh… I haven't seen that weapon before." The weapon had its own sheath strapped to her thigh and looked like a three-section staff a martial arts weapon he'd seen in movies several times. He didn't know much about the weapon, other than it looked impossibly difficult to use; but he did know they weren't usually bladed. Veronica's weapon looked like it had a heavy ball on one end and a spear blade on the other.

"Don't lie, you were staring at her boobs. Or was it the camel toe she's got going on?" Kaitlin responded impishly.

Veronica ignored her well, mostly but subconsciously adjusted the front of the body suit to pull it out of her girl bits. "It's a modified three-section staff that Sensei and I developed. It's a lot heavier than what humans use, and the chain runs all the way through the different sections. The weighted mace end balances the spear point, but if I pull the mace end hard, the three sections lock together, changing the weapon into a spear with a ball and chain on the end."

Stephen blinked in response, impressed by the weapon and that she was obviously comfortable enough with it to take it into potential combat, but parts of him couldn't stop looking at her in the body suit. To be honest, his eyes kept wandering to Kaitlin as well. The body suit hugged her and teased at his senses. It was like she was standing there nude but subtly not at the same time. Sure, he had seen her nude many times now all three of them, actually but he couldn't help but be captivated by the idea of seeing them like that again.

"I can take this back off, or maybe you want to watch me take Veronica out of hers instead," Kaitlin teased, using a slightly mocking bedroom voice as she trailed her fingers up her own body and then reached out toward Veronica.

"I… uh…" Stephen stammered.

It was Kara who came to the rescue. "I know we all enjoy making Stephen squirm and try to talk his way out of being human, but we are on a clock," she interrupted, then stared at him expectantly. Teasing time now officially over, the other two girls returned to a more formal vibe and looked at Stephen. It took a few seconds before he caught on.

"Oh! This is one of those Alpha things, isn't it?" Stephen replied, finally getting the idea that they were waiting on him.

"What are your orders, my Alpha?" Kara answered in confirmation.

This… this was a tactical operation, not unlike things he had done at work over the years. This he could do. "Kaitlin, Veronica, I need you on perimeter. You'll need to relieve Deon. If this is a trap or they have some kind of surprise in store, I want to know but don't get seen. I'm sure he'll have goblins there too, and that invisible trick isn't even fair. Make sure you pack some spare clothes as well. The body suits may cover all the bits and pieces, but it'll still get people's attention. As soon as you're packed, I want you two to leave first. Be in place before we get there at 3." Veronica and Kaitlin bowed slightly from the shoulders and then went back into their rooms to grab clothes. About a minute later, they both returned wearing the leather harness that Kaitlin had shown him a few days ago. With the harness and the body suits, they could shift into wolf form and still be prepared to shift back. When they came back into the living room, Stephen met them at the door. "Nothing fancy," he said to both of them. "I don't want either of you hurt." He then moved forward and kissed each of them gently. Both girls smiled before they shifted and disappeared into the night.

"They'll be fine," Kara answered when both girls had disappeared down the driveway. "Most they have to worry about is getting seen by a human, and they're both very good at avoiding people."

"I know," Stephen answered, still looking out the open door into the night. "I trust them both more than I trust myself, actually but I can't help worrying about the people I care about."

"Part of being the Alpha is knowing that you're putting your people in danger and that it's necessary. We live in a deadly world much more than what you were used to as a human. Malcolm had trouble with that," Kara said, her voice drifting off with her memories. "He was so focused on keeping his people safe that he sometimes avoided doing what needed to be done. They're warriors, all of the werewolves are. We know the rules from the very beginning; maybe that's why we live so freely we know there may not be a tomorrow. This is just a meeting, and all they are doing is security. It'll be fine."

Stephen turned and closed the door behind him as he tried to close the door on his worries. By the time he turned back to Kara, he had hardened himself to what had to be done. "I'm sorry our date ended like this. I really had a great time."

"Me too," Kara answered, smiling. "Maybe next time I'll ask you out."

"I look forward to it."

Chapter Fourteen:
F Around and Find Out

Stephen parked the car and looked out over the park. Baker's Memorial Park was founded on the original Baker homestead, one of the founding families of Moser City. The park was quite large, almost two thousand acres set on the northwestern edge of town. The side facing away from town actually butted up to rural country side, making the natural appearance of the park even larger. There would have been no way the city could have afforded to maintain such a huge park if it hadn't been for the Baker Park Foundation, a private organization that maintained the park using an endowment from the Bakers. The family had been quite wealthy sheep farmers and had chosen the land for his rolling hills and access to water. The Clear Water river flowed through part of the park, along its northern edge. This drew weekend campers and fisherman from around the area who came to enjoy the park and get in a little bit of outdoor recreation before they had to go back to their urban life. Stephen had chosen the main parking lot, closest to town and nearest to the more urban attractions like soccer fields and the disk golf course, that also overlooked the basketball courts. There in the middle of the many courts was a table, complete with tablecloth and chairs. Across from the table sat a pile of dirty laundry. Stephen assumed that had to be the Twilight Marquee but the young woman standing next to him was a question.

"Are you ready," Stephen asked?

"Of course, the Marquee is an ass and dangerous, but not anything I haven't seen before. The most he'll do is leer and make some inappropriate comments. The real question here is are you ready? He'll try the same thing, he'll try to get under your skin, and you know you can't react to him," Kara answered.

"Now that I've read the Accords, I think I have a handle on most of the rules," Stephen answered with resolution in his voice. "Invoking the Accords is essentially creating neutral ground, anyone breaks the peace and all the races have justification to go to war against the violator. So, he can be an ass all he wants and so can we, but we just can't attack each other. Any idea who the neutral third is going to be?"

"Since we're here at the park, I'd guess it'd be Balthazar or one of his family," Kara answered like that would explain it to Stephen, then sighed heavily as she got out of the car and pulled the hem of her dress down. "It's almost time, we can't be late."

"Who or should I say what is a Balthazar?"

"He's a troll," Kara answered as she walked away from the car. Stephen blinked at her a couple of times in surprise but then gave up with a shrug. After the last few weeks, meeting a troll shouldn't be a surprise anymore.

Stephen and Kara walked arm and arm, unlike how they had just a few hours ago, every bit of the lovely couple. Stephen couldn't help himself and looked around expectantly.

"Relax, the girls are out there," Kara answered. They walked together until they met the closest walking trail. The parking lot overlooked the basketball court but to get to the court you had to go down and then back up a hill. The Marquee had chosen the site well; in order to reach the table, Stephen would have to walk up the hill while the Marquee looked down upon him. It was subtle, not something others would notice, but in the psychological gamesmanship of diplomacy, it set a tone. As they started upon the trail, Deon stepped silently out of the surrounding trees, causing Stephen to jump a little.

"How the hell do you do that," he asked in frustration.

Deon smiled and gave a little chuckle as he fell in step beside Stephen. "You just have to have an understanding with the dark." Again, Stephen wanted to question, but it was just too much effort right now. Deon could have been teasing, but he was about to have a meeting with a goblin which would be overseen by a troll, so why the hell couldn't Deon have an understanding with the dark.

The three walked around the trail until they finally had to step off the path to start up the hill towards the ball court. Now a little closer, Stephen could see that the woman with the Marquee was in fact a young teenager, probably not more than thirteen or fourteen. The girl's hair had been recently butchered, whoever had cut it short, didn't know what they were doing or did a bad job on purpose. She wore…very little, nothing more than a gossamer cloth wrapped around her and tied behind her head. The cloth did nothing to hide her small swollen breasts or the bits further down but to Stephen's surprise, a newborn baby lay sleeping in its folds. Werewolf Alpha Stephen knew that there would be some kind of trick or insult coming. He knew that he had to ignore it and move on with the mission, that like Kara's presence, the girl was here to get under his skin. Cop Stephen, the part that had spent most of his adult life trying to protect the innocent from people like this, wanted to do "other" things to the Marquee. As they stepped upon the basketball court, Stephen began to speak.

"Twilight Marquee, in accordance with my responsibilities under the Accords, the King of Wolves has come to speak with you," Stephen said carefully using the formal title allotted to him in the accords. In response, the pile of dirty laundry stood and shook itself with effort. The voice that came out of the buried pile was not the gravel sound of Authorabanak but a fuller, more baritone sound that bordered on human.

"King and Queen of Wolves, how very good of you to come and join me so very late at night," the Marquee said as he waved an arm at the single chair across from him. "I do hope that our meeting won't disturb your work in the morning at the police department."

"I'm sure that I'll be fine," Stephen answered as he took the offered chair. "Good thing about being the Chief, you're never late for work." This drew a small chuckle from the Marquee that again was all too human in nature.

"I must admit though," the Marquee continued his voice now taking on a more hard, almost threatening tone, "that I am quite put out at you Chief Butler. Here you have become the Alpha of your pack for almost two weeks and yet you have failed to seek out the other leaders in your territory. You have done us great dishonor by ignoring us, and I for one shall not forget that we are apparently beneath your notice."

"Then I must humbly apologize...I'm sorry I didn't get your name?"

It was Kara that answered for the Marquee. "Twilight Marquee is his name, my Alpha. When the previous Marquee is no longer able to rule, a new one steps forward and takes the name. Their name before is forgotten and the Twilight Marquee continues, immortal."

"Ah…," Stephen replied, using his own lack of knowledge to his advantage. "Then I must apologize twice, Twilight Marquee, as you can see my human upbringing has ill-prepared me for the ways of a paranatural world. If I have given offense due to my lack of acknowledgment of the other leaders, then I must blame my insult upon my ignorance. I'm certain that if I had been in your shoes, I too would have been offended; but I guess we must both be patient with my current lack of understanding." Stephen had been a cop for twenty-five years. He'd talked down dozens of suicidal parties, had resolved hundreds of disturbances, and even talked a dozen or so junkies into getting real help; he knew the art of diplomacy. The first thing he had learned was that being in a position of authority made it harder to relate to someone and the best counter was to appear more human. Admit to your own shortcomings, then empathize how the other person feels, acknowledge that you and the other person are in the situation together; and slowly they begin to see the problem as a team event. Diplomacy and the art of coercion had its non-verbal skills as well as just verbal. A good cop knew better than to stand toe to toe with someone, instead they would stand off at an angle, making the other person turn towards them to talk. Pointing or directing the person's gaze was also a simple action, that began to draw the person into getting used to following instructions. The most important tip though, was to use the person's name anytime you wanted to change their thinking. The brain automatically locks onto names and that short little pause can be enough to interject another course of action. Put all together, a well- trained cop can find ways to talk themselves out of most...but not all situations. There were always those people that just wanted to do things the hard way.

"Your ignorance is not my concern, your disrespect is. If the werewolves have chosen an Alpha that is ill prepared to lead, then that is their sin, one that you shall be responsible for; but fear not, I am not without forgiveness, for a price."

Deon's cell phone dinged and buzzed, breaking the Twilight Marquee's dramatic delivery and drawing an angry glance. Deon only shrugged at the goblin as Stephen and Kara turned to look at him and the modern-day intrusion. "Sorry, thought I had turned the darn thing down," he answered to the Marquee as he turned and read the message. Deon started to type back an answer but then paused and deleted the message. Stephen couldn't help but chuckle inside at the timing. The goblin had been all amped up in indigent righteousness only for a cell phone to mess up his delivery.

Another tip in diplomacy is to take your time. It takes emotional effort to be angry and that effort can be exhausting. If the other person is angry, let them vent, the more energy they expend the less anger they can maintain. "I can understand your feelings, and again, I meant no disrespect to you or any of the other leaders. Please don't let me compound my mistake by violating the Accords on my first formal discussion; should we not wait for our Arbitrator? I believe section six subsection four requires that meetings under the banner of the Accords must be attended by a neutral Arbitrator who shall oversee that the negotiations are fairly agreed upon and documented. As the party requesting the meeting, I assume you have arranged for an Arbitrator to attend?"

Now it was the Marquee that had to take a pause. Stephen had just quoted the chapter and verse of the Accords, letting the Marquee know that this discussion would be at least on a level playing field. He also hadn't planned on Stephen being so accommodating or even taking blame for the slight. Other werewolves always had to be in the right, had to have the power, and here Stephen was admitting not only the insult, but taking full blame. This was not what the Marquee had been expecting. It was time for his distraction. "Yes, you are quite correct, King of Wolves; the Arbitrator should be here. I'm sure you do not know but your Queen will attest that trolls are notorious for being late. They seem to have their own sense of time, the big rock heads. While we wait, may I introduce my new son," the Twilight Marquee said with a wave of his arm. Now this close Stephen could see the girl fully, and thirteen may have been a high estimate for her. She presented the child, who couldn't have been more than a couple of days old at best, but she never dared to raise her eyes. "We found this girl on the streets, a forgotten runaway, like so many others the humans throw away. She was sick and almost starved to death when my people brought her to me. I fed her, gave her shelter, gave her clothes and medicine and in payment; she spread her knees. The human men that used her paid me good money for that slit between her legs. I'm not sure why, it was barely even fully covered in hair when we took her in."

Stephen had been prepared, or so he thought. He knew the girl was there to piss him off and make him sloppy; but damned if it didn't work anyway. His wolf was already standing and walking towards the creek in the inner space where he dwelt inside of Stephen. Kara must have felt it because she chose that time to interrupt him. "Stephen, do you think we can hurry this up, you were supposed to fuck me after our date tonight and I'd rather be doing that right now instead of talking about some flat chested little girl's twat. Believe me, mine is a lot more interesting."

Stephen almost bit his tongue and his wolf thought about other things beside tearing this heap of shit covered in dirty clothes into little pieces. Even the Marquee stopped dead in his tracks as the lump of clothing turned so fast part of his face coverings fell. What Stephen saw there was far from human. The creature's eyes were pure black and shimmered like a doll's but the rest of the face was the dark green of pine needles with deep pot marks where some kind of disease had left its mark. His nose was longer than normal, yet thin and ended in a sudden downward hook that gave it an almost beak like shape. The Marquee's mouth though, that would give the greatest of Great White sharks reason to pause. The mouth was filled with rows of jagged and broken teeth, with replacements growing in behind them. The goblins may be small and driven by their greed; but the mouth was all carnivore. Stephen couldn't see the rest of the head but that one glimpse was more than enough for his nightmares.

"Soon my Precious," Stephen answered as he reached out to her and ran his hand down her back. "We both know that the Twilight Marquee is more important, we can have all the sex you want later, but we need to focus on this for now."

"Yes, my Alpha," was Kara's reply but she said it in a voice that Stephen had never imagined could come from Kara, submissive.

"Dead just a few months and already she has moved on to fresh cock," the Marquee said with a hint of greed in his voice. "She sure must have loved Malcolm so very very much to jump on you that fast. Weren't you two friends before he took the cowards way out and blew his own head off? I guess you must have broken her quickly, a pity, I thought that the great Wolf Queen would have been a harder piece of ass to break."

Now it was Kara's turn to tense under Stephen's hand. He didn't have long before she'd lose her shit and spray goblin bits all over the court, so he did the only thing he could, he grabbed her ass. "Kara," Stephen answered is a low slow voice that threatened no disagreement, "is no one's piece of ass. There is no 'breaking' her or any of the other women that live with me. They choose who they want and who they don't; and I respect them all the more for their choice. If my Queen wishes to join me in my bed, then I thank my lucky stars that I've been blessed to share it with her."

Again, the Marquee was flustered and pushed the only button he had. In a flash of speed Stephen didn't expect, the Marquee grabbed the girl beside him and yanked her off her feet and onto his lap. He had grabbed her so hard that if she hadn't been holding onto the baby with both hands, she would have dropped him. Before even the baby had a chance to make a sound, the goblin ripped away the sheer cloth that the girl had been wearing and forced her legs open.

"But you see Wolf King," the Marquee said as the baby began to wail, "there is beauty in a woman whose only thought is to please you." With those words he shoved his rag covered hand between her legs. She looked like a little girl sitting on her abusive uncle's lap. "Give them their free will and all they want to do is complain. Let them think for themselves and they'll just think of ways to betray you, but a broken spirit, that can be molded and shaped into something better. You can make her into something more than what she was before, give her a greater purpose than what she was born to, and in the end... she'll thank you for it." The girl screamed in pain, her child had just been born a few days ago, as the Marquee's hand violated her and was being purposefully rough. Yet she still held her body still for fear of what would be worse. It was a voice as deep as the ocean that stopped Stephen from killing the Marquee.

"I see the Earth Mother has delivered me at my appointed time," the troll said in a voice that could be felt and heard. It was that voice that shook the group back from the brink of war.

"You're late," the Marquee said as he flung the girl off his lap and she tumbled to the ground while still clutching the baby to her chest.

"I disagree friend goblin, I have arrived as I was meant to arrive, in time to save you from a quick end and to preserve the balance." As the troll stepped into the light, Stephen could see him clearly and was surprised at what he saw. The troll was human for the most part but scaled up several times the size of even Deon. It stood close to ten feet tall and was almost as wide, with large, thick, hair covered arms that were slightly too long for the body. His face was wide and flat, with a broad nose several times to big. Surprisingly, the eyes were bright and even golden in color, like two polished nuggets set in his face. The troll had a small beard that was patchy on the cheeks and only partly grown in but the hair on his head flowed back in a torrent of locks the color of wood ash. His skin though, was rough and gravelly in texture as if it was covered in hundreds of lumps that looked like some kind of rock like skin disease. It gave the creature the overall appearance of a man covered in stone. "I am Balthazar, and I bear you welcome King of Wolves to my hills."

The sight of the troll had been enough to force Stephen's rage back into place, but just barely. Still, he had been given a second chance, and he realized just how close he had come to starting a meaningless war that his pack didn't need and maybe couldn't win. The Twilight Marquee was a raging maggot covered piece of shit, but he had almost destroyed Stephen and the pack. "Balthazar, it is very good to meet you and if the Twilight Marquee's words were correct, I owe you and your people my apologies for not coming to meet you earlier. I beg your forgiveness, I wasn't even aware that trolls…or goblins…even existed until just a short time ago. I'm afraid that I'm still being reminded that I'm still all too human in some regards."

"Most," Deon and Kara chimed in together, forcing each of them to smile before they remembered their place.

The giant smiled a wide toothy grin and bowed slightly from the shoulders as Stephen had watched his own people do. "The Wolf King honors us with his words, we trolls know that all things happen in the time and place appointed by the Earth Mother, and our meeting was meant to be now. We do not fault you for the nature of your birth but rejoice for your people in the hope that a cure can be found for their condition," Balthazar answered in a slow melodic manner that showed no hint of being rushed. "Now, in compliance with the Accords, I accept my role as Arbitrator of these proceedings. Twilight Marquee, as the caller, you shall speak your words first."

Balthazar's presence seemed to calm even the Marquee or perhaps having a witness was more than what the Marquee had wanted. It wouldn't have surprised Stephen if the Marquee hadn't planned on Balthazar being late from the very beginning, just to have the chance to push Stephen and learn his limits or weaknesses. "Arbitrator, I too act by the will of the Accords and call upon the King of Wolves to fulfill the duties assigned to the werewolves. A threat walks the night and endangers my people, a Kludde. The King of Wolves must perform his duty, track this demon down and destroy it."

Stephen knew that there was a provision in the Accords that commanded the werewolves to act in certain cases, but he had no idea what a Kludde was or why it was a threat. He turned to Deon.

"A Kludde, my Alpha, is an evil spirit that often takes the form of a black winged dog that walks on its hind feet. In ancient times, they were often tricksters, but their tricks were often deadly. They can be spirits of vengeance or rage, and if that is the case then it will kill anyone it comes across. It will likely start in the dark places, away from humanity and in places where there won't be any witnesses. This would make the Kludde a threat to the goblins."

"But this isn't one of the races that you told me about," Stephen said, his eyebrows narrowing in confused thought. "Where would something like this come from and why is in the city now?"

"Kluddes are evil spirits and so are exceedingly rare. It's said that they are often formed from the spirit of a witch that was burned at the stake."

Stephen got a chill at the thought. Karen Ashter had been a tormented and evil woman, a witch, and she had died by fire. If this nightmare of a fairy tale was true, then Karen's spirit hadn't passed on but had become a winged dog out for vengeance on anything living it could find.

"Then the Wolf King admits his duties, we'll expect your people to take care of the problem immediately. If not, then I shall lay the death of any of my people or kin at your feet, and we will expect just payment."

"Kluddes are extremely dangerous," Deon continued. "As spirits made flesh, the body doesn't die like a normal creature, and they often have other magics or curses. Hunting this thing will be very hard and even if we can put it down our people could die."

"My people will certainly die if you don't and the Accords command it," the Marquee commanded in a flourish of a dismissive arm wave.

Stephen paused and then turned slowly back to the Marquee. "No… they don't."

The Marquee jumped to his feet and sputtered as he tried to answer faster than his tongue would allow. "Section nineteen subsection eight," the Marquee began but Stephen cut him off.

"Only says that the werewolves are empowered to take any action necessary to protect the combined races from a threat that endangers more than one race. Assuming you are correct, Twilight Marquee, and this Kludde thing is in fact in the city, then I'm forced to wait until there is proof that it is a threat to your race and at least one other. Then I am the one empowered to take action as I deem necessary. The Accords makes no demand that I must act, simply it empowers me to take any actions that I deem justified to answer a threat to more than one race. In this case,

I'm afraid, friend goblin," Stephen said in a mimic of Balthazar's earlier greeting, "that the King of Wolves sees no threat to more than one race at this time. Perhaps this thing is out there hunting goblins, perhaps it is not, but I have no proof that it has any desire to hunt anyone else. Even if there was clearly a threat, the Accords do not demand that I answer that threat, merely saying that I may."

The Marquee visibly shook with rage and this time it was him that was inches away from breaking the Accords. The Twilight Marquee grabbed the table and squeezed until the plastic folding table mashed in his grip. "Then you would let this thing hunt amongst my people, slaughter goblin and human alike without your response", the Marquee asked is a slow voice that dripped with promised threat.

"No," Stephen corrected, "I never said that I didn't see a need to respond to this threat, I just simply made it clear that I'm not commanded by the Accords to do so. I'll be more than happy to hunt this thing down and do what I can to bring it to an end…for a price."

The Twilight Marquee flopped back down in his chair and sneered at the werewolf sitting across from him. Never in his life had he ever heard of a werewolf like this man. The Marquee didn't like it, not in the least. Stephen was changing the rules concerning werewolves and the Marquee suddenly felt like he was at the disadvantage. Still a negotiation for a job was something that he did all the time. This he could control.

"If the werewolves would debase themselves so far as to demand money from us, I'd be forced to let the other races know just how untrustworthy this new Alpha appeared to be. Why, never has there been a Wolf King so low as to demand a payment for a duty prescribed in the Accords."

"I'm afraid I don't understand. Marquee, doesn't the goblin people work off this very principle, that risk must have its rewards? You ask the werewolves to take on the risk that you are too frightened to address yourself. You tried to hide behind the Accords to force me to risk my people to save yours. Now I will hunt this Kludde down for you Marquee, but not for free."

"Then name your price," the Twilight Marquee answered coldly.

"The Onimaru Kunitsuna," Stephen answered. "I want it back and I'm betting that you could do that for me."

"The goblins didn't take that thing," the Marquee countered. "I can't give you what I don't have."

"No, but I doubt that there is a pick pocket in this whole city that doesn't answer to you somehow. If the goblins didn't take the sword, you know who did, or at the very least you can find out. You deliver the sword and I'll go after the Kludde."

"I'll deliver what I know about the sword, but after the Kludde is dead."

"Oh no," Stephen countered. "You deliver valid information leading to the sword's recovery first. I'll even bargain with you...we'll start our hunt, try to locate the thing and warn your people to stay away from it. Once I have the sword back in my hands, then we go in for the kill but not before."

The Twilight Marquee's black eyes narrowed to slits as he stared at the Wolf King and worked the angles. He didn't have the sword, but it would be a simple task to give it over to the werewolves. In truth, it would be to his advantage. The "people" that did it were too big for their britches anyway. Give over the information, the wolves get back the sword, and then they take all the risks to get rid of the Kludde. If all the angles worked out in his favor, the goblins were about to win big. In a flash of motion, the Twilight Marquee's hand darted out across the table. "Agreed" he said firmly. After a short pause, Stephen took the creatures' filthy clawed hand and gave it a single shake.

"It brings me joy that your differences could be settled through the Earth Mother's peace. It will be good for this evil to be returned to the great cycle," Balthazar said in obvious pleasure. "If there are no other topics, then I'll call this meeting to a close."

Stephen, Kara, and Deon wasted no time walking away from the goblin on the other side of the table. All they wanted to do was get away from the nasty thing and try to get at least an hour or two of sleep before the sun came up. They had only gotten a few paces away before the little pile of dirt called out to them.

"Don't even think about breaking our deal wolf. You fail to keep your word, and I'll come after you and your precious women. I'll add them to my harem and there won't be a thing you can do to stop me."

Stephen froze and both Kara and Deon prepared to grab him if he started to Shift. Instead, he answered calmly without even turning around but in the cold voice of command that he had used at the ascension trial. "Goblin you can threaten me all you want, come after me I don't care, but if you think about laying one of those dirty fingers on any of my family…I'll declare war on every goblin in this city. I'll personally hunt them down one at a time until they give you up. Then…then I'll give you exactly what you want…I'll give you Kara. Just remember one thing though, the last person who tried to subjugate her was a werewolf and he's lying in a hole right now torn into small little pieces by her hands." Now Stephen turned very slowly to look back at the goblin. "So, I'll give you one piece of advice Twilight Marquee, you be very careful what you wish for, I just might give it to you." Stephen slowly turned back and walked back toward his vehicle with Deon and Kara in tow. Part of him honestly wished that the Twilight Marquee would do something stupid but the rest of him feared that he would.

Once they were out of goblin earshot and Balthazar were no longer in sight, Deon spoke. "Kaitlin texted; we have a problem."

Chapter Fifteen:
Diplomatic Immunity

Andy Thomas was a professional and he was proud of his skills. The only thing he valued more than his skills was his good looks. He had had it all in high school sports talent, brains, popularity, and all the girls he wanted. Now, pushing thirty, he still had the looks, but the brains had failed him once the nerds weren't there to do his homework and the teachers didn't pass him just so he could play ball. He was tall, with sandy blond hair and broad, muscular shoulders. He worked out daily to keep up the appearance and because he needed to be big sometimes to intimidate his way through life. His day job was working as a private investigator, one of those sleazy, ugly divorce types that made their money catching other people in the act. He didn't mind his work and didn't care what other people in the industry thought about him; he made serious money doing his job and that was all that was important to him. Sure, other people would have problems with minor inconveniences like morals or ethics. Andy didn't give a rat's ass about any of that crap. If the money was right, he'd do anything to get the job done, even if that meant he had to set up the photos himself.

The hunt for money had almost gotten him killed well, several times but the worst was two years ago. It was two years ago that he was on a stakeout waiting for his current assignment to slip up. It was a rich people divorce, the kind where hundreds of millions were on the line, so he had been paid to find proof the wife was sleeping around. Andy had followed her for almost a week before he figured out her pattern. The wife had been careful always watching for tails, always changing her routes but Andy had been better. When she drove her Mercedes into the wrong part of town, he knew he had her. What he didn't know was that the thing she was going to meet wasn't human or worse, that the thing had superpowers. Somehow the monster had heard the shutter click on his camera. That was how he met Commander Maxwell and found out there were secrets in the darkness that even he didn't know. Andy still tried not to think too much about that night or the nightmares would come back. The monster had been on top of him, about to eat him alive, before he begged Maxwell for a job. It was idiotic a stupid Hail Mary pass play, the kind that even looked dumb on paper but football coaches still tried but it had worked. Kaden Maxwell, the monster, the werewolf, the Alpha werewolf of the Maxwell pack, had decided to hire him. That had started two years of fear always watching out for his employer's moods, and always afraid of being lunch if he failed. His current job: follow Chief Stephen Butler of the Moser City Police Department and dig up everything he could find about the man.

Andy had guessed that the Chief must have a thing for leggy redheads based on their date earlier. He'd followed them through the crowd, popped a couple of candid shots, but had been careful never to get too close. Keeping an eye on them at the little dive jazz bar they went to had been difficult, but Andy had skills. If Kaden was interested in Stephen Butler, then this Butler guy was bad news too, and Andy would be damned if he ever got caught again.

Andy watched as they pulled up in Baker's Memorial Park from a safe distance. He had followed them to the park, but at that hour there wasn't much traffic to get lost in, so he had to stay farther back. By the time he caught up, Chief Butler and the tall redhead were already out of their car and walking toward what looked like a clandestine meeting.

His car rolled to a stop as Andy parked on the side of the road, well away from the parking lot. He had disabled the interior light long ago, so other than the noise the car door made, he was able to slip out into the darkness, assured that no one had noticed him. Andy slipped his bag over his shoulder and grabbed the can of scent blocker from the car as he closed the door only enough for it to stay shut but not fully latched. He'd learned certain tricks over the last two years of working for Kaden Maxwell, one of which was that there were things out there that could smell you from a distance. The scent blocker had been made for hunters so they could hunt animals. In this case, Andy used it so the animals wouldn't hunt him.

Silently, he slipped around the back of his vehicle and slid down the steep embankment beside the road and into the drainage ditch at the bottom. He couldn't see them now, but that meant they couldn't see him either. Andy stayed low and moved quickly, but as quietly as he could, toward the tree line not far ahead. He had been lucky the drainage ditch crested right at the tree line on the other side, so he could slip into the cover of the trees without being seen. The tree line was the hard part once he slipped into the trees, branches and brush started to pull at his clothing and snag the bag over his shoulder. This forced him to slow down and move more carefully as he made his way through the trees, across the small walking trail, and then to the edge of the tree line on the other side.

Andy lay on his stomach and slowly opened the bag he was carrying as he locked his eyes on the basketball court. Inside the bag were the tools of the trade: a pair of quality binoculars and a sound-amplifying microphone with recorder. The binoculars were even the high-dollar digital kind that could take photos while being used.

Whatever this meeting was about, he could see and hear it clearly meaning that Kaden would be shelling out big bucks for this info. His heart pounding with excitement and so focused on his prey, Andy didn't see the random brush pile to his right begin to move. He didn't see the thing stand no taller than his waist and begin to move slowly toward him. Andy definitely didn't see the beaten and battered kitchen knife that appeared from the goblin-shaped walking brush pile.

Kaitlin slipped through the night so quietly she didn't even disturb the sleeping rabbits. She loved her wolf form loved the feeling of being wild loved it so much that, of all the werewolves in her pack, she was the best with her wolf. When she and Veronica arrived, panting from their long run at speed, Deon set them to work sweeping the area for any threats to Stephen or Kara. Already she had found three of the Marquee's goblins, which meant there had to be at least half a dozen more she hadn't found yet. Not all the little bastards knew the secret to invisibility or whatever trick they used to make you think they were invisible. So far, the ones she found didn't appear to be much of a threat. Goblins weren't to be underestimated, though, so she didn't get too close to them either. But from what she could see and smell, they weren't carrying anything overly dangerous. Kaitlin guessed they were there mostly for numbers. If the Marquee pushed Stephen or Kara to blows, they'd jump out and mob them; probably mob them just long enough for the Twilight Marquee to slink off into some hole somewhere. Goblins were vicious in numbers or when cornered, but they weren't famous for being ready for a stand-up fight.

It was the whiff of old motor oil in the air that caught her attention during her goblin hunt. Stephen was more careful with his vehicles and kept them maintained regularly; this vehicle was well past due for an oil change. What's more, the smell was new a new vehicle had arrived just after Stephen and Kara, and with the unusual hour it probably wasn't someone out to enjoy the park. Kaitlin turned her nose to the smell and bounded through the dark, no longer trying to sneak past sleeping rabbits. Her wolf moved through the park and stopped flat on its stomach as it looked down over the road leading to the parking lot. There was a human there, judging by the smell and the sudden hiss of a can of scent blocker. Kaitlin watched as the human gently closed the car door and slid down the hill toward the tree line that Kara and Stephen had just walked through. Somehow a human spy had joined their late-night meeting, and the spy knew enough about what they were to try to cover his scent.

Kaitlin slipped down the small rise overlooking the roadway and moved up to the rear of the intruder's vehicle. With just a thought, she slipped out of her wolf skin and back into her human form as she crouched behind the vehicle. "The one bad thing about being a wolf," Kaitlin thought to herself with a smile, "no thumbs." Gently she slipped her phone out of the bag strapped to her back and made sure the light from the display was pointed away from the human now creeping up the drainage ditch. She disabled the camera flash, used just the streetlight to illuminate the license plate, and snapped a quick photo. Making sure she could read it, she sent a quick text message to Deon with the words "human spy" attached to the pic, then shifted back into her wolf. By the time she was done, the human had slipped into the thicket of trees.

She didn't need to slide down the ditch; Kaitlin took a few steps on one side of the ditch and then bound to the other. With the human wearing scent blocker, it was harder for her to track him by smell, but she roughly knew where he was and, more importantly, what he was likely doing. Slinking low and quiet, she slipped into the issue the human had had moments before. The trees and brush all wanted to be her friend and wanted to snag on her gear. Kaitlin's advantage, though, was that she could just lie flat and creep forward, staying below most of the friendly brambles and branches.

The human wasn't far ahead of her now one well-timed leap and she'd land right on top of him. Kaitlin watched as the spy stared through the binoculars and pointed the sound-amplifying microphone toward the meeting. She was torn: she couldn't let the human spy on them, but at the same time she knew Stephen wouldn't want the human hurt. Kaitlin was trying to figure out her next step when she saw the goblin. It was hidden in a brush pile, and from the knife it was slowly drawing, it looked like it was going to make up her mind for her. The small creature started slinking slowly toward the human, who was too engrossed in his spying to notice that death was approaching. She didn't have long to decide, but with the human listening to the conversation through the headphones attached to the microphone, she thought she could risk it. Slowly she rose just a few steps away from the goblin, well within striking range of both the goblin and the human spy. All it took was the first murmurs of a low growl to catch the goblin's attention and freeze it in place like a statue. She couldn't see much of the beast, hidden in his brush-pile camouflage, but the two black-pearl eyes snapping wide to face her were enough confirmation that it got the hint. Just to make sure, Kaitlin slowly raised her top lip, baring the row of teeth and the promise of a bloody death if the goblin wanted to push its luck. Wisely, the creature backed off and slipped into its brush-pile blind.

Andy watched and listened, eyes wide at the secrets he was recording, as the meeting drew to a close. Goblins and trolls were real, the Chief of Police was a werewolf, a Kludde was hunting them, and the Chief was trying to recover some stolen Onimaru thingy. Several times he thought they'd all end up killing each other. He had never seen a goblin or a troll for that matter but it was clear that werewolves didn't get along with goblins. When the giant they were calling a troll appeared, Andy had almost dropped his binoculars in shock. It was only the money that kept him from running for his car. This was exactly what he'd been paid to find. He could imagine Commander Maxwell's reaction when he dropped all this on the table. Maxwell was terrifying, but he could be quite generous for work well done. Counting his chickens before they hatched, Andy almost lost track of time as the meeting broke up. He had to get back to his car and get out of the area before they noticed him. He had a lead on them, and Butler and his posse didn't seem to be in that big of a hurry. Andy threw his stuff back in his bag and turned to head back to his car. The reddish-gold-furred wolf standing just a few feet behind him seemed to have other ideas.

"Um… hi," Andy said and half asked. "Guess you're kind of wondering what I'm doing and maybe thinking I might even taste good." The wolf's eyes raised in what he hoped was disgust, but he didn't want to run the risk of being wrong. "See"

Kaitlin yipped a quick bark, interrupting the terrified human who, now standing this close to him, stank of unwashed sweat and fear. Her bark had been enough to terrify the human into silence again and let the others know where they were hiding. As she waited, Kaitlin watched the goblin slink off, obviously deciding that staying out of wolf business was a good idea. In just a few moments, Veronica came bounding through the woods at a near run in her wolf form, and the others were not far behind. As for the human, he appeared to be mostly concerned with remembering to breathe.

Deon stepped forward first, putting himself between the threat and his Alphas. If the spy did something stupid, he'd be the first to take the damage instead of them. Seeing the cowering man just a few feet from Kaitlin's jaws relaxed him a bit but only just. Without preamble, Deon strode up to the man and snatched him off the ground with one arm. Andy gasped in terror as the black man lifted his two-hundred-and-sixty-pound frame without a hint of effort.

"Who are you?" Deon asked, his normally low voice now a rumble of distant thunder.

"Andy… Andy Thomas. I'm a private detective," Andy answered, his feet dangling in the air.

"That means someone hired you to spy on us," Deon stated, already working the angles and deducing Andy's background. "If you're here, that means someone has told you what we are, and you're dumb enough to get involved anyway."

"Well, more like I didn't have much choice but to get involved," Andy corrected, his terror beginning to relax now that they were talking.

"Then I'm going to assume you'll have no problem telling me who hired you," Deon said. "Since you already know what we are, you know you were dead the moment you decided to come here. Your only chance of walking out of here is making sure we're happy with your answers."

Andy paused for a moment, his mind blazing through all the possible outcomes and angles. The thing he had feared most had happened he'd gotten caught again, and all the old terror came screaming back to life. Shit, he'd even been threatened with death several times; but this time it wasn't a threat. This time, Andy knew this man meant every syllable. The problem was, so would Kaden; if he talked his way out of this problem, he'd be talking his way into another problem, and either way, there would be monsters trying to kill him.

"I can't," Andy answered quickly. "I really want to, 'cause I sure as shit don't want to die, but he'll kill me too if I say a word."

Deon's face hardened. "Then I'm very sorry to hear that," he responded as he drew back his left hand and pointed it like a knife toward Andy's chest. It was clear half a heartbeat from now, Deon was going to rip Andy's heart out with his bare hands.

Stephen was half a second behind Andy in speaking out. "Wait," Andy screamed.

"For?"

"I was hired by… another werewolf… someone who is very interested in learning all he could about Chief Butler. I was supposed to come here and follow you guys around and learn everything I could about you," Andy said quickly as he turned to Stephen. "That's it nothing more. I'm not a threat, just a guy doing a job. All he wanted to know was what kind of man you were, what you were like, maybe if there was anything he could use to his advantage. That's all, serious!"

Stephen turned to Kara, and she answered for him. "Kaden Maxwell. We knew there would be interest from the other packs, and with him wanting a meeting we knew this was likely to happen."

Stephen turned back to the terrified human and, for just a moment, let himself empathize with Andy. He wasn't much different in his own way a "human" caught up in the world of werewolves neither of them having much of a choice. All Andy was doing was trying to survive and make a buck, to get through the night alive, same as Stephen. The difference was that Stephen couldn't walk away; he had a pack now, people he was responsible for a family. The monsters in the night weren't hiding under his bed; he had become one. Somewhere Andy had gotten dragged into this world, but he at least had the choice to try to get out, to run. Stephen couldn't even do that much. With a shake of his head, Stephen tried to push the human away mentally so he could be the werewolf he had to become.

"How long have you been following us?" Stephen asked calmly.

"Just a couple of days not long."

"And if I decide to let you go, what will you tell Kaden?"

Andy paused but didn't dare hope not yet. He could have tried to lie, but at times like this he had always found it better to just tell the truth. "You're smart you dealt with that goblin and beat him. You got him to promise to give up this Onimaru thing even though you had full intention of going after the Kludde anyway. You're a cop first, so running to the rescue is what you do. You came up from working the streets and, from what I hear, you did it well, so you're not shy in a fight. You would have gone after the Kludde just because it was a threat. I've talked to some of your cops and they all love you, so you're at least a decent leader. Somehow you didn't use to be a werewolf, everything I can tell, you were born completely human but now you are, and I don't know how. There's nothing in your past even remotely paranatural, but here you are leading the pack. You can get your hands dirty but only when you're forced to, which makes you dangerous because you think before getting all slasher-movie on people. It also makes you weak because it makes you slow to react. You're a straight shooter with people but not the best at playing politics. You were married once, but your wife died, and until you met these three you weren't interested in getting back into the dating thing. Now… you're crazy in love with her" Andy nodded toward Kara "and I think you have feelings for the other two as well."

When he stopped talking, Stephen let the air go silent for a few moments before he spoke. "Not bad, Mr. Thomas. Looks like you've done your job pretty well. I didn't know I was such an open book. So, you know Kaden pretty well too, I'd guess. You did a pretty good job summing me up. What do you think he'll do when you report back?"

Andy didn't hesitate to answer. "He'll lose his shit if he finds out I got caught. He'll see it as a military defeat, and since you guys already beat his people once, he'll be pissed and worried. He hates not knowing what to do or having to worry that he's not as powerful as he thinks. You're a question mark, and you sure as hell don't act like a normal werewolf. He won't know what to make of you. Part of him will want to think you're a weak or scared human; but the other part of him will see you as so confident in your strength that you didn't care what he learned. Either way he's going to think you dismissed him as being a threat, and that's what's really going to get him. Either way he's going to have to react or he'll think he's losing face in front of his pack. He won't do anything before you guys are supposed to meet, but afterwards unless you can get some kind of advantage he'll come."

"So even if I kill you and drop you in a hole, Kaden's going to know he lost again and it'll force his hand," Stephen answered. "If I let you go, it's an insult that will elicit an attack because he'll think I don't care about him being a threat. Either way, it sounds like he's just a nut job playing soldier and schoolyard bully at the same time.

He's so worried about his power and being disrespected that he'll go to war just to prove he can."

Andy didn't answer; instead he just stared at Stephen and waited for death or maybe something worse. It was Deon who broke the silence.

"Maybe we use that," he said. "Just like a street thug confront him head-on and call him out. Shame him for the behind-the-scenes crap and sending in spies. He's setting himself up for a head-on confrontation anyway what do we have to lose?"

"But what would confronting him gain us?" Veronica asked.

Stephen stood quietly for a few seconds and worked the angles. He had years of experience working the streets and working in administration to apply to the problem. He'd hate to admit it, but a good part of being a police administrator was balancing all the alpha-male cop egos, and really this problem was no different. "First," he answered, "it'd buy us time." Stephen turned to Andy and nodded for Deon to put him down. Once he had Andy's full attention, he continued. "I think we can help each other, Mr. Thomas."

"How's that?"

"You want out from under Kaden's thumb, and I want him off my back. So, here's what I have in mind. I want you to go to him and tell him right up front that not only did you get caught, but I let you go with a message for him."

"Oh, hell no he'll lose his shit," Andy proclaimed, imagining his violent and quick death.

"Just wait hear me out," Stephen interjected. "I want you to tell him that I called him out. That I said he must be nervous if he had to send in a hit squad and now a spy into my territory. I want you to tell him everything you found out about me, and I want you to tell him that I told you to tell him. Then I want you to tell him that if he has any more questions for me, all he has to do is write them down and give them to you so you can deliver them to me. Tell him you're now our official courier between the Butler and Maxwell packs kind of like an ambassador, maybe. Last thing I want you to tell him is that I'm standing right here no tricks, no secrets, just waiting on him to set the time and place for our Alpha meeting. Until then, unless you come over with a note from him, he can stay the hell out of my territory, because the next people he sends go home in bags."

Andy Thomas stood there with the blood draining from his face. He had no idea what to think or how to respond. Elation at walking out alive was replaced by gut-wrenching fear that he was being sent back to Kaden. His only other choice was to run and hope that Kaden or his pack never crossed paths with him again.

It was Kara who put it together first. "Andy becomes untouchable," she said, wide-eyed. "Kaden's first response will be to lash out in anger, but if you're our official courier basically our diplomat then he'd be striking a declared neutral party. Plus, with you being human, you're obviously not a threat to him, so even if he wants to kill you, he can't claim any kind of self-defense. Plus, he'll know Stephen has gotten to you and made this deal, so everything you tell him no matter how true he won't be able to trust. And since you're human and not a werewolf, he won't be able to sense if you're lying. The only thing he'll learn is that Stephen is standing nose-to-nose with him and daring him to say anything about it. We're using his very public meeting plans against him. His pack is the one that called for the meeting, and we're just responding by sending his spy back as our representative."

Now it was Andy who started to put it all together. "So, I do what claim some kind of diplomatic immunity or something? I make my report and deliver your message and hope he's not pissed off enough to take my head off anyway?"

"He can't touch you without his own people thinking him weak and all the other packs knowing he can't be trusted. This is the exact same thing he has done to us. As long as everyone knows he's offering to talk, we can't strike him without baggage from the other packs," Stephen answered. "You do exactly word for word what he asks of you, and I answer everything he wants to know, just like you promised, and he can't strike our neutral diplomat."

"And when this is all over and you two have your talk then what?"

"Then we either work it out and we're playing nice, or we're elbows-deep in each other's guts. Either way, he's too busy to deal with you, and you either hit the highway or keep working for me. No matter how it ends, he'll never try to use your services again because he'll never know if you're telling him the truth or what I want him to know."

Andy paused and stared up at the night sky like he was praying for salvation. "I don't know… you guys don't know him like I do. He's not as worried about what everyone else thinks as you guys are. He'll probably tear me apart anyway. Maybe, if I talk to Ted first kind of warn him what's about to happen then maybe Ted could calm him down. Ted's the real brains he'll see what this is and that I'm just a pawn."

Kara answered, "Sure, it's a risk. It's not a perfect plan, but you died the minute you got caught here tonight. Maybe Ted can help, maybe he can't. You decide you don't like this plan and there's nothing stopping us from name-dropping you at our meeting with Kaden. All his people have to do is suspect that we caught you, and you're a dead man walking. That leaves you either trusting the plan or jumping in your car and driving until you run out of money or gas. All that does is leave you looking over your shoulder for the rest of your life until he finds you or we do."

"And if he's as paranoid and Rambo-hard-charger as everyone thinks, do you really think he doesn't have a way to keep track of you?" Deon asked. "You think he's going to let a military asset like you roam around without having his thumb on you? Even if it isn't true, as long as he believes that you know secrets about his pack or him, he's going to be on your tail for the rest of your life… or you get your diplomatic immunity."

Stephen almost felt sorry for the man as he squirmed and paused, trying to find any other angle. He really hated the idea of using Andy like this, but there wasn't much choice. Like Kara said, Andy died the moment he got caught. Using Andy sucked, and blackmailing him into the decision almost made Stephen sick; but what choice did any of them have? He would either be forced to kill Andy an almost-innocent human or he'd have to risk letting the man go and lose any advantage he had over Kaden.

Andy's knees gave out and he dropped to the ground, staring out into the middle distance. Mental overload was dangerously close to making him puke all over himself. Stephen and the group just stared down at him and waited. Finally, he looked up at Stephen.

"I guess I missed one thing in my assessment of you. You're a cold-hearted son of a bitch too. You should have killed me right here, he would have, any of his pack would have; but you're worse. You're not killing me you're making me willingly walk back to my own execution."

Stephen stared down at the doomed man, nodded slightly, and then turned and walked away.

Chapter Sixteen:
Gossip

Stephen rolled out of bed as late as he could, but after the night that he had, sleep hadn't really been an option. Deon had told him that being a werewolf meant that his physical body would be stronger, faster, and more durable than when he was just a human, but somehow no one had made that message clear to his brain because all Stephen wanted to do was sleep. Still, the balancing act of Alpha werewolf and Chief of Police would require more days like this in the future.

Standing in the bathroom wearing just a pair of shorts, Stephen stared into the mirror and looked at the changes. He was bigger than he had been just a few weeks ago; his muscles were beginning to show more definition, and he thought he was even a little slimmer. Stephen worried for a second that the people at work might notice the sudden changes and think he was adding steroids to his workout diet. Of course, he couldn't tell them that he had just gotten a dose of better genetics. Sure, he'd always hit the gym like it was a religion, but lately he'd been slacking off and he was still making progress. He wondered just how much his body would change if he had the time to hit the home gym downstairs like he used to do. For that matter, with his new better genetics, he wondered just how much his bench press had changed.

He didn't really start waking up until he hit the shower and the hot water started to soak into his tired body. "So many changes," Stephen said out loud to himself as he reached for the shampoo. His life was just changing so damn fast, but really, he wasn't complaining about most of the changes. He'd found so far that he really enjoyed the girls' company, and true to their word, they didn't seem to care that he was open about his feelings for all three of them. Stephen smiled as he thought back over his date with Kara. She had been so…alive on the dance floor. He didn't really do much dancing either, but once she had finally let go, she exploded to life. He was amazed as he watched her, and every other man in the place, along with a number of the women, couldn't keep from watching her too. Kara moved and laughed like the stoic Ice Queen had finally melted and there was a joyous riot of a woman underneath. He'd never really imagined seeing her like that, like she could have danced all night and never touched the ground. Stephen rinsed his hair; a wide smile still plastered to his face. Kara was such a powerful and amazing woman, so full of confidence and strength, but buried inside she was just as much of a kid at play as Kaitlin. He looked back over the other changes in his life over the last few weeks. Just a few days ago he would have felt guilty or worried about his feelings; now he marveled at all the happiness he had found in the three women. A lifetime of human rules was beginning to fall away, and Stephen wondered just how much more he'd change before it was done. He didn't think he was ready for all his new duties as the Alpha of the pack. The idea of bedding the other women in the pack, even the ones in relationships, just seemed alien to him. Kara, Veronica, and Kaitlin were different though; somehow, he was getting more comfortable with them. Still, change is always scary, and even though he truly enjoyed the girls, he also still feared the change that they brought as well. Being Alpha meant that he'd have to make more hard choices, choices that would cost or take lives, and he feared that he'd change to a point that it wouldn't bother him anymore. At what point would all these changes change, who he was beyond now being a werewolf and no longer completely human? Which change would be one too far?

Shaking off the heavy thinking this early, Stephen stepped out of the shower and toweled off. He was the Chief of Police and the Alpha werewolf; self-doubt and second-guessing himself were luxuries he didn't have time for anymore. He had places to go and people to see, which led him to his closet and his work clothes. It was time to start the day.

Deon had pack stuff after work, so Stephen started his own car and drove into work alone. Even though he enjoyed his time with Deon in the mornings, he kind of missed driving. It was a pleasure in his life, the feeling of driving and the quiet time it gave him. He thought about last night again, about how close he had come to killing the Twilight Marquee, and just how easily he had come up with the plan to doom Andy Thomas to either life on a knife edge or an open death sentence. Andy wasn't wrong Stephen was turning cold-hearted; maybe that was what happened when you had something in your life that was so important that you'd cross any line to protect it…to protect them. He had to admit, even if he was turning into someone different, someone harder, he was happy for the first time since Becky had died. He just hoped that he wouldn't change too much become something that Becky wouldn't approve of or wouldn't understand.

Stephen went on autopilot all the way to the office, only to come back to the moment when he closed his office door behind him. He'd been in a daze, deep in thought, and the sound of the closing door was finally able to get his attention. It was time to start his day.

Two hours ticked by, and it was shortly after nine when he was pulled out of his computer by the intercom. Mathew, his personal assistant, needed his attention.

"Yes," Stephen answered as he pressed the hands-free button.

"Chief, Lieutenant Wong to see you."

"Oh, excellent timing, I was just about to come find her."

Michelle Wong walked into his office with an armful of folders and her yellow legal pad of holding. Michelle seemed to have the magical ability to never run out of space on her legal pad and knew where every scribble was and what it meant. Stephen, on the other hand, had to make notes to remind him of what other notes meant. Michelle kicked the door closed behind her and almost ran across the room to drop the mound of manila folders onto his desk before they could hit the floor.

"Your morning caseload. Glad to get that pile of crap off my desk," Michelle twanged in her Texas accent. How that kind of accent could come out of an Asian woman's body just never seemed right to him. "So…you're dating again…," Michelle said, totally ignoring all the work she had shoved off onto him, as if that one statement said everything that needed to be said.

Stephen tried to catch the pile of work before it slid off in one direction or another, only partially succeeding before his mind caught up to her. He hadn't really thought too much about how to respond to this, but he knew sooner or later he would have to have an answer. His face was known around town, and there would be people who had seen him and Kara out last night. Just like there would surely be people who would see him out on a date with Veronica sooner or later. Kaitlin's words came back to bite him on the ass unless Dad wanted to take his daughter to the movies, he'd never be able to date her publicly. When he didn't immediately answer, Michelle cocked her head and gave him her best criminal interview stare.

"Well, it's kind of complicated," Stephen answered honestly. "I'm actually seeing a couple of women right now, and before you ask, yes, they both know I'm seeing the other, so I'm not cheating or two-timing anyone."

"OH…MY…GOD," Michelle answered in her best valley girl from the edge of her seat. "Stephen the lady-killer player! So, what are they like? Names, socials you know we have to run full background checks to make sure they're good enough for our Chief to be dating."

Stephen smiled good-naturedly on the outside as he panicked just a touch on the inside. The way she had worded that sentence meant that him leaving the office for date night had already made it around the office. "Well, her name is Kara Hughes. She owns the Bit and Byte coffee shop downtown. I met her there when Malcolm took me for lunch just before he died. We sort of hit it off, and I asked her out."

Lt. Wong stiffened slightly at the mention of Malcolm. Stephen had taken the death hard, and everyone was just a little on edge about the subject.

"How you doing…you know…with the death?"

Stephen's smile faltered but soon returned. He sighed before he answered. "Like with everything else, there are good days and bad ones. Honestly, work has been a blessing I've been so busy that I'm kind of processing it slowly. Kara has been a huge help too; she and Malcolm dated before I knew her, so she's been there for me to vent. It's been good to have someone to talk to who knew him as well as I did and cared for him. I've learned so much from her."

"You're good with dating his ex then?" Michelle asked. "I know how close you two were; I thought that might be kind of hard, always being reminded about him. I assume she's OK with it too?"

"She's mostly OK with it," Stephen answered. "I'll admit at first it was kind of rough on both of us. We both had some drama to work out between the two of us, but we've mostly gotten over that, and now we're putting it behind us. In a way, Malcolm makes it a little easier sometimes too, since we both have him as shared memories."

"And…the second girlfriend, you dog," Michelle twanged with a smile as wide as Texas, trying to lighten the mood.

Stephen paused for just a second when he suddenly realized the next problem they both had the same last name. If Michelle knew that they were mother and daughter, she'd lose her mind and it would be all over town in twenty minutes. The only thing in the known universe to travel faster than the speed of light was a juicy secret.

"Veronica, I met when I was in the hospital. She works in their lab and did most of my blood work. They were taking so much blood when the docs were trying to figure out what I had that she and I just started talking. Next thing I knew, we sort of liked each other. I'm planning on taking her on a date tonight or tomorrow if our schedules work. Now enough about me…what about your man?"

Now it was Michelle's turn to smile like a schoolgirl, so much so that she didn't notice the subtle change in topic before she got the chance to ask for more details. That was another cop trick the easiest way to change a topic is to get the other person to talk about something they liked personally. She had met Senior Agent Mathew Williams on the recent kidnapping case that they had worked together and had fallen for each other immediately; so much so that he had taken vacation time right after the case was closed so he could spend more time with her.

"We're really, really good," Michelle answered excitedly, "like I'm wondering if he isn't the one."

"Really?" Stephen answered in surprise. "Are you two talking marriage already? It's only been, what, a couple weeks or so now?"

"No, nothing like that, but I just can't imagine my life now without him. Plus, his vacation time is running out soon, and he'll have to go back to DC. Stephen, he's asked me to go with him."

"Are you telling me you're leaving us?"

"No… I mean, I'm thinking about it. I really love it here Moser City is awesome and I love this department but long-distance relationships suck. I don't know what to do," she complained. "I don't want him to leave, but I don't want to leave here either."

"Sounds like you two have a lot to talk about then. Whatever you decide, I'll never speak to you again if you decide to leave us, and I'll give you terrible reviews if you try to get another job," Stephen said with teasing in his voice. "Seriously, nothing is more important than your happiness. Just be careful and take your time. No matter what you decide, you'll always have a home here with us."

"I know, and I really appreciate that," Michelle answered, with a hint of a tear in her no-nonsense, Texas-bred tough-cop eyes.

Sensing that she wasn't ready to talk anymore about her possible change of career, Stephen moved the conversation forward. "So, other than dropping a bombshell and a pile of paperwork on my desk, did you need anything else?"

"Actually, yeah, I have some more. There's been movement on the case," Michelle replied, her professional exterior now back in place. "Most of the Feds have been concentrating on trying to locate a possible buyer for the sword, hoping to intercept it before it can get sold or moved out of the country. They've been looking for large, unusual cash withdrawals or transfers but haven't seen anything yet. State and FBI have also been looking at possible leads on the Japanese side as well; apparently there was some opposition to letting the sword travel out of the country, so they are looking at possible suspects over there."

"Don't know doesn't feel right for that," Stephen answered. "Do you think someone would get that messy for just taking a sword to the States?"

"It's just one angle they're looking at, but no, I don't think so either. I'm still leaning toward rich-guy private collector or maybe an extortion angle. We did get a break when we did the door-to-door around the Hendrix house. The neighbor across the street is also a single mom and knew Cindy really well; they babysat for each other to make the single working mom thing work. She reported seeing a large black crew-cab truck at Cindy's house the whole day of the murder. The witness said she remembered seeing the truck because it was a 'man's' truck, and she thought Cindy might be getting some action while the kids were at school. She also had a doorbell camera; we were able to get a shot of the truck and a partial plate when it drove past. We got three suspects getting out of the truck but no faces, and the angle was too bad to get any good descriptions."

"Any luck tracking it down?"

"Actually yes. With the vehicle and partial, we went back to campus cameras and started checking parking lots and entry points.

It's a damn good thing the campus did that sexual assault awareness drive a couple of years ago and expanded their cameras we found the truck coming onto campus three days before the break-in. We got the full plate, and we think the same three possible suspects on camera going into the library. We were able to pull fairly decent headshots, and the Feds are searching for possible matches." Michelle reached into her yellow legal pad and pulled three photos from between the pages. She handed the photos over to Stephen.

Stephen stood and took the pictures and could feel the cold fury starting to boil inside of himself. If his wolf was making him feel these feelings more intensely or more clearly than he had before, he didn't care. Looking into the faces of the people that slaughtered Cindy Hendrix and her family, he had nothing but rage in his heart. The cop side of him pushed that rage back down, pushed it back into the small box where all cops bury their feelings. If they were human, they'd get human justice; if they weren't…well, then he'd have to see what happened.

"Michelle, that's great," Stephen said sternly, not trying to mask his feelings for these men. "As soon as they can find facial matches, I want to know. I want you to call me before we make any moves on these guys if they are still in town. I want to be there when we get the guys that did that…evil to the Hendrix family."

"We're not there yet. We just got the faces from the campus security cameras about twenty minutes ago, so the facial searches have just gotten started, and there's no guarantee that we'll get a match. The photos are better than nothing but not perfect either."

"What about the truck? Who do the plates come back to?"

"A Mrs. Elenore Tidswell, but when we run her, she comes back as deceased about two weeks ago. I've got a detective tracking the death report down and trying to reach a next of kin to find out how her truck got involved. It's not reported as stolen, and neither are the plates, so we're not sure if anyone even knows it's missing or if her relatives are some of the three guys in the videos. We're starting on her surviving relatives, but so far, no matches from their driver's license photos."

"This is really good news finally we have something to work with," Stephen said, a touch of relief in his voice. "Have we gotten anything back from crime scene yet?"

"Well, our team and the Feds went over the place, but they didn't get anything. I'm not really surprised, though these guys feel like professionals, so making a mistake like leaving physical evidence doesn't feel right. Plus, with the number of visitors that've been through the exhibit already, it was hard to find anything usable. They're still looking at the house but we're not expecting much there either."

"I just have one question: why the hell didn't you lead with the good news instead of asking me about my love life?"

Michelle laughed. "Well, after telling you that I'm thinking about moving to DC, I needed to leave you with something good before the end of the day. Besides, if I told you first and then asked about your love life, there's no way you would have told me!"

Michelle left still laughing soon after, headed back to her office to hopefully keep up with the Feds and keep her agency in the game. Not all the federal agencies liked to play well with the locals, so Michelle had to keep on top of them. After she left, the rest of Thursday just sort of happened. Paperwork happened from one pile into another. Meetings happened about very important things. Emails about very important things happened and then happened in response. All of the very important things that the Chief of Police had to deal with personally all…happened. Of course, the definition of "important" seemed to be variable depending on who it was he was talking to; everyone seemed to think their opinions were important. Overall, it had been…a day.

Chapter Seventeen:
A Simple Dinner at Home

Stephen drove home quietly, a smile on his face for no other reason than he was getting to go home to his girls. It was a feeling that still wasn't lost on him. After Becky had died, there had been no one to go home to, no reason to smile after being off work. There were days now when he thought back on his life after Becky and still marveled at the fact that he hadn't become a raging alcoholic or something worse. At the time though, he never really noticed how much he hated to drive home, to come back to an empty house. Now that he had people to go home to, he noticed the difference every day.

The other thing about driving home was that he had time to think without being distracted. He still didn't have a clue what to do for a date night with Kaitlin, the obvious age difference being just too huge to go without notice. To be honest, the age difference between him and Veronica would probably start more than just a few whispers too. Publicly dating Kaitlin—that would get him called into the mayor's office with Human Resources sitting in. Regardless, he refused to leave her out. Kaitlin had spent the majority of her life being ignored or overlooked because of her apparent age, and he refused to hurt her like that again. Now he just had to come up with a plan.

His plan for Veronica's date had actually been easy to decide upon. Hers wouldn't be as public as his date with Kara. Not because he was trying to hide, but because Veronica wasn't that kind of woman. She wouldn't enjoy something as public as dinner and dancing; rather, Veronica was a more subdued personality in public. His plan for their date would be something more personal, and he hoped that it went over with the meaning that he was trying to share.

"Hi honeys, I'm home," Stephen called out as he opened the front door. He didn't need to say anything—werewolf senses were almost like superpowers, and he knew that the girls had heard him coming—but it still felt good.

"Welcome home, Stephen," Kara answered from the kitchen, a smile across her face. "You've got good timing. We're just about ready to eat dinner before Kaitlin has to go into the casino."

He could smell dinner from outside. His new senses were still hard to control sometimes. If he thought about them or tried to use them, his senses could overwhelm him, and they'd just about knock him on his ass; but practice made perfect and he was getting better with them. "Spaghetti with garlic bread. I do love Italian," he answered.

They sat together at the dining room table, Stephen at the head with Kara on his right and Veronica on his left. Kaitlin sat next to Veronica with a towel stuffed into her collar, trying to protect her work clothes. Apparently even werewolf queens made mistakes— serving spaghetti sauce on a night when Kaitlin had to work in her white tuxedo shirt.

They ate like a normal family, each talking about their day and just sharing time together. Kara talked about the coffee shop and the price of good coffee beans going up again. It was a struggle to keep pricing under control when she had to compete with the larger chain companies that could buy coffee by the trainload. If the price of coffee kept going up, she'd have to start passing the cost on to the customers, which she was loath to do. For Kara, her customers were important to her—not just for their money, but because they were the reason she kept the shop open. She loved being part of their daily routine and why she knew most of their preferred orders. For Kara, being a small-business owner kept her human and let her ignore all the other things in her life that weren't.

Veronica's day had been bloody, but her day was usually bloody when she worked at the hospital doing lab work. Normally she would be at work right now—the afternoon shift was her norm—but she'd covered the day shift for one of her coworkers and so was home early. Veronica preferred the night shift, which let her do her job without having all the extra day-shift people underfoot. The other reason she hated mornings was that she didn't like to get up. After they had gotten home from their little meeting in the park, Veronica had just gotten changed and gone into work early while Stephen had tried to get at least a couple of hours' sleep. Hers had been a day filled with making polite small talk with hospital patients while she helped fill in for the techs who were short-staffed. Then she'd take the blood samples down to the basement lab and run whatever tests had been ordered. It was precise and detailed work, but she was good at it and enjoyed helping.

Kaitlin's day had been spent in bed. Her work schedule wasn't normally as structured as Kara's or even Veronica's. Kaitlin worked full-time as a dealer at the local casino, but that meant she had to struggle for work hours sometimes. When the customers ran out of money, the casino sent people home, so she had to get the work when it was offered. It did make it a little easier on her to work around being a werewolf and the demands that put on her time, but she had bills to pay. Stephen had offered to help—he had more money than he would ever need thanks to Becky's talent with investments—but Kaitlin would always refuse. She'd always answer that an adult had to pay their own bills, a reminder to herself and anyone in earshot that she wasn't a little kid anymore.

Dinner that night had been an actual pleasure, and not just because Kara could make a mean spaghetti with garlic bread. They ate as a family and enjoyed it. Like all things though, it was over soon enough. Kaitlin wiped her mouth on her towel, checked to make sure her white shirt wasn't stained with spaghetti sauce, and ran for the door to head to work. Since Kara had cooked, she was freed from the cleanup duties, so in short order Stephen found himself mostly alone with Veronica in the kitchen.

"I have a question," Stephen began as he dried the plate she had just handed him with a dish towel. "Are you reading anything right now?"

"What, like a book or something?" Veronica asked.

"Well, that's what most people read unless you're into tech manuals or something," he teased back.

"Smart ass. Yes, I'm reading a book. Why?"

"Well, I just wanted to know if you were free tomorrow night to go on a date with me and if you wouldn't mind bringing your book?"

Veronica paused, and even though he had promised earlier to take them each on a date, she couldn't help but smile at the tingles she got in her stomach when he asked her out. It was like being in high school again, but this time the jock that everyone wanted to be with wanted to spend time with her.

"I'm not working tomorrow. I'm off all weekend. Only thing I have is my martial arts classes in the afternoon, but I should be done before five," she answered, with just a touch of excitement sneaking through. "I guess I can bring my book with me."

"Great," he answered, his own excitement leaking through. "It won't be very fancy, so just wear something comfortable and a pair of walking shoes."

"Gee, I have to take a shower and everything! So demanding," she teased.

"Well, I suppose you don't have to take a shower after your class. I can always drive through a car wash with the windows down," Stephen teased back.

"Or we can skip the date, and you can just join me in the shower," she fired back, but then paused and changed her mind. "No, I think I like the date more right now."

Veronica was so excited as she thought about what was coming that she almost dropped the next plate she handed him to dry and put away. She'd been out with men dozens of times, but here she was with butterflies in her stomach and feeling weak at the knees because he had asked her out. She felt silly when she thought about it more— her, a grown woman—and the idea of a date not being a surprise, but the butterflies were still dancing. "I'll look forward to it," she said assuredly, smiling so hard her face hurt.

Dishes done and put away, Stephen changed out of his work clothes and into something more comfortable. When he returned, Kara and Veronica were both downstairs in the entertainment room—what used to be called a family room. It wasn't a big room, large enough for a sectional couch and some large pillows on the floor with a projection TV slung from the ceiling. He'd never have dreamed of owning anything like this if it hadn't been for Becky;

she loved the old classic movies and liked having a nice place to cuddle while she watched. This evening was little different: Veronica and Kara both shared opposite ends of the sectional, leaving obvious room for him in the middle. The middle section was his favorite anyway since it could recline back and had a footrest. He hated to admit the number of times he'd fallen asleep on that couch while Becky watched her movies and hated more to think of all the time he wasted with her. He wouldn't be so wasteful this time.

"What are we watching?" Stephen asked as he flopped down and reclined the couch.

"It's Thursday, so we've got new episodes on the BBC," Kara answered as she leaned into his shoulder once he got settled.

"I've been looking forward to this all week," Veronica replied while she settled into his other shoulder, now both women snuggling comfortably against him. To be honest, he didn't care what they watched; he just enjoyed feeling them against him—and this time, he refused to fall asleep.

Chapter Eighteen:
A Book Under the Stars

Stephen stopped the car back at Baker's Memorial Park, not far from the same parking spot that they had used when they were meeting with the Twilight Marquee. He had picked Veronica up from the house when he got off work and turned back toward the park. Last time they had gone down to the basketball courts, but this time Stephen had a better destination in mind.

He had gotten up early that morning to rummage around in the basement for a couple of old friends long forgotten. After he had cleaned them up from their years of storage, he packed a change of clothes and headed to work. He'd packed a pair of running pants and a long-sleeve, tight-fitting shirt for their date. Not the fanciest of clothes, but he had told her to be comfortable.

Work had been a struggle. The Feds had hit another dead end with the facial recognition software from the photos of the three possible suspects. Michelle had told him during their daily briefing that they had started with a geo-fence of the database to cover Moser City and the surrounding counties. When that had turned up nothing, they broadened their search and still hadn't found anything. Now the Feds were looking at passport entry photos, thinking that the three suspects could be hired professionals from outside the country. Regardless, they had gotten nowhere so far, and Michelle said that the tension was already becoming an issue with some of the agents. With a high-profile case like this, it could make a career and even land the right agents speaking engagements for life. On the other hand, a theft of this importance that didn't end in an arrest could get someone reassigned someplace unpleasant.

As for Michelle's part, they had tracked down the lead the Feds had left for them—the black truck—but she too had hit a dead end. This lead was a little more unusual, though. It hadn't been hard to find the former owner's family. Mrs. Elenore Tidswell had owned the truck before she died and had lived next to a gated community in a decent part of town, so Michelle tracked down her son, Eddie Tidswell.

Eddie was a local scumbag, the kind that always seemed to be getting into trouble somehow and was good for everything from slinging dope to petty smash-and-grabs. Lt. Wong had worked a couple of cases with Eddie and had even used him as a CI a couple of times—with limited results. This time was different, though. Eddie could remember his mom having the truck, even knew how much she paid for it, but couldn't remember what had happened to it. What's more, if he was to be believed, Eddie couldn't remember where he got the five thousand dollars in cash that Michelle had found on Mrs. Tidswell's kitchen table. Eddie even seemed surprised by the money, like he just accepted that it was there but didn't really recognize that it had been there the whole time. It was kind of like seeing a picture hanging on the wall—it was just always there, so much so that people tended not to see it anymore unless something changed about it.

Even when she pushed him, all Eddie would say was that the truck wasn't stolen, but he didn't know why or who had it. Of course, this didn't make any sense, so the Feds had given a run at interviewing Eddie, but he stuck to his story. It took a little convincing, but Michelle had even gotten him to take a CVSA test, what most people called a voice-stress test. To everyone's amazement, Eddie passed with flying colors. As far as he knew, he was telling the truth.

After a day of getting nowhere fast, Stephen was even more excited for their date.

"I hope you don't mind a little exercise. It's a bit of a walk where I want to go," Stephen said as he grabbed an old picnic basket and a duffel bag out of the back seat.

"I like exercise," Veronica answered. She had struggled with what to wear for their date tonight. Stephen had said casual but to expect a little exercise by asking for the walking shoes. She finally settled on comfortable, loose-fitting yoga pants and a baggy shirt that wrapped around her and tied at the hip. She had always been a fan of darker colors, so the yoga pants were a charcoal color with her shirt being a lighter gray. "How far we going?"

"It's a couple of miles," Stephen answered. "If you want, I can rent a golf cart from the park store and we can ride."

Veronica smiled at him like he was being dumb for a second before she realized he was serious. "Stephen, I appreciate the offer, but… you remember we can sprint a couple of miles now, right?" Stephen flushed in embarrassment, and she could feel the wave of emotions off him. He was rattled—something more than just being on a first date with her. "You're flustered. I'm sorry I shouldn't have teased you."

He took a deep breath as they started walking the long, familiar path through the park. "You're fine. And you're right, I really wasn't thinking. I'm just… I'm not sure how to explain this without making it sound creepy or something."

"How about one word at a time, then? You know about my secret—not-so-secret—bedroom practices. There's not much I get judgy about," she answered with a reassuring smile.

They walked a few more paces before Stephen finally spoke. "I wanted to take you someplace special. But now that we're here, walking down this path with you, it feels like this might have been a bad idea."

"Do you want to go back?" she asked.

He paused again, deep in thought, though his feet kept carrying him forward. "No. I just want to make sure you're not weirded out or something. I want to take you someplace special to me— someplace that was special to Becky and me. This place we're going… it used to be our favorite spot. And when she got sick, I had to rent a golf cart because she couldn't walk it anymore. I know that sounds weird now that I'm saying it out loud."

"No," she answered immediately, emotion thick in her voice. "It's not weird. It's really special. If you want to share your special place with me, I… I don't even know what to say."

She couldn't find the right words, so she simply reached out and took his hand.

Together they walked, hand in hand—Stephen carrying the picnic basket in one hand, the duffel bag slung over his shoulder, Veronica holding her book. They walked in comfortable silence, just enjoying being close. Their feet had eaten away the first mile before either of them spoke again.

"This kind of reminds me of my inner space," Stephen said, looking around at the nature surrounding them. Away from the parking lot, the trees stood in natural clusters along gentle rolling hills, wild grasses swaying in the breeze.

"Your inner space?"

"Oh, it's what I call the place where Big Black lives. When I look inside myself to go to his place, it looks a lot like this."

"You can actually *see* that?" Veronica asked, a hint of remorseful envy in her voice.

"Well… yeah. I just sort of meditate and show up in his space. I don't really know how it happens. I hope that's not weird or something."

"You're not weird," Veronica answered quickly. "I'm the weird one. Kara and Kaitlin both have an inner place too, but I think theirs looks different from yours. I don't—I just go to this foggy place when I try to see where my wolf lives. I don't get to see any details. Or even my wolf."

"So you've never met your wolf?"

"No, I've seen pictures of what I look like when I shift, but that's really all I can see. Kaitlin especially has bonded really well with her wolf, and she can tell me all kinds of details about her inner space and her wolf. Sometimes she just goes to her inner space when she's alone to hang out with her wolf, and they play together. Obviously, I can shift, so we've bonded enough for that, but my wolf and I have never met. Really, it surprises me that you've met Big Black. From all the problems you've had bonding with him, I wouldn't expect you to be able to see details in his world."

"Well, maybe it's not based on how well you've bonded but on something else," Stephen theorized. "I've always been able to see his space, so maybe it's something Malcolm did with the injection. I didn't know you couldn't see more details. Is that unusual in the pack?"

"Not really. Kaitlin and Kara are the unusual ones, actually. I'd call you unusual, but that's a given," Veronica answered with a chuckle. "Most of the pack who can shift only get glimpses or shadowy places when they talk about their wolf's space. Malcolm used to tell me he didn't even see an inner space when he tried to meet his wolf, but I think he was lying. He always used to describe the inner space as some kind of genetic mind trick we'd all devised—like a mass hysteria—but I think he saw his inner space too. Malcolm never liked the idea of the paranatural world being a world of magic. He had to have some kind of science-based answer for everything."

"You don't talk about him as much as Kara does. Does it bother you to talk about Malcolm? I know you loved him too."

"Not really, it doesn't bother me," Veronica answered. "I loved him, but it was different from what he had with her. We loved each other, but in different ways. I was his safe space—the place where he could be the bottom, where he didn't have to be in charge. When we worked in his lab together, it was more of a partnership in most things. He'd discuss parts of the science with me in detail for hours at a time just so he could work it out in his own head. I caught most of it, but he was so brilliant that I wouldn't understand the rest of it if he explained it for a hundred more years."

"That reminds me of Becky," Stephen replied. "I'm not dumb, but the way she could track market figures and see trends was way beyond me. I used to think sometimes that she could see the future, because she always seemed to know when to dump a stock before it got toxic. She made a lot of money for people over the years."

Their conversation fell quiet then, both lost in their thoughts, both simply enjoying the peace of being around each other without pressure or presumption. It was an easy walk as they got further from the civilized world. It didn't feel long before Stephen's feet stopped on their own.

"It's off the trail here, through this way," Stephen said as he let go of Veronica's hand and pushed the low-hanging branches aside. A few steps off the path and they disappeared from view. He guided her through the woods only a few dozen yards before stepping aside to reveal the scene before them.

They stood beneath an old oak tree—the kind that seemed older than the rest of the forest around it. The tree sat on a bare hillock, its thick branches casting a wide, cool shade. The ground beneath it was clear. The hillock overlooked a broad bend in the river that marked the edge of the park and drew so many tourist campers every season. From here, they could look down over the water as it lazily made its way toward a distant ocean and forget the rest of the world existed.

"Oh, Stephen… it's beautiful," Veronica said when she saw his special place.

"Becky loved it here, even before she got sick. She said this place always brought her peace."

Without further explanation, he set the picnic basket and duffel bag down beneath the tree. Stephen opened the basket and spread out the blanket he kept inside. Then he leaned back against the oak and reached up to her.

"Come lie down. Put your head against my leg and just listen."

She did as he asked, settling onto the blanket under the ancient oak and making herself comfortable against his thigh.

"What page are you on?" he asked as he gently took the book from her hand so she could relax.

"There's a bookmark," she answered.

Stephen flipped open the book and found her place. Then he just started reading out loud to her. His voice meshed with the gentle sounds of the water flowing below and the forest around them. It had been amazing before, back when he was fully human, but now the sounds and smells were almost too much. His senses tried to overload him again, so Stephen tuned them out and concentrated on the book.

After several minutes, he reached over and placed the basket within Veronica's reach, urging her silently to explore it without interrupting his reading. She pulled out the light dinner he had packed and spread it on the blanket between them. Now, after every few lines, Veronica handed him a small piece of cheese or a roll of meat, which he ate from her fingertips so he wouldn't get the book—or his hands—dirty. After a few more pages, Veronica poured tea from the thermos and held the cup up for him. Together they repeated the process for hours, lying there surrounded by nature and the pages of a good book.

He read to her until the sun dipped low and the bugs started flying more aggressively.

"Stephen," Veronica said, breaking the spell of his storytelling. "You know I'm in love with you, right? Like really in love with you. Like hardcore, crazy in love with you. Wow... saying that out loud suddenly feels all crazy-stalker."

Quietly, he returned the bookmark and closed the book. "It still sounds weird to me to say it, but I love you too," he answered. "Even the crazy-stalker part of you. There've been so many changes, so fast, and if you'd asked me six months ago whether I'd ever see myself in love again, I would've called you crazy."

"Can I ask you for something special? Something greedy?" Veronica asked as she smiled up at him like a silly schoolgirl.

"Of course."

"I know you love Kara and Kaitlin, and I'm very okay with that. I even like feeling how it brings us all closer together. But… can I claim this place as mine? This place, in all the world—just for you and me." She paused, the words catching up to her racing thoughts. "Only if you don't mind. I mean, only if you don't think Becky would have minded me sharing this place with you," she rambled.

Stephen just smiled, reached down, pulled her farther into his lap, and kissed her into silence. It wasn't a hard or hungry kiss—just love, steady and warm. When he finally broke it, he answered. "I don't think Becky would mind. I actually think she'd really like you. So yes… we can call this our spot now."

Veronica smiled, tears forming at the corners of her eyes as she pulled him back down for another kiss. Again it was soft, full of affection, but they lingered longer this time.

"So… I've been dying to know," she said against his lips. "What's in the bag?"

"Just wait. It's getting close now—you'll see in a few minutes. Just lie back and enjoy the view."

She did as he asked, resting her head against his thigh. Stephen returned to the book, reading another dozen pages until it finally grew dark enough.

Out here—far from town, the city lights swallowed by the trees—the stars put on their show. There were more visible than even at his house. He'd seen this sky dozens of times from beneath this tree, but this was the first time he'd seen it with werewolf eyes. Above him, the entire universe seemed to gaze back.

"Oh, Stephen… they're beautiful," Veronica breathed.

"Guess we don't need the telescope in the bag anymore."

"No, but it was a good thought." Veronica wasn't looking at the stars anymore—she was looking at the man she loved. The date had been perfect, but only one thing could make it better. She shifted onto her knees, drawing his gaze away from the heavens and back to her.

Veronica swung a leg over and straddled his lap, leaning in to kiss him again—this time with more heat than before. Message delivered, she broke the kiss and leaned back slightly, reaching for the tie that held her shirt wrapped around her. With a shrug, she slipped the loosened garment from her shoulders and let it fall beside them, revealing a pretty light-blue bra underneath.

"Keep taking clothes off and you're going to get bug bites in tender places," Stephen teased, though he didn't move to stop her.

With a mischievous smile Veronica pulled the front of the bra up, her bare breasts falling free as she answered him. "Do these look like bug bites?"

Stephen never answered but the heat from his hands as he grabbed her breasts almost made her breath catch in her chest. His hands were strong and larger than hers, a man's hands, but she was used to this feeling from other men. What was different this time was who owned the hands and that mattered to her. Hungerly, he pulled her forward, pulling her down towards him and catching her mouth with his. He kissed her hard, like they had on the back deck just a few nights ago, when he was interrupted by his phone. This time, he'd called ahead, letting the office know that he wasn't to be disturbed unless an absolute emergency.

Her skin was intoxicating and the surge of sensations from his new senses made even the touch of her skin into an erotic pleasure that he'd never felt before. Stephen broke their kiss and let his mouth explore downwards, across the side of her neck and onto her shoulder. He kissed and gently bit a trail down to her collar bone but could bend no further. Instinctively she solved the problem and rared back, bending her back into an arch and letting him support her weight with his hands on the small of her back. Freed once more to explore his mouth traveled down further, down to the curves of the soft flesh of her breasts until he found their peaks. When his mouth closed around her pointed peaks, Veronica's voice escaped her lips with the sounds of pleasure. The sound was like blood in the water for a hungry shark and spurred Stephen forward, to bite and tease her body more, all to get those sounds from her again. He never noticed that his fingers were now digging into her sides, the strength of his hands adding just a touch of pain to her pleasure. What he did notice was that her hips began to thrust towards him and his body agreed with that idea.

Stephen pulled away from her just long enough to find his words. Veronica looked down at him and felt his need rolling off of him matched by her own and she knew what he was going to say. "These are in the way," she said as she stood and started to pull herself free from the yoga pants that now seemed to be way too much clothing. It seemed to take forever before they finally let go of her legs and she stood over him in all her naked glory. To her pleasure, Stephen hadn't wasted the few moments that they had been parted, having wiggled free of his pants as well. With just a little chuckle, she sat back down carefully onto his lap forcing her words to come out like a sigh. "I'm first", she said as their hips met and she felt the Major General slide inside her.

That's when it all started to go wrong. The pleasure of feeling him inside her threw her head back and tore another sound of pleasure from her matched by the low growl of his own voice. When Veronica leaned back forward and he pressed his hips towards hers, she felt it hit her like a wall, not the feeling of him or the pleasure he was bringing, but his wolf. It hit so hard that it knocked the breath from her lungs and Veronica fell forward onto him, only to be locked in place by arms that were several times stronger than when he was solely human.

"Stephen, your wolf," Veronica choked out into his ear, but he didn't seem to hear her as his body continued to move toward hers. With a thrust of her own force, Veronica pushed herself up and tore another scream of feelings from herself, but it gave her room and the feeling of her own wolf inside her gave her purpose enough to speak. "Stephen, stop! Your wolf is calling mine and if you don't stop him, I'm going to shift right here on top of you."

Her voice sounded distant to him, like she had called out to him from far away, but he heard her words and knew their meaning. Stephen looked around and found himself naked and in a different set of woods than where he left Veronica. He knew this place, this metaphysical place deep inside himself where his wolf lived. This time the brisk cold air was different, he could smell her on the wind, feel the heat of her body across his skin even in this inner space. He wanted her, wanted to go back to her and feel her with his own senses again, but her words still held meaning.

Stephen turned and ran over the rolling hills. Why he always seemed to appear in the woods a distance from Big Black's den he didn't understand, but this time it seemed to annoy him more than ever before. Things were different this time, more than just being able to smell Veronica on the wind, this time his wolf's voice joined with the wind. As he crested the last hill and looked down at the den on the other side of the frigid creak that separated him from his wolf, he heard Big Black's howl. At first it sounded sad, like it was the feeling of being alone, but then Stephen heard the other sounds buried inside, the sounds of longing and the feeling of love returned. The howl only stopped when Stephen reached the edge of the water and this time he wasn't met by the hostility of before.

Big Black looked at Stephen and turned away from him, jogging a few yards away only to stop and look back over his shoulder at the human. The wolf waited for his rather dim-witted partner to figure it out.

Stephen looked in amazement and then stepped into the frigid creek. He didn't know what would happen if he crossed over, they had only ever exchanged places the last time he shifted, so there was no telling what would happen to his body if they both were on the same side. Still, it was clear that Big Black was inviting him there, apparently needed him to be there, so Stephen stepped out of the water and onto the other shore. No matter how much he wanted to go back to Veronica, something inside him told him that this was important.

Chapter Nineteen:
Through the Fog

He ran hard after the black dire wolf as it led him further from the familiar inner space where it had always met Stephen. He'd never even dreamed of this space being as large as it appeared to be, but he'd been running full out behind the wolf for what seemed like an hour. Slowly though, the lands around them changed, but Big Black showed no signs of slowing down. Gone were the rolling plains and scattered trees, replaced by the denser forest of a mountainside. He could feel the elevation trying to rob him of his stamina, even with his new endurance, but he didn't stop because something told him that time was very short.

They ran together, climbing further up the mountain until the world around them began to fade, replaced by dense fog. At first Stephen thought it to be just that—fog on a mountain—but as the ground began to even out, he noticed that the details of his surroundings were gone now. The sounds of wind dancing through tree branches and the smells of dirt and rot had all faded to nothing. Still they ran, but not for much longer before Stephen started to make out a shadow in the fog. It wasn't much at first, just a patch of darker gray in the sea of swirling mists, but this patch didn't move. Big Black padded to a walk as they approached and reared his head up to let out a howl, deep and long. The shape in the distance turned at the sound and started to move forward toward them. He didn't know how, but Stephen knew who approached—though it couldn't be possible.

Veronica finally stepped close enough that the fog parted, revealing that she too was nude in this place. Her eyes, wide with shock, looked first to Stephen and then to his wolf, her mind stumbling over itself trying to process what was going on.

"Stephen?"

"Yes."

"But how?" she asked. "This is my space, the inner space where my wolf lives. How can you be here? How can Big Black be here?"

"I don't know," was all he could answer before Big Black lifted his nose to the wind and took in a deep breath. He seemed to answer them both when he let out a short huff of breath before he darted off into the fog without warning. Neither of them knew what to do or if there was anything that they should do, so Stephen simply reached out for her hand and waited. In the shrouded distance, they heard Big Black's voice call out again. This time the sound was pleading, urging, like he was trying to call home a lost loved one. When another voice answered, Veronica burst into tears.

"Oh Stephen," she cried, tears suddenly falling freely from her eyes. "That's her!"

Veronica grabbed his arm and steadied herself as they waited. It was hard to see through the thick haze, but Stephen thought he saw them first. "There," he pointed.

The shroud of fog seemed to part for Big Black as the dire wolf padded forward, a smaller female wolf in tow. The wolf was the reddish-black color of mahogany and moved with grace and power. She seemed to hesitate as the fog parted, revealing the two naked humans. She looked to Big Black for answers, but Stephen's wolf huffed dismissively and then promptly fell over and stretched as if looking for a comfortable spot to lay down. Just that fast, Big Black was now more interested in leisure than the events around him.

Veronica knelt down, tears still flowing down her cheeks as she reached out to the beautiful wolf. "It's OK," she said carefully, urging the wolf forward. "I'm right here, it's alright." Slowly, the female wolf inched forward and sniffed carefully at the outstretched hand. Then the wolf was on her, knocking Veronica onto her back as the wolf rolled its large head across her. Veronica cried out in surprise, but it was replaced immediately by laughter as she wrapped her arms around her wolf and petted the predator like a long-lost loved one. They rolled around on each other in jubilation for several moments, both lost in each other, until Veronica looked back at Stephen and seemed to remember.

"He called to her and led her out of the fog," Veronica said through her tears. "She had been lost in the fog for so long and I couldn't find her, but Big Black was able to call to her and bring her to me. Oh God, thank you," Veronica sobbed as she stood and fell into Stephen's arms. "Thank you for this."

Big Black rolled to his feet, apparently bored of all this drama, and padded toward Veronica's wolf. They met each other as lovers, each rubbing their face against the other, marking each other with their scent and forming bonds that were stronger than friendship. Then, as quickly as this had all started, Big Black looked around at the fog and shook himself like he was trying to shake off a long nap. As he did, the fog began to melt away as the first rays of sunlight pierced through. It didn't happen all at once—it would take time— but the fog of this place was beginning to melt.

The dire wolf shoved his side into Stephen's hip with a knowing look and started to pad off. "I guess we have to go back," Stephen said as he turned back to Veronica while she cried in his arms.

"I'll be a minute, but I'll be there," Veronica answered through tears of joy as she turned to her wolf once more.

Together they ran back through the slowly thinning fog and back down the mountain. Stephen followed his wolf through the woods until they once again transitioned into rolling hills, and then the sounds of water in a creek could be heard in the distance. Big Black only slowed when he reached his den and, with an exhausted look at Stephen, flopped over and curled into a ball to sleep. Stephen didn't understand what had just happened, but he could feel the exhaustion coming from his wolf. It had taken a huge effort to do whatever Big Black had done, and now all the wolf wanted was a well-deserved nap.

"You did amazing," Stephen said to his wolf. "Thank you." To his surprise, Big Black huffed back dismissively—or perhaps that had just been a snore. Stephen smiled in response and made it back across to his side of the creek.

Stephen could feel her on top of him again, feel the relaxed weight of her body and the dampness on his chest from her tears. He didn't try to move her; instead, he just held on and tried to process what had just happened. There was just so much there to think about, so much emotion, the least of which was that he and Veronica had finally had sex together. Well, technically they still were, since he hadn't tried to move her and was afraid that if he moved, it would somehow distract her from her wolf. He couldn't fully understand what all this meant for Veronica, but he knew that it had to be huge. Carefully he wrapped his arms around her and held her gently, and after a few more moments, he felt her starting to shake with sobs. Stephen held her tighter then and hoped that his presence alone would bring her some kind of comfort. He didn't totally understand the waves of emotion coming off her in that moment—they were so mixed and intense that they were hard to read—but he knew that she was overwhelmed.

"Thank you," Veronica whispered repeatedly, like saying those two words over and over was all she could do.

Stephen squeezed just a little tighter and stroked her hair, answering only with, "Shhhhh." Skin to skin and wrapped in his arms, they lay there together under the stars and the ancient oak tree until he felt her start to calm down, going from a sensation of overwhelming emotions to just being numb.

"Stephen," she said quietly and hesitantly, "I want to go home."

"Of course." When she moved, Stephen involuntarily made a little noise as she pulled away from him, drawing her attention. "Sorry, still sensitive."

In her befuddled state, it took Veronica a couple of seconds to understand what he had meant. "Oh, I'm sorry, we were...," she started but never finished her sentence.

"We were having an amazing date, and it's time to go home," he answered with a smile as he started to look for his clothes. They weren't far, and he got dressed easily, but had to help Veronica get herself dressed. He had been a cop for a long time and knew what he was seeing—a woman who had gone through something so emotionally charged that she was in shock. He helped her get dressed, collected their things, and then helped her to her feet. Holding her hand, Stephen led her through the woods and back to the trail. On the trail, surrounded by the trees, it was dark—dark—but werewolves didn't need as much light, and Stephen made his way without trouble. They were going much slower than the trip out, Veronica apparently so overwhelmed that she was having trouble keeping up with their walking pace. He knew that wasn't the case—her endurance and speed were better than his—but she was so out of it that she was struggling.

"Veronica, here—get on my back and I'll give you a piggyback ride," Stephen said as he put the basket down and bent down in front of her.

"No, I'm OK," she stammered in response, but even as she was saying no, she was climbing up onto his back and wrapping her arms around his neck.

Stephen stood, worry for Veronica taking up most of his brain's processing power, leaving only just enough to marvel about how easy it was to hold her weight now. He would have felt the strain of her weight a couple of months ago, but now, with all the changes in his body, she felt like holding a child. He grabbed the basket, checked the telescope bag on his other shoulder, and took off at a brisk walk. He could have run—could have sprinted—and not felt held back by carrying a full-grown woman on his back; but he was worried that the jostling would be hard on her. Instead he stayed at a brisk mall walk, which was still faster than his best walking speed would have been three months ago.

When they reached his car, Stephen got her seated, threw the luggage in the back, and set off for home in less than a minute. She didn't say anything on the drive home, just leaned against the window and stared out at the night. He thought she had gone back to the metaphysical space inside, that inner space where her wolf lived, but she made a few small voluntary movements as they drove, letting him know that she was still awake.

Even as he drove—faster than he should have been, Stephen was processing the next few steps. He'd have to get her home, ask for help to get her inside to accelerate the treatment phase, and notify the people in his life who had a much better chance of understanding what had happened than he did. That meant he needed Kaitlin and Kara—or maybe Deon, but he'd be at his own home and probably asleep. Stephen glanced at the time as he maneuvered around a slower-moving truck and figured that Kaitlin would be home and still awake after work. She always liked to take some time to wind down after getting home from the casino, which usually meant comfy clothes and comfort food. Kara worked day shift today but was off Saturday morning, one of her few mornings off from the coffee shop, so she would probably be asleep but could be woken if required.

Even as Stephen was slowing the car down in front of his house, he was already reaching out for help. He knew he had some new ability that only the Alphas of old used to have—the ability to transmit his emotions into commands. He didn't want to command so much as communicate his needs. Stephen focused on Kaitlin, imagined seeing her in his mind, and focused on needing her help. He let a touch of his worry seep through, a touch of the tension just below the surface, and hoped it worked as he dropped the car in park and started to get out.

He had just made it to the front of the car when the front door almost exploded open. Kaitlin had barely let the door get out of the way before she had tried to go through it, and even with her small frame, the heavy oaken door would have lost. She stood there, hunched over, her arms opened wide, and her lips curled back in a snarl that would have looked at home on her wolf form. She was in combat mode, ready to fuck up anyone that got in her way. It was an impressive sight from the small-framed woman—except for the open pint of ice cream in one hand, her My Little Pony cut-off shirt, and pink gym shorts.

Kaitlin looked around frantically, her brain processing first to identify threats, and second to find the critical needs. Seeing no threats, she saw Veronica limply lying against the car doorframe.

"V!" she almost yelled.

Kaitlin dropped her forgotten ice cream and, with a simple flex of her legs, leaped into the air like some kind of superhero movie, coming down on the other side of the car near the door just as Stephen reached it.

"What happened?" she asked as they both started to gently help Veronica out.

"Emotional overload," Stephen answered. "I don't think she's hurt, just in shock. We were on our date and some stuff happened that overwhelmed her." Kaitlin's eyes snapped to Stephen, a look of hard message in them that said, if you hurt my sister, I'll tear you apart.

"I'm fine," Veronica answered in response, her hand reaching out to rest on Kaitlin's forearm. "I'm just really exhausted. It wasn't his fault."

Threat forgotten, Kaitlin and Stephen helped Veronica out and into the house. Kaitlin immediately guided them toward the back bedrooms, but she surprised Stephen when she turned toward his bedroom instead of Veronica's. With a glance of question from him, Kaitlin answered, "Your bed is bigger than hers," and guided them into his room. Veronica regained a little of her clarity and walked the last few steps to his bed under her own power, only to fall down and sprawl across it.

"Strip her down and get her in bed," Kaitlin told Stephen, and when Stephen looked back toward her to respond, his words were cut short as Kaitlin was stepping out of her shorts, her My Little Pony shirt already discarded in a pile.

"Puppy pile," she answered. "Like we did for you."

"Kara?" Stephen asked.

"Already asleep, and she had a bad day at work so I don't want to wake her. I think V will be fine with just the two of us."

Stephen focused on undressing Veronica down to nothing and then dropped his own clothes on the floor. He gave her the middle of the bed—Veronica already asleep—and climbed over her to curl up on her right. Kaitlin slid behind Veronica and, with Stephen, curled up to hold her between them. For werewolves, touch, skin, and pack all had power of their own. They had done the same for him not too long ago, curling up to hold him. It had been one of the best nights he'd ever known, and it was his turn to provide for Veronica. They cuddled in close to her, his arm reaching out to cover her and touch Kaitlin at the same time. Kaitlin returned his touch and leaned up just enough to make eye contact, giving him the sorry look. Stephen winked back at her and then they both settled in to sleep.

Chapter Twenty:
Wolfing Down Breakfast

Stephen woke Saturday morning and didn't bother to even look for his phone or a clock. He hadn't slept that well since their last puppy pile and honestly didn't care what time it was, nor did he have any desire to move. Veronica and Kaitlin were still sleeping—both of these beautiful goddess-like women had shared his bed with him all night. Sure it wasn't a sexual night, well not since the park, but Stephen still woke up with the feeling of amazement and wonder at how lucky he was now.

He laid there in bed with his eyes closed and just… felt. He felt Veronica's skin against his. He listened to her breathing and to Kaitlin's. His arm still draped across both women, he felt the touch of Kaitlin's red and blond hair against his hand and the warmth of her skin. Kara was up already. He could hear her in the kitchen, hear her moving around, and could smell the breakfast she was making. He couldn't sense her emotions—either she was hiding them like she so often did, or she was too far away. Regardless, he was pretty certain that she knew something had happened; she always did. Somehow just knowing she was in the other room made him feel right with the world.

He had been warned that being a werewolf meant that his emotions would be more intense than before, more powerful and sometimes even overwhelming. He had almost lost his control at the office when he thought the Feds were dismissing the murders of a mother and her two children. His emotions had been so strong then that he almost shifted with the intention of killing them all. Maybe that was what he was feeling now, an overly intense feeling brought on by his new werewolf nature—but he didn't give a damn. He was happy, really happy—the kind of happy that other days would be measured against—and more important than even being happy, he was loved. He hadn't felt this good since Becky, and if this was what it felt like to live with three women who each cared for him, he never wanted it to change.

Unfortunately, no matter how strong the feelings he had, no matter how comfortable he was, or how terrible an idea it was to even think about getting out of bed, there was one power stronger than all of that, that would never be denied.

He had to pee.

Gently, and very slowly, Stephen unwound himself from the bed and the mass of covers. He had expected to wake at least Kaitlin, but both women just mumbled their displeasure and seemed to snuggle deeper into each other.

Mission accomplished, Stephen slipped out of his bathroom and grabbed a pair of clean clothes out of his dresser, moving as carefully as he could not to wake anyone. He really wanted a shower but thought the noise would be too much, so he dressed quickly and made for the door. Gently he pulled the door open and stopped to look back at Veronica and Kaitlin. He couldn't help but smile again as he stood there in the open doorway and watched them sleep. Movies and television tell lies that women sleep in perfect makeup and with their hair freshly styled. The truth was much more beautiful in his eyes. Their hair was a wild mess, neither ever wore much in the way of makeup, Veronica was breathing heavy enough to almost be snoring, and Kaitlin was drooling with her bare ass and one leg hanging out from under the covers. It wasn't a Rembrandt or some other famous painter's work, but it was a perfect picture in his eyes.

Kara slid up behind him and wrapped her arms around his waist, pulling him against her.

"You're transmitting again, and they love you too," she whispered in his ear.

"Sorry, I didn't mean to. I'm just feeling really affectionate I guess this morning," Stephen replied as quietly as he could.

"Happens," Kara answered. "Communal sleeping like that reinforces bonds and brings the pack together. A long time ago the whole pack used to sleep like that, but it's not as common anymore. The pack is spread out over a larger territory now, so we aren't together as much."

"I don't know how I would feel sleeping with a whole pack of naked werewolves, especially since I don't know most of them yet, but I like sleeping with the three of you. It might be the werewolf emotion thing still, but I'm feeling very blessed right now—for you especially. I don't know how I would have ever gotten through any of this without you. Each of you really, each of you makes me more, makes me better. Thank you."

Kara let go of him and reached for the door, pulling it gently closed before she took him by the hand and led him toward the front of the house. They would let Kaitlin and Veronica sleep longer, but there were things that needed to be discussed. Stephen didn't need werewolf senses to smell the morning coffee and the breakfast on the stove, which woke a hunger in him that he hadn't noticed before.

"Morning," Deon said in greeting from the table, his own cup of coffee in his hand and a steaming mounded plate of food in front of him. Deon was a huge man—bigger than he had any right to be—and that man could put away the food.

"Morning, Deon," Stephen replied with a smile. He'd missed sensing Deon in the house, proof that his new senses were still not perfect. It was becoming their Saturday morning tradition. Deon would come over for breakfast and Kara would be up early cooking. Since she worked morning shifts, it was her norm to be up before the sun, so she let everyone else sleep in if they could. When breakfast was ready, Stephen would join them and they'd eat together while discussing pack business. Stephen hated coffee, had never been able to develop a taste for it, so he had a cup of tea, and another plate of food was ready for him at the head of the table. Stephen sat down and was quickly joined by Kara, who had brought her own plate. Normally, they'd start talking almost at once, but Stephen's stomach would not be denied or delayed this morning. He attacked his food with gusto, almost forgetting that the other two were even there.

"I take it it's good," Kara said, half-teasing as she watched him eat at an unusual pace. "You know if you slow down a little bit, you might actually taste something."

Stephen stopped, a piece of bacon half hanging out of his mouth and looked back at her and then down at his plate. He hadn't even noticed what he had been doing. With a flip of his tongue, the half-eaten bacon disappeared before he answered her.

"I'm sorry, I'm not sure why I'm so hungry, but I just couldn't seem to resist."

Kara and Deon shared a quick glance before she continued. "It's pretty obvious something happened last night. Want to explain while I go get more food out of the freezer?"

"Yeah, I don't know why but I don't think you've made enough this morning," Stephen answered with a sheepish grin. As she went back into the kitchen Stephen started to explain. "Veronica and I went on a date last night. I took her to Baker Park and we set up a little picnic out by the river. It wasn't anything out of the ordinary, I read to her while we ate and then watched the stars come out. We uh… we kind of started messing around a little after that and things kind of just progressed… and—"

"So you were fucking," Deon answered. "Human… again."

"Hey," Stephen countered weakly, "it just didn't seem polite to give you details that you might not want to hear. I mean, we're eating breakfast."

"It might be an important detail and a step in the right direction for all of us," Kara countered from the kitchen. "Something important happened and we can't overlook details."

"Okay, fine," Stephen answered. "Yes, she was on top of me and that's when my wolf got involved. She tried to stop and said that Big Black was calling out her wolf so hard that she thought she was about to shift right there. She told me to stop him but before I could even try I was in his space and he was waiting for me. I probably haven't talked about it much before, but when I go there, it's kind of like being in a rolling tundra with trees and a little creek. He stays on one side of the creek and I have mine. I think it's just the way my mind tries to process having him inside of me and how I shift. When I shifted during the fight, I saw us in his space and we swapped sides of the creek. When I gave up my side and he stepped onto my side, I shifted."

"So, you can actually see this space, in that much detail?" Kara asked.

"Yeah, all the time. It's always the same space and he's always at his den on the other side of the creek when I get there."

"So what was different this time?" Deon asked.

"So I get there and he's excited about something and howling for something. He takes off away from the den and looks back at me like he's wanting me to follow him, so I cross over to his side and we run off through the tundra. We keep running and the landscape starts changing until it becomes kind of mountainous and it starts getting foggy. The fog keeps getting thicker and thicker, but I can see someone standing in the fog, so we keep going and it's Veronica. She's surprised that I'm there and we start trying to talk about it, but Big Black takes off into the fog. Then he howls again and another wolf answers. Veronica starts freaking out and Big Black comes back with her wolf, leading it back to Veronica. She starts crying and playing with her wolf, but it's really emotional for her, like it's super important. Big Black plays with her wolf for a second and then he leads me back to his den and I come back to the real world."

Kara almost dropped the food she was loading into the frying pan and stared hard at Stephen, then turned to Deon. Deon stared back, his mouth slightly open, before he turned slowly toward Stephen.

"Are you absolutely sure," Deon asked pointedly, "that is exactly what happened? What you saw happen?"

"Yes," Stephen answered, now just a touch afraid of their response.

"But that's not possible," Kara said, forgetting the food and only turning off the stove by reflex. "He shouldn't be able to go into someone else's wolf space like that—no one can. That would be like sharing souls or merging souls together. I haven't even heard stories anywhere close to this."

"Stephen, what did Big Black do after that? Did he do anything special or unusual?" Deon asked.

"Not really, he just flopped down and curled up to sleep like he was exhausted or something. I guess that was kind of unusual—he usually is more of an asshole when I'm there."

"So, whatever happened must have really taken it out of your wolf," Deon answered, "and based on your eating habits this morning, I'd say you're trying to recover for both of you."

"I feel great though," Stephen answered. "I haven't slept that well last night in weeks—well not since the last time we all puppy-piled together."

"You know what this means," Deon said, looking at Kara in amazement, "what this could mean for the pack."

"No," she answered. "Don't jump to conclusions. We don't know if it changed anything for Veronica or not. Even if it did, we don't know if Stephen can do it again. Maybe it requires them to be physically connected or a certain level of emotional connection. There's no guarantee that he can help the others or if he even helped her at all. I still can't believe that he was able to actually go there—to her space—like that."

"Okay, quit talking like I'm not here and explain it to me," Stephen complained, with just an accidental touch of a commanding tone in his voice.

"Well, we're not sure exactly what happened," Kara started. "It sounds like somehow you and your wolf were able to link yourselves into Veronica's inner space where her own wolf lives, but if you did, that'd mean you somehow touched souls. Remember how we said there are two souls in your body—yours and your wolf's? If you actually did find a way to connect to her space, that'd mean that you shared your soul with hers—the four souls sharing the same space for that time."

"I…" Stephen stammered, slow understanding beginning to take hold. "I don't know. I don't know how that was supposed to feel. It didn't hurt or feel hard or anything. I mean she was surprised when we got there but she didn't seem to be in pain, and her wolf actually seemed to know Big Black, like they were old friends or something."

"If you did connect," Deon continued, "that's an ability we've never heard of before. That's kind of… well, scary by itself, but if Big Black was able to lead her wolf out to her, that might change things for Veronica too."

"I don't understand," Stephen answered. "How does that change anything?"

"Veronica was late to get her first shift," Kara answered. "We weren't even certain that she'd ever shift. You know the problem about our birthrates declining, but we're also having a decline in the number of children that can shift. It's like their connection with their wolves has gotten weaker, and Veronica's has never been overly strong. She can shift, but it was a struggle for her to learn, and sometimes she still can't shift well."

"Veronica told me earlier that she never actually got to see her wolf, even in her wolf space inside. She'd never seen it. She told me she only knew what her wolf looked like because she had seen pictures of her in her shifted form. She was kind of jealous, I think, of you and Kaitlin, because you both have such a strong connection with your wolves," Stephen said to Kara.

"If you were in her space and Big Black led her wolf to Veronica, that might have strengthened their bond," Deon said. "If—and it's a big if—you were able to strengthen their bond, then she may be able to shift easier now."

"And you think that Big Black and I might be able to do that for the others in our pack who can't shift?" Stephen interrupted.

"Maybe," Kara replied. "Huge maybe. But if you can… I can't explain how important that would be, how much it would change for people. Being a werewolf and not being able to shift is like living as half a person. They're always going to be part of our pack—our family—but the people who can't shift have always kind of been second place. It's not that we try to treat them different or push them out, it's just sort of a thing that happens—everyone just kind of knows how it is. If you can do this again, can heal the people who can't touch their wolves, it would be massive for the pack."

"You'd more than double our forces," Deon continued. "The ones who can't change are still assets, but being able to shift is a huge gain. Plus our pack isn't the only one with this problem; all the packs have part of them that can't shift. So if news ever got out that you could heal the others, it would… well, our whole world would be different."

"If I can heal—or actually if Big Black can heal—then everyone will want it."

"Or want to stop it," Kara added, "to keep the balance of power intact and out of fear of you. If you keep developing these abilities, things that were lost or we've never seen before, then it's going to force the other Alphas to act. If word ever got out that there was a possibility of healing a damaged or broken link, their own pack members would leave them and seek you out to join our pack in hopes that you'd offer them healing."

"Kara's right though, this is all guesswork, and there's no way to know if this helped Veronica and her wolf at all. This might be just a one-time event," Deon said, trying to ground the conversation before hopes got too excited.

"I know he helped," Veronica answered, standing in the hallway wrapped in a blanket from his bed.

Without explanation, Veronica dropped the blanket, took two steps, and jumped into the air. As she leaped, her body just seemed to melt away—apparently as easily as any shift Stephen had ever seen Kaitlin do—revealing the large red-and-black colored wolf that was inside her. She landed, her wolf's claws clicking on the hardwood floor as it hopped a few more feet and leaped again, this time covering the distance over the couch and landing in front of the fireplace. The wolf turned once more and took a larger leap, covering the distance across the entirety of the open floor plan front room, and landed once again barefoot and naked in front of Stephen. When she landed, appearing human once more, she fell on her knees and wrapped her arms around his waist while burying her face in his lap.

"It's all different now," she said while she held onto him. "My wolf lives on a small rock bluff on the side of a mountain, overlooking part of the forest below. She gets down with a little path that winds down the side of the mountain so she can run in the forest. I can see it all now—like the fog was never there—and she greets me every time I go back."

The room was quiet as they listened, Stephen gently stroking her hair while she held onto him. For several seconds no one spoke until finally Kara broke the silence.

"Veronica, I'm so very happy for you," she said as she crossed the room and knelt down by her daughter, wrapping herself around Veronica.

"There is still no guarantee that this can be repeated," Deon said carefully, "but even if it's just for her, this is huge."

Stephen looked down and the dawn of understanding began to open his mind. He had never seen Veronica like this—so emotional, so vulnerable, or so happy that she was physically overcome. If Veronica, who could already shift, reacted like this, how would others react that couldn't shift at all? If he and Big Black could make those people better, what would that mean for his pack? What would that mean for the politics of the other packs?

He had been terrified of what Malcolm had done to him—genetically changing him into a werewolf with the hopes of being a cure for their problems. Stephen had feared that he wouldn't be a cure, and at the same time feared that he would be. Now he had a little bit of an answer.

What do you do when you suddenly feel like a werewolf messiah and one of the women you love looks up at you like she's seeing heaven?

"Oh Malcolm, what have you done," Kara voiced aloud sadly, somehow echoing the very thoughts that twisted inside Stephen.

Seeming to understand that there was more still to do and that Veronica needed more time, Kara stood, lifting Veronica back to her feet. "You need more sleep," Kara told her. "We don't fully understand all of this yet, and I don't want you to push yourself until we do. Regardless of how this happened, even Big Black seems to be tired, so I'm betting your wolf is exhausted too. I want you to rest for a while longer while we try to decide how to proceed and then eat."

"I'll take her," Kaitlin answered, not even bothering with a blanket as she stood in the hallway where her sister had been. Secrets were impossible when you had werewolf senses, and Kaitlin's ashen face told everyone that she had heard everything. She wrapped her arm around Veronica and they both headed back to Stephen's bedroom.

"This has to be a secret. No one else can find out," Deon said, a bark of command in his voice. "If anyone finds out, even our own pack, Stephen's safety is going to be a problem."

"You don't think our own pack would do something?" Stephen asked, his stomach growling like it too now had its own wolf.

"No, not directly to you, but getting their hopes up like that would be devastating if you can't reproduce this effect," Kara answered as she walked back toward the kitchen and the remembered food she was supposed to be cooking. "Plus, if anyone hears about it, then there's a risk that the other packs will find out and they most definitely will do something. If they hear even rumors, some will try to kidnap you and force you to do it again for their pack, while others will fear you enough to risk an all-out war to destroy you."

"Which is why we have other things to discuss," Deon replied. "I've met with what's left of Marcus's men—the ones that have been trained in personal protection—and they are all very glad to come to work for you. I think most of them thought that you were going to come after them eventually because you thought they were still a threat to your power, even after you assured everyone that you wouldn't. Having you voice your trust in them enough to bring them on like this basically cemented you as his replacement in their eyes. Our pack's construction company is also ready to get started on the house improvements. I assume you're still comfortable with changing this place into your personal castle?"

Stephen nodded as he answered. "I guess we need a safe place even more now."

"Good. They're scheduled to be here about 1000 this morning to get started. You should meet with them and at least look over their plans before you get started with anything else today. I've already seen the plans and they look pretty good but also something we can do pretty quickly. When I told everyone that you were personally interested in beefing up home security and needed them to do the work, they all just about jumped at the opportunity—which is why everything got done so fast. You're old hat to us, but new to the rest of the pack, and they need some face time with the Alpha."

Stephen looked at his watch; there wasn't much time before they would all be arriving. "I also have to go to a convention today," he said. "Leann invited me to the Magical Wizard Con today and said that the Cabal would be there to meet with me. She even gave me an all-access pass."

"Oh you're going to need some help with that," Kara answered over the sounds of her cooking. Her statement wasn't judgmental, like Stephen wasn't capable—more a statement of acknowledged difficulty. "You know we're not well liked, and the Cabal are a nervous lot to begin with. Goblins are easier—they just want power, money, and sex. Most witches are paranoid, terrified of us, and constantly looking over their shoulders at the best of times. Now after the Karen Ashter incident and the missing sword probably being a magic item, you're going to need one hell of a plan."

"I'll go with him," Deon answered. "It may not help, but I've at least been introduced to a couple of them. Leann isn't the most stable of people, but I'd call her a friend at least. We also need to get Veronica to the Keeper. If anyone will know what is going on, it'll be her. As soon as she's a little more fit for travel, I'd suggest Kara and Veronica go for a visit."

Kara dumped another load of breakfast on his plate with an agreeing nod to Deon, and Stephen wolfed his second helping down—almost literally. They were just clearing the plates when the sound of cars and heavier vehicles arriving outside drew their attention.

"Remember, you're Alpha here. Think like a King," Kara said as she and Deon took up their positions on either side of Stephen as they faced the door. When the knock came, it was Deon that answered with a simple "Enter."

Together, three men entered the room and carefully closed the door behind themselves. The moment the door closed, they each dropped to a knee with their heads bowed.

"My Alpha," was spoken in unison.

The first man Stephen recognized from his fight with Marcus. The man was young—or as a werewolf, just appeared to be young— with blond hair and a nervous air about him. This was Johnathan, Marcus' best friend and the first to turn against Marcus in the end. Marcus had promised to turn Johnathan's sister into effectively a sex slave to the Maxwell pack or to risk war with the Maxwells.

Johnathan wore a well-cut black suit with a white shirt and black tie. It was formal wear but looked more like something that a servant would wear rather than something designed to be impressive. Stephen had been a cop for a long time and didn't miss the tell-tale signs of the lines of a suit being ruined by hardware underneath. Johnathan had been chosen to be the new head of Stephen's personal guard, answering directly to Deon.

The next man wore the hard-worn work boots of a laborer, with battered jeans and a long-sleeve shirt. The man's dark hair was matted in a peculiar circular pattern that took a moment for Stephen to place, before he realized it was the adjustable band from a hard hat. He had a broad chest and thick arms, the kind of body that came from a life of hard manual labor. The laborer's skin was the color and texture of old leather, looking like it had never seen moisturizer and probably only rarely knew sunblock. The man's face was worn with age and weather, looking to be close to fifty, but he had a face that looked familiar and Stephen struggled to place it. He had met this man before, probably had been introduced to him by Kara prior to the fight at the pack meeting, but Stephen couldn't place the face.

Lastly, there was the youngest of the three men. He wore khaki slacks and a polo shirt labeled with the logo of a security company that Stephen didn't recognize. He wasn't a large man, smaller than the other two by several pounds, with slightly longer hair that had been pulled back into a small ponytail. The man had the air of intelligence about him—like his education had been beaten into him to the point that his brains were now part of his personality. He also had the air of nervousness about him. At first Stephen thought that it had to be about meeting the new Alpha, until he realized that it was because this man had made the mistake of ditching Kaitlin. This had to be the fool known as Elliot.

Stephen stepped forward and greeted each of them, starting with Johnathan.

"Jonathan, a pleasure to meet you again and under better circumstances," Stephen said as he reached forward and touched the man's shoulder just enough to guide him to his feet.

"Thank you, my Alpha," Johnathan answered as he rose and finally made eye contact. "I'm very glad that you have seen fit to invite us to work for you, and I assure you that we'll each give our lives for yours or your household."

"No, you won't," Stephen answered in stern reply. "I don't want guards who are willing to throw their lives away for me or mine. I want guards who will make our enemies throw away their lives. You will fight by our sides if that's what is needed, but you will not die for us. I want guards who focus more on life than on death."

"Yes, my Alpha," Johnathan answered, his eyes glowing with respect.

Stephen went to the next man, who stood when Stephen stopped in front of him. "I must apologize," Stephen began, "I know your face but after the events of the last meeting, I'm afraid your name has slipped my mind."

"James Maddox, my Alpha. Timothy and Elliot are my sons," the construction foreman answered. "They still speak of you and wonder when they'll get to play with you again."

"Oh, the twins," Stephen answered with a wide smile. "Those boys sure were full of energy. I haven't played that hard in years. I hope they are both well?"

"Very, and they're always running around at home," James answered. "My wife and I look forward to your visit, my Alpha. As a confirmed fertile woman, Alicia and I would be honored to add to our family."

It was like getting hit in the face with a bucket of water. Stephen had always known that he was expected to have sex with even the women in relationships, but he had never expected to be openly asked. James had just asked him to have sex with his wife and get her pregnant—without even batting an eye.

"I…" Stephen stammered.

"Stephen has many duties on his plate right now," Kara interjected. "I'm sure he looks forward to his visit with Alicia, but we're not in a position to make any formal visits to anyone right now. With Stephen's human upbringing, we have a lot of training and information to give him before we can safely turn our attention to social visits."

"Of course, my Lady Alpha," James answered with a shoulder bow.

Stephen mentally thanked Kara for the save and turned to the last man.

"You must be Elliot," Stephen greeted as the man stood, shock evident on his face. "Kaitlin has spoken of you and your talents as a security consultant. I look forward to reviewing what you have in mind for the house."

"Of course, my Alpha," Elliot answered, struggling to hide the shock at being known by name followed by the fear of what had been said about him behind closed doors. "If I may, sir, I have drawn up several plans that James and his crew are ready to get started on building."

The next hour was spent going over detailed plans for a multiple-phase construction plan that would come a lot closer to turning his home into the castle he had described. James's crew of almost thirty workers, all working on a Saturday, were ready to start turning dirt, so the plans were quickly reviewed and approved. Stephen trusted Deon with his life and now with his home, since Stephen hadn't had the time to look over everything, instead trusting Deon's prior approval. Even without the workers standing around on the clock, Stephen just didn't have time to waste.

The formalities over, it was time to go to a wizard convention.

Chapter Twenty-One:
Feeding

The body of a black dog that walked like a man and flew on wings powered by hate hid in the shadows brought by the coming dawn. Before it had a form, before it could think, the creature had just known to avoid the daylight. As the sun rose, it would simply sink into the nothing of a shadowed overhang and wait for the coming twilight so it could resume its never-ending search.

The form of a winged dog was stronger than the wisp of oily death that it had been before, and so it had thought that there was no more reason to avoid the sun. It had been wrong. The morning light found it before it had found a place to hide, and the light had not been kind. The dog's body hadn't burned or evaporated into smoke, but the light had still left the creature feeling weakened, like when it had just floated away from the flames of its creation. Maybe the light would have eventually killed it, but the nearby stormwater tube had been its salvation. The creature pulled the dog's body deep into the tube under the roadway and curled up, perhaps to die a second time.

Instead, the body simply existed, neither living nor dead. Now it just lay there in the deep shadows and waited. It waited, and it raged, hating all living things around it and hating even itself. The touch of the sun's light had left it weakened, and moving the dog's body took so much control and effort. It hated this new form, trapped in a body now. It had to wait for strength to return before the body would obey it once more. Even when the comforting darkness of night had returned, the body would not move, nor could the Kludde leave the form of the dog to float free once more.

It raged at being weak again, a weakness it had brought on itself by daring to let the light of day touch it. It had known better, but the hubris of having form made it reckless, and now it was paying the price. It took a whole day for the creature to recover from the sunlight's touch. When it could move again, it was hungry, and only the sweet taste of life could save it.

It emerged at twilight, the sun's rays now just an echo of their normal glory. The creature delighted in its fortune as it pulled itself from the drain. It had emerged to find dinner waiting for it.

The boy was young, maybe not even ten years old yet, but old enough to find the water. The drainage ditch held the water of several miles of runoff, so even though it hadn't rained recently, it still held water more than waist-deep on a grown man. The boy seemed fascinated by the water: the way the twilight danced off the surface, the way the water felt. The Kludde didn't know what autism was, nor would it care if it could understand; all it saw was that a young boy was being offered as its newest meal.

Autism was better understood now than it had been years ago. When the call had come out that an autistic child had wandered away from home, the police officers responding knew that, for some reason, autistic children were often drawn to water. That's why it didn't take them long to find the child's lifeless body floating in the water of the drainage ditch. There were no signs of a struggle, no damage to the body just a deceased child floating in the water. There wasn't even any real reason for an autopsy, since the coroner could plainly see that the child had fallen in the water and drowned. That's why they never found that the child's lungs were clear of water, the body already being dead from the Kludde's soul-devouring power before it ever hit the water. All that was left was the family's mourning and the community's well-wishing sympathy. No one would ever blame the Kludde or even know that it had been a murder instead of a terrible accident.

In the darkness, the Kludde disappeared into the back alleys of a city that was now its hunting place. The creature's never-ending rage was only slightly diminished by the death of the boy. Even now, the creature had forgotten about the child or the tiniest moment of pleasure it got from consuming him. It was on the hunt again. There were more souls to consume, more rage to be inflicted on the innocent.

Silently, the winged dog hunted the back alleys, but all the normal prey that should have been easy to find was missing. Gone were the homeless and forgotten people. What little it did find were mere animals, and their tiny lives gave it no more pleasure. There were others out, though people that walked down sidewalks and laughed in pleasant groups under the bright glow of streetlights but instinct told the Kludde that hunting people like that would be risky, and it had learned to listen to its instincts now.

No matter the temptation, it had learned its lesson from the sunlight. It could hunt the people as they traveled together, but it would be dangerous. If one of the prey were to get away, there would be others that would come to hunt it. The wolves would come. Part of it wanted them to come so it could do battle with them and taste the pleasures of taking their lives, but its creation had taught it rage tinged with the tiniest touch of fear. It loathed the wolves and feared them at the same time.

Quietly, it searched the back alleys and forgotten places looking for easier prey, and it wasn't until just a few hours before the coming of the cursed sun that it found some. It could smell them with the dog's keen nose the smell of unwashed human bodies huddled together. There was another smell coming from the old, abandoned building, an acrid smell of chemicals, of poisons. The humans were hiding in the old building, putting poison in their bodies to make them forget their lives. It didn't care about the reasons why; it just relished its good fortune. Here would be a feast. So many human lives to consume, and none that could escape it.

With a quick beat of its wings, the dog lifted into the air and glided nearly silently through the broken-out second-story window. Its first victim was an old man, barely conscious from the drug that coursed through his veins. With a single beat of its wings, the Kludde crossed the room and dropped down on the disgusting man as he lay in his own filth. The soul that it pulled free was tattered but still tasted so very sweet. Maybe it was the drugs in the old man's body, or maybe it was just the intoxication of the hunt, but the Kludde was almost drunk with the rush.

The building had more forgotten people, only four or five more and its hunger called it to them all.

The creature moved through the old building, room by room, victim by victim, hunting that next moment of release from the burning hatred inside. That tiny rush of pleasure it got from consuming life was its own drug, and in this place it fed its addiction. Even the cursed rays of sunlight couldn't stop it in this darkened, forgotten building as it killed over and over again until finally it reached the last of the drug-addled humans.

This one was a young woman, naked and abused in every way imaginable. She traded her body for the drugs that she craved to the point of near insanity. It was all killing her the drugs and the various diseases she'd gotten from all the men she had been with but neither drug nor disease would get to end her life, for the Kludde had come. This one fought back, the only one to do so, but that only made her soul taste all the better. It felt the flash of fear as it consumed her, the touch of regrets, and the acceptance that her terrible life was now over. For the briefest of moments, the dog's face smiled as it sucked the last of her soul from the battered body.

Sated, the spirit knew that it was time to find shelter, to sleep off its full meal. The Kludde found a small break in the old masonry foundation that was large enough to slip through. Hidden memories of the animal's previous life may have brought it to this place, may have remembered that there was a safe place to sleep beneath the floor here, but that didn't matter to the Kludde. It would spend the day sleeping off its feast beneath the very bodies of the people it had slain.

Chapter Twenty-Two:
Magical Wizard Con

The Moser City Municipal Auditorium was the perfect example of form and function coming together. It wasn't a fancy building, made of hard angles and harder concrete, but it did serve its purpose. On an average day, it sat empty, waiting for special events to come to town and fill it with spectators. The usual events were third-rate concerts, traveling rodeos, barbecue contests, or, sometimes, rare semi-professional wrestling matches. Today, this great public work was filled with magic.

Deon and Stephen had to go around the attached parking garage twice before they found a spot to park. Already, they could clearly see that excitement and spells were flying in the air, well, spells of imagination at least. People milled through the parking garage, making their way towards the entrance to Magical Wizard Con. These ordinary people, who had no idea that an entire world of darkness and monsters was right below the surface, had donned their finest wizard robes and pointed hats to get full enjoyment from their adventures. There were people pulling wagons loaded with collectible toys still in their pristine boxes, looking for that special guest signature to drive up the price of their collectibles, which they never planned to sell. Fathers walked through the crowds, leading their magical fairy princess daughters by the hand, their own hopes of finding that certain comic book filling their heads.

Stephen's head had other thoughts. He and Deon had discussed their plan on the way over, but he wasn't certain that they had a hope in hell of walking out of here with a win. He had decided to divide his goals into three categories: first, to feel out the witches to see if they had been involved in the theft of the Onimaru; and, if not, to seek their help in finding it. The second goal, and by far the harder goal, was to seek their help long term. Even if he was now some kind of werewolf messiah here to fix all their problems, it would take time. Even if a thousand new werewolves were born, they still had to grow, and that meant he needed a different solution. The third goal of the day was to simply survive the meeting and get out alive. His experience with witches to date had been measured with Leann Kingsly as the high-water mark, which wouldn't have filled a bucket, let alone a bathtub. There was no guarantee that he or Deon would be allowed to even leave without a fight. It was then that a teenage goth warlock walked by and caught his eye, the young man's toad familiar riding on his shoulder.

"I suppose that if the meeting goes badly, we could at least hope that they turn us into toads instead of kill us," Stephen joked half-heartedly. "Maybe we could make it home and get one of the girls to kiss us to break the spell."

"Ya, I'm not sure that it works that way," Deon answered glumly. "I still don't like that we are just walking in, without using the formal meeting protocols in the Accords. At least if we used those, we would have more protection."

"And it would take more time to set up; we'd have to find a neutral third party who could actually get inside with all these people here watching, and it would send the wrong message. I want them to know that we're walking in with our pants down, totally exposed and at their mercy."

"You think they won't start a fight because there's so many human witnesses?"

"I hope it never comes to a fight in the first place, but honestly, I have no idea if they'd risk witnesses or not. You're the expert on the other races, not me."

"Witches are the most human. They live and work as humans and have human lifespans, usually. That's about as far as it goes, though, with their common mental health issues and naturally paranoid nature, they are actually the least predictable of us."

Stephen didn't answer as they approached the front of the building. Stephen already had a pass, which he'd looped around his neck and was quickly waived in without a second glance. Deon's entry was a little more difficult; he had to buy a ticket like everyone else who hadn't prepaid. That line was a little longer and moving slowly, but he eventually got his one-day general admission pass.

The crowds inside were full of costumed people, everyone moving in generally orderly directions through the maze of stalls. Vendors were there by the score, each selling their own unique wares and various other commercially produced products. There were vendors selling fake swords, some selling handcrafted wooden wands, and still others selling specialized brooms for all your fantasy flying needs. That's when Stephen saw the beauty of the convention, the ability to hide in plain sight. He was certain now that some of the vendors were selling the real deal, that real witches and warlocks were walking through the crowds buying the tools of their trades. Suddenly, the convention took on a new light for him. Sure, some of the side rooms were dedicated to discussions of the current favorite fantasy television show or movie, but others discussed the basics of herbology or magical theories.

This was a convention, and an obvious cash cow, but also a place for those in the know to connect and learn from others.

"Where do you think we should go?" Deon asked.

"I'm guessing a back room, maybe a green room for the special guests, or maybe convention staff area."

"Or perhaps you should just come with us," a voice from behind them answered.

Stephen and Deon turned in unison to be confronted by three robed figures, the central figure with a lightning bolt scar drawn on his head. The three, two teenage men and a female, looked like they had stepped off the pages of a popular book series that even Stephen had read years ago. These three, though, each wore an all-access backstage pass and had an air of serious intent.

"Unless you would like to leave the convention, we'd ask that you come with us."

"Of course," Stephen answered and noticed that all three were holding their wands a little more seriously than any fan, kind of like they knew their wands would actually work.

The female of the trio led the way, warily glancing behind her to keep an eye on Deon and Stephen while not making too much of a scene so the other guests would notice. Deon and Stephen were, in turn, guarded by the remaining two male warlocks who followed behind. They were led off the convention floor, away from the crowds and past building security, who only gave a passing glance at Deon's limited access pass before they continued.

They continued on, leaving the carpeted public area and entering the bowels of the building, where electrical rooms and plumbing valves could be seen, until they reached the rear entrance of one of the closed meeting rooms. Here, they were met by two other guards who demanded that they be searched before they were allowed past. Stephen and Deon had expected this, both choosing to lock their service weapons in their car instead of trying to bring them into the convention. Besides, by leaving them behind, they wouldn't have to flash a badge to get past the security folks who didn't allow weapons into the convention.

Stephen and Deon were led into the large meeting room, which immediately reminded him of one of several law enforcement conferences that he'd attended over the years. The assembled crowd was all talking, some to themselves and some to other people, but the room was alive with a splattering of voices. The room was very sterile but functional, with a large stage area that let everyone in the room see the table and podium set up for those in charge. The rest of the room was filled with dozens of large round tables draped in white tablecloths and table service. It looked like any number of luncheons that he had attended, complete with the mass-produced convention food that bordered on decent only if you were lucky.

That is where the similarities with anything that he had seen before ended. The room was lit by electric lighting, but he could clearly see balls of light buzzing around the room above everyone's heads. The light balls only became something different when they stopped above a witch or warlock. Once they stopped, the light faded enough that Stephen would see small mechanical creatures that resembled fairies or sometimes little bugs. Each construct appeared to be carrying small rolled-up parchments, like tiny messages written out in an old-world fantasy style.

Then his surprise only increased when he saw one construct in particular zip back into what could only be a cellphone that a witch was holding. The amazements continued with the very wait staff. They were dressed as any normal waiter or waitress at this kind of event, white button-down long-sleeve shirts with black pants and a small black tie. The unusual part was that they were all manikins, the humanoid-shaped display models that clothing stores had used for years to display the latest fashions. They moved mechanically around the room, offering plates of food or refilling glasses of water or tea, the lack of eyes obviously not bothering them at all.

Around the room, there were at least two hundred or more witches and warlocks assembled, and more were probably still milling around at the convention or working the event, far more than Stephen had expected. Most were dressed in long robes adorned with various badges and symbols. These weren't magical symbols of some ancient alphabet; rather, they were modern lapel pins that advertised everything from baseball teams to smiley faces. One woman in the far corner had marked her robes with what looked like bumper stickers. The only sort of organization that he could see was that the robes all seemed to have colors in common. Some seemed to be trimmed in red, and others in brown or green, but they all displayed a single color trim.

"Oyez, oyez, oyez," a warlock yelled out over the crowd in a voice that almost boomed off the walls.

Stephen hadn't noticed the man at first, too distracted by the room of wonders in front of him, but the crier stood not far from him, near the door, and wore robes of scarlet trimmed in gold.

"Lord Mayor, gentle council folk, assembled guests, we announce Stephen Butler, King of Wolves and Deon Chase, the Alpha's Fang."

What had once been a splattering of voices had turned into the silence of the downtown library in a heartbeat. There was still noise, little ones, people reaching for wands or other magical fetishes, some reaching for more modern weapons.

The town crier motioned them to follow him, and he led them through the tables to stand in front of the stage at a simple microphone pole stand. There at the raised table sat seven dignified and regal people, the middle obviously being the Lord Mayor, whatever that meant. It was immediately apparent that these were the respected leadership, the Cabal, but their appearance was not what Stephen had expected. These people didn't wear the robes of the assembled crowd, rather they wore formal clothing, most of it at least a hundred or more years out of date. Unlike human governments, which tended to be filled with older white people, the Cabal was assembled from multiple colors of skin, genders, and ages.

The woman in the middle seat, stood from the dining table and walked to the podium. She wasn't overly tall, probably just a little over five feet, with black and purple hair, and looked to be no older than her early forties. Her dress was a floor-length purple-and-black affair that looked like hoops and corsets were involved. Stephen smiled to himself when he realized that the real magic in the room was the way she was apparently able to sit down behind the table in that thing.

"We welcome the King of Wolves and his Fang to our Cabal meeting," the woman said formally, her voice amplified by the microphone so everyone in the room could hear her.

In true seminar fashion, the microphone feedback only made a couple of people wince before it evened out.

"We must say, we were surprised by your appearance and without the formalities of the Accords. We are the Lord Mayor Stephanie Parks, and we welcome you to Magical Wizard Con."

"Lord Mayor," Stephen answered again, causing the microphone to whine in complaint until he stepped a little further back.

"I thank you for your greeting, and I must start by apologizing to you and the Cabal. I just became a werewolf and then Alpha of the pack just recently. It has been brought to my attention that I have had a lapse in manners by not seeking you out earlier to introduce myself when I became Alpha. I beg your forgiveness for any insult, and I assure you that it was due to a lack of understanding of my new world rather than a purposeful slight." With that said, Stephen ended his sentence with a slight bow from his shoulders, a sign of respect to the Lord Mayor that drew murmurs in the room.

"We have been told that you are not like the other werewolves that we have dealt with, and we see now that those whispers may perhaps be true. Your oversight has been forgiven for honesty, the less dealings that we have with the werewolves, the better most of us like it. Which brings us to the question at hand, why have you come to us now and who do you seek to punish?"

"Punish, Lord Mayor?"

"Surely the King of Wolves and his Fang do not come here without seeking blood payment for Karen Ashter's actions, or are we to be blamed for some other sin? You wolves come to us as thieves in the night and steal away our people for some breaking of the Accords real or imagined. Why should now be any different? So pray tell, King of Wolves, whose blood do you demand now?"

"I am here seeking only answers and perhaps your help," Stephen answered. "Karen's actions were wrong, and she paid for them with her life when her own creation brought her down."

"Lies," a voice in the crowd yelled. "You burned her with fire, like we've always been burned!"

"No," Stephen answered back, turning to the crowd to answer the accusation. "We were there to end her, I do not deny that, but Karen died by her own hand, not ours. I am by far no expert in your powers or spells, but she created a wall of heat with a wave of her hand and it was that heat that started the fire. She was brought down by Rick Bradshaw, who she had brought back from the dead. Rick charged through the wall of heat and his body caught fire as he grabbed her."

"So, you claim," the Lord Mayor answered. "But…your words do hold truth in them. The work that she was attempting would have put an unimaginable toll on her and losing control of her creation would be a possible side effect. If you speak true, then she has paid for her sins by her own hand. Still…you have not answered the question as to why you have come."

"I have come because you are right, I am not like other werewolves. Until just a few months ago, I was human and had no idea of any of the paranatural world. Maybe being human has given me a different perspective but I'm here to try and change how things have been done before. I don't come here to demand or to take, but to ask. A sword has been stolen, the Onimaru Kunitsuna, and I'm told that not only is the sword a tsukumogami and possesses a soul, but that it would be a powerful fetish for the working of Aether. I am not here to blame anyone wrongly for its theft, rather I ask for your help in finding the sword before it can be used to threated anyone, including your people. If it is an Oni slayer, then whoever stole it would be a threat to all of us." More murmurs spread through the crowd and this time they were louder and more insistent.

"And what would you do to those who stole the sword when you find them," Lord Mayor Parks asked.

This time Stephen turned back to the Mayor and made eye contact so that there could be no misunderstanding of intent. Stephen would accept no other outcome when the guilty was found. "If they are human, then they will face human justice. If they are not, then they will face my justice." This time the room broke out in open voices, most shouting out their displeasure at the idea of werewolf justice.

"Then perhaps you are not so different from other werewolves after all," the Mayor answered and tried to bring the crowd back to some kind of order by raising her hands.

"Before I was a werewolf, I was a cop, Lord Mayor," Stephen began, using the microphone to force his voice over the crowd. "I've seen the terrible, inhuman things that humanity does to each other every single day. This time, I saw a mother who had been tortured, her body covered with small cuts to bleed her slowly all day long. I saw her two children, who had gotten home from school, and walked into a room of bad people doing terrible things to their mother. I saw how these bad people stood the mother's own children in front of her and then blew their brains out one at a time. I was there to see how they cut the mother's belly open and spilled her guts out into her lap to let her bleed to death in agony as she stared down at the bodies of her children. So yes, Lord Mayor, I will bring these people to the justice that best fits their sins. If they were humans, then the human laws will have to do their work; but if they weren't human, then they will receive what they have coming. What more would you ask of me, or ask of yourselves? Have you all become so scared, so focused only on yourselves that you can't feel the outrage that I feel? Are any of us so much better than humanity that we can't feel for that mother and her children and demand that the guilty be held accountable? What would you do, Lord Mayor, if the burden of punishment was in your hands and not mine?"

This time, the room was silent as it waited for the Lord Mayor's answer. Stephanie refused to break the staring contest with Stephen, and no matter how powerful his words might have been, she didn't even blink. This was a hard woman, a woman whose multiple lifetimes had hardened her.

"We can see why you are the Chief of Police," she began calmly, not letting his words affect her reply, "you're a good public speaker. Regardless of your question, King of Wolves, the burden of punishment isn't mine, nor has it ever been allowed of the Cabal. You speak of righteous indignation for a mother and her children, but where were you when our children were taken? Where was your fury when humans came into our homes and burned them with their families inside at the merest whisper of the word witchcraft? Where was your punishment when werewolves came in the night to take and slaughter for no more reason than they could? So, we ask you, King Butler, if you and yours did not help us then, why should we help you now? Why should any of us be placed at risk so you can find a sword and punish murderers?"

"Why," Stephen answered, "because the werewolves can't do it anymore without your help."

Again, silence filled the air, and this time even Stephanie's face contorted in shock.

"It's no secret, everyone here knows, I'm just probably the first Alpha werewolf you've ever heard say it out loud. The werewolf race is dying out. Our women are not bearing children, and those that do, some of their children can't shift into wolves. Our entire house of cards, the Accords and all the years of peace that they have brought, is coming down around our ears, and it won't just be the werewolves that pay the price. How long will it be before one of the other races decides that the wolves can't protect themselves anymore and make the first strike? Then, when we're gone, who will they come for next? Which race will step up and form a new Accord? What if they don't? What if the paranatural world is suddenly allowed to go screaming out into the night, and humanity finally takes notice? You all know what will happen when humans figure out that there are witches and vampires out there. Even if the humans don't come, who's going to stand up to the other races when they decide that they should have the power? You asked where my fury was when werewolves came, I ask you where will your fury be when the other races come without werewolves to keep them in check? Will the Cabal be strong enough to stand alone against the threat? Look around the room, Mayor, does any of your people work well in groups right now? How will you organize a corroborative defense with a room full of free spirits who are constantly being distracted by the voices of their other selves?"

"Even if what you say is true, even if we are to believe any of this," Stephanie responded firmly, but there was fear in her voice, "what would you have from us?"

Deon had helped Stephen put this whole plan together. Stephen would show them the terrible future that they all knew was coming, but he'd be the public bad guy while Deon would be the solution.

The hope being that Deon's prior history of honorable dealings with the witches would help to offset their fear of werewolves in general.

"What we ask, Lord Mayor," Deon answered in a voice of confidence and strength, "is that you add your strength to our own. We know that this is a huge thing to ask, to ask for trust and cooperation after all our people's history. We know that my Alpha is a new wild card, and none of the races have gone out of their way to garner trust with the others. Why should anyone trust another right now? That is why we want to build that trust one person at a time. Let us prove to you that you have nothing to fear from the werewolves and that both of our peoples can gain from working together. We would gain your support in keeping the Accords enforced, and your people gain continued security and safety. At the bare minimum, the worst case, if the werewolf packs do eventually fall, the witches and warlocks that work with us will be better prepared for what comes next."

"You ask us to risk our own people to fight battles that you started," an unnamed council member blurted out. "It was you wolves that forced the Accords on the rest of us, and yes, I admit that they have worked well for everyone involved; but we have survived alongside humanity for centuries, why should we fear them now? Have you watched their movies and read their books? They love the idea of magic and wizards right now. They make stories about us and games to be like us. Why should we worry about what they might do in the future? If this all comes to an end like you say, I think it'll be the humans that we should be allying with, not the wolves."

Murmurs of agreement and of shock rumbled through the room. Witches and warlocks were paranoid for a reason, sometimes there are people out to get you. It had only been a couple of hundred years ago that being a witch could get you burned or dunked in a lake.

"I agree," Stephen countered, "that is a valid option. Break the Accords now, go to humanity publicly to gain their trust, and side with them. When you expose the entire paranatural world to them, you'll be their saviors and allies, for as long as they need you. I was born and raised human, you're absolutely right, humanity loves a good fantasy story, but ONLY as long as it's a fantasy. Sure, publicly, they'll be your friend, as long as they gain something from you, but privately, they'll fear your abilities. What they will fear the most is that anyone could be like you. So privately, they'll start to study you, try to figure out how magic works, and if they can use it for their own gains. I'm about as human as you'll find in our world, but don't believe me, look at humanity's own history. Anytime they have encountered something new, a new place or a new people, what has happened? Oh, I agree with you, the majority are good people that would accept you with open arms, but what about the ones in power that would see you as either a threat or as a resource?"

"We know this is hard," Deon resumed, "honestly, it's hard for us too, to admit that we need help. That's why we aren't asking for a huge commitment; let's just start small for now. Assign one person to work specifically with me. We'll investigate the stolen sword and bring those guilty to justice for their crimes. Then we go from there and see how this works for everyone. Then maybe, just maybe, we start to learn to trust each other, and together we start planning for what the future might hold for all of us."

This time, the murmurs were more uncertain.

"You have brought us much to think about," the Lord Mayor answered. "This is a heavy decision, one that we cannot make just on a whim right now. Perhaps we should table this idea and think it over for a while, then return and discuss it further."

The Lord Mayor was both a politician and a witch. She could see that this decision was going to be decisive, so rather than make the call, she called for a delay. Once she could properly read the temperature of the other witches and warlocks, then she'd make her call.

"Lord Mayor, I ask to speak," a warlock called from a short distance away. The man was tall and lean, with a slight muscular build, and he moved with a confident ease as he pushed himself off the wall where he had been leaning against an exterior door. He was of fair skin and had hair so blond that it was almost white or maybe even silver. Stephen wasn't into guys, but even he would describe the man as beautiful. Somehow, he seemed to move with an effeminate grace but still had the swagger of a male. What caught Stephen's attention first, though, was his eyes, a brilliant blue so intense that if someone had turned the lights out, they probably would have glowed. The eyes looked even more pronounced, accented with a pair of wire-framed hexagonal glasses. His wizard robes were black, edged in a yellow that was almost gold. Like the other warlocks and witches in the room, his robes were also adorned with various enamel pins and decorations.

"The Cabal recognizes the Reeve," the Lord Mayor replied.

That was a title that Stephen recognized from way back in his police academy days, back when he was being taught the history of law enforcement. The Reeve was an old Anglo-Saxon title for an administrator who enforced the laws on a local level. So, the Reeve would implement and carry out the administration of justice in the Shire where they were assigned. Combine the two words, Shire and

Reeve, and the word Sheriff would evolve. If the title held true, Stephen guessed that blondie was some kind of law enforcer for the local Cabal, probably something similar to what Deon was for his pack.

"Honored Council," the Reeve began, "I agree that this is a heavy and very unexpected question brought before us, one that will require a long and thoughtful decision. Until a final decision is made, though, I would volunteer to represent the Cabal and to work with the wolves. This decision will set our future and shouldn't be made lightly. Let me work with them on a trial basis, so I can report back what I have seen firsthand to the Council. If we are to believe that the Wolf King is predicting our future, we should investigate every opportunity."

Open voices of shock and denial spread through the room, and even the face of the Lord Mayor blanched. She had been trying to put this off, to punt it down the road and not make the decision. The Reeve, apparently a respected warlock, was forcing the issue. With a slight nod, the Lord Mayor turned back to the council members, and they literally brought their heads together in a tight circle to discuss the issue. That's when Stephen recognized another talent that the witches had that he hadn't considered: they always had a second opinion. He was shocked by the thought for a moment, the advantage that something like that would give.

Witches knew the real history because, in a way, they were living it. All the questions that historians were debating, they already knew the answers to. That's when he realized the next part: what if this wasn't the "current" time in Leann's head? What if she was a past self for someone in her future and what if she could talk with them? Is that how people like Nostradamus or Edgar Cayce made their future predictions, by listing to the future voices in their head?

Stephen didn't have to be a professional at reading body language to see that the discussion wasn't going well. Some of the Council was for it, obviously wanting to grasp any possible solution offered, but the others were very solidly against the idea of working with wolves. One in particular seemed almost violently opposed to the idea. In the end, though, it looked like Lord Mayor Parks was the deciding vote, if that's actually how their process worked.

"We must admit, the Council is divided on this. I personally am divided," Parks began, using the singular I rather than the group we. "I have feared wolves all my life and would have never dreamed that two would be here today, not demanding, but asking for help. Help that we will try to give."

The room exploded with noise as voices tried to talk over one another. The Mayor raised both her hands and waited until the noise had lowered enough that the audio system would still make her heard. "On a very trial basis," she added. "The Reeve is by far the best and most logical choice for this experiment and has held the Council's trust for years. We will place this in his hands with the understanding that he is empowered to end the experiment at the first sign of something not in his best interest or the interest of the Cabal."

"We thank you, Lord Mayor and the Council," the Reeve responded. "We will report back my findings as to the honesty of the wolves and our possible future of working together."

"I also thank the Lord Mayor and the entire Cabal," Stephen added, and even gave a short bow towards the Mayor from his shoulders. "The first step is always the hardest, and I will not forget your wisdom and trust you've shown us today."

"See that you don't," was the Lord Mayor's only answer. With a nod of respect of her own, the Lord Mayor dismissed the King of Wolves, and as he and Deon walked out of the conference room, the Reeve of the Cabal followed.

Chapter Twenty-Three:
New Partner New Mission

The three men walked together in silence until they had made their way through the crowds of paranaturals and humans alike. Once outside and away from the majority of those who could listen in, the Reeve began.

"I suppose I should introduce myself, my name's Louis Merritt," the Reeve began as they walked towards the parking garage. "I'm the Cabal's Reeve for this area, a title kind of like a police officer for witches."

"I recognized the title," Stephen responded with a nod. "The old English version added the word shire to the title, and it eventually became sheriff. I assume you try to keep the others in line and enforce the Cabal's orders or something?"

"Sort of like that," Louis confirmed. "You were dead on when you said that witches and warlocks were flighty, we aren't really very good at following rules, but I do my best to keep the majority of them from doing something to hurt themselves. It kind of goes against the nature of our work, though, where belief and imagination are the main driving force in magic instead of following rules."

"So how did you get to be the Reeve?" Deon asked with obvious interest.

Stephen hadn't noticed before, but Deon's emotions had changed; he was interested in Louis. The fact that Stephen could even detect the change in him, Deon normally being cautious with what emotions he let slip, only meant that he must really be interested in Louis.

"It's not a very high-demand position, but it's technically a council member post," Louis explained. "Most of us don't want to be bothered having to care about what the next witch is doing, and you've got to be stronger than almost everyone else to avoid fights. Usually, if someone is getting sloppy enough that I have to intervene, I just show up, and they quit whatever stupidity they were doing. Well, actually, they usually just get more careful so that no one notices anymore."

"So, you're like us, you're enforcing the Accords," Stephen said with growing excitement. From what he was hearing, the Reeve had the same kind of job that he and Deon had to do.

"Kind of, sorta, but not exactly. We don't usually worry about the details of the Accords; most of us are scared of you wolves bad enough that we don't get anywhere near messing with humans. Obviously, there are exceptions, but mostly I enforce the Laws of Work."

"Which is?"

Louis sighed before he answered, "The Laws of Work are the laws of physics, but for magic. Our formal title for each other is 'those who can work' or simply 'workers'. The Laws of Work are the agreed-upon rules of using Aether to prevent humanity from taking notice and to protect the worker. We call the process of using Aether, 'the Work,' because it's physically and mentally exhausting, but is something that drives us all with such a passion that most can't ever stop. When you're working with a matter/energy source as limitless and as versatile as the Aether, you have to have some kind of limits, or the worker or humanity can burn. That's why most of our community resents the Accords so much, our passion and drive for the Work is so overwhelming that anything that might be seen as a limit is automatically bad."

"But you have the Laws of Work, isn't that bad?" Deon asked.

"Most of us are trained from birth to see the Laws as just a safety net, stay within these lines and you won't burn up sorta thing. Unfortunately, as most workers get older, they naturally get closer and closer to pushing the Laws. Sometimes they get burned, sometimes they make a mistake, and you wolves get involved, but sometimes I can get there fast enough to pull them back from the edge. We all have an inherent drive to push the boundaries, to try new things or old things in new ways, and that catches up to most of us eventually. It's probably the reason you don't see a lot of really old witches or warlocks, but if you do, don't ever mess with them."

"You make the Work sound like an addiction," Stephen said, "kind of like a drug."

"A drug like you could never believe," Louis agreed. "I don't know if that's part of why so many of us suffer from mental health issues, or that's just a side effect of having heavy souls. I do know that the Work is… powerful. You feel like it's the heaviest workout you've ever done at the gym, but it all came easy; like you felt amazing, but you know you'd feel so much better if you could just push a little bit more. It's like the feeling of accomplishment you get when you do something that was really mentally difficult, and at the same time, you just won a race. I don't know, it's hard to describe, but there's a mental and physical component to it that almost gives you a high, and the harder the Work, the bigger the rush."

"I never knew that," Deon answered, obviously in thought, like the news suddenly filled in the answers to questions he had as well.

"That's why we have the Laws of Work, to keep most of the youngest grounded until they're able to better process what happens."

"And if they can't or won't, then you step in," Stephen added.

"And sometimes I can help, and sometimes I can't."

"It sounds like it's a good thing that working the Aether is so hard then," Stephen said. "If it was easier, then you'd have a lot more addicted people who could do a lot more damage."

Louis stopped and looked Stephen in the eye, obviously offended. "It's not like we're a bunch of Aether-crazed junkies trying to shoot fireballs all over town. You can't tell me that your precious humans are any better. Look at all the pain and suffering they cause to each other over their addictions. How many people die every year from overdoses, DWI accidents, or drug-related crime? Sure, we can change the shape of reality around us with our magic, but a box of ammunition and an automatic weapon can kill a lot faster."

Stephen also stopped and returned the look. He hadn't meant to offend, just the opposite, he was trying to acknowledge the obvious difficulties in the Reeve's job. "Louis, I'm sorry, I didn't mean to offend you, what I meant was that it sounded like you had a pretty difficult job and that the stakes were high. I didn't mean anything more."

This time, it was Louis who had to pause and breathe Buddha in and Hitler out. "No, you're right, I'm being overly sensitive. Generations of mistrust and hate don't go away in one conversation. I guess I was looking for something to piss me off. I'm sorry as well."

The three men walked in silence through the parking garage until they got back to Stephen's car. When they reached the vehicle, Stephen spoke. "So do you want to ride with us, or do you have your own vehicle here?"

"Oh no, I left my broom one floor down, so I'll just ride it," Louis answered in a serious tone.

Stephen and Deon just looked at him and blinked. "Guys, it's a joke! My motorcycle is parked one floor down, so I can just follow you guys, but what's the plan here?"

"I thought we could go back to the murder scene, see if you could give us a new perspective or something that we missed," Deon answered. "I've worked with Leann Kingsly for several years, and she's been able to help me on several cases before Stephen got involved."

"You can work with Leann? OK, I guess the rumors of werewolves going into killing rages if you piss them off must be false if you have the patience for her," Louis answered with a smile that lit up his eyes. Deon's smile was just as bright. Stephen didn't miss his cue.

"Why don't you two just ride together and go back to the house? I honestly don't want to go back," Stephen said, making an excuse for them to drop the third wheel.

"The Bit and Byte is just a short walk; I'll get a cup of tea and then catch a ride home. Just let me know if anything changes. Louis can always pick his bike up when you're done." When Deon moved to answer, Stephen's phone rang with the now dreaded work ringtone, cutting the big man off.

The conversation didn't take long, and his face fell with the news. "That was dispatch, the zone cars got an anonymous call. We've got six dead at a dope house at Montgomery and Twenty-Ninth Street. No signs of foul play except on one body, a nude woman that appears to have been sexually abused."

"Sex for dope?" Louis asked.

"More than likely," Deon answered. "That's not one of our best parts of town. Could be just a series of overdoses from some bad meth they were sharing, could be… something different."

"You think it's the Kludde?" Stephen asked.

"Could be," Deon answered gravely. "The Twilight Marquee was worried about it targeting street people. On the other hand, with Fentanyl getting mixed in with meth now, all it takes is one bad mix to kill. Could be that, or the Kludde found easy prey. We won't know until the coroner can do blood labs."

"What's a Kludde?" Louis asked with concern.

"Very rare old world spirit of rage and vengeance," Deon answered. "They used to be considered trickster demons, but the tricks were usually deadly. The old stories say that Kluddes are formed from the vengeful spirits of witches that died by fire. They usually take the forms of winged dogs with a chain dragging behind them, usually attached to an ankle or around the neck."

"And you guys think that when Karen Ashter died in the fire, she became this Kludde and is still out there killing people."

"That's our best guess," Stephen answered. "The Twilight Marquee believed it enough to demand a meeting with us and bargained for us to kill the thing, but how do you kill a spirit?"

"Spirit magic isn't my specialty," Louis replied, "but there are magics that can harm or trap spirits. Most spirits are echoes of souls that get trapped in the Aether instead of going back into the cycle of life. In this case, it sounds like the Kludde was formed by the strong Aetheric energy that Karen was using at the time of death, mixed with her emotional turmoil. Add in a witch's heavier-than-normal soul, and sure, I guess I could see something like a Kludde being formed. The Aether is wild stuff; you never know for certain exactly what will happen sometimes. Given enough time, I might be able to come up with something that might work on a Kludde, assuming that we're right about all this."

Stephen nodded. The partnership between werewolf and witch was already paying off. "You said it isn't your specialty. What do you specialize in and… what's up with the robes?"

"I guess that's a logical question, and I probably won't be giving away too many Cabal secrets," Louis answered with a half-smile. "There are different branches of the Work, each represented by a different color, in my case, the gold trim on my robes. I'm an artificer; my magic specializes in the creation of objects and binding aetheric energies to those objects. For example, I could make a pocket watch that would never need winding or batteries, or I could make a knife that never went dull. Now, all the various pins and decorations on our robes, those are personal achievements. We're not a very formal lot, except at Cabal meetings, so there isn't any way to get recognized for doing something that you're proud of, so we reward ourselves. Each pin or sticker on the robe is something special to us that we accomplished, and we want to remember. Like this smiley face pin, I awarded it to myself when I created my first aetheric device as a kid."

"So, the more decorations, the more experienced the witch or warlock," Deon said in summation.

"Or the more arrogant," Louis replied. "Like I said, they're self-awarded, so the value of the award doesn't compare person to person."

"Then in combat," Stephen asked, "you have devices to protect yourself instead of using spells like Karen used."

"Ya, that's pretty much right. I can use the flashy spells like the rest of the workers, but my magic works best and is strongest when it's bound to a device of some kind."

"That's really cool," Deon said, smiling broadly, showing his honest interest in the topic. "Maybe you have a device or something that can help us track down the sword. Stephen, how do you want to do this now? We still splitting up, or do you want us to go to the drug house?"

Stephen thought for a moment before answering. If the Kludde was to blame and was still in the area, then his officers would be in danger that they couldn't defend against. On the other hand, he really hoped that the addition of Louis and his magic might give them the lead they needed to bring the killers to justice.

"No, you two keep going back to the house and see if Louis's abilities find something that we didn't. I'll call a district car to come pick me up, and I'll head over to the flop house."

"And if the Kludde is still there or in the area, what's your plan then?" Deon asked, obviously not liking the idea of separating from his Alpha.

"Then I make up some excuse like it's a hazmat scene or something and get everyone out. I have no plans on fighting this thing, at least not until we know more about it and can figure out a better way to kill it."

"I'll make some phone calls too," Louis suggested. "I know some workers that specialize in spirit magic; they might know more about Kluddes and might have some suggestions on how to kill it. I know a lot of those old traditions always had some kind of weakness, like fire or silver, maybe there's a weapon we can use that it's weak against. I also need to stop by my bike, I'll need my work bag, and I want to drop these robes off in the saddle bag. Warlock robes are probably not the best way to go around in public if you're trying not draw attention."

Stephen unlocked his car and retrieved his sidearm from under the seat, then handed the keys to Deon. "The girls are all off this morning, so I'll give Kara a call too. If this is the Kludde, then we'll try and distract it until we can get all the officers clear."

Deon nodded as he strapped his weapon back on and slid the driver's seat back.

"Keep us in the loop," he said, his nervous emotions leaking through just a little. "I don't like the idea of you going in there alone, so at least wait for the girls to get close by if you need backup."

"Don't worry, I'll be safe," Stephen answered in a voice that reminded them of a teenager talking to his parents after learning how to drive.

"You two have fun together." Deon glowered in response, but Louis had the faintest of blushes appear for just a second.

Chapter Twenty-Four:
The Forgotten People

The passenger side of a marked patrol car is not designed for guests. The passenger side is usually sacrificed to make room for mobile dispatch computers and equipment organizers. That's why Stephen had to unfold himself when he tried to get out of the patrol car that stopped at the flop house. The building had been industrial at some point, a two-story affair that hadn't been used in at least a decade. This was probably one of those blighted buildings the city council kept complaining about at meetings, trying to get city staff to be more aggressive in getting owners to keep up the property or tear it down. The property owners, on the other hand, either used the property as a tax write-off or didn't have the money to invest in keeping up a property when they wouldn't get any return. Urban blight was a problem for all cities in this modern age.

"Thanks," Stephen called as he waved back at the patrolman, as the young officer started to pull away.

Stephen smiled briefly at the man's apparent anxiousness, having to drive through traffic with the boss riding along. The officer was driving like he had been taking his driver's test all over again.

There weren't as many cars or cops on scene as Stephen had initially expected. People tended to disregard the homeless or the people who battled addiction, like those who died. Stephen didn't even expect these deaths to make the news tonight, not unless the story was spun to talk about the horrors of the new fentanyl epidemic. It was just easier to ignore the people at the lowest rungs of society than to admit that society had failed them.

The most vulnerable people, the ones who needed the help the most, were often the ones who didn't get it, and in some cases, didn't want it. Stephen suddenly understood the goblins just a little bit better. They had seen this weakness in human society and learned to exploit it. Now the homeless and the addicted would be their eyes and ears in exchange for just enough resources to keep them alive and addicted.

Stephen walked past the scene tape and checked in with the officer stationed at the front door, giving his name and rank for the crime scene log. The moment he walked inside, his human senses could smell the tang of human waste in the air.

"Chief! I wasn't expecting to see you here," a female's voice said in surprise.

Stephen turned to the on-duty detective, Detective Shenequa Clark, and smiled in greeting. Shenequa was one of the junior detectives, having only been promoted from patrol a few months ago, which explained why she got the call and was working weekends. She was relatively tall for a woman, with dark skin the color of chocolate, and black curly hair she kept tied back in a bun most days. Stephen hadn't really gotten to work with her much, but knew her by reputation around the office. She was a hard-working woman, a single mom with two kids, who gave her all to anything she was doing. In Stephen's opinion, one of the finest in Moser City PD.

"Shenequa, guess you got the duty call out," Stephen said in greeting as he reached out for her hand. "I was out and about when dispatch called me, so I thought I would just stop by before I headed home. What do you got?"

"Six confirmed DOA, one was a woman. We found her nude and obviously sexually assaulted over a period of time, as some of her wounds were already healing. Based on physical appearance, she was a junkie like the rest of them. We don't have IDs on any of them, so we're running prints, and I've taken photos if I need to check with the various shelters and homeless support groups in the area. There's no obvious signs of assault or foul play on the other bodies, more like they just passed out and never woke up. You'll need to watch your step, though, we've got needles and shit everywhere, so it looks like this has been a flop house for quite a while. I've called out drug task force since this is probably a mass overdose. I know they were working with the Feds recently, trying to go federal charges on the dealers that provided the meth. We'll have more for them once we get IDs and criminal histories back. We've got a couple of baggies with residue that we'll get sent off to confirm fentanyl, but that would be my best guess right now."

"Any point of entry for a suspect, just in case this isn't an OD?"

"Nothing that we have found obviously yet, the back of the building had an unsecured door, and most of the windows are busted out to some degree. The bodies were all found on their bedrolls, so it looks like they did their hit, and then laid down. There's fresh track marks on all of them. Coroner's people are still going over the bodies."

"Have you talked with the officer that was first on scene? We sure there's nothing else here in the building?"

Shenequa blinked, trying to buy a moment to figure out why the Chief of Police was so interested, or why he had even shown up for that matter. There were the obvious insecurities; she was a new detective, and he was checking up on her, or maybe there was something here that he saw, and she was missing.

"I…uh, I didn't ask. They just told me what I had, and I started working the scene. I assume they've cleared the building, but I don't think that second floor is very stable."

Stephen paused long enough to see what had just happened. He had been a new detective once himself, and having the Chief on scene made everyone nervous.

"Sorry, I don't mean to walk all over your case," he replied, trying to dismiss her concerns. "I know you have this, and I trust you, like I said, I was already out, so I guess I just had to come be curious. I think I'll just take a walk around in case the city has any questions if they hear about it, and then I'll probably head home."

"Sure thing, boss. If we find something, I'll make sure you know."

"Thanks," Stephen replied with a wave as he started to walk away.

The building was divided into several rooms, maybe once having been an office building of some kind, or maybe divided into several storage areas, so it didn't take long for him to get out of sight. Still, Stephen walked well away from the sounds of people working before he tried to center himself. He wasn't very good at actively using his wolf senses yet, and in a place like this, he really didn't want to use them, but if the Kludde was here, then lives were at risk. Carefully, he chose one sense at a time, starting with his nose, and started to concentrate on what he was actually smelling. The wave of information slammed into his head, and he almost threw up from the putrid odors, but he kept his food down in its proper place. The smells all mixed together, but with effort and concentration, Stephen slowly began to unwind them like a ball of different yarns. There was the smell of dust, of rust, of old oil, the smell of human bodies and their waste, the smell of old wood and rot, he could smell the gamy odor of various small urban wild animals, and, lastly, the smell of the poison they had been using. Nothing smelled like a Kludde, if Stephen had even known what that smelled like. At least there was nothing that smelled like it was… evil, maybe?

Eyesight was next, and the moment that Stephen tried to concentrate on his vision, the room almost exploded in light, causing him to wince and narrow his eyes. It was daylight outside, and it might as well have been daylight in the windowless room as well. Immediately, his eyes were drawn to even the smallest of movements. The mice that scampered back towards their home when he got too close were all noticed. What's more, he could have estimated their distance from him to the inch and even could have guessed where the best place to intercept them was before they escaped. The part that surprised him the most was the change in colors. The colors of the shadows and the grays of the dust and old wood seemed to pop out more, as if the colors had even more defined textures.

On the other hand, blues and yellows were there but just didn't seem to be that important. The other colors, like red and green, he barely seem to notice at all. The end result was an almost superpower-level motion detection and shadow changes. He wouldn't be able to tell you what color the creature was, other than just a shade of gray, but if it dared move, even when buried in shadows, he'd see it.

When Stephen tried to focus on his hearing, he almost went deaf and grabbed at his ears in pain. This time, when his phone went off, it had been Kara calling instead of work. Shocked out of his concentration, his hearing returned to normal as he answered the phone.

"We're here," Kara's voice said in greeting. "Are you safe?"

"Yes, I'm still inside, and I'm trying to sort through my senses to see if I can detect the thing, but so far, nothing."

"Then this might just be a tragedy and not Kludde-related?"

"Possible," Stephen admitted, "but my gut is saying this is a Kludde attack. I don't know how, but I just…feel it, like there's something here and I just can't tell you how. Maybe it's the timing, six deaths, all junkies just like the Marquee talked about, it just doesn't feel like coincidence to me."

"I have Kaitlin and Veronica with me. I'll have to tell you about our conversation with the Keeper later when we aren't talking over the phone. She was very interested in your little trick with Veronica's wolf. How do you want us to proceed right now?"

"Man, this isn't going to be easy, three super-hot red head women hanging out in this part of town won't go unnoticed; but is there any way you guys can keep an eye on the building?"

"I did get the chance to ask the Keeper about the Kludde," Kara replied. "She says the pack hasn't ever faced one themselves, but there are oral histories about them being nocturnal. Assuming you're both right about this, it's probably bedded down somewhere nearby until nightfall. We can try and find someplace to set up, but do you want us to risk it?"

"No, if it's nocturnal, then let's let it sleep. I'll see if I can speed up the process here and get my guys out of here. The faster we can get the bodies removed the quicker we'll be clearing the scene. If Keeper thinks that this thing won't come out till night, then maybe you girls try and find some place to keep watch and then come back closer to dark, assuming that I'm right and it's here. This could be just one big waste of time."

"You're part wolf now, Stephen, part of that means you're going to have instincts that you aren't used to having. If you think it's here, you're probably right. I'll have the girls find a good observation point for this evening," Kara replied. "How did the Cabal go?"

"They reluctantly went for it, on a trial run," Stephen answered. "Deon is headed back to the murder scene with a guy named Louis Merritt to take a look. He seems like a good guy; he volunteered to work with us, but it's still touchy. It'll take some time to build trust. Good news is, I think Deon likes him, and he might be interested in Deon as well."

"I'm happy for Deon, if it all works out and turns into something, he hasn't had a guy in his life for a while."

"Maybe my Gay-Dar isn't working, but Louis seemed pretty smiley at Deon too, so I'm hoping they're both on the same page. Louis is what they call a Reeve, sort of a cop for witches, so I'm hoping he can be useful. We really need to get a break and find this sword. Let's just hope that Deon and Louis are having better luck than we have had so far."

Chapter Twenty-Five:
Getting to Know Him

Deon and Louis drove across town and chatted like two men trying to get to know each other. It wasn't a far drive, the house in question being in one of the many middle-income suburbs but they put the time to good use getting to know each other.

They started with business professional, talking about their work, then ventured into their personal lives a little. Deon talked about his hobbies, mostly watching movies and working on an old junker of a classic car that had been left over from a previous relationship. Louis talked about his current magical projects and his love for sci-fi movies. Neither were big sports fans, mostly because neither had the time to devote to watching, so they had that in common. The conversation was going well until Deon started talking about his family and his life in the pack. Louis immediately shut down, obviously refusing to talk about his own family or perhaps he was feeling threatened. Deon didn't know if it was him talking about being a werewolf, or maybe Louis didn't like talking about family, but either way, it wasn't a good topic. Instead, he switched the conversation back to work.

The topic started with a quick and dirty review of the burglary and the history of the stolen sword. Then he talked about their suspects, three male suspects driving a black extended cab truck, and even rattled off the plate number. Lastly, Deon went over the current political fallout between the United States and Japan. Louis listened carefully to the facts without interrupting for questions until after Deon had explained the murder scene.

"So very strong emotions over about ten or twelve hours for the torture and murder, then?" Louis asked.

"Roughly," Deon answered.

"And the neighbor's doorbell camera, did you guys take it or just the video?"

"No, the camera is still there, and we have the video. Does that matter?"

"It might, it's been several days now so I may not be able to convince the camera to remember that far back," Louis replied like he was expecting to have an actual conversation with the camera. "I'll probably get a better view from the house itself if we can get inside."

"Ya, that shouldn't be a problem, after the Feds did their crime scene thing they secured it, but it hasn't been released back to the family yet. Getting in without breaking anything will be the hard part since I don't have the keys."

"I can get us in," Louis answered. "I'm sure there'll be a lot of signal interference with all the emotions of the officers and crime scene guys all over the place, but I will have the best chance of getting something from the house."

"What exactly are you talking about? I'm confused," Deon said.

"Leann is better at it so I thought you would have known, I can try and track the souls moving through the Aether."

"Oh, you mean like the radar thing she does on her old broken computer. Ya, she's done that for me a couple of times, but she says time and too many people messes it up so I didn't even ask her to try this time."

"Leann is super good at it," Louis admitted, "a lot better than me. The way she can do it at such a long range is way beyond me, but if I'm close, like at the scene and there's been strong enough emotions involved, I can usually sort through some of the clutter to track back the souls."

"Kind of like the difference between a long-range and short-range scan on Star Trek," Deon answered, letting his nerd flag fly a little, "see, I watch sci-fi too."

Louis smiled in response as he replied. "Ya, actually that's pretty accurate. Leann has a much longer range and a wider view than I do but I can get more fine details if I'm close enough. She could probably get even better details than I can, but she rarely leaves the library."

"So do you do the same thing with the door camera?"

"No, cameras are a different process. Magic is more about belief than function, when humans use the words 'smart' or 'artificial intelligence' they're adding their belief to that thing. They have a collective assumption of what those terms mean so it influences the devices themselves. In a way, if a doorbell camera has image recognition software or one that can unlock a door based on the image of the owner, they actually do become intelligent, at least in terms of Aether. People believe that cameras can see and so they can, often better than what they were ever designed to do in the first place."

"So, you actually mean to talk to the camera and ask if it remembers seeing the three guys?"

"Pretty much," Louis confirmed. "I'll need some of my fetishes to help me interface with the camera, and kind of prompt it to remember in a way, but I've been successful with it in the past."

"Well, I can help you with fetishes," Deon joked in reply.

"I'm sure you can, but I'm talking more about the magical equipment I'll need to make a connection with the camera," Louis answered with just a touch of a wicked smile. "The higher tech the device the better in this case since they tend to have better memories. The camera still has to be pointed in the right direction; they can't remember what they couldn't see."

"So, do they actually talk back? Like you ask questions and then it answers?"

"Not quite like that," Louis countered. "It's not like a conversation, more like I input what I'm looking for and when it happened into my interface and if the camera remembers seeing that, then it'll show up on a screen. It's kind of like what the owner does by pulling up their cloud app. I'm just bypassing the cloud and asking the camera itself. The more details I can give the camera, the better the chances that it will remember."

"That's... well, just kind of weird, but I guess it makes a little sense too," Deon answered, both weirded out and amazed at the same time.

The idea that every camera he ever walked past might remember him and could tattle on him later if the right witch asked was just stalker-level creepy. He was going to have to remember to cover the various cameras on his tech at the house.

Deon drove Stephen's car to a stop in front of the house that Cindy Hendrix owned before she was murdered. It looked like any other house now, no different than any suburban home on the street, but this one would be neighborhood gossip for years. Even him pulling into the driveway was probably already being noticed by the nosy neighbors that were home on a Saturday afternoon. Assuming he was being watched, Deon made a big show of pulling his badge out of his shirt that he always wore on a chain around his neck and dropped it on his chest for the neighbors to see.

"Do I get one of those," Louis asked with a chuckle. "The Chief did say I'm the Witch Sheriff now so shouldn't I get a badge too?"

"Badges, we don't need no stinking badges," Deon fired back, quoting his favorite politically incorrect movie.

"Hey, I know that movie, that was an old one!" Louis had ditched the warlock robes and now was in a light blue T-shirt with the logo 'I believe in Magic' on the front and a pair of simple blue jeans. In other words, he really didn't look like a cop when he got out of the car. If he had pointed ears, he'd look more like some kind of modern hippie elf with his silver blond hair and fair skin. What ruined the image was when he reached back into Stephen's car and threw a black canvas bag over his shoulder.

"So that one of those magic bags that's bigger on the inside," Deon asked with a chuckle.

"What, a bag of holding for DnD? I wish, those things would be cool," Louis replied. "I know at least a dozen workers that have tried to make one over the years. Apparently, making something bigger on the inside isn't hard, it's getting your stuff back out that's the trick. Closest I've ever heard anyone getting is using a bag to shrink the stuff. This, just a normal boring black bag of tricks. So where do you want to start?"

"The camera is there, across the street," Deon said as he pointed out the house. "I think working inside might be better, fewer neighbors to ask questions, but I warn you, it's going to be kind of messy. Old blood smells and there's a lot of it."

"Not my first crime scene," Louis countered. "Get a bad spell backlash and the Aether will blow witch bits all over the room." They walked together to the front door which was securely locked. In addition to the locks, the door jab had been sealed with crime scene tape. The tape wasn't meant to actually hold anything closed, rather its job was to prove that nothing had been opened. The tape was delicate and rather than coming off, it'd just break, proving that whatever it was attached too had been opened.

"Any ideas on the tape? Stephen has more in his car, but it'll look different. I doubt anyone would notice though," Deon said. "It's designed so it can't be removed without ripping."

Louis looked at the tape for a few moments before he reached out and gently touched the surface. Perhaps it was Deon's imagination, but he could have sworn he saw the smallest arch of electricity jump between the tape and Louis' finger. When he pulled back his finger, half the tape had fallen away from the door frame, letting it open without breaking the tape. To Deon's surprise though, Louis sighed with maybe just a little disappointment or perhaps that was a result of effort.

"That's instant magic, what you would probably call a spell," he explained. "I can do little stuff like that but it's not as clean as my other work and it takes more effort than it should."

"How did you do that? That tape shouldn't have come off like that, or at least it should have ripped."

"The short explanation, I convinced the tape that it wasn't sticky on that one side, but it won't last very long. Give it a few minutes and you can stick it back down. Now, let's look at the lock." Louis unzipped his bag and brought out a small rectangular zipper bag made of old leather. Inside, there were a set of metal lock picks, like the professional locksmiths still used.

"You can pick a lock?"

"Well, yes, I'm good working with small machines, but I don't need to with this set." Louis inserted a rake, a small thin bladed tool with waves on the end, and then a tension bar.

Instead of working the rake to move the lock pins, he just touched both tools gently with his hand and closed his eyes for a moment. Louis didn't say any magic words, and this time there was no flash of light, there wasn't even a click sound; but after just a few seconds, Louis moved his hand and pulled the tools back out of the lock. When he twisted the doork n o b, the door came open.

"It's all about the belief more than the function," he explained dismissively. "People think lock picks can open doors, so they do. This is the difference in my work compared to the other branches. When I have time to prepare my tool, like these lock picks, my magic is much smoother and takes only a little bit of effort to get what effects I want. Other workers could do the same trick but not as cleanly or with as little effort as I can but I have to have the tools prepared. That's the blessing and the curse of being an artificer, given the time, I'm very strong, but only when I'm prepared."

"One of these days, I really need to learn how to do that," Deon said, obviously impressed as they both walked into the house.

The front room was still a gore-filled mess. The chair was still in the same place, not quite in the center of the blackened blood pool, but dozens of footprints were scattered across the carpet. It was impossible to work a crime scene like this and not get…dirty. That was one of the reasons that crime scene specialists wore disposable booties over their shoes. The smell was different now, too. It didn't reek of human waste and death as much, all the bodies being removed, but that stink still lingered. Death was a smell that would soak into the very house itself, which was why there was an industry of specialists who cleaned up crime scenes. The most powerful odor was the metallic smell of old blood and the putrid stink of decomposition. People who work with the dead or are first responders know those smells, the kind that sinks into your clothes and into your hair. It's the kind of smell that sticks to you, and you'll smell it all day until you can get a shower and new clothes. Deon didn't want to look, but when a large caliber bullet goes through a human skull, it blows people bits all over the room, and it was those leftovers that were starting to decompose.

Deon knew how nasty crime scenes could get; he'd worked them the majority of his life, so he was worried about Louis. The pale man didn't seem the type to be able to handle scenes like this, but to his credit, Louis didn't even blink. It wasn't something that Deon missed either, adding a little more street cred to his new warlock friend. In law enforcement, you always get those cops who try to one-up the next guy, the kind that have always done one thing worse than you. Those were usually the ones that blew chunks first on nasty scenes. Apparently, Louis wasn't one of those guys, giving a little more weight to his stories being true.

Louis went back to his bag and pulled out a set of welder's goggles. That's what they had started life as, a pair of dark gray goggles with black smoked glass lenses, but there had been certain additions made to the design. Now there were various bits of wire and what looked like a small antenna added to them. Electrical wires came out of the side and trailed down to a small battery box that Louis clipped to his belt. The battery box was also covered in additions. Little dials and switches covered one side, each labeled with a small tag to give the switch meaning. In total, the device looked very steampunk, like it had been kit bashed together by a weekend hobbyist.

Predicting Deon's questions, Louis began to explain. "Like I said, my magic works best through devices," he began, "and in this case, they don't even really have to do anything themselves. The dark glass blocks out outside distractions so I can better focus on seeing the Aether in the room. The antenna and little radar dishes symbolize drawing in information and seeing things invisible. The battery pack represents power and function, while the switches give me control over what I'm seeing. When I put a touch of Aether energy into it and focus my belief on what I want it to do, my willpower channels the energy into function."

"I'll, uh... I'll just stand back over here," Deon answered in a fake nervous tone, teasing his new companion just a little.

"Ya, probably for the best, this design hasn't blown up in at least a couple of hours, so it's probably due," Louis agreed with a smile and a tease in his voice.

He slid the goggles over his head and pulled them down over his blue eyes. Then his fingers found the switches on the battery box, and with practiced ease, he began turning dials and flipping controls. For a few moments, Louis didn't say anything, just kept working his fingers over the controls, turning dials further and further.

Just when Deon was about to interrupt with a question, he spoke again. "OK, I've dialed it back. The image is pretty bad, with all the people who have been through here, but I've been able to lock onto the mother's emotions. Life-changing emotions reflect in the soul, the kind of feelings that change who you are, and it makes it easier to see the soul. I'm going to try and fine-tune it a little and see if I can filter out some of this interference."

More switches were flipped, and dials were turned as little as possible before Louis continued. "There, that's a bit better. I can see her now, looks like she's in the chair, and I'm seeing two people standing over her. I think they're both men. Moving forward just a little now… ya, the two men go to the door… and two smaller souls, bright ones, come in. Those have to be the two young kids. The men grab them, and the kids are terrified, their souls getting agitated and stirring up the Aether. The two men bring them in front of the woman and… ah, hell."

"The bright lights go out," Deon said, filling in the blanks.

"Ya," Louis answered in a stilled voice. "The woman's soul is shaky now, like she's uncertain or exhausted to her very core, like she's given up and she wants to die too. Oh, there's the flash; she just took a mortal wound, she's fighting for life now. I didn't see the two men move though, you said she got disemboweled, right?"

"Yes," Deon answered.

"Then there's someone else here, someone I can't see," Louis replied. "I'm sure the two men who had the kids didn't move. They were still standing in front of her and wouldn't have been able to reach. I'll try and see if I can focus in a little more; there has to be someone else."

"We know there were three men."

"Ya, you said that, but I can't see the third anywhere; all I'm seeing are the two men." Louis looked around the room several times and tried to see it from different angles, but nothing seemed to help.

Still, he worked, fingers turning the fine control knobs as sweat began to bead on his forehead and he started breathing harder. "I'm almost at my limit," he explained. "I… ya, I got nothing."

With a sigh of frustration, Louis swept the goggles back and blinked as his eyes tried to adjust to the light. "Deon, I'm sorry, I just can't see the third person. I know you said you were certain there was three, but if there was, I don't think it had a soul, or if it did, the soul was very small, or I'm confident I would have seen it."

Deon went still. "Oh damn, how did I miss it!"

"What?"

"No, not yet, a good detective doesn't jump to conclusions, he lets the evidence draw the picture. If you're still up for it, let's go talk to the camera and see if it can tell you anything. I don't want to taint your work with my hunch."

"OK, but I'll need a few minutes to catch my breath. The Work takes a toll, and this one was hard."

Deon and Louis didn't want to wait around inside, not with the… well, the everything. Deon checked that the door was relocked and pulled it closed behind them as they both stepped back outside onto the front porch. True to his word, the crime scene tape stuck back down as if nothing had happened. The quiet suburban life seemed to be a stark contrast to everything they had just gone through. The violent nature of a werewolf's life and the esoteric strangeness of a warlock's heavy soul seemed to magnify the tranquil, mundane nature of normal people living normal lives.

"Do you ever miss it," Deon asked, "the idea of being normal? No magic, no werewolves, just going to work and having a family?"

"Honestly, ya, I think I do sometimes; usually when I'm having to do something really unpleasant like trying to get a worker to quit doing something dangerously stupid. We don't take being told no very well, and some of us struggle with our mental health more than others."

"You seem pretty well adjusted," Deon commented.

"I've got it easier than most, I think. My other lives kind of keep to themselves more, and I'm pretty ADD myself, so I tend to focus on a project so hard that I can tune everything else out. My parents got me treatment when I was young, so I got diagnosed with ADD and high-functioning autism, early enough that I learned coping mechanisms in my formative years. I still have my bad days like everyone else, but I'm better than a lot of the others."

"Is that why you don't talk in the plural about yourself like Leann and some of the other do?"

"When my other lives are talking, and we're doing something jointly, I use the plural, since we are all doing whatever it is together, but when they're quiet, I just use the singular. How about you? You ever miss being less furry?"

Deon smiled, but there was a twinge of sadness involved. "Sometimes, but I think I am who I was supposed to be.

Werewolves are pack creatures; we need other people in our lives. When I'm with the pack or socializing at work, then I'm fine; but when I'm home, and there's no one there, then I get too far into my own head, and I get lonely or mentally self-destructive. People always talk about wanting to live forever or just living longer but living longer than most everyone else just means you have to say goodbye more. I could live to two fifty, maybe two eighty, assuming I don't die in battle first. That's a lot of goodbyes to people I care about, so I guess sometimes it's easier just to not care. Don't even get me started on all the pressure I have to live with: work, my role as Beta, knowing that my whole race is dying. How does anyone learn to live with that?"

"So, you don't have a wife or girlfriend then? Kids?"

Deon chuckled, "I had a boyfriend for a while, but my hours and work didn't work out for him. That's where I got the junker of a car in my garage, I told you about. He moved on, but the car didn't, so I've got that to work on. Being gay is hard enough; trying to find the right partner isn't easy, but then I have to hide the werewolf side of me, and that just makes it worse. Anyone that I'm with usually thinks I'm cheating because I'm always having to run off for some reason, and I can't tell them what I'm doing. I blame it on work, but Tony, my last boyfriend, just couldn't handle the hours and the secrets. I knew it wasn't going to really work, though. I mean, how do I explain, say, living with someone for thirty years and they age, but I'm not as much? Eventually, I'd have to either risk trying to explain or walk away."

"You ever tried to date a paranatural? Someone who you didn't have to hide things from, and just like you for you?"

"Well, the pack is pretty focused on reproduction right now, so not being interested in women kind of puts a damper on that, and I don't know if you've noticed, but werewolves aren't that popular with the other races. If you have someone in mind that is into big black guys who turn into werewolves, then let me know, and I might give it a shot."

Louis smiled in response and pushed himself off the porch railing, where he had been leaning while catching his breath. "You know, Deon, I may just know a guy, but we have work to do, and I'm ready, so let's go talk to a camera."

Deon nodded with a smile, and they walked across the street together. When Deon reached the neighbor's house, he knocked, and after a short conversation, he was given access to the outside camera. He had to invent a story that Louis was a police technician, and that they wanted to check the camera's settings so they could try to rebuild the video quality. The story was complete bull, but the nice lady seemed to buy it and went back inside after Deon assured her that it would only take a few minutes and that there wouldn't be any damage to her equipment.

Of course, there had been questions about the investigation, questions that Deon answered with the standard, "It's still an ongoing investigation, so I can't discuss details," reply. After that, Louis set himself to work.

This time, the device he retrieved from his bag looked like an old handheld video game from the late 1980's, with a small LCD screen, a four-way thumb control, and two buttons to mash. Dangling out of the bottom were two wires that ended in alligator clips. Louis clipped the wires to the frame of the camera, not even to something like wires, just the plastic body, and then powered up the machine with just a touch.

"OK, I'm making connection with the camera," Louis explained as he started to mash buttons and move the four- way controller with his thumb. "This is actually a pretty good camera, so we might get lucky if I can convince it to be helpful. Not all cameras are very easy to work with; some of the imports, especially, can get uppity."

"Who knew that foreign cameras could get an attitude?" Deon laughed.

"Just try getting one of their cars to do something for you, that's a full-blown negotiation," Louis answered with his own chuckle, "and their accent is terrible." Deon let the man work and tried not to hover too much over his shoulder. Well, he tried to at least, but apparently, curiosity was dangerous for werewolves as well as cats.

"OK, here we go," Louis finally said and turned the display just a little bit more towards Deon.

The LCD display should have been in the original greenish grey, but instead it was in full vivid HD color.

"The camera remembers the truck, so I was able to get it to show me. I can zoom in and add some filters to it to sharpen up the images." Louis started the video, which showed the extended cab black truck as it pulled into Cindy's driveway. They watched together as three men got out and started for the front door.

"Can you zoom in on the faces? This is way better than what we got. I want to make sure we have the right men," Deon asked.

Louis thumbed the controls and paused the video, zooming in on each face and then sharpening it so well that it looked like they were standing right beside the suspects.

"I'm curious, there's three there, but I wonder where the third one went when we were inside, let me change filters," Louis said as his thumbs kept working. Within a few moments, two of the three men began to glow slightly. "Wow, damn good camera, I didn't think that would work?"

"What is it?"

"It's an aura perception filter; this camera must have a really good night vision feature built in. That light glow around those two is their auras, what most people call the electrical field produced by the human body. That third guy, though, he doesn't have one."

"It's because he's undead," Deon replied, his fear now confirmed.

"Vampires don't have souls or auras. I need to call Stephen."

"But it's daylight, I thought…?"

"Propaganda spread by the vampires themselves," Deon answered as he reached for his phone. "Sunlight only hurts the young ones. The older they get, the less it bothers them, and I'm guessing that one doesn't mind a bit. I was really hoping I was wrong when you said one soul was missing. This isn't going to be good."

Chapter Twenty-Six:
Vikings

The conversation hadn't taken long over the phone, just a few minutes to let Stephen know that they were all going to have a bad day. After that, it was a quick trip back to pick him up at the flop house, then turn back towards their destination.

"So, we think it was a vampire because it didn't have an aura and it didn't leave a wake in the Aether because it didn't have a soul," Stephen summed up as Deon drove. "Could it have been something else, maybe, some other kind of creature that doesn't have a soul?"

"No, it all makes sense now," Deon replied. "Vampires are highly organized, more so than even us werewolves, and they have resources that we don't. That's why the Feds' facial recognition search isn't turning up anything, because there are no records to find. They're super paranoid about modern surveillance. It's hard to be immortal when the government has your face on file, so they make sure to get hackers to scrub the data every few years or so. Then there's the truck itself. Michelle said it belonged to Elenore Tidswell, but when she interviewed the son, Eddie Tidswell, the guy seemed to be confused about the whole thing. He swore it wasn't stolen but didn't even remember the pile of cash that was still on the table from where he sold it. We thought he was just brain-damaged from too much drugs, but vampires can befuddle human minds as well. It's a side effect of when they feed on humans; something in their spit damages short-term memories and makes humans very susceptible to suggestion, like a chemically induced hypnosis. Elenore even lived right next to them. They own an entire gated subdivision that just happens to be right next door."

"And I'm guessing the two other people are what, human servants?" Louis asked from the front passenger seat.

"They use humans all the time," Deon confirmed. "In small doses, vampire blood is addictive and does all kinds of things to the human body. I've seen it turn humans into bodybuilders in just a few days, but once they get on it, they can't get off without the worst case of DTs imaginable."

"But why?" Stephen asked. "If they own an entire gated subdivision, they aren't hurting for money, why the sword?"

"Some of the older ones pass the time as collectors," Deon answered. "It's kind of a status symbol between them, to be old enough to have lived through that time period and own artifacts that no one else has got. Something as rare as the Onimaru Kunitsuna would be a huge win in their politics games. I'm guessing that our three suspects stole the sword on orders of their Exalted Great Grandfather or maybe as a gift to get their own political points."

"Their what?" Louis asked. "I've not dealt a lot with vampires. What's an Exalted Great Grandfather?"

"It's their version of our pack Alpha," Deon explained. "The process of making another vampire is apparently very difficult, so most of the time, the attempt fails, and the victim dies. That's why the world isn't overrun with immortal vampires. Making new vampires consistently comes with age, so almost all the vampires are in a way related to each other through their creator. Their direct creator would be mom or dad, then that vampire's creator would be grandfather, and so on. In town, the top vampire is called the Exalted Great Grandfather, so he's at least four generations back from the youngest ones. They're also highly organized in a tiered authority system based on age, with the Exalted Great Grandfather being kind of like a Don in a mafia family. Great Grandfather's word is law and enforced upon pain of death. Since their authority is age and power-based, there isn't a lot of upward mobility happening, so younger vampires play politics, and there is some pretty deadly back-biting is the name of the game. If you want to get ahead in vampire society, it's usually by stepping over the body of someone else."

Stephen's mood darkened so suddenly that it made Deon look up at him in the rear-view mirror. "It's pretty obvious that we have a breach of the Accords here," Stephen said coldly. "These three have to pay for what they did to Cindy, but it doesn't sound like this Great Grandfather guy will be overly willing to just give them up, or am I wrong?"

Now it was Deon's turn to pause and bring the mood down in the car. "He... might, but only if we have overwhelming evidence. The vampires have a lot to lose if the Accords fall apart, and it was them that proposed the Accords in the first place. If they fail to uphold their requirements then we can always go to the other races, which could possibly start a war. Or we would be in our own rights to enforce the Accords ourselves by going to war with the vampires. If the other vampire families found out that this one was breaking the rules, they might use it as an excuse to settle old scores themselves. Like I said, they're very much like a mafia family, and the families in other cities don't get along all the time."

"Uh... I'm not here to start a war with anyone," Louis said nervously. "I haven't been working with you guys for four hours yet, and we're talking about pissing off the head of the local vampire community and possibly going to war if he doesn't give up your suspects? I don't see that as being in the Cabal's interests right now."

"I will not let them just get away with what they did," Stephen replied, this time a little more forceful. "They knew they were breaking the rules when they went in and slaughtered that family, so if we don't enforce it, then what's the point of having the Accords. If they want to start spilling blood in my town, then they have to know that there'll be consequences.

"Your town?" Louis demanded. "Since when do you get sole ownership and the right to say what happens? How many lives are you willing to exchange for three humans? How many centuries of peace between the paranatural races are you willing to throw away? You asked us for our help to keep the peace, not to fight your wars."

"Guys," Deon snapped, redirecting their attention to him before Stephen could fire off another shot. "You're trying to fight a war that hasn't started yet. Stephen is right. We have to understand what we are walking into before we get there. Louis is also right, though, we have to use a little wisdom when we try to balance the scales. This is a time for diplomacy, not fangs and fireballs. Our first step is to warn Kara and give her everything we know about what's going on. That way, in a worst-case situation, then someone else knows what's happening."

Stephen paused and took a deep breath. "If peace is to be maintained, then they have to know that there is accountability. If not, then we risk them trying something bolder until we are forced into a war that no one, including me, wants to fight. What that accountability is, though… that will take some tact, I guess."

"Agreed," Louis answered, obviously not fully trusting the situation but still willing to work with it.

With that, Stephen called Kara and repeated everything they had found out, explaining that they were going to meet with the vampires about the sword. To say that Kara didn't like the situation would be like saying a nuclear weapon makes a little bang. Kara all but demanded that they stop the car so she could catch up, but Stephen had to tell her no repeatedly before she relented. He needed her on watch for the Kludde, if it was really in that flop house, and with the sun already getting closer to the horizon, he needed her there. The final point of logic that convinced her was that the three main leaders of the Butler Pack couldn't be taken out all at once. With her walking into the vampire's lair with them, there would be no leadership left to summon the troops.

Stephen's mind whirled as they drove the remainder of the way to the vampire's…subdivision. There had to be a way to get justice for Cindy and her kids, but no matter how sick it made him, he could also see the logic in what Louis had said. A war wasn't the answer, but neither could he let the vampires believe that he wasn't willing to fight one to do what was right. He didn't even notice that Deon had slowed down until the car turned off the main roadway and came to a stop at a heavily wrought iron fence that looked like it could have stopped a tank. Two uniformed guards stood on either side of the roadway just inside the gate, where they could watch while stepping out of sight if trying to keep a low profile. Then there were the cameras; no less than four were visible to catch multiple angles of the car. Deon had stopped by a small brick-in call box that looked like one of those mailboxes people brick in because they get tired of replacing them all the time. Above the call box was another small camera and a display. When Deon pushed the button, the screen came to life.

"Yes," the guard on the other end said neutrally.

"Stephen Butler, Alpha of the Butler Pack, King of Wolves, requests an audience with the Exalted Great Grandfather."

"And the other guests?"

"I am Deon Chase, the Alpha's Fang, and Mr. Louis Merritt, Reeve of the Cabal."

"Please wait," the unimpressed man replied, and the screen went blank.

They waited for almost a minute before the screen came alive again and the guard returned, this time a little more excited. "The Exalted Great Grandfather welcomes the King of Wolves to his domain. You are asked to drive to the end of the cul-de-sac, to the great house, and wait in your car. You will be escorted into the building after a security screening."

"Of course," Deon answered. A heartbeat later, the screen went dark, and the great gates began to open. The road was spotless, with not a pot hole in sight, and was lined with well-manicured lawns with perfectly groomed trees. It was like driving through a suburban paradise. Each home was freshly painted, with perfectly green yards, and not a dandelion in sight. Neighbors walked the street, waving and smiling happily, some even walking their dogs as Deon drove past. It was like some kind of idealist version of what the normal Midwest United States was supposed to be, like it was all a movie set instead of where families really lived.

The further they drove away from the city street, the more the houses began to change. Each house became just a little more, a little bigger, a little fancier; as if getting closer to the end of the cul-de-sac made the people who lived there more important. The houses had already started in the half-million range, which was an excellent price in the Midwest, but these houses were already in the million-dollar range. When Deon stopped the car, the house in front of them would have fit in with the mansions in Beverly Hills. The moment that the car stopped, guards, this time obviously armed, approached the vehicle. Stephen, Deon, and Louis all stepped out slowly, making it clear that they were willing to comply with the possibly trigger-happy men who had superior firepower. They were each patted down, Deon and Stephen surrendering their side arms, and when they were approved as safe, the huge double doors to the house opened.

"Chief Butler, what a wonderful surprise," a man said as he stepped outside with his arms wide in greeting.

Stephen almost choked on his tongue when the man announced his presence because he had seen him before in a surveillance photo. Here in front of him was one of Cindy Hendrix's killers, one of the monsters that slaughtered her children, the piece of filth that tortured her to death one cut at a time just for the political points of stealing a sword. Stephen's rage must have leaked out because Deon snapped a look back at him with shock on his face and even moved to intercept if Stephen was about to shift. The look was what he had needed to pull himself back from the edge of rage and gave him the second he needed to put on his game face.

"My father, the Exalted Great Grandfather, wasn't expecting your visit, but we're delighted that you have come. My name is

Jon Kolsson, regent for the family, and I welcome you on behalf of my father. Please, if you'll join me, I'll take you to him."

In person, Regent Kolsson was a fairly average man in his mid-forties, standing about five feet eight inches tall, with short-cropped blond hair and blue eyes. He had stocky farm-boy strength, with broad shoulders, but no clearly defined muscles like Deon's. Stephen wasn't sure if the pale skin was a side effect of being a vampire or if he was pale-skinned in his life before being turned. He wore a designer suit that looked expensive enough for Stephen's wallet, but what was even more impressive was that the man had been wearing it around the house since he wouldn't have had time to change.

"Thank you, Regent Kolsson," Stephen answered in his best professional voice, the one he used when he was trying to be friendly to rapists or child molesters during interrogations. "I do apologize for the sudden visit, but I'm afraid we are on a bit of a time crunch and didn't have time for more formal communication."

"That is totally understandable, Chief Butler, when you're a vampire, time is the one resource you never seem to run out of, so your visit is a welcome change to the day. Now, if you and your associates would follow me, I'll be happy to take you to the Exalted Great Grandfather."

Stephen, Deon, and Louis followed the child murderer into his home. The house was gigantic, the foyer alone being almost as large as half of Stephen's entire house. Walking through the various rooms was like taking a trip around the world, each being obviously dedicated to a different culture. The foyer had been styled after ancient Greek homes, with marble floors and pillars, mostly naked statues of ancient heroes, and a large central water fountain with a small pool around it. The next had been Victorian England, with long drapes, intricately carved wood furniture, and light pastel colors. Jon led them through room after room, as if giving a tour, or delaying for a time, which also gave Stephen and his friend's time to look around the place. Even for such a large home, there were people everywhere; some sitting and reading, others chatting, some playing various games, while staff did light cleaning or brought in refreshments. It was the staff that caught his eye, two more faces that he recognized from wanted photos. All three suspects were here, just inches from his fingers, with only politics in the way to protect them from justice.

Jon finally led them to a set of huge, floor-to-ceiling wooden doors so old they were stained a deep black. Still, the details of the carvings set into the ancient doors were sharp and well-defined, as if the door had been lovingly maintained throughout the long years it took for the wood to age. These carvings were unlike anything he had seen: images of wolves and bears, twisted knots, and runic symbols that reminded Stephen of Norse mythology. Stephen could smell a whiff of what he thought was incense at first, lavender and heather, the smell of wood fires, and of leather. When the great doors were opened, he found the sources of the smells. The Exalted Great Grandfather was holding his court in a room that was every bit an ancient Viking long house, complete with stone floors and old wood. Fur-covered skins hung on walls, and handcrafted wooden chairs set around tables that lined the hall's central fire pit. Along the walls and hung on every available surface were Viking round shields, weapons, and pieces of armor from all around the world. It was like a weapons armory and trophy room all in one, laid over the top of a long house. Most of the weapons were ancient, long-swords and axes, hammers and maces, but there were a few more modern trophies as well. Stephen saw a couple of glass-covered cases in the corner of one wall, displaying pistols and modern combat knives. This room would be the perfect place to display a stolen Japanese katana.

As Jon led them through the room, a dozen or more people milled around, but conversations had halted the moment the doors were opened. These people were mostly dressed well, many as well as Jon, but some had obviously been in a hurry and hadn't had time to change from more routine day wear. Men and women of various ethnic backgrounds milled around, and to Stephen's surprise, there were even a couple of teenagers who would have passed for maybe freshmen or sophomores at the local high school. No one seemed overly happy to be hosting uninvited guests.

As the group passed, the small crowd moved to the chairs lining the tables, apparently with assigned seating. Jon came to a stop at the far wall, where a throne of twisted driftwood and antlers stood, covered in the hide of what could have only been a polar bear. Hooked over the antlers was an ancient Viking longsword, still in its sheath but obviously so old that it could have been used in a Viking raid in the distant past. A faded round shield, stained red and painted with the symbol of a boar, hung on the other side of the throne, which framed the man who sat comfortably in the seat. He didn't look old, but Stephen could almost feel the age coming off of him, like old was something that could be felt rather than just seen.

The man looked every bit the Viking warrior that should be sitting on a throne in a room like this one. His blond hair was long and braided, held back from his face with leather straps. He didn't look to be thirty years old, but had a weather-beaten face, hidden by a long beard, which made judging his age a little tricky.

The man had thick shoulders and arms that bore both scars and muscle. Tattoos spiraled down his arms in a pattern of runes and Celtic spiral patterns, which probably held some kind of meaning that was lost on Stephen. His eyes were sharp and the same bright blue that Stephen had seen in Jon's eyes. That was when he recognized it, familiar genetics between Jon and who could only have been the Exalted Great Grandfather.

"Esteemed guests, may I introduce our Exalted Great Grandfather, Baug Kolsson," Jon announced.

As he said the name, the other people in the room erupted in a deep-throated guttural salute of some indistinguishable word. It all played out like some ancient salute to a tribal war chief rather than something that was happening in modern times.

"So, you're the new Alpha werewolf," Baug said in a rather neutral accent, which almost totally destroyed the atmosphere that had been built. "I heard that you had taken power. That's the problem with you werewolves; you never can get a good feel for them just by looking. One can be small or weak-looking, and then be a beast of a fighter in their wolf form. Which one are you werewolf king? Are you a beast?"

It was a challenge, right off the start; Baug was trying to set the tone of his superiority by forcing Stephen into playing to the man's strengths. Baug obviously saw himself as a war chief, and maybe he had been in the distant past, but Stephen wasn't that kind of man. In modern terms, Baug was playing the role of the football locker room bully, trying to size up the new guy and set the stage for who had the biggest dick in the room. Stephen had seen this type before and wasn't overly impressed, but it did give him an advantage; he knew how to speak this language. When confronted with an Alpha male who is trying to assert dominance, either face him head-on and expect a fight, or dismiss the chest beating altogether as being something that wasn't even worth responding to in the first place.

"Exalted Great Grandfather," Stephen answered, ignoring the man's previous comments, "I'm afraid that I'm here on a matter of an Accords violation. We have evidence that some of your household have murdered humans."

Baug's mood turned dark in an instant. Gone were the locker room antics and the casual bully turned into a real threat. "Careful with your words, wolf. This is my house, and to accuse one of my family with something like a violation of the Accords is not something to say lightly."

"I wouldn't have come here like this if I wasn't certain," Stephen answered firmly. "To be completely honest, they were sloppy, and now you and I are forced to clean up the mess.

This got a reaction from the room as a murmur went around. Stephen was obviously speaking from a position of strength, and that made everyone else nervous, including Baug Kolsson. There was a murmur of fear in the room now. The unspoken question on everyone's mind was what did the werewolves know.

"Present your evidence."

Stephen reached into his back pocket and pulled up his cell phone, carefully showing it around before he approached the Exalted Great Grandfather. When Baug nodded, Stephen stepped close enough that he could whisper to the bigger man while he showed him the photos.

"They tortured and killed a human woman and her two children, but they were sloppy and didn't think that there would be cameras. They did this to force the woman to give up the security codes they needed to get into the library, where the Onimaru Kunitsuna, a sword which is a prized Japanese national treasure, was on display. Perhaps you have seen it on the news. They stole the sword, and I'm guessing they have already presented it to you as a gift or will shortly."

As he spoke, Stephen thumbed through first the crime scene photos, which showed how Cindy Hendrix and her children had been butchered, then the photo of the truck and pictures of the three men going into the house, and lastly the photo of the truck and men when they had gone to the library to case the place.

After the last photo was shown, Stephen continued talking. "This isn't something that we can just sweep under a rug. The stolen sword has caused an international scandal between the US and Japan. The Feds are all over this, and they have these photos, too. I know you're very careful to keep your images out of federal databases, but how long until someone makes a mistake? The Feds can't give up on this, not until they have the sword back and someone to blame. All it will take is one of these people to walk past a bank, or maybe a post office, somewhere there is a camera the Feds have access to, and the hunt will start again. You can't even scrub their databases this time; this is just too big, and someone would notice when the evidence photos went missing. Even if I wanted to ignore the Accords violation, which I won't, we need a better solution."

His message delivered, Stephen stepped back away from the throne and got a better look at Baug, who had turned as white as the polar bear pelt he was sitting on. The room had gone silent, and everyone was waiting to see what would happen next. Without preamble, Baug suddenly stood from his throne and glanced over the room.

"Walk with me, Stephen," he commanded, but this time his voice held an edge of tension instead of a bully's arrogance.

When others in the room, presumably guards or perhaps his closest advisers, moved to join him, Baug dismissed them with a wave of his hand. Stephen, for his part, glanced back at Deon and Louis before he joined the Viking war chief.

Baug led Stephen silently through a door concealed in the back wall, which opened into a much more modern-looking office lined with old books and smelling of fine cigars. Baug didn't stop here, though, and continued to walk into a garden that was behind the huge house. Like the rest of the home, even the garden was bigger than it should have been, with manicured trees and rows of flowers in the full bloom of spring. Baug led them to a small trail, which was covered in small stones, before he spoke again.

"The other two are just human servants, their families having served for generations, hoping to be made into vampires. I don't care about them," Baug began as he started to walk along the trail. "Jon, though, I can't give you him."

"Your people called for the Accords," Stephen countered, "and were instrumental in founding the rules that we all live by today. You know his life was forfeit the moment he killed those kids. There was no need to kill the kids or even to slaughter Cindy; he did it because he wanted to, because he enjoyed it."

"I don't dispute that," Baug answered. "Jon was born in an age when might made right, and people were obstacles to be slaughtered if they stood in your way. He's so caught up in the superiority of being a vampire that he doesn't see humans as any different than humans see cattle. He isn't as modernized as I am. Jon's been openly chaffing against living under the Accords for a hundred years. Even with all that, I still can't give him to you."

"Why?"

Baug sighed, and it was a sound that held centuries of fatigue. "When I was human, my people, who most call Vikings today, raided and pillaged for whatever we wanted. We didn't respect any religion that wasn't our own, so we stole the gold from the churches of the new god and raped their nuns. If we wanted slaves, we took them; if we wanted their valuables, we stole them; all because we could. It was an especially hard winter after a summer of pillaging that forced me to do something stupid. I had spent my share of the gold we had taken, and my crops hadn't been very good. I told you that we didn't respect the other religions except our own, and to tell the truth, I didn't even respect ours; so, when my larders started to run as bare as my purse, I turned to stealing from our own religious places. I broke into a barrow, a place for the dead, and I thought I was going to get rich from people who wouldn't notice. I was wrong. The Draugr that was living there didn't take kindly to my visit, but I fought him to a standstill. I was unmatched with a sword, or so I thought at that time, and didn't really recognize that the Draugr had just been playing with me. Draugr was our word for the creatures of the night that you would probably call vampires. When he got bored, he beat me unconscious with his bare hands. When I woke up, I was filled with a fire inside like you could never imagine. I'm not talking figuratively either; it was an actual fire, like I was about to burn to ashes. He'd left me far to the north, where the ice was thick year-round, sleeping in a stream of meltwater. I lived like an animal, feeding off of any human I could find and sometimes off of animals, but I refused to be consumed by the fire. It took me three human generations before I had learned enough control over my own blood to be able to come back south and return home. I walked into my village a stranger; no one alive even remembered my name. Three human generations had passed like the blink of an eye to me, but by vampire standards, I was just a child still. Maybe that's why it tore at my heart so badly when I realized how much time had passed and that no one even knew that I had existed. To be totally forgotten was a horror that I hadn't ever imagined, and truthfully, it still frightens me to this day. To be so useless and small that no one would even know I existed eats at me. I was desperate to find something to hold onto, something that proved that I had been human and that I had mattered. Jon was what I found. My entire line had died out; none carried my blood except for Jon, and when I found him, he was on the edge of death. Plague had come, and it was about to take the last thing in the entire world that proved I had been human. I was still centuries from being old enough, to have enough control, to be able to spawn a vampire myself, but I tried to do it anyway. The thing that makes us vampires, the thing that lives in our blood, puts out enough heat to burn us alive, so we have to feed it human blood to keep ourselves cool. I had to give Jon the exact right amount of my blood, enough to turn him, without burning him alive. Too little, and my blood would poison him to death; too much, and he would burn to ash. It was a miracle that I was lucky enough to get it right on the first try. Jon, my biological great-grandson, became my first child, and I his father."

Baug paused in his story as he watched the birds overhead, the sun already getting closer to the horizon than Stephen would have liked. "So, you can't give up, Jon, because he's the last thing you have to prove that you were human," Stephen summed up. "Is this something you would really risk breaking the Accords for? If the other races found out that the vampires were refusing to follow their own Accords, it would be like declaring open season. Some would come after your people, and the others would just go wild themselves."

Baug nodded in agreement, "I'm sure some would see it as a perfect excuse to settle old scores. With your pack leading the way, me and my people in town would likely be wiped out; something I would truly like to avoid. I just can't give him up, though, not for the lives of a few humans or the risk of war. He's all I have left."

"And he's likely the first to fall if it were to come to war. You would lose not only Jon, but every vampire that you have sired since, every one of those people back in the house that look to you for leadership and prove that you still live. Even the ones that are in there plotting against you down deep know that you're the glue holding all this together. Even if he does stay, the politics in your own house would make you vulnerable."

Baug bowed his head. "Damn him," Baug snapped when he looked back up at Stephen. "Damn him for forcing me into this, damn his greed, damn his stupid political games...damn him for being my son."

"Baug, do you have the sword?"

"No, but my living birthday is coming up in a few days, I'm sure they have it hidden until then, meaning for it to be a gift. You've seen my weapon collection. A sword like that would have been a centerpiece in my collection."

"Then we start with getting the sword back, and we figure out a way that I can return it to the Feds in a way that they can believe. Your human servants have to get arrested; they'll have to be the visible fall guys that the Feds can parade around on camera. Do you think they'll keep their mouths shut about paranaturals?"

"They've been mentally conditioned since birth to keep quiet," Baug replied. "I brought their families into my home when I migrated to the US in the late 1880's, so I doubt they'll betray anything. Not to mention that I still have most of their families here if we need hostages to leverage their silence. My main concern though, is their need for our blood. They've been addicted to our blood since they became adults. Without getting fed regularly, they'll lose their minds from withdrawal in just a few days, maybe a week at most. The withdrawal may even kill them, it's been known to happen before."

"That may work in our favor then. If they aren't competent to stand trial, the Feds will have to drop them in a hospital somewhere, and they'll disappear from everyone's radar. I'll be honest, though," Stephen said, looking coldly at his host, "I want Jon dead. What he did demands nothing less, but I'm not sure if I can justify a war either. If he doesn't die, then the other races will know that I went soft on him, and right now, I don't think we'd survive that either. It's only fear of the werewolves of the past that is holding things together right now anyway. If the others think I'm weak, there's nothing left to hold them in check. If Jon doesn't die, he has to be punished, something almost worse than death, something that will make the others believe that I'll enforce the Accords by any means necessary."

Baug's eyes went wide in horror for a second before he controlled himself. The idea that had passed through his mind was so terrible he hesitated to say it, but it was the only viable answer. "If I could give you that punishment, would you agree to letting him live?"

"Only if the punishment fit the crime," Stephen replied. "Don't think I'll agree to exile or something like that; he needs to die."

"Then how about a living death?" Baug answered with tears in his eyes for what he was about to do. "We're immortal, as long as we get enough human blood to keep our fires cool, we won't die from most regular things. What if we buried him alive? We could give him a tube so we could feed him, then wall him off in the house for as long as you deem to be a fitting punishment. Kind of like you would do with human murderers, put him in a prison that he can't escape from, and let him serve his sentence. Then, when he's served enough time, we can release him. I'm...I'm not sure his mind will survive it though, being buried alive like that, it's...almost worse than death."

"You would still be able to watch over him, to make sure your legacy was safe, but everyone would know that he was being punished in a way that was in a way worse than death," Stephen answered. "It wouldn't be for just a few years, though; a human sentence won't compare to an immortal vampire's life. Like you said, three generations passed in a blink of an eye for you."

"Then a hundred years for each person," Baug suggested. "We keep him walled off for three hundred years. The only time we'd ever remove him would be if I were to die and he would have to take over the family, or if I were to move houses, so I could take him with me."

"No, if you leave is fine, as long as he's walled back off when you find a new home. If you die, though, someone else leads the family until his sentence is served."

Baug paused. If he was still human, this whole idea would make him vomit, but it was better than a war that would likely kill them all. "I hesitate to thank you, Stephen. I'm not sure that you deserve it, but I am grateful for his life. I only hope that what I get back in three hundred years isn't something worse."

"For your sake, Baug, I hope it works out for you. I don't blame you for any of this, and I guess in a way I kind of understand your need for your humanity. I'm still trying to come to terms with my own condition. Until just a few weeks ago, I didn't even know that paranaturals existed. I was just as human as everyone else. I'm still not sure how to feel about it. The idea of sentencing someone to be buried alive is a pretty inhuman thing to be doing, but here we are, and it's something I'm sure I'll be having nightmares about myself."

Chapter Twenty-Seven:
A Sentence Worse than Death

Baug Kolsson walked back into the Viking longhouse with a look of stern resolve. It was the look of a leader that was about to do something so terrible that he couldn't believe it himself. Stephen followed, only a few steps behind, but his appearance matched Baug's every emotion. Together, it was clear to all that something monumental was about to happen.

"Jon, go get your two accomplices and bring me the sword."

"Father… I…" Jon started, but never got to finish.

"NOW!" Baug screamed, and actual waves of heat rippled through the air around him. Jon's words cut off in his throat, and he ran from the room. Apparently, the thought of fleeing for his life never occurred to him because a few minutes later, he arrived with the two human servants in tow. Over Jon's shoulder was a long tube, something like a case that pool players used to carry their pool sticks. The three condemned men came to stand in front of the Exalted Great Grandfather, Stephen, and his group having stepped to the side.

"Father, this was supposed to be a gift for you, for your birthday," Jon began.

"A gift that you thought was reason enough to violate the Accords," Baug replied with such anger that steam could be seen coming from his mouth as he spoke. "You murdered three humans and stole an internationally important relic. Did you really think that you could get away with it? Did you think that the humans would just ignore that the sword was now missing?"

"We stole it cleanly," Jon replied. "There were no witnesses!"

"Are you stupid? No witnesses? If your theft was so perfect, then what do you think brought the wolves to our door? What do you think prompted even the Witches to join forces with them?" Baug asked, apparently just now acknowledging that a warlock was standing in on the side of the wolves. "Are you so ignorant to really think that in this modern age of surveillance, you could just walk in and steal it? The federal authorities have your photographs. They're conducted a manhunt for you even as we speak, but Chief Butler has found you first. Can you imagine the damage you would have done if you had gotten seen before he came here? Did you ever think about how your actions put all of us, everyone here, in mortal danger of being found out by the humans? No…you didn't think at all. You never do. You still think this is the Viking Age, when you can just rape and steal whatever you want because might makes right. I love you, you are my son, my blood, my family; but you're such a fool that I can barely stand the sight of you right now."

Jon didn't answer, and the two other men standing beside him were pale with abject terror at having so obviously displeased Boug. It was Stephen who broke the silence that had been weighing heavily in the air. "Jon Kolsson, you and your two human servants stand accused of violation of the Accords for the murder of Cindy Hendrix and her two children. You two men will be arrested by the federal agents and will face humanity's justice system. You, Jon, will face a different fate."

Jon's eyes snapped back to his sire's face with a look of horror. "Great Grandfather," he begged, calling upon their human connections for aid, "you can't be serious giving me over to them. He's going to kill me."

"No, my son," Baug answered, and this time tears started to fall as he spoke. "I won't be giving you over, and the King of Wolves has agreed not to take you. You will be buried alive, walled up in the foundation of this house, kept alive by being fed from the outside until you have served a sentence of three hundred years. It is only by the mercy of the King of Wolves that we do not all face annihilation from the other great races or risk war for refusing to hand you over."

As Baug spoke, Jon's eyes went wide with terror, and he stumbled back in shock, the sword falling from his arm as he recoiled from his sentence. The black case fell, but never hit the ground; instead, it was caught by invisible hands. The sword case hovered there for just a moment before the trick of the light faded, and a goblin appeared. Unlike the creatures Stephen had encountered before, this one did not surround itself with rags or other debris; instead, it stood there in a form-fitting black suit, like something from an old ninja movie, its face covered by a thick mask. Several people moved with inhuman speed to reach for a weapon, but before they could engage in combat, the creature spoke.

"Stephen Butler, Alpha of the Butler Pack, the Twilight Marquee sends his greetings and fulfills his bargain," the creature spoke in the most disturbing of sounds. Unlike the other goblins, who all tended to have low or gravelly voices, this one spoke with the twittering song of birds. The creature's voice alone was startling enough to shock the crowd into hesitation. With just a few steps, the goblin walked forward and held the case up to Stephen. By the terms of the agreement, the Twilight Marquee had returned the sword, even though Stephen had already found it. Numbly, Stephen reached out and took the case before he handed it to Deon.

"I…," Stephen began, but then the words cut off in his throat. Another question had come racing to the front of his mind, and the answer could have heavy consequences. "Jon, stealing the sword wasn't your idea, was it?"

"What," the doomed man answered, his mind still dumbfounded at being sentenced to a living death. "I…uh…no, it was Mark's idea. He said that Father would want the sword and that even if something went wrong, that you would be too weak or soft-hearted to do anything about it."

To his right, the human, presumably named 'Mark,' dropped to his knees and tried to bury his face in the flagstones that made up the floor.

"I didn't mean for any of this to happen," the doomed man pleaded before he dared to look up at the Exalted Great Grandfather. "They told me that it would be easy to do and even told me where to find the woman with the codes. They had the plan all laid out and told me how to do everything. All I had to do was get Jon to help, and you'd be so indebted to us that we could have asked to be made into vampires."

"Who told you this?" Baug asked.

"The goblins."

Baug moved like a flash of lightning, inhuman muscles answering to his will faster than any human flesh could move, but Deon wasn't quite human either. Before Baug could land a blow,

Deon was already standing between him and the goblin, who was just now beginning to try to slink away behind Stephen.

"Exalted Great Grandfather," Deon said carefully as he watched the crazed look of hatred and felt the waves of heat coming from Baug, who had just barely stopped from crashing into him. "Suggesting a crime isn't carrying it out. The goblins have not violated the Accords by merely suggesting to one of your servants that they could. If you strike him down, the goblins can demand a price in return."

"That's what they want," Stephen added. "From the very start, this was a double play. If I failed to return the sword, they would win, and the werewolves would lose face. They could give me just enough of a hint to bring me to your door, and I'd be indebted to them for their help. If I found the sword on my own, then you either gave up your son, or there would be war. Either way, you would either lose your Lieutenant, or there'd be serious casualties on all sides. The goblins win. That's why he's here, just to fulfill their bargain enough so the Twilight Marquee keeps his word to help me recover the sword, but also to be a witness. If I let Jon go, then the goblins spread the word. If not, then I make an enemy out of you, and he's here when the slaughter starts. All the goblins had to do was make a few suggestions to your people, make it sound so easy, and play into the natural greed of the people around you, then stand back and watch. Vampires are famous for your in-house politics and intrigues. All they had to do was lay the seeds, and your very natures would do the rest."

Baug's eyes never left the goblin, who wisely didn't make any sudden moves. If he had been any younger, if he had any less wisdom brought by the centuries of life he had lived, he would have torn his way through Deon to get to the goblin in front of him. Somewhere in the back of his mind, the political wisdom of generations of life was screaming that the goblin before him was just another layer to the game. If he ripped the beast apart, the Marquee would still win.

"Goblin, you are a trespasser in my house," Baug began as steam bellowed forth with each word, making him look more like a dragon than a vampire. "Leave this place and tell the Twilight Marquee that he's made an enemy this day that has a long, long memory. You tell him that I'm coming for him. Tell him the Skalds will sing songs about what I will do to him. Now leave before I change my mind and send you back to him one piece at a time."

With an imagined bravery, the goblin stepped out from behind Stephen and walked towards the great doors. When they closed behind him, Baug turned back to Stephen. It was Stephen who spoke first.

"We still have to return the sword. What was done, was done, and the goblins don't change what happened."

"Agreed," Baug replied, his control slowly becoming firmer. "The Accords must still be answered, but I promise you, the goblins will also pay a heavy price for this."

Stephen nodded, and all eyes fell back on Jon and the two other condemned men.

"Take my son and provide for his feeding, then wall him off in the basement. You other two, I cast you out. We'll arrange for their capture by the federal agents and provide the evidence they need to believe what has happened. King of Wolves, I leave the return of the sword to you, if only to prevent the goblins from trying to steal it away."

Jon collapsed to the floor and had to be carried from the room while inhumanly strong hands grabbed the two humans and dragged them to their fates.

"Once you're ready, I'm assuming the feds will get a tip leading them to the arrest," Deon said. "When the call comes out, we'll just happen to be in the area and chase the third suspect as he's getting away. He'll make it to the river, but the car won't make the curve, and over the side it'll go. Thankfully, we'll be lucky enough to recover the sword, but the suspect will get away, or maybe perish in the river, never to be found."

"If that will satisfy you," Baug answered, exhaustion and anger now trying to choose which was going to take over. Regardless, the ancient man slumped back onto his throne, begging for an end to this meeting.

"Baug…I'm sorry," Stephen said slowly. "Cindy and her family weren't the only victims here today. For what it's worth, you did the right thing, and I won't forget that."

The Exalted Great Grandfather lifted his head from the side of the throne where he had been leaning and smiled weakly.

"You've shown me that you're a man of honor, and I won't forget that either." In reply, Stephen, Deon, and Louis all gave a slight bow and turned away from the tormented man.

The house was quiet now except for the distant sound of a man screaming from downstairs, a sound that was only going to add to Stephen's nightmares. Perhaps it would have been more of a mercy to have killed the man, but Stephen's resolve firmed when he thought about the images of Cindy and her children. They were escorted through the last of the house, and when the double doors to the outside world closed behind them, Stephen's phone rang.

"Yes, Kara," he answered.

"It's getting dark here," Kara replied. "Kaitlin says she just saw the Kludde, it's still in the building, but seems to be smelling around the place like it's trying to figure out what happened. Stephen, she said it looks like a giant black dog with wings."

"Keep away from it," Stephen ordered, "but don't lose sight of it. We're on our way to you. When you talked with the Keeper about the Kludde, she didn't happen to tell you how to kill it, did she?"

"She said magic is our best bet, but we should also be very careful not to let it touch us. The Keeper said that from what little she found in her research, the one thing the records did keep repeating was that the process that twisted the soul into the form of the Kludde, would make it poisonous to normal souls. She said that the records were really old, but she thought that meant that it might be able to kill with a touch."

Stephen looked over at Louis, who gave an involuntary shudder at the look. "We can't touch it, so we can't kill it, but it can kill us with a though. Guess it's a good thing we have a warlock with us then. We're on our way, just be safe before we get there."

"We will."

Twilight was heavy when Deon parked the car not far from the ragged flop house where Stephen had been only a few hours ago. It had felt like a lot longer than just a few hours when they pulled up. The streets were thankfully empty already, like something in the air was warning all living things that death was near. In this part of town, working street lights were few, so much of the street was already turning dark. As soon as their car stopped, Kara stepped out from between two buildings, wrapped in a charcoal-colored cloak and wearing her combat bodysuit underneath. Even with all that was going on, Stephen couldn't help but be distracted by the glimpses of what he saw under the cloak.

"Kaitlin and Veronica are on the opposite two corners of the building, so we can see all sides. Unless the Kludde was able to find a way out underground, Kaitlin thinks it's still in there. She only got a glimpse of it right before I called."

Stephen looked to Deon as he asked the next question. "How are we going to keep this off of 911? If someone sees us or we have to use guns, I don't want this called in, and we have our own people to worry about."

"If we avoid shooting the thing, I think we'll be OK," Deon answered. "People around here tend to keep to themselves anyway."

As he spoke, Deon started to strip down, causing Louis to go wide-eyed at the brazen man who apparently was stripping on the sidewalk. As soon as Deon got his shirt off, his own bodysuit became visible.

"Bodysuits, so you can transform without having to be naked, I guess," Louis said. "Usually, when I've had to deal with werewolves in the past, it was just cleaning up afterwards. I didn't know you guys wore bodysuits into battle."

"We don't usually," Deon answered as he stepped out of his pants. "Nudity isn't a big deal to us, but when we're working around humans like this, we wear them just to keep from getting people calling the cops for streakers. They may look weird, kind of like we're a bunch of divers or something, but people don't usually call it in."

This time it was Stephen's turn. "Ah, hell, guess what I didn't even think of wearing this morning?"

"Still so human," Kara answered with a small laugh. "We'll get you in the habit sooner or later, either that or you'll get used to being the nudist Chief of Police."

"How was I supposed to know this was all going to happen? All I was supposed to do today was go to a wizard convention and try to make friends. After that, I was going to go home, mow the yard, and try and think up a date night for Kaitlin. At least I remembered to bring the Widow's Tears." With that, Stephen wrapped the strap around his waist that held the paired short swords in their scabbards across his lower back. The swords were shaped like teardrops, the grip set along the back at the widest part of the tear and were the traditional weapons of the werewolves.

"You wouldn't want to be home anyway; the construction crew have the furniture covered in plastic and have already torn the walls apart. Our new security staff are climbing all over the place, installing cameras and security gates, or they're trying to take over the basement for a security room."

"Really? They sure aren't wasting any time, are they? I guess they're taking their new duties seriously." Stephen moved to lock the car doors, but hesitated as he looked back into the car, seeing the black case lying in the back seat.

With one look around, he opened the door and grabbed the case, before he locked up the car. "I should probably leave this in the car, but with this neighborhood, I sure as Hell don't want to come back and have it stolen out of a cop car. We just got the damn thing back."

"That's the sword?" Kara asked. "Veronica's going to be happy; she's been worried about Jason since it was stolen."

"Well, I don't want to leave it in the car just in case someone tries to steal it again. I wouldn't put it past the goblins to try and snatch it back just so they can make me beg to get it back. Louis, you have any ideas here for the Kludde?"

"I'll do what I can if you guys can keep it contained long enough. The flashy fireballs and lightning bolts magic isn't very easy for me so don't expect too much, and it'll all depend on how dense the Aether is here. I'll probably have to have several seconds before I can cast anything."

"OK, so we fight a holding pattern," Deon said. "Keep moving, and keep it confused. Switch up whose got its attention, but stay out of reach until Louis can hit it with something that can put it down. If Louis can't bring it down, we back out and keep it in sight until we can come up with another plan."

When everyone appeared to understand, Stephen turned and led the way back into the abandoned building. He paused when he heard Louis gasp in surprise. When Stephen turned back to the man, he was flanked by Kara and Deon's wolves. That was when he realized that this was the first time that he had seen Deon's wolf form. Even in this form, Deon was huge, almost as large as Big Black. He had expected Deon's wolf to be black as well, but instead it was the color of charcoal across the back that faded into a light gray across the belly and legs. The darkest parts were the tips of the wolf's ears and tail. Louis apparently was a little intimidated by just how large both wolves were this close up.

"Ya, I had the same reaction the first time I saw a shift," Stephen confirmed. "Werewolves are a thing of terrible beauty."

"Uh… ya, that's what I was thinking," Louis answered unconvincingly.

Stephen found the door that he had entered earlier today and held it open for Louis and the two wolves. When he entered behind them, Stephen concentrated on his hearing for just a second, risking being overwhelmed by a passing car, or even more scary, a passing police siren. Thankfully, it only took him a second to hear Veronica and Kaitlin, who were spread out in other parts of the building.

"Louis, you stay with me. Kara and Deon, you're on point. Let's go find this thing." Stephen tightened the strap that held the sword case across his back and then drew his twin short swords.

They set out in near silence until Louis spoke softly. "Uh…I can't see a thing. Watch your eyes, I have to put out some light, or I won't be able to help."

Louis reached into his pocket and produced a small metal wind-up tin helicopter, the kind that used to be sold in children's stores before everything was replaced with plastic. He gave the small spring three quick turns while whispering something, almost like he was talking to the pilot, and then threw it in the air. The spring released, and the rotor blades spun, but instead of falling, it hovered in the air and then flew out a few yards ahead of them. Once in place, a tiny search light turned on and put out way more light than should have been possible.

"Sorry, I know that blows any surprise, but I was afraid I'd walk right into someone."

Stephen only nodded in agreement while Kara and Deon spread out further, like they were avoiding the light themselves. Slowly, the group moved through the first floor in search of their prey.

The Kludde had awoken almost an hour before, still a little drunk from the heavy meal of souls that it had enjoyed. The winged dog lay beneath the floorboards of the vacant building and listened as the small creatures fluttered through it. It loathed them, all living things actually, but it hated the wolves above all others. That was why it had stayed under the floor for this long, because it had smelled the stink of a wolf. The Kludde's nose knew that the werewolf wasn't there when it had first woken up, but it and several humans had been in the building while it slept, and that alone was enough to hold it in place. If a werewolf had gotten this close, had almost found it, then there was the chance that it might return, and the Kludde could seek its vengeance. The creature didn't fear death anymore, and only the smallest lingering emotion of fear of the wolves still held on in its charred soul from when it had been Karen Ashter. Now it longed for them, dreamed of their return so it could know the pleasure of consuming their souls. The creature lay in the dark and dreamed of that glorious day when it would hunt them. What little conscious thought it had begged for their return and the taste of their screaming souls. It begged so hard that it almost missed the creaks of the floorboards under the weight. The terrible black dog sniffed at the air, and the scent of wolf answered in reply. This time, it wasn't just a single wolf, but five had come. Somewhere, deep in the darkest pits of what it had once been, the parts that vaguely remembered being Karen, it recognized the wolves that had come. It knew four of the wolves, had known them from before, and its hate consumed even the smallest bits of reason that it had left.

Veronica moved through the dark in her human form, but with her level of eyesight, it might as well have been full daylight. She moved quietly, careful not to startle the small rodents that moved around her as she stalked through her part of the building. She had thought about entering in her wolf form and was even wearing her bodysuit if she needed to shift, but had decided that she might need to have a weapon at hand instead. Now that Stephen and Big Black had strengthened her connection with her wolf, she didn't fear not being able to shift when she needed a different form. Veronica held her three-section staff, the specially built martial arts weapon that her instructor had taught her to use. This was a special weapon, unlike anything that humans could use, just due to the sheer weight, if nothing else. To her, though, it was as comfortable as an old friend, which is what protected her.

The Kludde lunged upwards, blasting the old wooden floor to splinters and struck out with its terrible claws, only to feel them scrape across steel instead of soft wolf flesh. Veronica took the blow with her weapon and rolled backwards with it, gaining some distance as she rolled back to her feet. If there had been time, she would have been afraid of the black-winged dog with its oily fur and claws the size of a bear's. Thankfully, there wasn't time to think, only to react as the thing sprang at her again from its back feet. This time, Veronica was ready, and the creature's gaping mouth met a steel ball. Her weapon was made of three shafts connected by a chain link. On one end was a weighted steel ball; on the other, a spring-loaded blade would snap out. If her weapon wasn't formidable enough, Veronica could pull the weighted ball, which would tighten the chain links until the three sections snapped together, turning the weapon into a spear.

The weighted ball slammed into the monster's mouth and drove its head back, but Veronica didn't wait for another attack. Her weapon danced in her practiced hands as it spun around her shoulders and back into her hands, this time bringing the bladed section to bear. If the blade actually cut the Kludde, it took no notice, instead it slashed out at her again with its claws. They missed her flesh by only by the narrowest of margins, which only enraged the beast more. Its prey was teasing it, so very close, but it couldn't touch the prey's skin. It was like teasing a child with candy, and the Kludde reacted in the same way. The beast roared and lunged forward again, ignoring the woman's weapon completely. If she had been a half-second slower, Veronica would have died under the thing's touch, but she was able to spin away at just the last moment. The creature turned on a dime, spinning back towards the tricky woman, but she was no longer alone. One of the other wolves had arrived, this one in her wolf form. Its fur was reddish-gold, and the creature moved with supernatural grace and speed. Kaitlin lunged in and snapped at the Kludde's legs, careful not to actually touch it, only to distract it while Veronica was able to get set for another round. The Kludde turned on the wolf, slashing at it, but the wolf sprang back a dozen feet, growling in response.

Light filled the room, surprising the Kludde for just a moment, allowing Veronica to pull the weighted ball tight and snap the three- section staff together into a spear. She lunged at it, driving the spear tip into its shoulder, but the monster took no notice even as black blood oozed slowly from the wound. When she withdrew the weapon, the Kludde lunged forward to follow it back to its owner, only to be intercepted by two more wolves.

These, too, snapped at its legs or danced in front of it, maddening the beast to the point of insanity. Here they were, its most hated enemy, and it couldn't kill them.

"Clear," Louis yelled as he struggled to draw in enough aether to bend its power to his will.

The moment the werewolves were clear, he used the aether to pull electrons from the air around the Kludde and built them up at the tip of his outstretched finger. When the charge was high enough, physics did the rest as the lightning bolt formed and arced back towards the positively charged creature. Its body pulsed and shook, tearing a scream of pain from the thing, a feeling that it had never had up to this point. The instant the lightning passed, the pain stopped, but the Kludde was left smoking and its skin charred. The effort left Louis panting for air; flashy magic like lightning bolts weren't his specialty, and Stephen hadn't been the only one unprepared to go into combat. If he had time to collect the correct equipment, the battle would be different.

The smoking body of the Kludde shuddered and then leaped at Louis, its fangs and claws outstretched to tear the human apart. It had no idea what the human was, only that it had caused it pain, and so must die first. Stephen stepped in front of the monster and took the charge on the blades of his short swords. The blow was so heavy that Stephen was thrown back into Louis, and they both landed a dozen or more feet away, with Louis taking the lion's share of the damage.

"Stephen," Veronica yelled, and again stabbed out, this time striking the beast in the back between the wings. Instead of pulling the spear back, she rammed it forward, pushing the creature forward. The Kludde's body was never really designed to walk on two legs, so the thing fell forward fairly easily as she pushed it down harder, trying to pin it to the floor. Veronica pushed with such paranormal strength that the steel shaft of her spear began to bow under the strain, but it still wasn't enough to hold the creature down. Now on all fours again, the Kludde just pushed off the ground, driving its own body further onto the spear until it ripped through the front of the monster's chest. With a sudden violent twist of its body, the Kludde threw Veronica like a rag doll, using her own weapon like a lever and leaving it behind as she slammed against the far wall.

Stephen hit the ground hard when he and Louis had been thrown by the force of the Kludde's attack, hard enough that it had rang his bell for a few moments before he could orient himself again. When he looked down at Louis, who had landed underneath him, the other man looked worse. His arm was twisted badly, obviously broken, and Louis wasn't moving. The warlock had been their only weapon, and now he was unconscious in a heap. Even if he woke up right now, the man wasn't going to be of any combat value anymore. He knew very little about magic or the Aether, but he knew what had happened to Karen Ashter when she had tried to cast while injured. Stephen looked back at the combat with the Kludde and grimaced. They were losing badly. Veronica was down for the moment, and the other three couldn't attack without risking the Kludde's touch of death. He needed to get back into the fight, if only to take some of the pressure off the other three before one of them got touched by accident. Stephen looked around for his Widow's Tears that had both gone flying when they had been ripped from his hands by the impact. If the weapons hadn't been torn away from him, he probably would have broken his hands in addition to being thrown when the Kludde had hit him, but all he had now was a tingling sensation. He found the first one easy enough, but it was several yards away, and the second was still missing. Onimaru's case was still in reach but looked a little worse for wear being partially crushed when Stephen had landed on it.

Stephen's focus snapped back to the fight when he heard the wolf's voice scream. He didn't see the actual hit, but Deon's limp form rolled several feet away from the Kludde and lay still. Stephen snapped. Conscious thought left him as he stared at the form of one of his closest friends and partner officer. Stephen had lost his first and closest friend just a short while ago to suicide. He refused to lose again.

Desperate for a weapon, Stephen mindlessly grabbed the closest thing at hand, the case for the Onimaru, and ripped it apart. The millennial-old sword tumbled naked onto the dirt-covered floor. The weapon's beauty was lost on him; the elegance of its lines, the perfect curve of its form, meant nothing. All Stephen saw was another weapon, something to strike back at the Kludde that had just killed Deon. There was no Ito, no Tsuba, not even a Habaki; just the bare-naked steel blade lying there in the dirt. Stephen didn't care if there was no hilt, grip, or guard, and without a scabbard, there was no need for a blade collar to lock it in place. He grabbed the bare metal and launched himself forward, roaring his anger from deep inside, and caught the Kludde unaware.

The spirit beast had its attention focused on Kara, who was standing between the monster and Deon's motionless body, just like a Queen should. What Stephen lacked in form, he made up for with rage. According to centuries of Japanese beliefs, the Onimaru Kunitsuna was a living thing, and it had a purpose again. It knew its job, and it did it well. The blade could feel the demon nearby and wanted with all its soul to do its duty once more. It didn't care that a samurai wasn't wielding it; the hands and arms that swung it now would do. Stephen swung almost blindly, but the blade cut deep into the Kludde's back, slicing one wing completely off, as it ripped through the nightmare's side. This time, the monster's blood sprayed freely, coating Stephen's chest and hands, but the man just ignored it. The spirit beast screamed in pain and rage, arching its back until its dog face was turned towards the roof. Stephen's rage wasn't spent yet, and he locked his front foot in place, using his momentum to pivot all the way around until he faced the monster almost eye to eye. This time, the Onimaru came slicing upwards with all the force that Stephen could muster. The supernaturally sharp blade caught the Kludde under the jaw where the dog's face met the neck, and sliced upwards until the blade exited at the top of the head. The Kludde's dog face fell free from the rest of its head, and a torrent of blood and desiccated brains sprayed from the wound.

The Kludde fell forward, already dead… again. The part of it that raged, that hungered, that loathed had never been stored in the dead dog's brain. That part was in its soul, and even as the beast fell, that part of the monster lived on for just a few moments longer. For the first time in its short existence, the Kludde felt peace. Gone was the need to consume the souls of the living, gone was the soul's burning rage. Karen Ashter's soul found…contentment for just the briefest of moments. By the time the body hit the floor, the soul was already fading into the Aether, to travel back to where all life came from, to maybe find a better life next time.

Kara shifted first and was scooping up Deon's still form into her lap as she fell to the floor. When Stephen was certain that the threat was over, he numbly dropped the ancient relic and rushed to her.

"Is he?" Stephen asked in a whisper.

"He's not breathing. I can barely feel his pulse," Kara answered with tears in her eyes.

Kaitlin helped her sister back to her feet, and the two women joined the group huddled around Deon's wolf.

"Look at his side," Kaitlin said as she pointed in shock.

There, under her finger, was a line of snow-white fur that marred the wolf's normally charcoal colored hair. The very tip of the Kludde's claw had caught him at that exact spot, but just for the smallest of moments as Deon's wolf had dodged the attack. That claw tip touch had almost been enough to kill him outright.

"What do we do?" Stephen asked, desperate for answers.

"Let me," Louis answered through gritted teeth, the pain causing sweat to bead on his forehead. Instinctively, Stephen grabbed the man and carefully held him.

"You can't," Stephen replied. "You're in too much pain, and I don't want to risk someone else. You said it yourself, a warlock that pushes too hard burns."

"I won't," was all the answer he gave, and Stephen was too desperate to argue.

Louis pushed through it all, the pain, the fear, the racial bias, and pushed the Aether through his body and down to his fingers. It didn't have to be much, nothing compared to the lightning bolt from before, just enough of a spark. A small crack sound popped from his fingers as he touched the wolf's side just behind the front legs. Instantly, the wolf's body tensed and then relaxed, and then...nothing. Seconds ticked by, and then the wolf's side flexed as it inhaled deeply. No one moved or made a sound as they all watched.

There was the first breath, and then a second, then the third.

The tension in the air popped like a balloon with the fourth breath and the flutter of eyelids as Deon's wolf woke up.

"Shhh, we almost lost you," Kara said quietly as she petted the wolf's fur. "Don't shift yet, just lie here for a bit. Stephen got the Kludde, and we're all OK. Just lie there and breathe for a while."

Stephen looked back at the body of the Kludde, the beast that had almost taken Deon from him, and watched as it slowly turned to oily black smoke. The creature dissolved bit by bit until the chain around its ankle was all that was left.

When it too finally evaporated, Stephen turned back to Louis. "I don't...I'm not sure what to say."

"I do... FUCK, THIS HURTS!"

Stephen laughed despite himself and nodded in agreement. "We need to get you to a hospital, and then I have to get the sword back to the Feds before Japan goes to war with the US."

"Just give me a ride, I know a witch who is better than any hospital, heck of a lot cheaper too," Louis answered as he choked back the pain. "Dammit, how am I going to get my bike back home?"

"I'll give you a ride, hell, I'll even run code," Stephen answered with a smile. "Don't worry about the bike, I know a guy who has a tow truck."

Chapter Twenty-Eight:
Burger and Fries

A week had passed since the Kludde had been killed. Just as Deon had suggested, Stephen waited until the vampires' tip came through that the suspects had been found at a no-tell motel. Stephen made sure he was "close" and called out that he saw a suspect fleeing on the radio. Kaitlin had a blast playing bad guy in the 'borrowed' car that they were using. She tore through the streets of Moser City, Stephen close behind her with his emergency equipment screaming until she got close to the river. His heart almost skipped a beat when the girl jumped from a moving vehicle just before it hit the water, but she just rolled with the impact and let her enhanced natural healing do the rest. By the time the first patrol cars had arrived, Stephen was pulling himself back out of the river, holding onto the Onimaru Kunitsuna. The fire department called their rescue divers, but when they arrived, the car was empty, and the door was left open.

The Feds had a field day with the arrest of two suspects and the recovery of the sword. The suspects admitted everything right off the bat, but as soon as their confessions were signed, they never said another word. News broadcasts from around the world covered the story of the lost demon-slaying sword, how it had been stolen but then recovered. The Japanese ambassador to the United States was even on hand to officially receive the returned sword from the Secretary of State himself in an official ceremony.

There would be a dozen federal agents writing books about the investigation and how an unknown tip had led them to make the arrest. The feds even did a media campaign to ask the tipster to come forward to collect the reward, but no one ever did. By the following Tuesday, the entire alphabet soup of agents and special agents had packed up their command centers and headed home. For Stephen, it was the most glorious week that he could recall in recent memory. Crime had almost gone silent, and even a few of the rookie cops had dared to use the "Q" word, but never around the Chief. Using the word 'quiet' around cops was just asking for trouble and stern looks from the veterans who knew better than to tempt fate.

Another good thing was that Deon was back on his feet. The close call with death had put the big man down for a couple of days, even with his werewolf constitution. That was good news, but the great news was that Deon had asked Louis out not long after he shifted back into his human form. Maybe standing on death's door had made the big man realize that life was short, even for werewolves. Louis, for his part, was also back, with two functional arms, though one was still tender from where he had broken it. Warlocks didn't regenerate, but apparently, magic had its own way of accelerating the healing process.

Much to Stephen's surprise, Veronica hadn't come to ask for the chance to complete their session in the woods. He'd expected that she, or maybe Kaitlin, would have tried to sneak into bed with him. Admittedly, they both had busy work weeks, and there was something... else going on. It kind of surprised him that he was a little disappointed they didn't try to sneak into his room, but apparently female werewolves also had that time of month, based on the amount of ice cream they had gone through. If Kara was also cranky, she never let on or said anything about it.

By the time Saturday had rolled back around, Stephen finally had a plan for Kaitlin's promised date night. He found Kaitlin downstairs in the entertainment room, with a bowl of cereal and cartoons on the big-screen television.

"I thought you weren't playing the little kid bit anymore," Stephen said, a large box only partly hidden behind him.

"Who says adults can't like anime? They've got some really good story lines, and animation can tell stories that live actors and special effects can't," she answered as she hit the pause on her show.

When she looked up at him, her eyes widened slightly at the sight of the box. "You taking out the trash or trying to hide my birthday present?"

"Birthday, is it your birthday? Oh shit, I didn't know," Stephen stumbled over his words.

"It's not, I'm just messing with you," Kaitlin replied with a smile. "So, what's in the box?"

"I hope you like it, and I hope it fits. I had it made, but the girls had to help me with the size. If you don't like it, you're welcome to wear something else, though."

Kaitlin set her breakfast aside and took the offered box. When she opened it, she gasped slightly at the dress that was carefully folded inside. The dress was essentially two pieces: an inner dark red leotard with full shoulders, leaving the arms bare, and shorts at the waist. Over the leotard was a black lace cocktail dress that would end just above her knees. The lace was densely woven, so the red of the leotard would blend with the black patterns, creating the illusion of a single dress. Where the shorts ended, just below her hips, her bare skin would peek through the lace.

"I wasn't exactly sure about your sense of style in dresses, so I made my best guess. I couldn't see you wanting to do the floor-length kind of thing, so I went with something shorter. Honestly, I didn't even think a dress would be your thing at all, but I gave it a shot. It's not really a traditional kind of dress either, but you're not a traditional kind of woman. I did think about adding sequins, but Kara talked me out of it."

"I...I love it," Kaitlin answered, but still obviously confused. "Why did you buy me a dress?"

"Because we have a date tonight and I would be honored if you would wear it when we go out."

"Stephen, we talked about this, I'm not going to ruin your career by making you look like a pedophile in public. I know I look like I should still be in high school, and there's no way we can go on a date together."

"Well, maybe not in human public, but what if I took you somewhere else, somewhere that people didn't care about what you looked like or if I was old enough to be your father. You and me, a formal dinner, and then some fun afterwards, and I can be just as affectionate to you in public as we want, without judgment."

Kaitlin blinked, trying to process it all and not daring to get her hopes up, but she had never known Stephen to be cruel before. "Seriously, you could kiss me, and no one would say anything?"

"Wouldn't even blink an eye," Stephen promised.

"Yes," Kaitlin screamed, as she jumped up into his arms and spilled the dress on the floor! Stephen caught her easily and hugged her tightly before letting go. "What time, oh I've got so much to do, I've got to get my nails done, and…oh I have to shave my legs…"

"Let's say 6:30, and you could go wearing a trash bag and still be beautiful to me, so don't kill yourself here," Stephen answered with a smile.

"Oh, you are so getting lucky tonight," Kaitlin only half-jokingly promised as she snatched up the dress and ran for the stairs.

Stephen followed her back upstairs, where Kaitlin squealed as she told Veronica about the date and showed off the dress. For the next several hours, Stephen made himself scarce, giving the women their space while still trying to stay out of the way of the construction crews, which were just about to finish up. Stephen had agreed to fortify the house, and the pack even had its own construction crew, but the amount of work being done was far more than he expected. Not only the work, but the rate at which it was getting done was shocking. Apparently, having strength and endurance that bordered on superpowers made construction go much faster. More than once, Stephen had seen members of his pack just pushing the nail in place with their thumb instead of bothering with a hammer.

In just one week's time, the drywall on the outside walls had been removed, bullet-resistant panels installed, and the walls were put back together and repainted. The windows were all different now. They'd been replaced with high-impact shatterproof glass that would stop bullets and hurricane-powered flying debris. New hardened garage doors were added, electronic door locks could now remotely close and secure every security door in the house, a state of the art AI based security camera system was added that could identify the allowed residents and staff by facial recognition, and an air scrubber machine had been added to the heating cooling system that would defeat most of the common air borne threats. There was even a security room set up in the basement now, manned full-time by his personal security personnel. He was told that they were still waiting to install the emergency power system and backup water storage because the parts were on backorder. Stephen didn't want to think about how much it was all costing; the ballistic paneling in the walls alone probably cost a fortune, but Kara assured him that the pack had more than enough money.

Stephen kept an eye on his watch, and when it was getting close, he made his way back to his bedroom to get himself ready. Veronica and Kaitlin had been at it all day, laughing and having a good time, but Stephen only needed an hour or so to get ready. Now freshly showered, shaved, his beard trimmed tight, he blew out his lightly graying hair and ran a brush over his teeth before he walked out of the bathroom. He knew exactly what he wanted to wear and only hoped that the old thing still fit. He hadn't worn this suit since before his wife Becky had died, and he apparently had been adding some muscle recently. Kara was just walking through the front door when he slipped on the dress shoes and gave himself one final look in the mirror.

"Oh…wow," Kara said, gob smacked when she saw him walk into the dining room.

Stephen wore a classic black tuxedo with a white shirt and black bow tie. Black buttons lined the white shirt, and the jacket was accented by a white pocket square over his left chest. "Stephen, you look…wow. Please let me come home to you wearing that more often!"

"I figured out a date for Kaitlin," Stephen answered with a little blush and a wave of emotions that Kara could feel. "I know black tie isn't her style, but I think she'll have a good time."

"Well, if she doesn't, she's stupid," Kara replied, still taking in the view.

"I'm not stupid," Kaitlin answered as she walked up behind Stephen, followed by Veronica.

If Kara had been gob smacked by his appearance, Stephen was almost knocked to his knees by Kaitlin's. The leotard hugged her perfectly, and the black lace teased at revealing her form, but didn't quite let you see too much. The lace dress is cut off just right at mid-thigh, making it short but not too revealing. She had teased out her short, cropped reddish gold hair, so it framed her face but left her neck bare. Her makeup was elegant but heavier than her normal wear, which added a few years to her appearance. Here was the Kaitlin, a decade or two from now, a woman who had walked away from the girlish looks of her youth. She was a couple of inches taller, too, height added by a pair of dark red heels to match the leotard. The outfit was completed by a simple red clutch purse on a gold chain.

"Mom, I hope you don't mind, but I borrowed your clutch purse."

Parent-child relationships were different for werewolves who would could live two hundred and fifty years or more, so it wasn't often that Stephen heard Kaitlin refer to Kara as her mother.

"You look amazing," Kara answered as she walked up and brushed her daughter's cheek affectionately. "I stole your choker for my date, so you're welcome to the purse."

"Kaitlin, you look… I don't know the words," Stephen replied, letting his emotions say what language could not.

That was one of the advantages of being a werewolf, being able to read each other's emotions, let them communicate in ways that humans would never understand.

Kaitlin blushed, a rare sight for such a flamboyant woman. "Thank you, but I haven't eaten, and before I pass out from all of this, you need to feed me."

"Then right this way," Stephen agreed as he offered her his arm.

"They look like they're going to prom," Veronica said appreciatively.

"Ewww, prom sucked," Stephen and Kaitlin said together, and then the room broke out laughing.

"Come on, we have places to be," Stephen said when the laughter stopped.

Stephen drove through town and smiled when he noticed that Kaitlin was scrunched down in the passenger seat. "You can sit up, you know, you're not a dirty little secret."

"But what if someone sees us, one of your officers or something. I'm sure they all know your car."

"Then they'll see me out with a beautiful woman and can be jealous when they start spreading the rumors. Until then, I'm not overly worried about it."

Kaitlin smiled and sat up, looking out the window as the city passed them.

"Uh, you sure are taking me to a great part of town," she teased as the neighborhoods became lower and lower income. "Wait, are we going to Gluttony? Stephen, are we going there?"

"I have reservations for two at seven o'clock," he confirmed.

"Oh my god, I always wanted to go there, but Malcolm wouldn't let me. He said I wasn't old enough for a place like that." Stephen just smiled in response and pulled his car up to a stop in front of the abandoned building that housed a unique establishment. The last time he had been here was with Deon, and Deon had peed on the tires to mark the car as belonging to him. This time, the business was open, and the parking lot was full of cars. There was even a valet service. Other than that, the building still looked like the same vacant derrick building that looked about ready to fall down. Even the broken neon light sign out front, which simply read "Gluttony," was the same.

Stephen handed the key fob to the valet and led Kaitlin into the building on his arm. Instead of going to the green door in the back alley like Deon had shown him on their previous trip, this time the front door was unchained and stood open to greet them. The front entrance was night and day from the outside. Gone was every sign of being a forgotten building. The main entrance was spotlessly clean, with serving staff walking around, pouring drinks for guests as they milled and chatted. Many of the guests wore masks, making the room look more like a masquerade ball than the lobby of a hedonistic delight. Across the room was a simple desk, not unlike the front desk of an old 1920's hotel, manned by a single person who appeared to be looking over the guest list. When Stephen and Kaitlin approached, the man looked up.

"Stephen Butler, I have a reservation for two at 7 pm," Stephen said in greeting.

"Mr. Butler, we're honored by your presence with us tonight. I've been asked by the Ogre to tell you that your money is no good here tonight, consider everything on the house in celebration of your recent success dealing with that problem with the vampires," the greeter replied. "Now, if you and Ms. Hughes would follow me, the Ogre has selected your table this evening personally."

The man led them to an old elevator, all polished brass and red felt wallpaper, the kind you'd see in old gangster movies. The trip down was quick, and the doors opened into another lobby, this one more of a central hub than a waiting room. Here, there were seven doors made of polished brass that gleamed in the light. Each of the brass doors was marked with a single-word label, one for each of the seven deadly sins. In the center of the room was another desk, once circular and manned by a man and a woman. Their guide brought them to the circular desk and introduced them, making it clear that they would be the personal guests of the Ogre tonight. The woman nodded in understanding and immediately guided them to the doors marked with the word 'Gluttony' in gilded lettering.

The moment the doors opened, the most delightful smells filled their noses as Kaitlin and Stephen were guided to a special table along the far wall. The dining room was packed with people, all chatting happily and eating anything that their hearts desired. Stephen looked around the room and recognized several faces from social media or the news. There were famous actors and politicians, leaders of governments, and even people who he wasn't certain were even remotely human. All seemed to be having a great time, and several greeted each other like old friends.

The host brought Stephen and Kaitlin through the crowd to their reserved place of honor. The table was isolated from the others, both by its location and by the hardwood cubicle built around it. Even the cubicle was further isolated by a thick curtain that covered the entrance. Here, they could be alone while still in a crowded restaurant.

"I can't believe I'm here," Kaitlin said, smiling so hard it looked like her face was going to bruise. "I've heard so many stories about this place. Did you know there's a gladiatorial arena down here where people can fight? Some of the pack have been down here before and told me some of the stories. When I was off limits from the rest of the pack, I really wanted to go to the Lust room, just to prove that I was an adult, but Malcolm wouldn't let me anywhere near this place."

"Deon told me about the arena, and I've already seen Lust," Stephen replied and then blushed nervously at what he just said. "Deon and I had to walk through the room when we came here earlier. We came in through the back door. I haven't been, like, there or anything but I did see… a lot. It's, well, let's just say it's not on the menu for this evening."

Kaitlin smiled hungrily as she leaned forward to get closer to Stephen from across the table. "You're cute when you're being human. So what exactly is on the menu tonight? I can recommend at least one person who's ready for her turn. I don't have as much experience with it as Veronica, but if you went through the back door to visit Lust, I'm not against you visiting mine."

Stephen stammered and was about to answer when a slight rap on the wooden wall announced the server's approach, just before she pulled the heavy curtains open. She was a beautiful woman with flowing green hair, dressed in the black-and-white outfit of the other servers. It was the hair that caught Stephen's attention first, but when he saw her webbed hands and what could only be gills on her neck, he really paid attention. He had no idea what she was, probably a mermaid if those actually existed, but just for her timing alone, she was so getting a tip tonight.

"On behalf of the Ogre and the staff of Gluttony, we welcome you to our establishment. My name is Ivet, and I'll be your personal assistant for this evening. It is my job to ensure that you both have everything that your hearts could desire while you stay with us, so please do not hesitate to ask me for anything. To start with, what would you like to order for this evening?"

Kaitlin blinked and then answered a little sheepishly, "Uh, we didn't get menus yet."

"My apologies, Ms. Hughes, there are no menus here at Gluttony. We pride ourselves on our extensive kitchen and our ability to have whatever you may desire. So please, simply tell me what sounds good tonight, and let our chefs do the rest."

Kaitlin looked at Stephen, who only smiled in response and gave her a quick nod in reply. "So, if I wanted a peanut butter and jelly sandwich with bananas, you could do that?"

"Of course, and if you wanted your peanut butter sourced from a specific region or perhaps a certain strain of the peanut plant, we could do that as well," Ivet answered with a smile. "If you wanted jelly made with only Muscat grapes, which are prized for the exquisite sweetness, we are ready to serve you."

"Stephen, I… I don't know what to order. I'm more of a fast-food wrapper than a fancy grapes kind of girl. What am I supposed to order?"

Now it was Stephen's face that hurt from smiling too much. "How about something simple then? How about burger and fries?"

"Ya, that sounds great," Kaitlin answered and then turned back to Ivet. "I'll have a burger and fries then, oh, and a Coke."

"She'll have a Wagyu beef burger, medium, with Roma tomato ketchup with just a touch of fresh mayo. For fries, she'll like Yukon Gold potatoes, hand-cut please, and fried in fresh peanut oil. If you would, she'd like the Coke to be hand-mixed rather than bottled, please," Stephen said, adding in some details of her request.

"Of course, Mr. Butler, and for yourself?"

"I'll have the same, but add a real vanilla bean milkshake for dessert to mine, and she'll have…" Stephen said and then turned to Kaitlin to fill in her desire.

"Caramel, milkshake, please," she answered.

"Of course, please give us just a few minutes to prepare your meals to perfection."

Kaitlin was all smiles as soon as Ivet closed the curtains and departed. "That was so much fun! Do they really have all that, just in the back, waiting for people to order? I mean, what if someone asked for something totally weird like fried crickets or blue whale steaks?"

"I don't know," Stephen admitted. "I've never been back there, but from what I've seen when I met the Ogre with Deon, I wouldn't be surprised if they didn't have stuff like that, just waiting. The Ogre really likes his food, so I wouldn't put it past them to have just about anything you could eat."

Stephen and Kaitlin talked and just enjoyed each other's company as they waited for their food. Gone were the human worries about the difference in their age, or the pressures of keeping up social appearances; it was just a man and a woman enjoying being around each other. Kaitlin may have only been twenty-three, but the pressures and violence of being a werewolf had grown her up faster than human girls. Either the company was so good that time had flown by, or the kitchen was faster than expected as well as being overstocked, because it didn't seem like it had been very long before Ivet returned and served their food. The second they had assured her that the food looked perfect, Ivet disappeared again.

"Oh...mouth orgasm," Kaitlin moaned as she swallowed her first bites of her burger. "I think they've ruined my taste buds now. I'll never be able to swallow drive-through again!"

Stephen's response was just a sigh of contentment as he enjoyed his fries. They ate together in comfortable silence, neither needing to talk, and the quiet felt reassuring rather than awkward, unlike normal conversations. The only sounds that broke the silence were the occasional moan of pleasure from the next taste. It was only when Kaitlin sat back, cuddling her fountain glass filled with caramel milkshake, that she broke the silence.

"That was amazing, I didn't know a burger could taste like that," she sighed in contentment before taking another pull of milkshake from her straw. "My only regret is, I can't eat anymore. I think this dress might have shrunk just sitting here."

"Good thing you've got the leotard under it then, plenty of stretch," Stephen joked, his own tuxedo shirt just a little smaller than he would have liked. "So, what do you say we go work off some of these calories then?"

Stephen opened the curtains and then slid out of the booth to reach out to her, helping Kaitlin to her feet. As soon as she was standing, he cupped her chin and lifted so that she would look up at him before he kissed her there for anyone to see. When he finally parted from her, Stephen smiled down at her wide-eyed stare. "See, didn't even smudge your lipstick."

"I..., I guess you aren't worried about who sees us," she replied, and then tears started to wet her eyes. Stephen felt her emotions even before she tried to explain them. There was a touch of fear, then surprise, and finally relief mixed with gratitude. "I know people don't talk about what happens here, but I didn't really think you would kiss me."

"You deserve to be kissed and admired by me or any other man you choose and deem worthy of the chance to kiss you. I'm just glad to be the one standing here with you now."

More tears started to wet her eyes, and just a couple escaped down her cheeks. "You're going to mess up my mascara."

"Then let's go have some fun then?" Stephen suggested. "I know you work at the casino, but I'm told that Greed has a lot more than just gambling to offer. When I made the reservations, they told me they had every video game ever made, and several that were currently in only demo versions. I know it isn't dancing or going on a nature hike, but I thought that you might like it."

"Every game," Kaitlin said excitedly, "even Demon's March Three! It's not even out in stores yet!"

"Let's go find out," Stephen answered and offered the woman at his side his arm. Together they walked through the crowd with heads held high, looking for the room called Greed.

Chapter Twenty-Nine:
Ogre Issues

Gluttony was a marvel of culinary delights, the likes of which no five-star restaurant could ever dream of matching. The Greed Room was a marvel of its own making. This was what every Vegas showroom wished it was but would never become. Every game of chance imaginable could be found, each wrapped in flashing lights and glitter. Men and women worked the crowds, bringing every sort of drink and dressed in everything from black tie to Vegas showgirls to servers who wore nothing at all. Even more impressive was that it seemed each guest or small group had their own server to meet their every need. There were slot machines by the thousands, card tables by the score, and so many television displays that the ceiling disappeared in some places. The screens themselves displayed every kind of sport humanity had come up with, and then found a way to apply betting odds. The most popular betting display was from Gluttony's own gladiatorial arena in the Rage Room. Millions of dollars changed hands in this room every hour, but other things, more meaningful things, were lost and won as well. Sure, fortunes could be made, but favors could be bet, and if the gambler was sure he had the winning cards, even lives could be used to up the ante. In some back rooms, Stephen was sure that people would be betting their very souls if there were creatures out there that could take them. After fighting a Kludde, betting souls seemed like a real possibility.

Stephen and Kaitlin weren't interested in the wagers; instead, they played every video game they could find, from classic stand-up arcade games to the latest in immersive virtual reality. The cooperative virtual reality games were the most fun. Sure, the graphics weren't as good, but the immersion sucked them in pretty quickly, until they forgot where they were, even until the next jump scare made one of them make some embarrassing noise. When the last zombie wave had been beaten back, Stephen had to take a break.

"OK, I gotta find the little zombie killer's room, I'll be back," he said as he slipped the headset off.

"Be careful saying that too loud, there's probably a couple of zombies here tonight too," Kaitlin said so seriously that Stephen wasn't exactly sure if she was joking or not.

"Seriously, real, 'I'll eat your brains' zombies?'"

"Sure, where do you think zombie movies come from? Heck, after what you said earlier, Gluttony probably even carries gourmet brains just for them."

"I…" Stephen began, still not sure if she was messing with him or what, "need to pee. I'll be back."

"You human," Kaitlin said with a smile and one more shot at him before she slipped the VR headset back on.

She was still killing the first wave of shambling zombies when she felt his touch on her shoulder.

"Stephen, you…"

If she hadn't been distracted by the game, she would have noticed the difference sooner. The hand on her shoulder squeezed and yanked her around while another hand tore the VR headset from her. Kaitlin barely had time to orient herself before a hand wrapped around her throat with almost bone-crushing strength. In truth, the hand was so large that it completely wrapped around her neck and left fingers over for part of her shoulder. Without any effort, the creature that now held her lifted Kaitlin from the ground.

"I found you," the creature's voice grumbled through speech so accented that its words were almost garbled gibberish.

Kaitlin finally got a good look at the thing and tried hard not to show her shock. The creature had a large head with long, heavy black hair and thick, burly eyebrows that were so close they almost touched in the center. The creature's skin was dark, like the color of blood just before it dried, and pockmarked with various blemishes. For such a large head, the eyes were fairly small, like two black glass marbles; but its mouth was unnaturally wide and dominated by two upward-facing tusks that came out of the bottom jaw. Hidden in the mass of black hair were a pair of twisted horns that only extended a few inches from the forehead.

Kaitlin had only seen a few of these creatures, but she recognized them as ogres, specifically oriental ogres, sometimes called Oni. The word "Oni" had different meanings, but this one was an ogre with more bestial features than their western cousins. The difference was only skin deep, though, both being famous for their dark nature and their voracious appetites for flesh. Like all ogres, the creature was huge.

"I found you, and now I claim you. Good and caught you are, fairly mine. Now let's go."

The creature turned and lumbered forward, swinging Kaitlin by the neck like a child carries a rag doll. She grabbed at the fingers and tried to hold herself still, or the creature was going to break her neck just from swinging her around. If this had been any other place, the room would have been filled with screams, but this was the

Greed room in a business called Gluttony, where anything goes, and few cared to pay attention. The beast had almost made it to the door before a voice called out to halt it.

"Mr. Gojou, I'm afraid you can't take our guests. Ms. Hughes is a guest of the proprietor, and he would be displeased by you touching her without her consent." The ogre, Mr. Gojou, turned towards the voice, which also brought Kaitlin into view.

There, standing calmly a few steps away, was Ivet, the green-haired waitress who had declared herself their personal assistant for the evening. "Ms. Hughes, do you consent to becoming Mr. Gojou's property?"

Kaitlin was almost struck dumb by the question, but was barely able to choke out, "No," before the huge being squeezed her neck so hard the air was cut off.

"There, Mr. Gojou, she obviously does not consent, and by the rules of Gluttony, she cannot be forced to participate. I must ask you to release our guest, and I've notified building security that Ms. Hughes is not a willing participant," Ivet said a little more forcefully.

Gojou just looked at the small woman and blinked before he moved faster than Kaitlin had expected. With a single backhand, Ivet's body launched into the air and came to a sudden stop when it smashed into a row of slot machines about twenty feet from the door. The sound of smashing glass and bending metal was more than enough to cover the sounds of a smashed skull and spine. The poor woman had died the moment the stop sign-sized hand hit her so hard that she had left her shoes behind.

If the sight of Gojou carrying off a woman hadn't gotten attention before, the sound of smashing machines and the sight of a broken body was enough. Screams started to spread from the immediate area as people tore themselves away from their current wager and took notice of the murder. Gojou turned back toward the door, obviously ignoring the screaming guests, but stopped just as quickly. Air that could be measured in cubic feet was sucked into the creature's wide nose as it took in the smell of fresh blood.

"Can't waste a good meal, she will be good eating if I skin her fast enough, even if she's already dead," the monstrous man said as he turned back towards Ivet's broken body.

He was just bending down to pick up her battered body when Stephen's voice cut through the noise.

"Mister, I don't know who you are, but you better put Kaitlin down, now."

Gojou looked back up, now ignoring the fresh meat at his feet, and saw the small man a few dozen feet away. Gojou looked at Stephen, and at a glance, dismissed the smaller man completely. "She's mine. Run away before I kill you, too. I don't like eating men, but I've got kids at home that'll eat anyone."

"Gojou," the Ogre's voice boomed so hard that it hurt Stephen's ears.

Stephen didn't know the man's real name, only that he was called the Ogre, and knew that he owned the place. They had met just a few weeks ago when Deon had introduced him. The Ogre was a monster of a man, between eight and nine feet tall, and probably close to five or maybe six hundred pounds. He was well dressed, in a tailored gray suit, with long, neatly combed hair braided into a single line down his back. The Ogre's broad face was covered by a thick beard that was also neatly trimmed and braided. When Stephen had met him before, the Ogre had been eating a small mountain of food; now, he looked every part of a mountain-sized businessman.

"This woman is my guest, release her... now!"

"I don't care," Gojou replied defiantly. "Have you smelled her? She's... so... good. She's ripe this one, like she's begging to be eaten. I caught her, and she's mine, fair and square."

"Gojou, you don't know who she is, who he is, release her and I'll forget this," the Ogre demanded.

"No, Ojisan, I've followed your rules and did what I was told, but she's mine, and I'll have her if I have to eat her here and now." Gojou's open hand grabbed at Kaitlin's chest, and in an effortless motion, tore her dress and leotard away to the waist, exposing her body for all to see like the huge man was peeling a fruit.

"Gojou, these are my guests, and I'm their host. You will honor the laws of hospitality or suffer the consequences. You are insulting this place and embarrassing me. He is the King of Wolves, and that is his woman," the Ogre threatened desperately, and as Stephen watched, he could have sworn that the Ogre's already ruddy colored skin was getting darker with rage.

The King of Wolves was a title that even Gojou knew to respect, and he turned to Stephen, now rethinking the smaller man. To everyone's surprise, Stephen didn't seem upset at all; he had already noticed the change in Kaitlin.

"Gojou, you don't understand what you just did," Stephen began so calmly that it was almost cold. "Yes, I'm the King of Wolves, but it's not me you should be afraid of, because I know something you don't. I can feel her emotions, and unfortunately, you can't, but if you could, you would know how bad you just fucked up. Kaitlin, I think he's done touching you now."

Kaitlin moved in a blur of motion as she pulled up her knees and then slammed both of her feet against the outside of Gojou's knee, driving the heels of her shoes into the flesh. The knee buckled even as Kaitlin's hands latched onto the oni's ring finger on the left hand around her neck. Sure, the Oni was massive and probably way stronger than a dozen humans, but Kaitlin was a werewolf and was deceptively strong in her own right.

Kicking off his leg, Kaitlin twisted away from Gojou as she pulled hard against the weakest finger on Gojou's hand, pulling it back until it forced the rest of the hand to come open. For his immense size, though, Gojou wasn't slow either, and as Kaitlin came free, he began to turn and reach out for her with his free right hand, even as his left knee continued to fail him. Kaitlin wasn't done, though, and used her momentum to ride the Oni's outstretched arm like a lever, pulling the finger further and further back until her momentum snapped it out of place.

Now almost fully behind him, Kaitlin released the finger and grabbed two handfuls of greasy hair as she ran up the side of the row of slot machines like she was in some kind of action-adventure movie. With one final push, she launched herself over the Oni's right shoulder, twisting his neck to its maximum deviation before pulling the already off-balance man off his feet. When Gojou landed on his back and stared up at the ceiling, Kaitlin was standing on his chest with one hand pulled back and held rigid straight, about to jam it like a knife into the Oni's left eye.

"Please," the Ogre pleaded in a voice so loud that those closest to him could feel the impact. "Ms. Hughes, please, I apologize for my nephew's unforgivable manners, but I beg you to spare him. His father, my brother, has certain connections that would be displeased by his sudden death. I do not value these other people over your friendship obviously, but they could make my business…complicated. I assure you, he will be punished for violating the laws of hospitality, and I can promise you he'll never bother you again."

Kaitlin answered in a cold fury that didn't give two fucks for the Ogre's inconvenience. "He killed Ivet, and all she did was try to talk him down!"

"Please, Ojisan, can't you smell her? I couldn't help myself," Gojou pleaded, not daring to move, only now fully understanding how dangerous a werewolf could be.

"Stephen, please," the Ogre said as he turned and to Stephen's surprise, knelt down on his knees. "He is under my care, a favor for my brother, and if you knew what she smelt like to us, what it does to us, you'd understand more. My people are very selective eaters by nature, our favorite meats being from intelligent people, and Ms. Hughes smells extremely inviting. The most primitive of our people still eats only human flesh, but the rest of us have broadened our palates. Gojou still struggles with his more bestial impulses."

"Kaitlin?" Stephen answered, not as a command but as a question.

"He tore my dress," she hissed.

"A simple matter to repair, I assure you," the Ogre countered. "I'll have my staff do it for you while you wait, and you'll never notice the difference. Believe me, my rage with my nephew matches your own right now. He's forced me to violate the Laws of

Hospitality, and that alone will damage my reputation for years. I'm already indebted to you for his actions, but I'm willing to give you anything within my power if you would spare him."

"Kaitlin," Stephen answered, and this time it was a tone of command.

"Fine, but they better fix my dress," she snapped with a twinge of pout in her voice, and just like that, the dangerous predator that was inches away from taking Gojou's life, disappeared into a free-spirited woman.

"Ogre," Stephen said, trying to hide the hint of a smile that he got from watching her, "you don't owe me anything. Friends don't hold grudges, and I would very much like to be your friend. There's been enough commotion for our date already, so I'd rather not add any more to it. Any debt you feel that you owe, I forgive."

The Ogre stood and looked down on Stephen with a look of both confusion and admiration at the same time. "I knew that you were different, but I guess I didn't fully understand you before," the Ogre mused. "No paranatural would freely forgive a debt like this, but you do because you don't wish to disrupt your date. Either you see no value in what I have to offer, or you do not understand what it is you are giving up."

"No, I understand," Stephen replied, "but I value you more than I do your debt. You know the trouble the werewolves are in right now, probably know it better than we do, and I'd rather have a friend at my back than someone who just owes me a favor. So yes, I forgive your debt, and I really would like to just ignore that any of this happened. I also hope that maybe someday, you'll consider me a friend instead of just a guest."

The Ogre paused as he considered Stephen once more before he answered. "Friends with a werewolf, now that would be an interesting flavor to add to my life. Perhaps we'll try that one day." The Ogre turned away from Stephen and bound over to Gojou, just as the man was reaching his feet. It was like watching a sumo wrestler move. Sumos only look heavy and out of shape, but their size hides finely honed bodies of champion athletes. The Ogre had one of these bodies. With a backhanded slap, the Ogre smashed his nephew back down into a heap on the floor, blood dripping from the side of his face. "I brought you here as a favor to my brother. You swore to him and me that you would behave and not dishonor any of us, but here we are, and look what you've done. You know the Laws of Hospitality; you know what a host's responsibilities are to their guests. They are my special guests, I promised to honor them, and instead, you slay one of my employees and assault Ms. Hughes because you can't keep your appetite under control." The Ogre paused, visibly shaking with rage as he all but screamed down at his nephew.

With effort, the huge man brought himself back under control before he spoke again. "You owe me your life, a debt that I do not forgive. You owe Ivet's family a blood price as well for taking her life, and you'll pay every cent of that debt. Now, get out of my sight before I kill you myself, my brother be damned."

Gojou got to his feet and almost sprinted from the room, running back to some inner workings of the business. Once he was well out of sight, the Ogre turned to Kaitlin.

"I'm afraid I'll have to ask you to remove the dress before we will be able to fix it. Perhaps I could interest you and Mr. Butler to partake in our services in Sloth for a couple of hours. Our staff there specialize in making you forget your troubles, and we'll do our best to salvage at least part of your date tonight."

Sloth, as it turned out, was true to its name, a place of relaxation and pampering. Their care began with changing out of their stuffy formal wear into some of the softest bath robes Stephen had ever felt. As soon as she stepped out of the remains of her leotard, one of the staff took off with her dress at a run. Next came the full-body deep-tissue massages, followed by hot stones, and finally a session of suction cupping over their major stress points. Then came the mani-pedis in the aroma therapy room, followed by laser dermal facials, all the while being fed honey-covered pastries and aromatic cheeses with berries. Stephen was fine with all that, but when they were led into the communal bath area, he got a little uncomfortable.

The place was huge, built in the Greco-Roman style, with marble columns and nude statues. The bath actually started in a sauna room, where they were allowed to sweat out their toxins and open the pores. Then came a cooling-off room where they were cleaned. They weren't even allowed to bathe themselves when they came out of the saunas; staff were there to gently scrub and exfoliate every nook and cranny of their bodies for them. That had taken some patience on Stephen's part, and a look from Kaitlin which clearly translated into "human" in at least three different languages when he tried to protest. Then came the actual pools of hot, then cold, and finally a pool of gently warm water for soaking. All the while, Stephen was surrounded by men and women who wore only a small white towel, some carrying it over their shoulders or in their hands.

Communal bathing was acceptable in many cultures, but none that Stephen had ever joined, so when he slid into the water to soak himself, he had his eyes closed until Kaitlin called to him.

"There you are," she said, getting him to look up at her as she bounced over to him. "Isn't this place amazing? I feel great, and that massage, I think I'll sleep for a week!"

Stephen looked up at her and couldn't help his reaction. Kara had warned him about her when they moved in together that Kaitlin was probably a nudist at heart, so it was no surprise to anyone but Stephen when she carried her towel instead of wearing it. In a heartbeat, though, he totally forgot about his embarrassment or just how uncomfortable he had been through this whole process. The woman moved with such smooth grace that he couldn't take his eyes off her. Kara moved with strength and confidence, like a queen. Veronica moved in two ways: first, passively, as if she wanted to be invisible, but then, in a flash, she could move like a fighter poised to destroy her opponent. Kaitlin moved like flowing water around rocks, letting nothing stand in her way and making it look easy. For some people, their bodies just seemed to fit them better, like grace and precise control came so easily that it was insulting to everyone else. Kaitlin could have been a world-class dancer. It was something about her energy, the power of her personality that accented and enhanced the already amazing beauty of her body. If he wasn't careful, he could get addicted to her, to all of them, actually, but she'd be the easiest to get lost in.

"Stephen, if you don't stop looking at me like that, then we're going to Lust and skipping the bath," Kaitlin said, almost skidding to a stop when she felt the waves of emotion coming from him. "I don't know if that was admiration you were feeling or if I was prey and you the predator. Don't get me wrong, I'm good with both, just tell me where we're going."

"I'm sorry," he stammered, shaken back into the present, "I guess I just kind of got lost there for a second. You're… just really beautiful, and I guess I was just appreciating the view."

Stephen reached up to her, guiding her down into the pool, expecting her to sit beside him. Instead, she moved in front of him, between his legs, and leaned back against his chest as she wrapped his arms around her waist.

"This is nice, and the water's perfect," Kaitlin said as she leaned into him, and he adjusted to hold her more comfortably. "I never imagined in a million years that we'd be here, doing this with so many people around, and no one cares how I look."

"Oh, they care," Stephen corrected, "they're just hoping no one else catches them looking."

Kaitlin's mood changed in an instant as she settled against him, and by reflex, he held her a little more tightly.

"Good, let them look, because I'm exactly where I want to be. You've changed so much of my life, and I'm so happy it scares me sometimes. It's like I'm almost looking for the downside, something about you that I don't like, or something for us to argue about, but I can't find anything. I try real hard to keep myself grounded, to think with a clear head, but it's almost impossible with you. I'm in love with you, Stephen, all the way down deep in love, and I can't help it. I've loved other men before, but never anything like this, and I don't ever want this feeling to stop. You don't know how much you've done for us, all three of us; we're so different now. Veronica is so much stronger and outgoing. I used to have to push her, sometimes with both hands, just to get her to go out, and now she's the one leading the way. Kara, wow, she's like a totally different woman now. She used to always be so serious, like she was holding the entire world together, and now she's... free, I guess. Before Malcolm died, she was always so exhausted but never let anyone see it; now she's smiling and laughing again. I know you never wanted to be a werewolf, Malcolm didn't ask before infecting you with his serum, but I'm so glad that he did it."

Stephen squeezed her even harder for a moment before he started to answer. "Kat, I... I'm not really sure where to start. I was angry with him for what he did to me, the way he killed himself, and all I could do was watch. I was angry at myself for not being strong enough to stop him or wise enough to notice how much he was hiding. I'm a cop, we're supposed to notice people's cues. I even knew he had struggled with depression from the first time he tried to kill himself, but I was lucky enough to be able to stop him. I had no idea it was coming again, not to mention that he was a werewolf. So, ya, I had a lot of dark feelings about being genetically altered without my consent, sometimes I still do, but then I look at all that I've gained. I have a purpose again, something bigger than just work. After Becky died, there was nothing for me, just work and then home to a huge empty house. Now, I have you girls, and Deon and I are even closer than we were before, plus a whole pack of people to get to know."

"Carnally," Kaitlin interjected, teasing.

"OK, that's still a work in progress, so I'm not rushing that yet. Seriously, though, I did lose Malcolm, but he's given me a lot in return. I love you too, and that's not something I thought I would be able to say again after Becky. I wasn't expecting to fall for anyone, and then the three of you came through my door, and my life changed. I love you, and Veronica, and Kara; and I never thought I could ever say that out loud. Wow, that was... that was weird. I can't believe I just said that."

"Was that good?"

"Yes, that was good! I'm in love with you. I'm in love with Veronica. I'm in love with Kara, and loving three women is OK."

"Feels like you just had a breakthrough," Kaitlin said as she lifted his hand and kissed the back of it. "I don't think you had totally accepted that before."

"I did, well, in my mind I had that squared away, but ya, maybe deep inside I was still struggling with it. Now, it's just… there."

"There's still something else inside," Kaitlin answered, picking up on his emotions. "You're still worried about something. I can feel the stress. Are you worried about the meeting tomorrow?"

Kaden Maxwell, Alpha werewolf of the Maxwell pack, had finally settled on the terms of their meeting. Stephen had never met another Alpha werewolf before, and the meeting was serious, so serious that war was a very possible outcome. The Maxwell pack had tried to assassinate him when Marcus had hired them to eliminate Stephen. Marcus had been the next in line for the Alpha position of their pack until Malcolm's genetic cocktail had bumped Stephen to the front of the line. Marcus had been a shit to begin with, a bully, a drug dealer, and very likely a murderer; so hiring an outside pack to come in and do the dirty work was easy for him. Marcus had even offered to pay them with sexually viable women, the only currency that werewolves really respected right now. Now, Stephen had to meet with Kaden to hammer out some kind of peace arrangement.

There was another mission, though, one that was probably going to be harder. Malcolm had left Stephen with an assignment, one that he couldn't get done himself. Stephen had to convince the other packs to try Malcolm's treatment and hope that it actually worked well enough to bolster their declining numbers. There hadn't been any evidence before, but now Stephen was living proof that Malcolm could make a werewolf. Now it was Stephen's job to convince the others to trust that he could stop their pending extinction.

"Ya, I'm stressed," Stephen admitted. "Deon and Kara have been briefing me on him for the last few days, everything from the way he thinks to the military strengths of his pack. He's aggressive and believes in might makes right, so he may just be looking for a reason to fight. Somehow, I have to talk him down without looking weak and still convince him that Malcolm's treatments work. Tomorrow we could either have an ally working with us, or we could be at war. They have another plan too, but I really don't want to talk about it."

"So, no pressure, right?" Kaitlin half-heartedly teased.

"Nope, none at all."

"You know, I can think of one way that's a proven way to relieve stress and is even nature's most effective sleep aid," Kaitlin teased as she slid her fingers up the outside of Stephen's thigh under the water. "I did promise that you were going to get lucky tonight."

"Down hormone," Stephen teased back, but still grabbed her hand. "You tease me now, and we'll be stuck here in the pool for a while because I am not getting up while I'm... flying the flag."

"Ms. Hughes," the voice of one of the staff members said, interrupting their teasing. "We have completed your dress, and I believe you'll find it satisfactory."

"Sounds like it's time to head home," Stephen replied, bringing an end to a delightful date night.

"Ya! Home to bed," Kaitlin fired back as she jumped to her feet, wiggling her bare butt in Stephen's face for a second before stepping out to towel off! "This night just keeps getting better and better."

Chapter Thirty:
Diner in the Middle of Nowhere

"Stephen, you two have to get up," Kara called through the closed door to his bedroom the next morning. "Security is already in place at the diner, and Deon should be getting here in about an hour."

Stephen woke easily and looked down at the woman, still curled up in his arm, her short, red and gold hair sticking out in all directions. He couldn't help but smile at her while she slept. She was going to be so pissed off when she woke up.

"I'm up," Stephen answered.

"Thanks for announcing that," Kara replied with a rare joke, "unfortunately, Kaitlin won't have time to fix that for you before we have to get going."

"I'm not that up," Stephen corrected, "I'm awake."

"Don't think I can't," Kaitlin answered without even opening her eyes. "They call them quickies for a reason." With a moan of displeasure, she rolled over onto her back, freeing Stephen's arm. "Wait… did we… oh, no fucking way!"

"Yep, Miss Raging Hormone got her first one, and fell right to sleep," Stephen confirmed teasingly.

"No… no… those bastards must have drugged me, or maybe…it was that damn massage!"

"Don't worry, performance anxiety happens to everyone at a certain age. It doesn't make you any less of a sexually attractive woman. Just because you fell asleep after I let my fingers do the walking, doesn't mean that it wasn't worth the trip."

"No! Oh, hell no! Come here, I'm getting to pound town right now!"

"You don't have time for that," Kara corrected through the door. "He's got to get cleaned up and ready so we can make the meeting at noon. It's a bit of a drive the way it is, and we still have to get food, so get your ass out of bed and get dressed, young lady!"

"Dammit, yes, Mom! You so owe me," Kaitlin answered and then grumbled at Stephen. "I can't believe you let me fall asleep right after we just got to third base and everything."

"It was a really good massage, but you were nodding off on the drive home. Sleep happens, and there will always be other days. I'm not going anywhere," Stephen answered with a smile, "and I am serious, I enjoyed myself."

Kaitlin smiled in reply. She'd been worried that, for all his talk before about seeing her as an adult, that at the last second he'd back out when it was time to touch her like an adult. Stephen hadn't hesitated. She was still pissed at herself for actually falling asleep, but there would be other days.

"Fine," she said resolutely as she dragged herself unnecessarily slowly across his body as she climbed over him to get out of bed, "but I'll guarantee that it'll be you begging for sleep next time."

Stephen had just gotten his morning tea and a couple of slices of toast down his throat when he heard Deon's car turn off the highway and onto the drive. The new security gate that had been installed opened with a distinctive groan, and Deon's car needed some engine maintenance. Just the fact that he could hear all that now and that easily made Stephen smile. He wasn't ready to don tights and a cape yet, but he was getting better with his superpowers.

Deon opened the front door without even knocking and was greeted by his pack. They all wore serious faces and were dressed for battle. The Maxwell pack had agreed to both parties being armed, likely meant as an offhand insult that, even armed, Stephen or his people didn't threaten them. Even Stephen was wearing the bodysuit this time. He had added a pair of pistols with extra ammo, each strapped to a thigh, and the Widow's Tears swords crossed behind his lower back. The appearance was meant to send a message, not just be ready for firepower. It said, "If you want war, we're ready to give it."

When Stephen saw Deon, he suddenly found himself looking at his friend in a totally new light. Deon was the Alpha's Fang, a title meaning that he was Stephen's personal protector and weapon. For the first time, Deon looked the part. He wore a full body harness over his body suit, complete with a matching pair of pistols, at least two large knives, a half dozen smaller throwing knives, and a sword across his back. There were probably a dozen or more pouches spread across the harness, each holding something nasty. The bodysuit was tight, showing just how much muscle Deon normally hid under loose-fitting clothing. It made him look like some comic book superhero, or maybe in his case, a super villain. It was the first time Stephen had seen his Fang armed and ready for deployment. It was the first time that it struck Stephen full in the face that Deon was a deadly weapon who would die or kill at Stephen's command. It was something that Stephen would have to process later.

"Are we ready?" Stephen asked.

"Your Praetorian Guard has been deployed since before dawn and have eyes on the diner and surrounding area. They've already located at least three other observation posts from Kaden's people, and two from other packs, but nothing that says ambush yet," Deon answered. "We knew a meeting like this wouldn't go unnoticed by the others, but it looks like so far everyone is just here to watch."

"We have to come up with a better name for Johnathan and his crew," Stephen complained. "Praetorian Guard, that just sounds so… Roman."

"It works, and it was your idea," Kara answered. "It reminds them of their duties and lets everyone else know what they'll be facing if they come after you."

"I kind of like it," Veronica added. "Hail mighty Caesar, Emperor of Rome!" Veronica even added a little salute to Stephen just to make him smile and lighten the mood.

Stephen smiled along with the rest of his new family, and it was that feeling, the feeling that these people were his family, that gave him the strength to move forward, to consider going through with the plan. They had a plan in place, something that he knew needed to be done, but a plan that was still twisting his guts worse than when he had to battle Marcus. Kara and Deon had come up with the plan, but they had waited until recently to bring him in. That was something that he was going to have to change. If they needed to make a plan, something this drastic, he wanted to be in the loop. Kara's answer had been valid, though; he couldn't micromanage everything, and it was the job of the Beta and the female Alpha to protect the pack. That meant that sometimes, they'd have to do some dark things, so he wouldn't have to do them.

"OK, people, the barbarians are at the gates, time to find out if Rome stands."

The meeting place was over three hours from Moser City, a fact that drove home just how big his territory was now. The pack was spread across the entire territory, sometimes so thinly that there wouldn't be another werewolf for a hundred miles, sometimes a lot more. It was just too much land to protect with too few werewolves, to keep both humanity and the paranaturals safe. The meeting itself was going to be in a small roadside diner, the kind that used to be popular in the fifty's and would be a source of inspiration for famous artists of classical Americana culture. What the artists didn't show was just how boring the landscape around the old dinner was. Gently rolling hills, miles and miles of row crops, and long-haul eighteen-wheelers were the only entertainment for the majority of the road trip. Stephen wasn't in a very talkative mood; there was too much weighing on him, and he wasn't even trying to hide his emotions. Kara and Kaitlin were both in the back seat with him and just cuddled up against him to reassure him the best they could. When they finally arrived, Stephen was ready to get out of the vehicle but still wasn't excited about what he agreed had to be done.

Deon stopped right in front of the double glass doors, but left the vehicle parallel to the building rather than parking like a normal person. He paused for a moment, listening to the radio speaker that was tucked into his ear, before he opened the driver's door. Like a chauffeur, Deon walked around the back of the vehicle and opened the back door, letting Kara exit first from the passenger side. As soon as she stood up, Veronica got out of the front seat on the passenger side. Stephen slid out behind Kara as Kaitlin got out on the driver's side. In all, it looked very much like a presidential motorcade, with security personnel looking around for threats and ready to shove Stephen back into the vehicle at the slightest provocation. As it turned out, there was really no need.

The whole front of the antique dinner was plate glass, and Stephen could see two men sitting at a table. Around the room were three other men, all dressed in loose-fitting military fatigues with at least two weapons of some kind visible and probably several more that weren't in the open on each person. Stephen had seen the briefing photos and recognized the man on the right, with the close-cropped military haircut, as Kaden Maxwell, the Alpha of the Maxwell pack. The other man had to be Ted Branson, Kaden's Beta and personal adviser. Assuming that the Maxwell pack had the same setup, it also meant that Ted was Kaden's Fang. What caught Stephen's attention as strange was that he didn't see any women in the group. Whereas he'd never dream of coming to a meeting like this without Kara, Kaden hadn't brought his Alpha female. Their intelligence reports said that Kaden didn't get along with the woman, but he'd still expected her to be at a meeting of this importance.

Deon opened the glass doors, and the traditional metal bell hung above the door frame announced their presence. There was no fanfare when they walked into the room, but every eye was following his every move, and judgment wasn't hard to see. When they reached the table, Ted stood to greet them.

"Stephen Butler, may I introduce my Alpha, Commander Kaden Maxwell," the Beta said with a wave of his arm.

Kaden also chose to dress in military-style attire, much like his other soldiers. The shirt was a simple olive-green button-up, worn with a pair of black BDU-style pants. Kaden hadn't done anything as tacky as wearing medals or ribbons, but they would have probably fit in with the overall look the man was trying to portray.

"Commander Maxwell, may I introduce my Alpha, Stephen Butler, and our lady Alpha, Kara Hughes," Deon said in introduction, apparently another part of a Beta's duties.

"Kaden, it's good to finally meet you," Stephen replied and extended his hand over the table in greeting.

Kaden didn't move to take it and just stared back at Stephen until he withdrew his hand and sat down. Stephen sat in the middle, directly across from Kaden, and was flanked by Deon to his left and Kara to his right. Veronica and Kaitlin stood a dozen or so feet behind them all, watching the room while they in turn were watched by the other guards. With Kaden and Ted sitting, three guards stood not far behind them. It was a classic Mexican stand-off, and anyone who made a sudden move would turn the place into a bloodbath.

Once Stephen and his party settled, Kaden finally spoke. "So, you're the artificial werewolf. When Malcolm claimed that he could make a perfect werewolf and that it would fix our problem, I thought him to be even more insane than the reports said he was. Then he came to me with this fool notion of a medical treatment, like we need some kind of treatment to solve our fertility problem."

Stephen didn't like this man to begin with. In one opening statement, Kaden had insulted him and the memory of his best friend. Still, it was a conversation, and that was better than shooting.

"So, I assume since your people called for this meeting that you had something you actually wanted to talk about," Stephen countered. "I had thought you would start with some kind of apology or excuse for sending assassins into my territory."

The response was forceful, more than Stephen would have usually started with in a negotiation with this much on the line, but Kara and Deon had both suggested that Kaden would respect strength more than diplomacy. He hoped, no, he prayed that Kaden could be reasoned with and the plan wouldn't even be needed.

"That was a regrettable decision by some of our younger members," Ted replied, obviously trying to play the good cop. "It was never meant to be something as provocative as an assassination, but it appears that your own pack was making moves against you. I think his name was Marcus or something. He reached out to our scouting party and unfortunately convinced them into taking some rather rash actions. Their orders from us had nothing to do with violence. I would propose that, since members of both packs have apparently made regrettable mistakes in judgment, that have already been paid for with their lives, that we could put this matter behind us."

"Regrettable decisions!" Kara interjected. "They came to our lands, right into our backyard, and tried to kill us. You call that a regrettable decision! The fact remains that they were your people, on our lands, for the sole purpose of taking out our Alpha."

"Alpha candidate," Ted replied. "It may be a matter of semantics, but I believe it is only fair to point out that Mr. Butler was not an Alpha at the time, and therefore it wasn't even his territory. With that in mind, though, we do…"

"NO!" Kaden yelled, interrupting his own Beta as he slapped the table in an act of dominance, "it was totally us, on our orders. We were offered payment to take you out, and you somehow got lucky enough to live through it. I won't apologize for taking advantage of your weakness. If you were really as strong as you're trying to convince us, my people would never have even gotten that close. Malcolm said he could make you into a great werewolf, the savior of our people, but all I see is human weakness. You let your woman talk for you instead of standing on your own. Now the only question is, what are you going to do about it? You want a war, then here we are, just say the word."

The room was so silent that a pin dropping would have sounded like a brass band falling down stairs. Every eye turned to Stephen as several hands were already reaching for their weapons.

His next words would make or break two packs today. "So that's how you want it," he began. The nervousness about their plan was fading quickly. "You're so excited to play soldier that you can't see the big picture. We're dying, all of us, one day at a time, and there aren't enough babies to keep us going. We're going extinct, and you want to speed up the process by starting a war."

"What's wrong with it?" Kaden answered coldly, staring so hard at Stephen that it dared him to even flinch. "It's the law of nature, we're dying because the weak have been allowed to breed for too long. We don't need some genetic freak to save us or some human science bullshit; we just need to cull the weak and let the strong breed. Right now, all I'm seeing in front of me is weakness that's begging to be culled."

Stephen hated this, every second, every wasteful second that brought them all one step closer to ending it all. He had come here to broker peace, maybe friendship if he got lucky. If he had pulled off a miracle, maybe he would have gotten them to at least try Malcolm's treatments on an experimental scale. Instead, they were looking at mutually assured destruction, unless Kara and Deon had been correct. In their planning sessions, this had been the worst-case scenario. Now he understood why Kara and Deon had planned for this possibility and had laid the groundwork. The only glimmer of hope was the small fraction of a second that Ted had let his emotions slip. The Beta was disgusted with Kaden's actions, just as much as Stephen was right now.

"You're a fool, Kaden," Stephen answered with frustrated fatigue in his voice. "Even now, you're so interested in playing soldier that you are waiting for me to make the first move so you can play the proud general defending his people. Either that or you think we're so weak that you can slaughter us without any real risk."

"Your defeat will be all the sweeter if you make the decision to start the war. We both walk away and ready our forces, then let the glorious battle begin. I promise you, my pack is ready for war. No one will be able to doubt my strength when you strike first, and I destroy you utterly."

Stephen turned to Ted and focused everything on him before he continued. "What about you, Ted? Is this really what you want. Mutually assured destruction just to feed his ego? You know as well as I do that this can't end without needless death, deaths that we can't afford. Is that how you want all this to end?"

This time, Ted paused so long that even Kaden was forced to turn towards his Beta. Whatever was going through the man's mind, it made him hesitate until he found an answer.

"It doesn't have to be war, surrender the women we were promised. That's the price for peace. If you really want to avoid war, then that's the cost."

Kaden sputtered in disagreement before Stephen spoke first. "Fine," Stephen answered in frustration, and then backhanded Kaden with all the speed and force that he believed his body could produce. His training with Kara and Deon paid off as his arm moved so inhumanly fast that he didn't even have time to register his own movement before the blow landed against Kaden's head. The force threw Kaden and his chair back in a twisted heap at least ten feet away from the table. "You wanted a war, but no one has to die but one of us!" Stephen yelled and then launched himself over the table.

The room erupted into violence as Stephen reached for his Widow's Tears even as Kaden rolled ass over tea kettle before stopping on his feet. Guards reached for weapons even as Kaitlin and Veronica both leaped forward and shifted in mid-air like twins instead of just sisters. Even Kara moved to the attack, launching the chair that she had just been sitting on towards the third guard, who had just been about to intercept Stephen. Ted was the slowest to move to defend his Alpha, but he did move.

"Wait," Deon pleaded as he grabbed Ted's arm. "You know this is what's best. You know who Stephen is and what he would mean for both of our packs. Can you honestly say that Kaden is the better Alpha?"

Ted paused and looked back at Deon, surprised by the firm but non-damaging touch of his fellow Beta. Ted wasn't the fighter that Kaden was, but he was the brains of the outfit. It only took him a second to realize that he had been played.

"You did this, all of this, this was all a setup. You wanted me to see our intelligence reports; that's why you never stopped our spies, you even had them hand-delivered by Andy. You wanted me to read those reports, to question my Alpha."

"It was Kara's idea more than mine, and she only came up with this after Stephen had chosen to return your detective back to you as our ambassador. How doesn't matter right now, you never answered the question, is Kaden better for our packs than Stephen is?"

"That's not for a Beta to decide; it's our job to be loyal to the Alpha and carry out his will," Ted answered and then started to pull away to help defend Kaden.

"You're wrong!" Deon almost yelled in reply, demanding Ted to pause again. "A Beta follows the Alpha because the Alpha is supposed to be the best of us, not just the strongest. Our job is to protect the pack by following the best Alpha. Kaden's forgotten that; he's supposed to be the best of your pack, not just the strongest. So, I ask you again, is Stephen the better man? Is he better for the packs, for our future?"

Ted didn't answer; he just stared back at Deon. When he didn't move, Deon pressed forward. "Let this be between them. No one else has to die in a needless war that neither of us can win. It's a pack challenge, Alpha vs Alpha, and nothing more."

Ted turned back just as Kaden was launching another attack. Kaden was his Alpha, even his friend in some ways, but Kaden wasn't the better man. Even as the guilt of betrayal stung him, he knew the answer.

"Alphas have the right to challenge Alphas for ownership of the pack," was all that Ted said, and Deon finally let go of his arm.

Kaden had rolled back to his feet even as Stephen was leaping over the table at him. For just a moment, shock and even a touch of fear escaped him before he controlled his emotions. It wasn't from the sight of an oncoming attacker, it was from the sheer power of the blow that had just broken bones in his face and hopefully in Stephen's hand. In just that moment of fear, Kaden doubted, before he moved to attack. Kaden's weapons weren't the traditional Widow's Tear short swords; he had a different preference.

Kaden drew his twin trench knives and readied his defense. The knives were shorter than Stephen's short swords, but they had been designed in World War I as pure killing machines. The blades were shaped like daggers, measuring six and three-quarter inches long, with full-tang handles. The handles had been built into brass knuckles, so the fingers would be protected when fighting, and the knuckles could also be used as punching weapons. Lastly, the knives were finished with a small, pointed tip on the butt end of the handle, there to be rammed into the skull in a hammer-fist type of attack if the blades or knuckles weren't enough. They were deadly weapons, a weapon made for the trenches, when you had to look your enemy in the eye while you killed them.

Stephen's attacks weren't as sloppy as they had been when he fought Marcus, and they were so much faster than before. His brain wasn't perfectly up to speed on what his new body could do yet, but it was a lot better than it had been before. Blade met blade in a flurry of motion as Kaden's trench knives met Widow's Tears. Stephen didn't have the years of practice that Kaden had, but this wasn't a battle about finesse or form; it was about trying to stab the other guy, and Stephen's blade found skin first. It wasn't a deep cut, but the tip of his sword sliced neatly through Kaden's shirt and drew a red line across the other man's shoulder.

Kaden groaned with the sting of pain, but turned that pain into action, pushing himself harder and taking advantage of his smaller, faster weapons. Now it was Stephen who was twisting away by half an inch from dagger points or desperately pushing blade against blade to deflect lethal hits. Even as fast as Stephen was now, blow after blow found at least some bit of flesh as Kaden's violent nature pushed his attacks and he started to bleed Stephen to death by a thousand cuts. Still, it wasn't enough for Kaden, and he roared in triumph as his dagger blade scored a solid hit against Stephen's thigh. Stephen groaned out with pain and stumbled forward, the damaged leg giving and pulling him forward, bringing him even closer to Kaden. Now, almost on top of each other, Stephen's longer short swords were at a disadvantage compared to the shorter and faster trench knives. Kaden wanted blood, he wanted victory, he wanted everyone to see him as the warrior that he was, the next Alexander the Great. With a quick hooking jab with his right arm, he moved to finish the fight by burying his dagger in the side of Stephen's neck.

Stephen's nightly beatings, as he liked to call them, were really supposed to be practice sessions. First, Kara would beat him senseless with her swords, and then Veronica would teach him her martial arts until he wished for a call from the office, so he'd have an excuse to escape. Now, those beatings were keeping him alive. Stephen took the cut on his thigh and had even turned the knee into the angle of the blade, just as Kara had shown him, so the cut looked worse than reality. He had wanted to be close, because Widow's Tears weren't just swords, a fact that Kaden must have forgotten in his greed for victory. Widow's Tears were shaped like teardrops with the grip cut into the top of the blade at the widest part. With his wrists twisted downwards, the blades were swords, focusing all their energy on the tips for stabbing and quick slashes. When Stephen twisted his wrist back into a punching angle, the thick part of the tear drops turned the weapons from swords to bladed boxing gloves.

Kaden's arm arched forward, driving the dagger blade of his knife towards Stephen's throat, only to be stopped when Stephen twisted and struck out with a right hook at Kaden's forearm. The Widow's Tears blade struck home, fueled by strength far greater than Stephen had ever known. The punch drove the blade into the forearm and out the other side, slicing Kaden's arm off just above the wrist. Stephen didn't have time to hear Kaden's scream as he withdrew his punch and then threw a left hook towards the man's throat. The blade sliced neatly through the man's throat with a cut so deep that it scraped against Kaden's spine on the way through.

Kaden dropped his sole remaining trench knife and grabbed at his throat with his remaining hand, his eyes wide in terror as blood sprayed across Stephen and soaked down Kaden's chest. The man stumbled back a few steps before he fell on his ass, still staring at Stephen. Kaden tried to speak, to beg for help, but only bubbles of blood came out from his destroyed throat as he drowned in his own fluids. It was a race to see if suffocation or blood loss would take him first, and in the end, blood loss won out.

As a final mercy of fate, lack of blood flow to the brain caused Kaden to pass out only a few seconds after the fatal blow was struck, but it would take a few minutes longer for the body to actually die. Stephen's hands had also gone numb, dropping his blood-soaked blades to the ground as he knelt in shock and watched the other man die. He wanted to reach out, to grab the man in front of him, to try and hold the injury closed so the blood would flow correctly; Stephen was too numb to move. Dumbly, Stephen blinked and looked around the room, the fighting stopping immediately when Kaden fell. His mind refused to register that his girls were all safe.

It didn't notice that Deon and Ted were on their feet, walking towards him and Kaden. His mind only noticed when his eyes returned to the body of the man in front of him, a man he had just killed in cold blood.

Ted leaned over the body of his Commander and checked it for a pulse, one that he knew he wouldn't find, there being more blood on the floor than left in the body. Stephen was still on his knees, not even noticing the blood that was soaking through his pants, as Ted turned to him.

The room had gone deadly quiet, making Ted's words sound even more harsh and grating when he spoke loud enough for all to hear. "The Alpha is dead, and a new Alpha has come to take his place. Kaden Maxwell is dead, long live Stephen Butler, Alpha of the pack!"

Ted and every werewolf in the room dropped to a knee and bowed to Stephen, who didn't even notice.

Chapter Thirty-One:
Aftermath

"Summon the pack," Kara ordered as she stood and looked at Ted. "They are to meet their new Alpha in one week at the Knotty Pines Resort."

"Yes, my Alpha," Ted answered as he bowed at the shoulders to his new queen. "There will be some pushback from this; not everyone will be willing to follow Stephen. Kaden's Alpha female in particular won't easily accept her loss of position to you."

"Will she challenge?"

"Perhaps," Ted warned. "I wouldn't put it past her. She was a royal bitch at the best of times, and they could barely be in the room with each other. If Kaden was a warmonger, she's power-mad, but she's no fool. If she doesn't really believe that she can beat you, she'll keep to the shadows until she thinks she can."

"Then I'll deal with her at the meeting if she wants to challenge there," Kara replied. "Until then, honor your dead, and prepare your pack's records; it all belongs to Stephen now."

"Of course."

Her work as queen was done, Kara turned to Stephen and leaned over him as he sat there on his knees in a pool of Kaden's blood.

"Stephen," she said gently as she carefully touched his shoulders. "We have to go, it's still not safe here. There are still wolves from two other packs out there, and they'll be able to smell the blood. We have to go home."

Stephen turned with unblinking eyes and looked back up at her with tears cutting trails through the blood that covered his face. He looked at her like a child would look at its mother for solace, like he begged her to undo this, to make this reality not real. He looked at her, and part of Kara died inside for making him do this terrible act. Killing Kaden had been necessary and, truthfully, the only choice. Once the man had sent in the assassins, he had chosen war with Stephen. She had always known that there would be those in other packs who would see Stephen as weak or worse, like some kind of monstrous experiment. There would be those, people like Kaden, who would come for him; they would come, unless he was strong. Kara knew the truth, had known it way back when Malcolm had talked incessantly about how great Stephen was. Stephen was strong, but he wasn't a killer, not yet. Stephen was a cop, and she would have to turn him into a killer. When he had ordered her and Deon to track down and kill Marcus, that had been analytical, like ordering someone to do a job. This had been personal, this had been messy, this had been real.

At his heart, Stephen wanted to serve and protect, even those who were trying to hurt him. He had always been trained to use the least amount of force necessary. He fought to win a fight, but not to seek death. If death was forced upon him, he would meet it with equal force, but he'd never seek it out first. Kaden had sought death, had brought it to Stephen's doorstep, but this was the first time that Stephen had ever had to return it in kind. That had been Kara's and Deon's plan within a plan from the very start. Stephen had to meet Kaden's threat, not with peace like Stephen had wanted, but with extreme violence. They had convinced Stephen to try peace, but if it didn't work, he'd have to fight Kaden and kill him.

He, of course, had resisted, had tried to think of any other way, but in the end, it was the lives of both packs that would hang in the balance if he didn't do what was needed. That was what had gotten him to agree; he had a duty to protect his people, even if that meant he had to do something terrible. That had been the truth, but she hadn't told him that she and Deon had hoped for this outcome. It wouldn't just end Kaden's threat, but it would also set back anyone else who thought Stephen was weak. This one death would buy time, and maybe dozens of lives. She had forced him into becoming a killer, and part of her hated herself for it.

They rode home in silence and cared for him as Deon drove. Kara and Kaitlin had brought a change of clothes and wipes to clean up with, expecting someone would be messy and not wanting to have to explain it to a random cop during a traffic stop. Stephen never resisted, only allowed himself to be moved as they needed, so they could clean him up and check him for more serious wounds, just in case Kaden had left a parting gift. There had been plenty of small cuts, the thigh being the most serious, but they had already stopped bleeding, and many were already starting to heal. For his first fight to the death, he had come out pretty well off overall, and it didn't take long to get him cleaned up and changed into fresh clothes. Stephen stared out the window, and little by little, his brain rebooted like a computer with a fresh update. When he finally did speak, Kara almost jumped from the sudden change.

"That won't be the last time, will it?" he asked her, not even turning from where he was still staring out the window.

"No. This is the life we live, every single day. Werewolves rarely live to old age, and now you can see why," Kara answered solemnly.

"He didn't give us any choice," Stephen said, almost like he was reminding himself of the facts. "Ted wouldn't have ever overthrown him, and Kaden wouldn't have ever quit, not until there had been so much death that there was no one left to fight. Kaden had to die so no one else would have to."

"There will always be threats to us out there. Kaden was just the most obvious, but he won't be the last."

Stephen turned to her, and for the first time, she could see the change on his face. His emotions hit them all like running into a wall.

The Stephen that he had been before, the one that they had grown to know and love, was different now. Stephen looked at her like the shadow of death itself.

"Then I need to be stronger," Stephen answered coldly, "and heaven help anyone who comes to threaten us again."

www.ingramcontent.com/pod-product-compliance
Lightning Source LLC
Chambersburg PA
CBHW070204310726

48976CB00001B/213